Praise for *Half a Heart*

"A master of her craft…[Her] genius lives in her ability to create complex characters."
—Rebecca Sodergren, *Pittsburgh Post-Gazette*

"Rosellen Brown is a master at portraying the tentative joy and edgy heartbreak of family relationships. Her character Miriam is one of the most human and full-bodied women I've come across in literature in years, and Veronica (Ronnee), with her foibles and defenses, one of the most complex in recent fiction. Rosellen Brown is a dream!"
—Anita Shreve

"It would be easy to be overwhelmed by the novel's complex themes and its many heart-wrenching scenes and miss the book's low-key humanity and gentle honesty. The resolution of the novel's overlapping conflicts is handled with delicacy, care, and precision. This is the power and grace of Brown's most introspective, accomplished work to date."
—Robert Fleming, *Bookpage*

"*Half a Heart* shows Rosellen Brown's power and compassion, her commitment to exploring the real life of relationships under pressure from their secrets."
—Floyd Skloot, *San Francisco Chronicle*

"It delivers its truth with sensitivity and humor, and that is this: We begin entwined; we unravel; we can entwine again."
—Susan Salter Reynolds, *Los Angeles Times Book Review*

"Brown is a master at rendering the tentative dynamics between mother and daughter, two of the best women characters to come along in years. It's good summer reading. Enjoy."
—Anne Stephenson, *The Arizona Republic*

"A perceptively rendered tapestry of tensions: between parents and children, blacks and whites, husbands and wives."
—Phoebe Hoban, *US Weekly*

"A fiercely candid novel, surely one of Brown's most challenging, intelligent, and masterful accomplishments. [She] brings events to a suspenseful climax through a nightmarish situation and its shattering aftermath."
—*Publishers Weekly* (starred review)

HALF A HEART

ALSO BY ROSELLEN BROWN

Some Deaths in the Delta

Street Games

The Autobiography of My Mother

Cora Fry

Tender Mercies

Civil Wars

A Rosellen Brown Reader

Before and After

Cora Fry's Pillow Book

ROSELLEN BROWN

Half a Heart

Picador USA
FARRAR, STRAUS AND GIROUX
New York

www.picadorusa.com

Picador® is a U.S. registered trademark and is used by Farrar, Straus and Giroux under license from Pan Books Limited.

For information on Picador USA Reading Group Guides, as well as ordering, please contact the Trade Marketing department at St. Martin's Press.
Phone: 1-800-221-7945 extension 763
Fax: 212-677-7456
E-mail: trademarketing@stmartins.com

Designed by Abby Kagan

The lines quoted on p.168 are from "Black Art" by LeRoi Jones (Amiri Baraka).

Library of Congress Cataloging-in-Publication Data

Brown, Rosellen.
    Half a heart / Rosellen Brown.
        p.   cm.
    ISBN 0-312-27830-6
    I. Title.
PS3552.R7 H35 2000
813'.54—dc21   00-022926
                                                               CIP

First published in the United States by Farrar, Straus and Giroux

First Picador USA Edition: May 2001

10 9 8 7 6 5 4 3 2 1

For Adina, for Elana,

from my whole heart

One of the things I learned is that I had to bend or else break. And I also learned that it is possible to bend and break at the same time.

RAYMOND CARVER
"Fires"

And it seemed as though in a little while the solution would be found, and then a new and glorious life would begin; and it was clear to both of them that the end was still far off, and that what was to be complicated and difficult for them was only just beginning.

ANTON CHEKHOV
"The Lady with the Lapdog"

HALF A HEART

I THERE IS NO SUCH THING as beginning at the beginning—just when would that be, and who would tell the story? But some moments in a life suggest a kind of punctuation: quick-stop comma, full-stop period, or the in-between caesuras of colon and semicolon.

Summer was a parenthesis that opened for Miriam Vener. Soon her children would split off from her, one by one by one, for what they loved to call sleepaway camp. First Evie would go with her best friend, Kendra, packed into the back of the Pearlsteins' van, to make off in the general direction of the Grand Canyon and points west. She would end up delivered to camp in California, reunited with the bunkmates she wrote to avidly all year long in envelopes festooned with cartoon stickers. She and the Pearlsteins' dog, Charlotte (named for the spider), liked to hang out the back window, their heads nearly identical. She always waved hard, looking tremulous, but Miriam knew she was so solid she'd be over it by the time they turned the second corner.

Then the boys, Seth and Eli, would go off together on their noisy way toward their summer of swimming, snakes, computers, food fights—whatever the clichés of camp life, they embraced them with enthusiasm. Young boys are not interested in distinctiveness; that comes later. She'd hug them to her, one to each side, and they'd pull, as hard as they could, away.

She had no respite from her mother's presence, though, a fact

that alternately irritated and frightened her. The final period, she
knew, might be placed at any moment, even, unimaginably, in the
middle of a paragraph.

It was June and the Houston summer was still benign; it was
sometimes cool in the morning and the sun that came splashing in
at the door was not yet murderous. She had just hung up on a
dispiriting conversation with her mother, who had called to say
that Miriam's father hadn't come home all night and that she was
afraid he had met with some disaster. "People are being shot out
there all the time," she reminded her daughter in a dire, terrified
voice, and that was certainly true. Miriam wasn't worried about
her father: he had been dead now for almost five years. Her
mother was the one who concerned her. She couldn't convince her
she had been dreaming, and finally had to tell her—by then she
was sounding a bit more harsh than she meant to—that the reason
she was so sure he wasn't coming home was that he was in his
grave. *Safe* in his grave, she heard herself saying.

That was when her mother gasped, "Oh my God," as if she
were hearing this for the first time, and began to cry. "I want to be
with him," she said finally. "I've had enough of this. I want to go
where he is. Are you preparing my grave yet? You ought to be if
you're not." She urged this on Miriam gently, the way she might
request that she buy something for herself, or for the children.
And that was when (because this was not the first time her mother
had abandoned reason, or rather, it had abandoned her) Miriam
understood that her mother, frail and lethargic and eighty-two,
was truly entering her final days, wishing, even when she was fully
awake and more or less sane, to die.

THEIRS WAS A PERFECT HOUSE for subtropical Houston, low
and white and hovered over by old live oaks on the front lawn and
generous greenery to cool and shade it. The house was fairly new,
elegant, "contemporary"; it had been around just long enough so
that the shade had grown lush. Miriam and her husband, Barry,
had moved there only a few years before, when Barry's ophthal-

mology practice began to take off. They owned some nice things—
frankly flat-out beautiful furniture whose price, like the price of
their cars, she had to turn away from, the glare was so great. Pretty
carpets created by dozens of small subcontinental children
hunched double making knots, a lifetime of knots. (Needless to
say, Barry went berserk when she described it that way.) The good
toys in the playroom that she did not regret, only wished she
could spread around to everybody's children: blond wood, un-
flakeable paint, the kind you can't lick off. Some judicious art, including the de rigueur pieces denoting Israeli themes; these were
the badges of belonging. Miriam resisted having a decorator do all
this, by threatening to leave her husband if he kept on insisting. I
can do it, she said. There are harder challenges. One living room
was there for you never to go into, like the old-fashioned "parlor"
her grandmother used to keep for company. The family room got
all the traffic; it was where you could take off your shoes. The big
sort-of-modern print, framed in gleaming silver, picked up the
color of the couch. The dried flowers and the huge lamps on the
end tables echoed the carpets—it really isn't hard to do, Miriam insisted to her friends, but they were afraid to believe her.

Her mother loved this house. When she had shucked their old
overstuffed foursquare in the Third Ward like an outgrown coat,
Jews were not living out here; in fact, when Miriam was growing
up, nobody was, there were no gatehouses, no curving sidewalk-
less lanes where every family wore their stock portfolio like a
mask. Where she grew up was mostly slum now, the neighborhood
of swarthy Jews given over to people of serious color. A few intrepid black householders kept their places beautifully there, against
great odds, their flower borders blooming, the trash fenced out of
the yards. Their dignity, Miriam knew, probably cost them some.

This section of Houston was called Memorial, a name whose
irony occasionally overwhelmed her. Here in this house, for which
she should have been—she was—grateful, what with this room of
her own and her walk-in-closetful of terrific clothes, she was mortified that her old dear friends (no longer her friends) would have
trouble getting past the gatehouse Gestapo out there unless they

looked like they had arrived to do some heavy cleaning. Angry, no, disappointed, no, bewildered, she didn't know the adjective, that she had once lived contentedly with the barest belongings and a sackful of books, and was happy.

Barry admired that in her, but he had to remove it. She asked him continually (he would have said naggingly) if *this* was what he had worked for, and though he couldn't imagine what was wrong with *this*, he always said (and she believed him), No, no, Miriam, how can you ask that? I am the best doctor I can be and this is the concomitant. That was the word: the concomitant. This is the reward that simply follows, like what? He would think for a minute, very earnestly. His earnestness was one of the things she liked best about Barry—he did take her seriously, or at least took her distress seriously, either because it made her unhappy or would ultimately make him unhappy, or a little, maybe, of both. Like ballplayers with their million-dollar contracts, he said, though of course they were not talking millions here. A lot of them play for the money, they play to get out of the ghetto, Miriam said. Sure, he acknowledged every time, having grown up in Dallas with a pool and a maid and a garageful of disgracefully good cars. But you can't tell me that's why they give it what they do. Next time you see Hakeem or Michael in flight, flat out, or everybody steaming down the court in a fast break, try calling it the money. What would you like me to do, turn the money down?

But this was a discussion they might have had sitting at the side of *their* pool, sipping, snacking, cooling off. They might even have been with friends. This is what everybody wants, he would say. Especially those who don't have it. Don't be sentimental.

He wasn't trying to make her look foolish. As the eye is formed, Blake said, so shall we see. He tried to see her, sitting there in her perplexity. But instead of basketball players, Miriam thought of one of the machines his patients looked through at the office that wouldn't show them certain images their eyes were too myopic or astigmatic or color blind to see—butterflies that came and went, depending, and geometric shapes. They were in there, but no matter how hard the viewer squinted, they were so totally not there if the wrong eyes sought them out that it was spooky. So he looked at her as hard as he could but there were certain memories, certain loves and hates and qualifications on this good life that were beyond his powers of sight, and it wasn't his fault, and she always ended up apologizing.

NOT THAT, A DAUGHTER OF ENORMOUS PRIVILEGE, Miriam was exempt. But (however unrealistically) she always thought she was immune to a sense of entitlement because her parents didn't move to their dream house until she was about thirteen, when her father began to mint money, as her mother not too subtly put it. The only thing she remembered liking about the move was that her sister, Joy, and she were finally severed, each to go her own way in separate rooms, Joy to her makeup and Toni permanents and nonstop phone calls from boys and she to her books and her dreaming. How predictable, she thought, safely on the other side. The Baby Intellectual. She wished she'd been more original. Her closet looked like a boy's compared to her sister's: jeans and boots and sneakers, and a Colts hat that she rarely took off. They got along better with a little space between them. Their brother, Alan, was never a part of their combat; he stayed as far away as he could.

Everything Miriam's parents loved about that house embarrassed her. They had a fraudulent little pond in the back yard with lily pads and live fish in it, gold-streaked flat-sided swimmers who seemed captive, who darted around hysterically nosing for an exit into larger waters (though a trip to the aquarium would have shown her that, at times, all fish corner abruptly and look frantic).

They furnished the huge sunken living room with chinoiserie, so that it didn't feel anything at all like her friends' comfortable scruffy houses, and then began to "entertain" lavishly. (What a peculiar word for the coming together of friends, the breaking of bread.) Her mother's parties were very popular; people coveted a place at her generously set table. As for the "Chinese element": sophisticated, everyone called it. Ahead of its time. But it was forbidding, everything lacquered and hard to the touch. Even her mother began to affect a vaguely Oriental look; she put her lovely shiny black hair into a severe bun held together with something like

ivory chopsticks. Miriam certainly couldn't appreciate what all this
elegance might mean to a pair of immigrants—her father was actually the one immigrant between them, having come to Galveston
when he was six, direct by boat because so many powerful East
Coast German Jews had made it plain that they'd like their Eastern
European compatriots to camp elsewhere, with their unsavory
poverty, their inferior language. Texas was far enough away.

How happy her mother was to help him to attain a black enam-
eled breakfront with recessed lighting that poured a cold fluores-
cent light down on tiny mincing figures in kimonos—who cared if
the country was slightly wrong, they were all Oriental, weren't
they, quaint yellow people? Was it any wonder Miriam couldn't
appreciate this for what it was, a kind of certificate of ultimate arrival? Except that they could have ice cream any time they wanted
it now, not only on birthdays, she couldn't name a single thing she
liked that money had bought them. There was no arguing against
the evident facts: that they lived in one of those privileged neighborhoods where the help bore, for a small price, the white man's
burden. *White*, she used to think, twitchy with rage. *Man. Bur-
dened.* It was a wonder she didn't set fire to the whole thing, she
sometimes thought, the scrolls with misty mountain scenes on
them, the shiny cabinets and hobnailed trunks presumably con-
taining tea or silks or something equally preposterous. If her parents hadn't been better-than-decent people who gave away so
much money in philanthropy they were always being cited and
given plaques and dinners and awards—United Jewish Appeal,
Hadassah, the brand-new Israel, that famous old Jewish hospital
for respiratory diseases in Denver—they'd have been ripe to be
hated. She was a mighty good self-righteous hater, a teenage zealot
with passion aplenty but no politics. She hadn't found her cause
yet, and optional poverty would have been inconvenient, if not
hypocritical. She was willing to wait.

AND THIS, she sometimes forced herself to think, if she subtracted the best and worst days of her life, was what she had
waited for:

Deb and Ernie Pinsky, Mona and Sam Cherkoff and their daughter, Shari, carried their coffee and cake out through the open glass doors to sit beside the pool. "Close those doors!" Deb called over her shoulder to Shari. "You let any of this heat into the house, you'll never be invited back."

"This is just at the edge of tolerable," Barry said. "I give it two weeks before we're done with fresh air for the duration." He was stooping over a band of Spanish tile to inspect one of the lights that was supposed to be shining on the bright blue water but was not. He tapped it experimentally and it flickered.

Loose connection. "Honey, we've got to call the electrician," he told Miriam, who was stooping to set a tray laden with ice cream on the glass table. He meant, she knew, You have to call the electrician. It was their trade: Miriam, who had a good bit of disposable time, commanded on her husband's behalf a small army of retainers to counter his helplessness in the face of the material world (though it baffled him only at home; in the office his fine motor coordination was remarkable).

She made sure everyone had coffee, if they wanted it, iced Texas style (hot, over ice cubes that crackled with the shock as she poured), and passed around the sugar and cream in their pretty flowered pitchers. Shari, health-conscious, drank herbal tea, for which her mother gently taunted her. "I tell her she wouldn't need to sleep so late if she had a little caffeine in her veins to get her going in the morning."

Though she said this cheerfully, her daughter glared at her. Shari had been living at home for a while, trying to decide whether to go to law school or, in the style of her grandmother's generation, to simply wait, more and more anxious by the day, for her wedding. The wedding was to take place on Labor Day weekend, after which she would launch her career of leisure, childbearing, and volunteer work. That she would consent to come out with her parents on a summer evening like this seemed like practice for a life identical to theirs, or perilously similar.

Shari, Miriam decided, was trying out a slightly petulant expression, familiar among her friends' older children, that said, I am accustomed to certain pleasures and I will continue to be a pleasant

friend/relative/co-worker if I have them, and only if. It was a lan-
guid look. She was a good-looking girl, large eyed, pale skinned,
her dark red hair cut in little points all around a heart-shaped face.
She was a bit too tall to be the gamine she seemed to want to be,
but really, more than her bone structure, what separated her from
Audrey Hepburn was her singular lack of energy. She was going to
widen quickly after those children, that lovely skin the one thing
she would bring from her youth; she would lounge in her Victo-
ria's Secret pajamas, Miriam thought, into middle age, and let the
help deal with the children. Her mother was probably right, she
lacked the drive to propel her out of bed in the morning into a
world that she believed needed her. Her brother, Ari, was learning
investment banking; he already knew how to fly a plane, taught
Sunday school at the temple, was considered one of Houston's eligible young bachelors—he had enough drive to pull an eighteen-
wheeler.

Deb and Ernie had a boy, Jordan, who was going to Princeton
in the fall; tomorrow, in fact, was his graduation, when he would
be draped with honors for debate, for Latin, for student government—for what his father called "the big-mouth awards of a
lawyer in utero." Another, Joel, was about to depart for camp with
Miriam's Seth. And there was between the boys a daughter, Lisa,
so solemn and political she was a throwback to another generation.
It was Lisa's peculiar distinction that she liked to claim she had
never been to a mall, had never watched a sitcom or a soap opera.
Her parents seemed to be afraid of her. They were more comfortable with the boys, especially with the one Lisa called Joel-the-
jock. All winter long he and Seth had worked on their free throws
in the middle-school gym. They were dogged, inseparable, borne
forward on their ambition to go to the NBA together. "Two Jew-
boys from Houston on the Knicks, right," Barry would say, but
never to them, because ambition was not a thing to kick around.
When it transformed itself into something useful and less improb-
able, not to mention remunerative, as it would in time, all those
shots to the rim would prove to have been good training in discipline, focus, and need. Need was the irreplaceable spark. Anyone

who accomplished anything burned with it, Barry knew, as he had, however unspecific his burning had been.

Miriam, swirling the ice in her tall glass of cooling coffee, looked at her friends across a great divide. Their unruffled placidity unnerved her.

How could one generation have delivered them all—she had to include herself, though she gave herself a few points for her discomfort—to such a sense of entitlement? Seated deep in that lounge chair, legs out in front of her, slowly turning a sweating glass in her hand like Shari, as if for confirmation she made herself attend to the conversation, which was cheerfully indicting the Houston school system. That was always fair game. Debbie contended that the growth of religious schools—Jewish day schools were the ones she cared about—was a sign of a deepening spiritual search, of what she called, like the title of a sermon, a quest for values. Miriam had trained herself to wait for someone else to represent her own view. If she did it herself, intemperate, she would end up red faced, breathing hard. A lot of people who don't give a damn about religion are abandoning the public schools, she wanted to say, to escape from the influx of black kids and Hispanics. Thank God for this community that there's a face-saving alternative they can even sell themselves.

They were good souls, liberal, she supposed, by most standards, "social-justice junkies," Ernie called them, when clean-hands causes and political campaigns begged their support. But they could not imagine lives very different from their own. True, all of it true, but she had no right to take out after them: her old activist's credentials were brown with age, and she hadn't renewed them. Two years in Mississippi close to twenty years ago in the long hot season of civil rights had prepared her for nothing, now, but hypocrisy. There was no worse disappointment, Miriam knew, than being stuck in the middle, neither this nor that. I am not one of you, my friends, but neither am I so unlike you that I can renounce a single thing we have in common.

Evie and Eli were sleeping in a tent tonight on the far side of the yard. They ran in periodically—for ice cream, for good-night kisses, and finally for their parents' adjudication of a territorial dispute concerning the placement of their sleeping bags. Barry got up reluctantly, his face grim to frighten them into peaceful negotiations, and followed them out to their little homestead, the white top of the tent that still glowed faintly in the falling light. Only her children made Miriam feel at home with her apparent friends—when it came to the perplexities of parenthood they were all equal.

It wasn't fair, and she knew it, to be so angry so much of the time just because she kept from them the details of her disaffection: Imagine "Power to the People!" here on her acre-wide lot with its elegant, gardener-shorn plantings, its expensively buried sprinkler hoses, its outbuilding full of shining tools, a more solid little house than many she'd come close to in her Mississippi days that held families of five. Deeper still, closer to the bone: out of the fervor of those days, she had a lost child to account for, and would not, could not, do so. Possibly the irony that tainted her vision was a consequence of her knowledge of herself, which was guilty; of the world, which was cruel; and of her secrecy, which was cowardly. Her friends were given no way to suspect that her children were replacement children, her life a replacement life, her love a replacement love. Sometimes she felt as though she lived beside a graveyard that she circled the long way around, holding her breath, to avoid walking through it.

Suppression of her outrage, her endless outrage, was costly; her depressions testified to the price. They floated across the horizon like thunderclouds and made it hard, weeks at a time, to speak, though she would not traumatize her children by not speaking. Each time she emerged from that semi-darkness, Barry suggested she get some help, but she didn't want air and light, some stranger to finger her secrets and tell her she needed to change her life. She wanted her life to be whole and it had been rent and scarred, healing.

Tonight, when no one ventured her opinion for her, she delivered it quietly; she forced herself to sound offhand. "Miriam! How can you think such a thing?" Debbie began. Debbie's definition of spiritual, Miriam thought ungenerously, probably included séances or the vow to refrain from shopping for a week. "Although it's true there *have* been plenty of problems lately, especially in the middle schools." And out rolled a stream of incidents and incitements in which the white kids were, with an amazing consistency, blameless, and ending in the inevitable: "Wait a minute, weren't you talking about putting Seth in someplace private, which one is it? Kinkaid? next year?"

Miriam took as deep a breath as she could manage. "Barry was thinking it. I was not and am not thinking it." She licked at him with a glance as rapid as a snake's tongue. She knew how thin lipped and smug she must seem. It was the best she could do with her anger. Could she be shortening her life by spending so much time in toxic waters?

"Well, dear," Mona chimed in, looking gravely back at her. Mona was very large and serene, with an untroubled forehead, and she never perspired; Miriam sometimes wondered if Mona was missing an organ or two, the ones that made *her* so vulnerable. While she struggled for calm, if anything disturbed Mona's composure Miriam had not yet discovered it. "Don't forget, you're lucky enough to live in a . . . safe . . . part of town. Your schools out here can concentrate on quality instruction, not subjecting your children to metal detectors to get through the front door." She sighed dramatically. "You have a charmed life, in case you don't recognize it."

Which led them, as it was intended to, to property values in southwest Houston, where anyone could buy a home—the inconveniences of democracy!—in spite of every discouragement the realtors could report or invent. Miriam didn't argue. She was used to putting forth her ideas once and then, for the sake of peacekeeping, falling back without following through. She thought of it as her punishment. She had nothing to be snobbish about; unbeknownst to most of the world, there were people around town far more radical and outspoken than she on every measure, passionate old-style Texas progressives, though you could probably fit most of them in one big room. But she couldn't dare align herself with them for fear of letting a dangerous come-hither chink of light into her cell. She remembered reading an interview with the jailed Argentinian journalist Jacobo Timerman in which he said he refused to receive visits from his family because they made his captivity too hard to bear. She had learned the conciliatory smile, the display of her omega belly to the alpha dogs. It was safer that way, all of it.

What would happen to their innocently noxious opinions, their complacency, their friendly assumption that they understood their lives—that they understood her—if they had a hint of the phantom child who'd haunted her through every season, almost as invisible to her, after all this time, as she was to them?

CLEANING UP, collecting the glasses and the plates studded with crumbs and painted-looking swirls of melted ice cream, she did not feel large enough to contain so many conflicting emotions. She had been large enough once, an age ago—had been a chance-taker, passionately alive in mind and body, but that woman, so foolish, so defeated, was long dead. She allowed herself to remember that self as rarely as possible, and when she did she realized that she had become a myth to herself, amazing to contemplate, implausible and complacent. Frightening, crouched hidden and silent behind her shield of superiority. Frightening and useless.

Barry called her, sometimes, on her inconsistency. Tonight he wasn't talking but she knew he hated it when she zoomed like a missile out of nowhere, aimed at her friends. "You're so damned superior," he could have said, he did say often enough, "but you don't do anything with your advantage." He was defending himself, indirectly, against her arrogance, but he happened to be right, she couldn't deny it or do anything about it. He called it negativity; she called it neutrality.

She considered her life, the one she had allowed to be wrecked as insidiously as if she'd invited a snake into her bedroom, a creation she had botched. She had gone forth with so much, with intelligence and education, with goodwill and the financial resources to support it, and look what she had done—had brought forth life and then forfeited it. Shamed at what passion and impulse had done to her, she would make no unconsidered moves ever again. Would be, she had decided . . . what could she call it? *Actively passive.* Was there such a thing? No? There was now. It was what you got when you married anger to depression, natural hopefulness to deadened possibility.

She couldn't step up and take part in anything that demanded she participate in person. She had failed at Mississippi, about which she had cared too much; had had the caring knocked out of her. Miriam made sure that the volunteer work that came with her marriage she could perform more or less anonymously, that she signed on, a cog, to do only those things others could do just as well: addressing envelopes, setting tables at the homeless shelter, visiting children on the cancer ward who didn't care what her name was. She kept herself to herself.

And she wrote checks. The checks, she made sure, came from a tiny account of her own, her small, private, informal foundation. She wanted the giving to pass through her like electric current, numbing her, a painless jolt of energy: Take this, she said to whichever cause she was rewarding, the Children's Reading Association, the building fund for a preschool, a student about to drop out of college for lack of funds. It is all I can give, it is mine and it is not mine. And she thought it interesting that when you gave money, it stood for you without apology or explanation and no one much cared about your history, unless you cared to contribute your story. Her fingerprints were gone, she thought. Effaced. Left on her baby's skin.

Miriam trotted across the grass to the children's tent to make sure they hadn't done away with each other. They lay on top of their sleeping bags in the heat, their faces frosted with sweat. Kissing their foreheads turned her lips salty.

Back in the house, the detritus of the evening went into the dishwasher, the inside lights on their dimmer were turned off, and Miriam moved down the long tiled hall toward the bedroom. She had arranged her life like an invalid's, so that it contained as few surprises as possible. Having swallowed the evidence of her biggest surprise, she would not be shocked again. One drama in a lifetime was very possibly one drama too many.

THE CONVENTION CENTER, red, white, and blue, looked like a giant bathtub toy, a pretend ship with portholes and smokestacks.

From a distance, the bright blue robes of the graduates streamed toward it, a skyful of birds en route to a single tree, their dun-colored parents rushing along beside them. There was a wind, blast-furnace hot, unusual for early June. Most students' elbows were cocked to keep those weightless mortarboards on. (The wary carried theirs.) One boy, hurrying just in front of Miriam and Barry, watched his sail off like a Frisbee into the parking lot, where it rolled, point over point, under a car.

Inside, out of the searing light, they had their choice of auditoriums. Debbie and Ernie Pinsky's son Jordan was graduating with his very good high school, before the most soberly dressed audience of friends and family in the building. Some of the other halls held ceremonies for less affluent students, whose celebrants were far more festive: little sisters in communion white, mothers and grandmothers in joyous silky flags of color. Gaiety prevailed most where the students were saying goodbye to school forever.

Miriam and Barry met a good number of people they knew, so many of their friends' children were in the same class of '86, having started together in nursery school, continued up through their Bar and Bat Mitzvahs (though sometimes in different synagogues and temples), then driving lessons, succeeded by shared terror over SATs and ACTs and other diabolical rankings, and finally into the angst and chatter and doom and reward of the year of college application-and-acceptance-or-rejection. One girl, who had not been invited to her dream Ivy, was a post-failed-suicide-attempt. Another had been on the cover of a national magazine in honor of her savvy combination of looks (euphemistically called "style") and academic power, which was, with undeserved optimism, pronounced prototypical of "today's have-it-all seniors." A boy with a mellifluous Indian name had already figured out how to finesse

The Market and was near the achievement of his first million. All this was, of course, rumor. Barry and Miriam had no high-school-age child to gather up the gossip firsthand. It had come to them in the elaborate game of telephone that ties communities together: the buzz, the dirt, casually dispersed, overheard, unverified, believed.

And now the graduates were here in the first ten rows of the audience, backs to their loved ones, too many to be assembled on the stage. En masse they made a huge bank of blue with golden tassels, like the famous Texas bluebonnets Lady Bird Johnson had ordered planted on the margins of the highways connecting Houston and Austin, where so many of these sons and daughters were soon to be headed.

Miriam sat more stiffly than she tended to. She felt a small brooding shadow descend on her mood, like the intrusion of shade on a day that had promised to be fair, clouds thickening out of nowhere. The award-granting was interminable, the awkwardly self-confident valedictorian making all the right moves, those choreographed gestures of respect. She was somebody's perfect golden girl, and she spoke the syllables of her finely worked speech so slowly and clearly they could have been kindergartners in her charge.

Why, Miriam asked herself angrily, had it not occurred to her that she couldn't come to a high-school graduation and survive it? How far down did she dare think she'd pushed her single, unapproachable, unquenchable grief? It wasn't true that she had no teenage child like this one: her child would be exactly the age of these children on this day of June, 1986. Her daughter, whom she could hardly imagine beyond her eighth month, whom she so rarely allowed into her imagination, could have been a classmate of Jordan Pinsky's, and of that glowing peach of a girl bestowing, with such preternatural poise, the valediction. "As you go into your assorted lives, some to college, some to work or travel, know that you can be master of your destinies. You are not helpless if you have discipline, energy, self-confidence, and a plan. They say that luck favors the prepared mind: Then be ready! Think out your moves. Believe in yourself. You and only you are the captain at the helm of your life."

Oh, little girl, Miriam thought, squeezing her eyes shut on the banality of the girl's earnest, uncynical face. Little dreamer, who didn't have the first clue about what might be waiting for her and her trusting friends. Someone ought to stop her from making false claims to the gullible. Someone ought to show her what fins, what teeth, and, under her little boat, what a neck-breaking tail might just come swimming. Cruel, this exhibition of unprotected innocence.

Though she often teetered on the edge of tears when memory stole up on her, today she was purely angry at her deprivation, angry at no one but herself that she had walked into this morning so innocently, thinking she was beyond grief.

What would be the look of her girl walking across the stage, reaching for the principal's handshake? Short or tall, vivid or nondescript? Even from back here, some of these children radiated charisma. A few—would she be one of them?—had poured their energy into outlandish hairdos or had decorated their gowns—flowers and secret symbols barely legible from a hundred feet—which was against the rules but all the better, these being teenagers. One boy—a boy!—accomplished a wild balletic kick just as he reached center stage, which set off a rolling wave of applause for his audaciousness, and a grumble behind Miriam that he ought to have attended the arts high school if he thought he was so talented. But most of them moved sedately forward at the calling of their names, as they would move through their lives, without challenge to convention. Though the principal had asked that there not be, there was applause after each name, some of it showering down proof of popularity, some barely dribbling the shame of having no raucous friends, only a bit of family, an embarrassingly uncelebrated existence. And then they threw their mortarboards up toward the roof, which seemed to loom miles above them.

In the lobby she saw a small just-graduated girl, golden skinned as if she were from Bombay, though she clearly was not, with the whitest smile an amateur beauty could have. The girl had a slightly apologetic look, abashed by shyness. She seemed to be answering questions quietly, with a shrug that said she couldn't bear to be taken too seriously. Her neck was frail where it poked stemlike out of the collarless blue gown, younger than the rest of her, sign, somehow, of a gentle spirit. Her legs were skinny, too, her ankles wobbly in heels that must not feel familiar. Bony ankles, bony wrists: a modest, diminutive girl who smiled a bit for approval as she spoke.

Her people came to meet her then, her mother much darker, hair in a neat roll (schoolteacher, Miriam thought; had to be), and an earthy-brown younger sister—maybe a sister, but firmer, stouter, in an authoritative fuchsia jumper. She threw her arms around the graduate and squeezed, and the one who looked—oh God, how she looked!—the way Miriam dared imagine her daughter could look, were she here today, stared straight at Miriam as she endured the embrace. And then, with a quick turn, tucked under her mother's arm, no father in sight—he'd have been white, unless they were creole; they might be, so near Louisiana—she went on her way, bouncing on her heels with only half-suppressed excitement, headed for the doors.

Watching the girl's ankles, flint sharp, vulnerable, disappear in those grownup shoes as the door closed behind her, that was the instant a vial of loneliness and unresolved longing broke inside Miriam's chest, something hot, moving through her unstoppably. She had never, since the first months after her daughter was gone, been felled by a wish so sudden, so wrenchingly complete. Was this what religious longing felt like, the blow that struck people off their feet in the aisles of tents and churches? And did it have anger in it? She wanted to cry out that she had a girl like that. Had had. Pluperfect. Historical past. She stood staring at the heavy door through which the girl who was not hers had vanished with her little family, and the dull, quenched light that infiltrated through its porthole window.

Debbie and Ernie shouldered through the crowd, Jordan in tow, smiling as though they'd just won him in a lottery. He let his mother hold his hand. Barry stepped forward to take care of the congratulatory embraces, the manful back-thumping, the gush. She had no right, she knew, to begrudge them their pleasure. It was just like Jordan not to look abashed by their pride. He still had a bit of boy in him; with effort she could find his child's soft face behind those solidifying bones. But he was standing square-shouldered in his shiny blue robes, making a man's sharp profile, scanning the lobby like a politician awake to his public obligations. Miriam hugged him and hugged his mother, and was grateful that the brimming of her eyes simply looked like the emotion that would, on such a special day, capsize the face of any loving friend.

2 PACKING THE CAMP TRUNKS had changed since Miriam had gone off, as a child, to the cool woods of Wisconsin. She really had had a trunk, black and heavy, scarred, its sides studded, corners reinforced with dark gleaming metal, and a thick, round brass lock that folded down with great formal finality. Everything about it was portentous, as if its contents were far more valuable than those frail cotton shorts sets and balled-up ankle socks.

Sometimes she discovered she'd brought along a stowaway salami, hidden in the bottom swathed in the *Houston Post* to keep her clothes separate from the smell of garlic so welcome at home, so alien out here in the splintery, piney, goyish woods. Always, however, she could rely on finding candy. Her mother, all year long, railed against the effect of sweets on her teeth, but when summer coaxed her children outside her line of vision into who-knew-what depths of homesickness and the suspicion of abandonment, she knew how to console them. Each, she and Joy and Alan, found somewhere in the middle, between bathing suits and summer pajamas, a round tin stuffed with translucent coffee-ettes and other nonmeltable reassurances that someone loved them, even if they couldn't see her or hear her voice, someone who wished them moments of stolen sweetness. Usually she reminded them to share their goodies with their bunkmates, but every now and then if she'd included a one-of-a-kind like a giant chocolate cherry, futilely hoping it wouldn't melt, she'd send with it what she called a whisper, a little note that said "Ssh. This is a secret just for *you*!"

Now, though, the new generation dragged duffels, bumping along the ground and up the steps of their bunks. They were weightless, too clean and new and poorly sewn to suggest their military provenance. If you'd asked Eli or Evie or Seth why they came in what Eli called "that weird puky green," they'd have had no idea. Duffels could be flung, they could be folded and crushed, empty, into the dusty dark under the camp cots, and they could be decorated with unwashable laundry marker when their mother finished her interminable back-of-the-neck labeling, which was faster than the sewing *her* mother had had to accomplish, but still irritatingly slow.

Miriam found it tedious too, but she enlisted the children in helping. The boys were impatient and Evie sat with her labori- ously printing her name inside her underpants as if it were an honor; she looked on it as a craft which took concentration and an attitude of gender superiority. "Let 'em go, Mom. If they don't want to help, let them go do their dumb stuff. Their writing's such a mess anyway." She sighed at sad reality. "Eli can't even spell his name right. Sometimes he does *E-I-L*." She changed pens, from black to red, just for the fun of it. "Hey, what do you think would happen if we didn't put any names in at all?"

"I guess they'd just have to go naked." Miriam was squinting at a delicate job, printing Evie's name as lightly as she could, inside a sheer blouse. She had had to do this to her mother's lovely clothes when she moved to her assisted-living apartment, lest she lose it all when they took her wash and delivered it again. It hurt her to have to write in the collar of her mother's favorite beautiful silk blouses, but they were probably not being worn much anyway these days, sullied or not. "But I don't think going naked would be very com- fortable for, what, softball. Or if they ride horses."

Evie laughed. "But swimming! That would be so good! And no sand in your bathing suit."

They were out on the sunporch, making piles of *Done* and *To Do*. Evie was so wonderfully into the thick of her not-quite-little-girlhood, articulate, emphatic about her enthusiasms and dislikes, a true companion.

Sometimes it was hard sledding to be the only girl in the family because the boys got out of control once in a while, tumultuous, raucous, and physical, or nastily sexist, trying to tell her what she could and (primarily) couldn't do as a girl. Miriam explained to Barry that Evie was getting some necessary grittiness training. His tendency was to protect her, try to create a safe little space around her in which she could be soft and adorable—he was a Southern daddy, after all, and she was his Puffball, his Miss Dimity—but Miriam thought she should learn to fight, to put her brothers in their places, to take nothing from them that she hadn't invited. Evie, no puffball, was a gymnast, she had a wicked arm on the softball field, no girl's flabby overhand; she played her clarinet with clear, strong, unwavering breath. Miriam was beginning to be able to talk to her about people and what it meant to be a good person, to be a friend, all those subjects she could only demonstrate to the boys, because, except occasionally, usually in a crisis, they didn't tend to stop for much talk. The only thing she held back from their closeness was that when Evie was very little, a baby, there were times when, bathing her, kissing her warm perfumy neck, she was shocked by the look of her and thought of her, fleetingly, as a little white girl. Of course I'm white, Evie'd have said. "What else could I be?"

Miriam would take a deep, unsteady breath then, would close her eyes and wait until her expectations, simplified, clicked back into place.

WHEN THE FINAL URGENCIES WERE FULFILLED and the duffels were stuffed solid and zipped, they went out for a valedictory dinner (no fast food, no Chuck E. Cheese's—they had taught their children to like pretty-good Italian). Then, after the last of the children had left and the house was quiet, Miriam went to see her mother, as if that way, whether it went well or badly, she could get her sluggish circulation going. Times when the children were gone weren't good for her; she slept too much, she was bored and irritable, she felt herself swallowing back the possibility of flight, not the usual reasonable summer withdrawal to another address but real flight, panicky, dangerous, undiscussable.

Miriam's mother, in these latter days, lived in an apartment house called The Gardens, where she could take her meals in a big cheerful dining room with other "seniors," looking out on a plot of begonias and pansies. The flowers, a nice idea, were all short and regimented, tough, perfect little blooms that looked as if they'd been planted by the military, with a stone fountain in the center that sent forth a wild soft spray like dandelion fluff. That morning it was windy; the fluff was being blown off to one side. Miriam found it disconcerting, as if the fountain had had a stroke.

Someone at The Gardens kept an eye on her mother and her housemates and called Miriam if there was a problem. (Her sister, Joy, lived in Hartford; she didn't have the right to resent it but right hardly entered in: she simply wished Joy were there to help.) The calls were getting rather frequent, too: her mother forgot her key, she got stuck in the elevator because she didn't remember where to get off, she was found with hoarded food that she had brought up to her apartment in a raggedy paper napkin and left, seeping or drying, on the counter until it was probably lethal. She argued that she was being starved when it was taken away from her.

They did not say the "A" word. Neither did Miriam. Instead, she took comfort from the things her mother had left, a memory of where to find her toothbrush and what to do with it, a continuing preference for clothes that matched, and her daughter's phone number, which on some days she used a dozen times, leaving messages if she wasn't there that were sometimes rational and sometimes not. She always remembered to instruct her to kiss the children for her.

Miriam hated to use her key. It must be jarring for her simply to appear in her mother's apartment—there was such a thing as rudeness even to those without memory—but she had knocked and knocked and now she was worried.

But there was her mother, awake and ignoring the door. She was lying on her gold brocade couch, which she had moved from the old living room. Her lovely face was pouched and worn, but there was no mistaking the beauty she used to be: dark eyes with a saber-flash in them even now, and a sweet, rather high forehead, domed and innocent as a child's. She had tried to pull her white hair back into her famous Asian bun—Miriam was cheered that she remembered—but it was too wispy now, the ends too broken, so it flew around her face as if she'd been out in a hard wind, and the barrette meant to hold it clung to a few short hairs. It was the futile barrette that did it—Miriam was overcome with affection born of pity for a woman who had never asked a moment's pity in her lifetime.

"Why don't you ever call me?" her mother asked first thing, belligerently. Her features had always been sharp and clear, softened by that irresistible brow; now they were hard, eagle-like. Her green mules, topped with puffs of fur like rabbits' tails, sat side by side, lined up neatly on her cotton robe, right where her knees must be.

"I called you this morning. I called you yesterday." Miriam heard herself: The privileged whine of the dearly beloved. She would never be able to deal with the irrationality of this, the way her mother's mind—but only sometimes, unpredictably—had begun to resemble Eli's "magic slate," the plastic sheet he could pull up with the sound of a torn-off bandage, obliterating everything he'd painstakingly written on the little blackboard.

They wrangled a bit about this, and Miriam trumped her by reporting what her mother had told her in the last day—food, sleep, bowels, a slight at the hands of her friend Lillian, who'd called her a stubborn ox at dinner last night. Lillian was one of the constants of Miriam's childhood; she had a permanent place at that laden table—in fact, Miriam couldn't stop calling her Aunt Lillian until long after she was grown. This her mother remembered, and called Lillian a shrew and a harridan from way back, but without withdrawing her claim of neglect against her daughter.

Miriam yanked open the blinds and looked out on the empty

garden. It was too hot in this season for flowers to do much good for anyone.

"Stop that. The light hurts. Slices, those stripes between the slats. Like layer cake, vanilla between chocolate."

"It *is* bright in here," Miriam conceded. "I'm sorry, I thought you might like that." She tilted the slats back halfway. "Why are you on the couch? Oh, Mother, did you *sleep* out here?"

"Distress, Miss Mistress Distress, always sounding shocked." Her mother raised her eyebrows, which she had penciled in at two queer angles, unmatching. "Have you finally decided to get me out of this place?"

There is only the cemetery ahead, Miriam thought, and she found her heart racing, with maybe a brief visit, first, to the nursing home. She had watched her friends' parents vanish before their eyes, some sucked back into infancy and then gone, others vaporized in an instant. There was nothing original about this torture. "No, you're not going anywhere. Good God, let's get you cleaned up. Ma?"

Silence as punishment.

"Mother." She looked around at the unlived-in room. At least they kept it moderately clean, if you didn't look too closely. Sometimes it smelled of disinfectant, the kind they use in public places. Her mother's gorgeous, pompous living room! "Doesn't anybody come up here to be sure you get your breakfast? They're supposed to."

"I don't want breakfast. Bring me some iced tea, would you, dear? I'm all stuck together here."

God only knew what to expect to find in her refrigerator these days, shameful, anything could be growing in there. Miriam brought a cold glass of tea, but her mother bucked at it and it spilled down her front, brown stains on the pale green sweater buttoned wrong over her robe. She cried out. Anger? Surprise? Pain? All her sounds were falling together, too. Miriam rubbed at the sweater with a towel but the stains were like trails forking out. Paths downhill.

"Where did this sweater come from, Mom, it isn't yours, is it? I don't recognize it." She unbuttoned it while her mother tried to throw her hands off. She couldn't get it buttoned again without getting slapped.

"What do you care about that? You never come to help me pee."

"Whose sweater is this?"

"I traded."

"What does that mean, you traded? You gave your clothes to somebody?"

"I have to pee but it's too heavy to move my legs. Come help me up. Quickly, quickly." Her voice rose in alarm.

So much must happen like that now, Miriam thought. Everything just falls on you. Her mother was all knees, her legs like tree stumps. Cypress knees. Had they been this heavy before? They'd yanked stumps out of the ground in a neighbor's yard when she was little, the big forks came up like yanked teeth. She would get scared way down her legs, to her ankles, when the stumps came up out of the moist ground, always moist under there. When my mother's in the ground it will be like that, she thought, wet and dark as coffee grounds. For all eternity under coffee grounds! Her mother always did like her coffee, owned eight coffee pots, glass, porcelain, silver, and the cutest little square Chinese teapot, pewter, she kept them all ranged on the buffet. Horrified at herself, she couldn't say a word, only tugged at her mother's monstrous knees.

Dark blossoms of tea, or was it pee, bloomed on the sculpted brocade couch. "Take me, hurry, take me to the bathroom."

"Mom, where are your—"

"Come, before I have an accident!"

Miriam shouted, pulled at her, there were dark splashes on the rug, pushing, shouldering the door to the lima-bean-green-tiled bathroom, turning her at the toilet, trying to lift her soaked nightgown. It dripped on her heels. "Too late," her mother said, and laughed. "Something you didn't know about your mother," she went on proudly. "You leave me here peeing and peeing, I can't stop. I'm finished stopping."

"Ma . . ."

"Oh, it's all right, darling. You know what it's like? It's like ly-ing down in a bath of your own smell, not someone else's. It's all right, really. Sshh." She seemed to be listening, there on the toilet in her drenched gown. "A little more. Hoo, it goes dripping down warm like blood. Good, good. There. The stains on the sweater don't count."

Miriam thought, I am so useless at this, how have I raised all those children?

"But the smell is going to linger," her mother said thoughtfully. "You can never get rid of that. Here, get me up. Remember the cat?" She was trying to stand but couldn't quite lift herself. Miriam got her under her arms. "That Lansing, that old red cat, the vet said that's the one thing that will outlast us. Cat smell on the up-holstery. In the carpet. No, not the one, I hate to contradict, dear, I told him, but there's a second. Roaches. Cat pee *and* roaches. He laughed. Dr. Hooligan. Houlihan. Hool-something-Irish, but nice anyway."

"Come on, Mom. Let's get you into something dry."

"I wish I could go to a vet instead of those doctors, they speed me in and speed me out again, they hate old people, hopeless peo-ple they can't help, they only love our money. Vets always love their animals. Last visit Dr. Eilenberg walked in one door of the examining room and out the other—'So how are you, darling?'— and he didn't even wait for the answer. Forty-five dollars for the conversation."

Miriam went to the closet for something to change her mother into. A meager selection, unfamiliar. Where had all her good clothes gone to? She found something dun colored, like a uniform. "Do you—I don't see a lot of your clothes in the closet. Your nicest clothes." She wished she had ten hands, she wasn't gentle, either, she felt like a rough nurse, unbuttoning, pushing the new duster on—there was a word they didn't use anymore. *Muumuu, housedress,* what else? A gray duster, scratchy, starchy, plain as a busboy's jacket. "Whose is this?" her mother said, staring down. Miriam saw that her mother's breasts barely fit into it, even smashed down the way they were now, like fried eggs with their yolks winking up. Sunny side up. "This isn't mine." She tried to shrug out of it. You could see the way it cut into her arms.

"That's what I was asking, Mom. Whose clothes are these? I don't recognize any of that stuff in your closet. Where's your nice satin robe and your sweaters, that blue one I gave you, and the cherry-colored—"

"I told you. We traded."

"Who's 'we'? Who's got your clothes?"

"The girl. Who comes here."

"What girl?"

"I don't need that look," her mother said sharply. "The one that works here. Cleans and takes nice care. She gives me a bath. Of course she can't get the cat smell out either, but that's okay, nobody can."

"The—woman who helps you took your clothes?"

"Traded. It was a deal, don't worry. I got more than I gave, Dad would have approved. Although some of it I'm frankly not in love with. The *schwartze*. A nice girl. Tina. Tweena. Something strange, they all have funny long names. Twee-anna maybe. The management sends her to me. She has a sweet little boy she brought with her last time, the cutest little boy, he played all by himself, didn't bother Mommy, so quiet. He made pictures, he made one for me, isn't it on the refrigerator? He put it up there."

"Mom—"

"But very dark. A pity. Very dark. Which would be his father's fault, Tina is—"

"Mom. Please."

"What is the matter with you." She tossed her daughter's hand off. "That agonized look is not becoming. Can I ask you to change the sheets, please. I get too tired when I do it." She said this with so much dignity that it seemed to exhaust her. "Let me sit there. *There.* My chair."

Miriam put her shoulder under her mother's arm and helped her across the room. Seated, her mother pulled at the front of her sweater, as if, out of modesty, she had to hide the swell of her breasts. "Didn't you—" She stopped and looked at Miriam, focusing as if she were far away and had to strain to see her. "I remember—you once had one of those, didn't you?"

"One of what?" Her mother sat flat-footed, as if she couldn't feel her legs; Miriam stooped to arrange them. "What did I have? A sweater?"

An I-told-you-so laugh. "A colored one. A little *schwartze. Schwartzediche."* Black. Blackish. "I never saw her." Her expression hadn't changed; neither had her voice. She could have meant a sweater.

Miriam's chest lurched.

"You had a—what was her name. Something Italian. Exotic."

Miriam nearly sat right down where she was, but she struggled backward to lower her weight onto the soggy couch. She would rise smelling urinous. "You remember her." Why *now*? Why after all this time?

"Not *her*. You never showed me *her*."

"But—Veronica."

"The little colored one. I said, the *schwartze*."

She had never called her that before. That was never her kind of language; in fact, she deplored it, and made that clear to those who used it. Had living here with Lillian and the others infected her or was this what she always thought, back when she condemned Miriam's pregnancy but said not a word about its particulars? Miriam nodded, trying to recall her mother's kindness, her comfort, her refusal to ask too many questions, and bile rose into her mouth.

"Where is she? Is she coming here?" Her mother began to pat the chair all around herself as if she had to prepare this instant for a visit. As if she had to hide everything. All she came up with was a crumpled tissue from between the cushions. She held it to her mouth to keep the shock in, but her eyes were on Miriam, furious and a little frightened.

"Do you remember—" The words seemed to come from someone else, they were so unfamiliar in Miriam's mouth. "Her name is Veronica." The banished name, the eradicated sight of her baby's tiny brown shoulders, the tender little wing-bones whose darkness against her clean white undershirts sometimes took her by surprise, but which was far more beautiful than the vague pink she'd been taught to call "flesh colored." If there was a line between sentimentality and honest feeling, she knew, a woman who had lost a child—no, any parent who had been cast aside—would shimmy across it out of control at the drop of a name, a familiar smell, a flicker of hope. They were not paragons of restraint or even good taste where their vanished children were concerned. She fell toward the sight of her abandoned child as she'd have fallen into a well.

"Veronica," her mother said, listening to it neutrally. "Wasn't there a comic you used to read, you and Joy, someone and Veronica?"

"Archie. Archie and Veronica." Where in the world did that surface from? Her mother's mind was like an agitated sea that might throw anything up from its depths.

"And Veronica Lake. The one with the hair over her eye. A terrible actress, but she had that hairdo. Why did you give her that name? It's not a Jewish name, is it? Veronica, harmonica. It sounds like something Italian."

She was so weirdly fixed on these irrelevancies Miriam dared to think she might actually escape without a death blow.

"I don't know," she said to her mother, stroking her hand, which was covered with skin as thin and transparent as leaves of phyllo. "I liked—we liked—the sound of it. I can't tell you—rain in the trees. Wind. It had a nice music to it." She had named the baby herself, of course. By then there was no "we," not a functioning we. She never knew whether Eljay liked the name or not, nor did she care.

Her mother pulled her hand away. "And for this, wind in the trees—like an Indian!—you had to break my heart. Lying down with a—"

"Don't say it," Miriam warned her, old shame flooding her cheeks. She saw that she had raised her index finger like the caricature of a teacher admonishing a disobedient class. "If that's the way you're thinking, don't you say a single thing."

But her mother, like a cat, bore grudges for her own reasons now, not in response to admonition. "That girl must be all grown up by now." She gave her daughter a long-suffering sigh. "Did she look like our family?"

"*What?*"

"The daughter. Who did she favor? You always kept her to yourself."

Miriam couldn't speak. "Did you want to meet her? You never told me." An understatement. Was her mother manipulating her for the pleasure of it? She was such a flirt, she had been known to utter insincerities to get her way—but what was her way in this?

Her mother was giving her a mournful look. "Oh my darling," she said. "Who knows what I said? Who knows what anything means. It all disappears anyway." She waved her hand as if she were wiping herself away. "I'm sorry to bother you so soon, dear, but you'll have to take me back to the bathroom. I get there myself on a good day. I'm sorry."

Miriam half pushed, half pulled her across the room. Her mother's heels didn't seem to want to come off the rug. When she'd lowered her to the seat, her mother put her head on her knees. All her needs, now, seemed to concern plumbing: food in, food out, and in between, confusion. Closing the door, retreating, Miriam thought, God, don't bend over like that, you might crack. People's backs do, she'd heard of backs caving in like toothpicks at this age. Someone just stands up and crumbles.

Her hard knuckles on the door. "Are you finished, Mom? Need some help?"

"Leave me, I like being alone as long as I can just sit. It's soothing, it's better than sleeping." Miriam, peeking in at the door, saw her reach back to flush but go on sitting. Another quick turn and her back, thank God, was still in one piece, something to celebrate. The things you have to be grateful for. "At your wedding, all the maids of honor wore burgundy and Barry's bow tie and cumberbund matched, remember, and you accused me of flirting with him, my own daughter. But you were smart, you were always too smart, because it was true." She had a new kind of giggle, a gurgle, really. "Well, I never had a son, after all. No, wait, of course I did, that wasn't—Alan? Babies, babies, no wonder my stomach's flabby now, all I ever did was have babies, and where is that skin going to go, after?"

When she was back on the couch she said thoughtfully, "I'm going to tell you something a mother shouldn't say to her child. But I'm going to tell you anyway. You want to hear this?"

"Sure, Mom." Miriam sat at her feet, stroking them. Good bones, her mother had always had delicate bones, and the skin on her feet was young, just as young as her own.

"Sometimes I wake up missing Irving, missing your father, just like there's an arrow through me, front to back. Maybe you'll know this feeling some day when Barry, God forbid, is gone and you're still here. Which is the way it seems to work out, the widows' club. Some days it's like nothing is real if he's gone, and my Mama and Papa are gone, and my darling little brother Abe that you never met, this is all a game in the sky, wherever that is. Out the window. We play it. We have to." She blinked in Miriam's direction. "Are you listening?"

Miriam's face was wet all the way to her chin. "I'm listening."

"So, Irv used to bring me presents, each one a surprise—this was, you know, very early on—and here's the part a mother shouldn't tell. I would dance for him to thank him, wearing what he brought, and only that one thing. If it was a bracelet that was what I would dance in, or a cashmere sweater, bare everywhere else. Once, during the war when they were hard to get, it was a pair of the world's most expensive stockings, he called them. Their seams felt like black velvet ribbons. They were smoother than my own skin, believe me. I pulled them on and very slowly, you know, I pinched them around those tabs—you remember the little knobby tabs?—on my garter belt, very gentle and tender so I wouldn't snag them, and then we locked the bedroom door and he got such a dance out of me, that was the night we made you, darling. Or it was Joy. Well . . . no matter who. In the stockings I was someone else. Somebody nobody knew but Irv, my boy. Even I didn't know myself like that." She had her hand over her mouth to keep her tears in. "He took everything with him into the earth, even the sight of me. Nobody else saw that, nobody knew, and I'm the only one who can remember, and he has it down there with

him, it just disappeared under the cemetery beside that highway, the
stupid noise of all those cars hurrying home, in that coffin with no
nails. That beautiful wood we bought, remember, you have to bury
them in such a hurry, with the star on top, and then into the ground
so fast there's no time to say goodbye. The wood just slipping away.
As if they never were. Worse. Skeletons, my Mama and Papa, and
Irv, my boy, my sweetest boy, if I let myself dwell on it I know he's
just a skull." She looked at Miriam, finally, right in her face, her eyes
swamped. "None of it's real, darling. You only think it's real."

She was slipping off to sleep. Miriam covered her lightly with
the thin blue summer blanket she found bunched on the floor beside the couch.

Her mother was right: when it passed into memory, reality
flickered like light through a row of trees. She had wondered,
sometimes, if she had dreamed that daughter. Her depressions,
those mysterious miasmas when everything turned slow and
leaden, the atmosphere weighted like a rumor of sirocco, of ham-
sin, a fierce drop in the barometer, those were causeless, she was
sure. She did not dwell on Veronica. She felt emptied of any
thought at all, trapped in a weather that moved her about, picked
her up and put her down elsewhere, like an object, by the sheer
force of inertia. But this burning lump in her chest was so real it
must have come from somewhere. For her heart to beat this fast,
there had to be a reason.

"You don't leave the men. Today you think the men will love
you no matter what. Can't you see how you lose them to somebody close by, somebody warm. The couples I know. Broken over
the years from neglect. They can go off any time. Though Irv told
me only in the army, girls without voices, he was honest, in the
army but not one other time. Why not believe him."

"Ssh, Mom. Just sleep." All these years and she'd never heard
anything like that. Not remotely. "Sshh, just close your eyes and
sleep."

SO SHE CLOSED THE DOOR quietly behind her, saying to herself, This may be the last time you're seeing your mother—any

time, these days, could be the last—whom you have loved for so much of her admirable life, and one of your last gestures, imagine, will have been—_shwartze, schwartzediche!_—a threatening, accusing finger and a disgusted snarl. She wondered, going down in an elevator full of other people's mothers with their clanking walkers and their pacemakers and their flowered muumuus that made them seem like a slow-moving human garden advancing on the lobby, her mouth clenched against tears, what she had come to in these seventeen years since she had seen her Veronica. She had come, she finally decided, to comfort, which was all these mothers asked for their children; all she asked for her own. Her mother had simply abetted her. And if comfort killed, it also saved; like so much else, it was two edged, two hearted. She had lived, these seventeen years, with half a heart, but comfort had provided the other half, had kept her alive.

As for her mother: she had warned her to silence with her upraised finger. That will fix you—she didn't think then but did think later, way later after it happened—for getting ready to abandon me.

BACK FROM HER MORNING AT THE GARDENS, Miriam got down to a task she'd put off a long time, packing away her youngest child's early books; they were into "chapter books" now, in which real stories had time to unfold and characters, for better or for worse, had pasts and futures. She riffled the pages of one of his crib books, which had taken up room on his shelves all these seven years, huge, bright photographs of animals on cardboard, so that Eli's teethmarks had done no more permanent damage than to leave great archipelagoes of stains at the edges. Seth was twelve, Evie was ten. She was all out of babies now. Even her littlest could manage without her as long as he knew she was there to come home to.

She was used to the circumlocutions it took to _get over_, as her black friends had called their mere survival. She had even arrived at the point after a few years, it must have been after Seth was born, that she could think _baby_ and see him instead of Veronica, his sharp and rather delicate features, that sweet, thin-lipped mouth, those funny boy-ears, the turtley wrinkled neck he still had and was becoming self-conscious about. His birth didn't obliterate Veronica's but buried it in fresh sensation; she couldn't wait to be pregnant again, could have gone on having babies until it became unseemly and exhausting, because the vividness of pain, the particulars of the various urgencies of each delivery—each demanded more than her full attention and left her little time for remembering. Seth came with brutal speed. Evie was breech. Eli's heartbeat slowed, nearly stopped, as if someone were squeezing it, and then as suddenly and inexplicably he was released intact, born with a vigorous cry. You could not go through labor without feeling, which was a balm.

Her mother had said, in her new complaining voice, "You never showed me her." Awkward, like a translation. No, I never showed you her, you couldn't have borne it. And then—snap of the fingers, so fast, so unbelievable—she was gone. Too late so early. And Miriam's mother, true, would never see her first granddaughter, the one who wasn't supposed to be, and who, then, conveniently was not. Unreal, her mother had said, the way death undermines actuality. And it had been a death, like one. Actually enough.

Except that she was out there in the visible world, Veronica was, favoring (what a word!) *someone*. Eljay's eyes, her mouth? Perhaps her mother's expression, that incalculable thing more like a passing wave on water, more like a scent, than a feature. Veronica? She didn't, couldn't say her name aloud. Instead, images tumbled by, impossible to stop them, the possible, the probable Veronica, like a kidnapped child on the side of a milk carton, aged by computer.

Her friends, she thought, as she stretched tape along the bottom of a collapsed cardboard box so that she could pile Eli's infancy into it—her friends thought they knew her. Pressed, they'd say, all right, she was a bit more liberal than they on social issues, though hardly rabid. All right, she had a recurring streak of something, not quite a depression, but something suspicious, troubled, not entirely accounted for. She knew that Mona and Debbie wondered about some unsavory family relationship—could there have been a smarmy bit of sexual abuse? Lord, they hoped not. Not confessing to them (Yes, I have a daughter, a bi-colored girl, a shame and a grief too deep to claim among you), how could they truly be her friends?

She was not so melancholy with her children around her. But they were not around her now.

And her mother was going to die without ever laying eyes on her little girl. She stopped to consider: "laying eyes on" was such a tender and tangible way to say it. Still, her mother would go into eternity with her first grandchild only a stain in her mind, only a shadow. A strange-named shadow and a shame. That would be the end of something for Miriam, too—some last chance missed, some opening not taken. Back at the beginning, she'd have had to force such an opening, like jimmying a lock.

But now. What if—just say, what if—she looked for Veronica and found her before her mother disappeared for good? Surely she had enough safety in her life for that. What was the worst that could happen if she went to her and said, "I am your mother," stark as that? "You have a place in this line." It *was* a line, whether she had ever thought of it that way or not. Everyone had a history and a posterity, even if that was all they had. She would present Veronica to her mother. "Here is my child, your descendant. It is so late now. Forgive us."

IT WAS A MEASURE of the lack of urgency in her life that no one demanded an explanation from Miriam when she planned to go off on her summer holidays alone, so many of her friends did it. It was the old tradition of the non-working wife retreating somewhere delicious with the children while her poor husband stayed behind to go to work, to sleep alone (she hoped), and, depending on distances, to visit the family in the country on weekends. For those Houstonians who could afford a vacation, the weekly reunion was sometimes difficult because, if they didn't drive the quick hop over to Galveston or a few hours northwest to Wimberley, they so often flew as far afield as Aspen or Vail or, like the Veners, to the happy contrast of New England, where the nights demanded a blanket and the water was sometimes too cold to swim in. But the separation was still worth suffering to spare women and children at least a fraction of the terrible summer in the moist and dripping South Texas hothouse, the painful moment each night when a mother would bend to kiss her sleeping child only to find beneath her lips such a rain of perspiration that it felt like a fever.

Her children had gone off to their summers of their own free will. The older they got, the more socially demanding they had become, and who could blame them if the attractions of summer camp won out over small-town New Hampshire life. It was inevitable that their status as visitors would begin to be uncomfortable when playing ceased to be anonymous, something any child would happily accomplish with whoever happened along. The first time Seth discovered that his softball team had acquired uniforms in his absence (TINKER'S LUMBER AND HARDWARE), it was a week before he would speak to his mother, who had brought him there one year too many.

BARRY DROPPED HER AT THE AIRPORT, kissed her goodbye. He was the good husband, you could see that in his eyes, his posture, his hands. She meant no contempt, thinking that. He chucked her under the chin as if to say good luck. He had never been jealous of her first love, and never disgusted at the knowledge that their child, hers and another man's, was out there somewhere in the world. Helpless, at a necessary distance, he had always grieved for her as best he could. He made it impossible for her to get angry at him. She must, she thought, be hard to be married to, but in the end, oddly, for a passive man, safe. She came with better-exercised defenses than most wives. She had had to learn self-control, how to live with deprivation and make the best of it. She was schooled in sublimation. The same thing that protected her protected him.

But—no surprise, really—he had shown her a look of subdued alarm when she unfolded Veronica's first letter before him.

"You wrote her? How did you know where she was?" His constant readiness to smile had vanished, Barry for whom Veronica had always been more than a rumor but less than a reality.

She cataloged the technicalities: How she had phoned Parnassus College, in Rowan, Mississippi, which she had fled seventeen years ago like a refugee before an invading army; had told the Parnassus College operator that she was trying to find an old faculty member's address—employed in the late sixties, though she didn't know when he had left—and been informed that they were not at liberty to give out addresses.

"Of course," Barry had serenely assured her, as if he'd emerged from such a wrenching experience unruffled. "Every institution has to protect its employees."

She had hardly been thinking of bureaucracies and their protective policies; Parnassus hadn't felt like an institution just then: in her imagination it was no larger than her own kitchen, where she had sat stunned with pain, her baby gone. She had had to plead that, if she sent the college a letter to forward, it be addressed not to Eljay Reece, the ex–faculty member in question, but to his daughter. Somehow, begging, she had prevailed. The operator, who had a soft and forgiving voice, must have known desperation when she heard it. "I'll see what they can do for you," she had said. "No promises, but I'll try."

She had torn up page after page of apology and unbecoming grief, and finally settled on terse, flat statement: I am, you are, we can. "Will we?" was her only question, "soon" her sole suggestion. Her restraint was an enormous triumph. She said "please" just once.

Waiting had been harder than she'd expected because there was no way to know if her words had been heard. Dramas in which people missed each other's messages had always torn at her— Romeo and Juliet, Othello and Desdemona, *The Wild Duck*—the ease with which lives could be deformed by bad timing and bad guesses, not to mention the ill intentions of tormentors! Not knowing if Veronica had received her message, she felt like someone with a disease that could not be diagnosed, let alone prescribed for. Maybe she had just marched at her high-school graduation, simple, on track, exactly as the calendar dictated. But really, she could be anywhere: Living in Dakar, where her father had wanted to go. Somewhere in a commune, making jewelry or planting herbs. A miserable runaway in a crust of dirt, crouching behind a Dumpster. A musician (it ran in the family) awake in some club at 3 A.M., head in a swirl of smoke. A mother herself, baby in a crook of her arm. Not unlikely. (Which would make *her* a grand-mother—that was a laugh.) How could anyone dream up enough possible scenarios?

Did a mother who had to invent her daughter's life deserve to know the answers?

BUT ONE DAY, when she bent to gather the letters that had scat-tered like a rain of dogwood petals on the hall floor beneath the

mail slot, among the usual bills and advertisements, a large elaborate invitation to Dr. and Mrs. Barry Vener to attend the Grand
Opera Ball at sufficient cost to clothe a small Andean village for a
year, so on and so forth, there lay a sunflower-yellow envelope
that at first she thought was for Evie, to be forwarded to her at
camp. She read, in a young handwriting, slightly ornate, MS.
MIRIAM STAROGIN VENER, and in the corner, on a printed sticker
with a unicorn facing away:

> Ms. Veronica Reece
> 516 Bergen Street
> Brooklyn, NY 11219

She took it, hands shaking, to the sunporch to read. The morning
was always quiet here in her underwater castle. She put two ice
cubes carefully in the bottom of a glass and poured Red Zinger
over them. Her hands trembled so badly that she splashed tea the
color of diluted blood across the countertop. Nothing was out of
place when the children were gone. She had her choice of white
wicker chairs and the little love seat with its bright blue pillows,
prettier than they were comfortable. God, oh God, she had nearly
died of the loss of this child. She was afraid she would faint before
she got the letter open, but she would not tear at it like an animal;
she found the ivory letter opener, breathed in deeply, and slit it
smartly along the crease. Veronica had been eight months old
when she last saw her, held her. She had had no words.

But she had them now, by the dozens. They erupted with exclamation points and underlinings. It was a *coincidence*, a weird but
happy one, that her mother was looking for her just now because
she had so much wanted to write to *her*. She prayed that her
mother really wanted to meet her because she had an adopted
friend whose "real" mother wanted to meet him only so that she
could warn him about some horrible disease that ran in the family.
Then she gave what she called her "basic facts": that she had graduated two weeks ago from St. Helen's Episcopal in Brooklyn,
where she was salutatorian and had won the theater prize. She
planned to attend Stanford University in the fall. Could they

meet? She hoped it wasn't too late to get to know each other—
"Better late than never." She signed her letter *Ronnee (Veronica) Reece.*

She was alive. She was well. She was friendly. The coincidence seemed a trifle suspect, but, Miriam reasoned, either it was true that Veronica—Ronnee!—had gone looking for her or she had wanted it to be true. *Wanted* with an underline. She took it for a sign.

"Have you been thinking of doing this a long time?" Barry asked her. How long, that would mean, have I been alone here and not known it?

She wanted to reassure him, reached out to put her hand on his cheek. "I don't have to abdicate *this* family if I want to meet her, you know. There's enough of me to go around." But she had a double consciousness, always had, always would have: There was now and, never entirely forgotten, then, or at least the shadow of then, like the world before he was born. He was, he had always thought, her second husband, de facto.

"Are you going to—"

She didn't want to recognize the panic that darkened his denim-blue eyes. "Don't ask me anything, Barry. I can't answer a single question. Whatever it is, I don't know."

"But how do—"

"Please?" He meant, Don't leave me, even if the leaving was retroactive. His face calmed when she slowly, soothingly, traced his nose and lips with her finger. He closed his eyes, not assuaged, she supposed, but resigned.

She hadn't called Veronica for fear of colliding with Eljay, nor did Veronica seem to want to speak to her. They planned their visit by mail, postponing their nervousness. They would drive to New Hampshire, to the summer house, alone, a perfect, cool, relaxed way to get to know one another. Veronica seemed to relax a little in her final letter, asked if there would be bats (in which case she'd bring along her Mets hat) and hoped that Miriam didn't smoke because she had "occasional" asthma. Unsolicited, she went out of her way to say that her father had not been consulted about her plans; neither, she promised, would he be in evidence when Miriam came to pick her up. "It's a *long* story." Miriam didn't doubt it. But not as long, she had smiled to herself bitterly, as it would be if I took you back to the beginning.

This was, for her, a moment when her first life and her second touched, quivered like the pointer on a scale, and balanced.

IN HER SEAT on the plane, Miriam was jittery, distracted. The last week, since the exchange with Ronnee, had been the longest of her life, and the next would, she was sure, be the shortest. All she could do was fall asleep, especially because she had spent these last nights twisting in her sheets, staring into the dark, pouring warm milk down her throat to no avail. She dreamed Ronald Reagan was sitting on her front step drinking apple juice, which probably had something to do with the flight attendant murmuring blandishments in her direction. She shook her head and slept.

AT LA GUARDIA Miriam rented them a car, a red one with a speedy-looking shape. Then she squinted hard and tried to find Brooklyn. When she had found her way, the first thing she noticed (after all the junked papers blowing around the off-ramp of the highway, the disgusting unprideful mess people seemed willing to live with here) was how the whole look of everything was different from Houston, the light and the density and the pace. Everything was ancient and impacted, but mostly it was busy, busy, unfamiliarly busy to her eye, the architecture of a dozen things, starting with the hulky buildings, the barred and grated windows, the rusted trash cans, the storefronts with their maze of signs and posters. And how the music changed! When a car sat revving beside her at a red light, the bass that rose from it seemed to shake her own little car—no music, just a warlike thumping.

Color, turmoil, grit. She called up none too kindly the clean, white, slightly blank memory of her part of Houston, her Memorial, though it wasn't fair to challenge inner city with outer suburb, not here, not anywhere. What was the busiest section of Houston, though? It was hard to find one, unless it was six-lane traffic near the Galleria or the Astrodome, maybe, after a ball game.

And then the people. When she found what she thought— guessed—was the right neighborhood, peeking out from under her disheveled map, black faces bloomed everywhere, on the street, on the stoops, in the windows. Maybe a goat—was that a goat?—hanging in front of a butcher shop. She cruised slowly by, attracting attention, as if the car were a boast. She saw a few African outfits and a woman with her head wrapped in a brilliant blue, yards to it probably, a Caribbean something, drifting down the street.

She was dressed carefully, in something well cut and slightly, but only slightly, matronly, two-piece linen, green and blue. Junior size, because she worked to keep her figure; went to the gym with her friends, cultivated the slenderness of her class (though fortunately not the tense chicken-stringiness of the overexercised, the overtanned). Once upon a time she had studied the necessary details for her masquerade costume. By now she was beyond having to think of them. Color-coordinated bag and shoes: she had changed places with her sister, sensitive to the role she played in what her husband liked to call her "larger life," which she thought of as her smaller one. Her haircut was very good; she wore it like a product. (The tip she left Kenny every couple of weeks would have fed her for a month when she lived in Mississippi.) So there in her little red dream car, which she parked in a panic because she was being watched by a stoopful of lounging men who were probably laughing at her, she was not exactly the dun color of a female bird among the fine feathered males but she was also not what they called—they still called them this, didn't they?—a fox.

Okay, Miriam, Bedford-Stuyvesant. When you walk down the street here, she thought, you're on your own. She moved on down the sidewalk, fast.

SHE HAD TO HESITATE in front of her daughter's house, this brownstone that was actually a weary, flake-pocked green, to decide whether to ring the downstairs buzzer inside a little black gate or go up the stairs. There was a little pot of marigolds on the upstairs porch chained to the porch rail. You wouldn't think a flower could grow in chains. Veronica had used the word *hope* three times in her letter: hope we can meet, hope we like each other, hope we can make up for lost time. These flowers, Miriam would lay a bet, belonged to her.

She walked up and there was a bunch of buzzers; this was a lovely old house, subdivided to death. The outside door was ajar. She felt as though her blood had invisibly run out of her and her starved muscles had collapsed. Shoulder against the wall for support, she made herself breathe deeply. What if she fainted right here for terror? Terror and delight. She could imagine being found, a white husk lying in a puddle of clothes wearing a good watch, a fine gold chain, a walletful of credit cards in her shoulder bag, victim of nothing but anticipation. Let me see her first, she prayed. Loot me later, but let me see her first!

Like a whiff of vinegar, that straightened her up. She rang REECE—the buzzer was a nasty rasp, and the door needed a rude push. She heard footsteps, squinted into the hall, got a whiff of somebody's burnt toast, and her daughter came out of the shadows just the way an image in the darkroom floated up out of the developer, feature by feature. Miriam was so dizzy with urgency she couldn't think of any words at all. Face-to-face, smiling stupidly—surely the girl must have felt as stupid as she did—all she could do was take her hands and grin, raise them shoulder height, holding on, and grin some more, although her cheeks were soaked with tears that felt as if they surfaced from her skin, not her eyes. Seventeen years. Seventeen years. Unreal, impossible: the human brain was not made for encompassing this. Miriam said that about a lot of things, actually—not made for going to sleep in New York and waking up in Rio or Rome or Karachi, or not made for flying to the moon and coming back, though she was obviously wrong about both. The mind adjusts.

But this time, light-headed, she thought she might finally be right.

THE GIRL was not tiny.

She was expecting someone very delicate, that wraith at graduation, breakable, unfinished, finely strung. In Miriam's dreams

Veronica was a dancer. Probably that was because her father was rather slight: thin, fine boned, actually, a man always self-conscious about his size. When he could finally crawl out of his tweeds and into a dashiki, he swelled up. Pride, maybe, but mostly fabric.

Or maybe she just couldn't imagine a child of hers bigger than she was, although they would all tower over her in time. After years of practice, she had managed to age her baby well past eight months, which was when she had seen her last, but not to have grown her up fully. Oh, not without herself!

Veronica was solid, almost square, someone who couldn't be moved, Miriam suspected, if she didn't want to move. Her hair was cut very, very short to show the bones of her head. She must have been wearing a dozen tiny gold rings on each side; her ears looked like tambourines. Her skin was the color of—she didn't know what, that would take some thought. Every comparison felt like a cliché. Coffee the way she liked it? Some kind of wood, some kind of spice? Cinnamon, maybe. Cinnamon was closest, though nowhere near right, too red. Honey was too dark. The delicate tan of the cedar that lined the inside of a cigar box, how about that? Miriam had stockpiled her father's wonderful-smelling cigar boxes, worn the gold paper rings on her fingers. That fragile papery wood . . . This is the person who grew inside me, she thought dumbly. She is half me. Those were just words, but this was about body; her heart was beating so hard it made her weak. Absurd, inadequate, insulting, almost, to describe her feature by feature, her this, her that, the way you do a stranger casually met. But she was a stranger. And since she was, Miriam could say (and would say) and be believed, Her face is beautiful.

"I'm all ready to go," Veronica said, then, her first words to her, Miriam realized, in her life. She registered the accent, deep-dyed New York, the syllables bunched tight in the mouth, dark the way the air was dark here—and she tried to catch the timbre of her voice but five words weren't enough. She was waiting for an invitation inside but she didn't hear one. Veronica was on her way up the stairs, rudely, or maybe just awkwardly, thoughtlessly, leaving her mother alone in the hall. So she ignored the lapse, if it was a lapse, and came along behind. The girl hesitated at the front door. Miriam could see how embarrassment colored her face, made her smile tensely, but for her it was now or never. Slow down, slow down, where are we going so fast? The going isn't the thing. You're here, I'm here. Stop.

"Oh, look, Veronica. Ronnee. Excuse me." As if there weren't enough distance between her baby and this girl, the name, someone else's, sat strangely in her mouth. "I'm not here to check out your apartment, really I'm not. But I'd love to—I could, sort of, see where you've been living, you know? Try to—imagine." She was desperate to look around, no way could Ronnee begin to comprehend. She didn't expect her to. The girl stepped out of her way.

The place was not bad. Better than it looked outside; it certainly was no slum. She saw, she saw, that Eljay was still, or rather once again, the intellectual fool he called himself—books, photographs, posters on the wall, enough shelves of LPs for a radio station—before he gave it all up for "natural soul." She wondered if he'd gone back to bow ties. It was a comfortable, lived-in place, walls a dingy golden color, a brightly striped couch, a wooden rocker. A vivid rug dimmed by wear. And sloppy and cluttered as it was—much looser than his tensely tidy room at Parnassus had ever looked—it was more alive in its way than the gorgeous embalmed houses that clustered around her gatehouse back home. She wished she knew why they lived here—solidarity? finances?—and not in what would be called a "better" neighborhood. She would not get to ask Ronnee's father.

"Your room?" she asked her, as casually as she could. Her trembling had begun to subside, though her mouth was still so dry she could hardly speak.

Veronica hesitated. She was wearing one of those gathered, diaphanous Indian skirts of many colors that were made for smaller girls, and a sleeveless purple T-shirt. Her arms were strong, possibly the arms of someone who lifted weights. Miriam could imagine her standing in front of her closet this morning trying to choose. How odd it all was, enough to drain the meaning out of the words:

Dressing yourself to meet your mom. My God, to meet your maker.
Reality can ask too much of us.

So, if she began "Her room was neat," that said as much about
herself as it did about her daughter. Such self-consciousness priced
every experience out of the market. Her room was neither neat nor
not neat (she could finesse that way); it was crammed, though:
posters, a paperweight collection, a Japanese paper parasol floating
down, open, from the ceiling from an invisible string. A dozen
framed photographs of friends. A pretty typical girl's room. Also
the room of a black teenager, recognizably American and recognizably middle class, every image, every icon black. Sade, so lus-
cious you couldn't imagine she could sing too. One of those
Jackson sisters, every Jackson a *J*—Janet?—and Judith Jamison,
more *J*'s (maybe she did dance), toothy and elegant, looking stern
enough to make paint peel. Well, why not?

Her friends were mixed, at least the ones in the group pictures,
undoubtedly school friends. Two or three leaning-together-
laughing shots—she remembered those so well herself—were of
girls with young, sweet, dark faces.

"You must love plants," she stumbled along, because the win-
dowsill was crammed with pots, violets burgeoning, ivy, ferns,
philodendron. She thought, I like this girl, she's busy with com-
mitments, pleasures, energy.

"Well, these are all going to be dead, probably, when I get back.
My father does *not* love plants." She went over and touched the
furry leaf of a violet, tenderly, the way you'd tweak a cat's ear. And
Miriam was thinking, Imagine how it felt for me to leave *you* with
him, Veronica. This was all flying by too fast. The girl was going to
be sucked back into nothing again as soon as Miriam left her.

"My grandma," she said, and hesitated. "My dad's mom, I mean,
in—where she lives in Alabama? She has all these plants, these are,
like, their babies, you know, their cuttings that she made me? She
says you're not supposed to thank anybody for giving you a piece
of their plant, you just name it after them." She was squatting
down beside the little forest of greenery and eyeing the leaves as if
they were faces. "So when I water them or whatever, some of

them, I say 'Good morning, Ma Thelmie'—that's what we call her, you know, Ma Thelmie. 'How you doin' today, Ma? Not so good? Sorry to hear that.'" She peered at them, making a resigned little face. "Of course I keep forgetting I'm not taking them to school with me anyway in the fall, so I guess they're done for."

"Well, give them to somebody, why don't you? Then that person can say hello to you whenever she waters them." I'll take them, she wanted to say, but that was too foolish.

"Ha! If they can make it through the summer with this man in charge."

Then she showed Miriam her collections—the paperweights and the wooden African animals full of precise detail, and her photographs, including a dozen names and places, and finally Miriam asked her, "Do you have a picture of your father anywhere? I'd like to see him after all these years."

She looked around. "Well—I don't, but—" and Miriam saw into his room, a dark little lair, which was as sloppy as a teenage boy's, the bed unmade, the floor littered with underwear and books, ah books, in a scattered pile beside the bed. On the wall an ancient SNCC poster with its corners riddled with tack holes that testified to how many times it had been moved and rehung. A black fist, with the figures of men, women, children sprouting out of it as if they were being squeezed. A strange image, if you thought about it; the fist that extruded them ought to be white. But maybe they were supposed to be flowers, blooming out of their chains like Ronnee's marigolds.

"Oh wait, yes," her daughter said suddenly, and dug out of a box a magazine, it looked like, and riffled its pages. "Here, look. He doesn't keep any real pictures, but see, here he is behind me. I'm getting this award—"

"Veronica, what's this? What are you getting here?"

She shrugged. "Oh, it's just—it was a theater piece, my school won this citywide contest and I was in the play, so—but look, see? Here's a good picture, he's sitting here cheering."

Indeed he was, the same man and yet not the same man she had loved just long enough or just a little too long, depending on what you thought of the outcome. When she knew Eljay he was a slim, intense, fiercely focused man, the color of a chestnut warmed in the palm. He wore tweed jackets, tight-collared white shirts, bow ties, and he was so nervous all the time that he jingled the coins in his pockets until the day she told him he sounded like a miser counting his money. Then he stopped cold turkey, proving, she thought, that we have more control of our bad habits than we think we do. He was the first seriously intellectual Negro she had ever met, back when *Negro* was the best word they seemed to have. Her journey from Houston to Smith to Michigan had not been studded with black male scholars, though of course she'd read Kenneth Clark and John Hope Franklin and all the rest, and she was so impressed she was helpless before his intelligence long before she asked herself whether he was a good or kind or likable man. It took her many years to recognize what a patronizing act it was to love him for being unique. It took her a few more to realize that he'd worked hard at that uniqueness and that he thought (at the beginning, at least) that having her love him was proof that his efforts had worked.

"This picture is how old?" she asked Veronica.

"Oh, just last year. End of my junior year."

He was a nice, ordinary-looking man, clapping his hands, smiling broadly. Of course he had thickened up. His hair was short, his glasses different. He had a close-cropped, responsible-looking beard. Mostly he looked like he had relaxed. He used to be a clenched fist, not, at first, in defiance like the SNCC poster, but in tension, frantic effort, wild unassuageable lust for the Ph.D. he couldn't seem to finish while he worked full time and then some, and all the imagined respect it would bring with it, the world on its knees at his feet. Eljay's childhood had not been an auspicious one, to say the least. It haunted him like a doom, like a self-fulfilling curse. She had never been sure how much forgiveness its outrages ought to buy him. That, of course, was turning out to be the question of the century, not simply of her love affair with Eljay Reece: how much love, how much compassion do we owe in return for struggle and pain? Sometimes she felt she'd been part of an experiment to find that out. Apparently she had not suffered enough pain before he met her, so he taught her, helped her to catch up. And here she was, speechless, hushed as a spy in his half-dark room.

"Has he changed much?" his daughter asked. Miriam couldn't imagine what she was conjuring up behind her own eyes.

She laughed. "Oh, honey, he was wearing a dashiki the last time I saw him, with a big sort of rainbow burst all over it. He had hair like—" She didn't want to offend her. "Well—" She gestured as if she had a huge crown on her head. Wider even: a cooking pot. "Let's just say he used to look like he was being electrocuted. I have some pictures along, for later."

When Veronica laughed, her eyes crinkled, her face got pudgy. "His hair's getting thin now, you ought to see the top. He hates it! He's very vain, I think—for a man, I mean."

"And the room—he was incredibly—compulsively—neat. This is . . ." Miriam shook her head. He had to be more at home with himself to live in a slouch like this.

She hit the magazine photo gently with her index finger. "He must have been very proud of you." It was the kind of scene that made her tear up just to think of it. She could hardly cross the threshold of her children's school on the day of any performance without needing a hankie. She had humiliated herself on more than one occasion.

But Veronica's face stiffened at that. "He was proud, but I told him he'd better not bother. I didn't even want him at that ceremony, but they said I had to let him come. 'He's your *father*.' " She made a bitter-lemon face. "Why don't we—let me save it, okay? It's a long story. They're all long stories."

So they went to pick up her duffel and her backpack. She said, "Let me just make sure everything's off that's supposed to be off," and made a practiced-looking once-over of the bathroom and kitchen, with a quick snatch at the oven controls to be sure they were straight up. Without teenagers at home, Miriam didn't have a lot of girls to compare her to, but she had herself, and the girl struck her as remarkably self-reliant. Not casual, not cool. Solid. Open. Eljay must have done something right.

How pathetic, to gather clues to the simplest facts of your daughter's life. Anger splashed up in her chest like something flung from a great height.

Just as they were leaving the phone rang. Veronica picked it up and said in a flat voice, "We're just on our way out. Right." No enthusiasm. "I don't really want—all right. Yeah, right." She put the receiver to the side for a minute. "Do you have a phone number where we're going? My father wants it, just in case. My grandmother's sick . . ."

"You don't need a reason," Miriam said, and gave it to her. The man she made this young woman with was on the other end of the line not asking to speak with her.

"Well, you won't," Veronica was saying to him. "Forget it, I couldn't care less. I've got to go now. What do you mean?" She hesitated, taken by surprise. "I don't know yet. We'll see." A long pause. "Anyway, what do you care?"

She was shaking her head as she put the receiver down. "He wants to know what I'm going to call you. As if he should care."

Miriam hadn't earned the tears for her daughter's theater prize; she got them for that instead. "I don't know, Veronica. Maybe it's a little early to decide."

"Well, on the subject of names. Ronnee. Ree. Call me Veronica, it's like I call you 'Mrs.—' " She hesitated. "Vener? Am I saying that right?"

"Sure," Miriam answered. "As in 'venerable.' " A very old joke, suddenly stupid. "Well, that'll get me to call you Ree if anything will. What do you call your father?"

She was pushing her luggage out the door, setting its three locks. (O New York.) "Asshole," she said, and followed her mother down the stairs. What Miriam registered, way back behind her eyes, was disappointment at the thought that Veronica had called on her alternate parent just at the point when her main man had become impossible.

MIRIAM WATCHED the way her daughter skipped down the front steps. Her lightness and speed felt a little studied, maybe, either for her—*See, this is what I've looked like, living here. This is how I move, quick, into my life every day*—or was it for the chorus of spectators? How wearing it must be, that endless clump of aimless, provocative viewers who hung out around the stoops, heckling, saluting, taking note. Here I go, she seemed to be saying, bumping her duffel down, step after step, scraping up its bottom, not caring.

She could see that Ronnee liked the car—a good parting gesture, the way she threw the bag in back, came around, and sat down breezily. Slammed the door firmly and watched those heads turn toward them curiously. Ronnee and this white lady in a car red as a trumpet blast? What's going down, Ree? Running out on us? None of your nosy business.

Then what?

"Have you eaten?" Miriam asked, and just as quickly regretted it, maternal habit that could never be overridden, not by the world's funkiest car.

"I'm okay," Ronnee said.

They couldn't look at each other then. She fussed with the air-conditioning, turned down the radio, down, not off, which would have seemed too obvious a plea for conversation. How were they going to *do* this? It was impossible. Oh, honey, she wished she could say, this is like giving birth: Now that we've started, there's no going back!

She asked Ronnee about her graduation, asked her about her school, her choice of college, why they lived in Bedford-Stuyvesant—wouldn't Harlem be more likely? (Because for years her father had taught jazz to kids out here and they got comfortable. He still played with some of them once in a while)—huge questions tumbling out as if she were asking, Do you like chocolate? She *interviewed* her, marking time, and Ronnee, looking as if her mouth was drying to cotton like her own, the way it will when something important is going badly, answered mostly looking straight ahead, sullen. Since she could see out and it was her city, Miriam wished she'd warned her that they were getting lost.

It took her a while to admit that she didn't know where they were. "I guess I can't talk and drive at the same time." She looked at Ronnee for help but the girl was so passive it felt to her like hostility, a sudden chill.

Or maybe she was just lost in thought. "Hmnn?"

"Do you have any idea where we are?"

"What are you looking for?"

"The Belt Parkway," Miriam said, feeling defeated. She was not sure why she thought it mattered, why she needed to impress her daughter as if she were running for Mother and had to look qualified. Her own children—she stopped that thought, horrified—her other, her subsequent children?—had known her for a thousand thousand minutes. She didn't have to build her personality for them. In fact, she couldn't escape it if she wanted to.

"The Belt Parkway. Oh, I don't know. I don't drive, so I don't pay a lot of attention to highways and stuff." She was looking around, baffled. "We don't have a car anyway."

"You don't?" Of course, we're in New York, not Houston. People survive very well here without their own wheels. But she realized she had a raft of questions about Eljay for her and this was not the time.

They were deep into a depressing neighborhood, battered and rusty, a bit of bleary water a few streets down. This was the New York that wasn't on the Gray Line tour.

"I think this is Gowanus," her daughter said. "With that stinking canal over there. You don't want to be here." Miriam didn't know if she meant that it was dangerous or just wrong, but it didn't strike her as a place to inquire of other carless people, so she drove around and around in search of a gas station and finally, in despair, pulled into a transmission shop—at least they lived in a world of cars. She called out to a young man, who was standing outside wiping his hands on a rag and looking into the middle distance. When she called out her question he came over and leaned an elbow above the car window so that he could hang his face close to hers. His uniform said *PEDRO P.* "Whatchu pay me if I tell you?"

She caught herself at the edge of outrage just in time to see he was kidding. He looked into the car at Ronnee and did an exaggerated double take. She was giving him no expression at all.

"Oh hey, lady, you got a *beauty* in here witchu. This is a whole 'nother *story*." He laughed, all spit and glinting gold. "Now we might do a little business, wow, okay. Where you taking her, lady? Whynchu just leave her here with me, I take good care of her!"

He kept his eyes on her while he told Miriam where she needed to go—he had admirable lashes, thick as paintbrushes—until finally the excitement of the directions drew him in. People can get very involved in trying to recreate the little map they carry in their heads; it must, she thought, be a sort of teaching challenge. When he finished, he was nearly out of breath. "Hey, sweetheart, can you say that all back to me?" He waited a beat, then actually, earnestly, made kissing noises at her. Ronnee rolled her eyes and looked out the other window.

"Lord, Ronnee, is that what you have to put up with?" They were on their way, a right and two lights, then a left.

"That wasn't bad compared to some of them. At least they can't get their hands on you when you're in a car."

Miriam had never been beautiful enough for that. In Italy, maybe, where it didn't matter what you looked like. Or things had changed for the worse. They drove on in silence.

After a while, on the Hutchinson Parkway, the green began to take them in, shaggy trees and neat cropped grass, like someone's lawn. Considering what it took to keep a front lawn tidy, Miriam mused, envisioning their St. Augustine grass that demanded endless tending by Horacio, whom Barry insisted on calling "the lawn boy," there should have been crews of hundreds ceaselessly plying the highway's edge. But it was one of those strange things—you never caught them at it.

"Do you ever get out of town?" Miriam asked.

"We used to go to my Grandma Thelmie's, in Alabama? But we haven't for a few years. I'm not sure why. I guess 'cause she's sick and we'd be a bother. She's not one of those people who'll sit down and let you do for her."

"She lives in the country?" She strained to remember, but the only memory she had of Eljay's mother, whom she had never met, was that when he was angriest he would blame her for living in her little town, a sad, one-streetlight place called Euphrates, Alabama; he would blame her for her never-ending poverty, for her arthritic body that made it hard for her to work even then, never mind her pain—he only remembered the pain when he'd been drinking or when he called to wish her a happy birthday or a merry Christmas and sentiment would flood over him and stifle his self-pity: Eljay was a desperate man, crab-clawing his way up the slick side of a bucket. Then his mama would blame her troubles on Satan and he'd find it convenient to believe her. Probably around the time they quit each other he was guiding her toward a salutary hatred of white folks instead, but Miriam didn't hang on long enough to hear whether the lesson ever took.

"She lives in a terrible little town, but I always liked to go there because she was so good to me. I have an aunt—well, actually, a second cousin or something, Darita, and they and all her friends would sort of spoil me, you know? And because it's really country all around. Not gorgeous country, I don't think—it's kind of flat and scrubby?—but still—" She gestured outside the car. "Green."

"Did you get to spend a lot of time there? Summers?"

"Oh, lots. Summers. And once I was down there just about a whole school year. That was pretty different."

"Why did you—"

"My daddy went to Africa. He had to go to Dakar. I was afraid we were going to move there, but he came back."

Miriam wondered if she was going to elucidate on all that but she said not one word more.

"But then, the last few years—she's really old and weak now and I don't think she's going to get any better—we haven't been there at all. I call her pretty often, though."

Miriam would have liked to tell her how her father used to rant against his mother, but she couldn't. In fact, the things she wanted to say kept rolling in like waves and battering up against some inhibition that stopped them, because it felt as if reticence was the better part of wisdom for now. You're less than two hours into this relationship, she told herself. There was no script for this. Not even an adoptive mother's script would do.

Her daughter, beside her, had drifted off into something like invisibility. It was a fascinating thing, actually, to see how far out of her body someone could drift and still be sitting there with her eyes open. I will have to learn how to read her, Miriam thought humbly, hoping she could slow herself down, chasten her expectations, let it be.

Ronnee had drawn into herself, almost catatonic in her distance and stillness and clearly under no pressure to perform: perfectly unmoving, hands loose in her lap, in a nest of soft many-colored fabric, the slightest frown creasing the sweet place between her eyes. Again Miriam thought of a dancer, someone in absolute control. She wished she could whisper to her, "What are you thinking, Veronica Reece?" but she didn't feel she had the right yet to intrude. *You said you were looking for me, too,* she said to her, but not aloud. What did you want of me? The girl had no curiosity about her; she hadn't asked a single question. Miriam felt she'd failed some test, though which one she couldn't guess.

Finally she turned on the radio, faced the problem of choice, confronted her most profound feelings about democracy, decided Ronnee was too far away inside herself to really care, and found some Schubert, simple on the surface and full of sorrow, which laid a cool hand on her brow and said, Patience, patience. You were never good at patience but you'd better learn it now.

SUDDENLY RONNEE WAS WIDE AWAKE, looking surprised, though Miriam couldn't tell whether it was her absence, asleep, or her presence, awake, that surprised her. Maybe she was just sleepy, not trying to disappear. Or the motion of the car was irresistible, the way it was to young children. Maybe that's the way she got ready for sleep—they had no past to tell her. "I'm not used to being in a car, you know, *going* somewhere!" She sounded jubilant.

"If you lived where I live, you'd never be out of one for long," Miriam told her. Finally questions, however impersonal. Ronnee wanted to know what Houston was like; she told her that, too. There were long patches that reminded her of those conversations you tend to have on planes, trains, and long bus rides, enjoying a little glimpse into a stranger's life, someone you'd never see again after you got where you were going. "Have a nice day," one of you says, and you pick up your luggage and go down the aisle. Lovely girl, you might think. Bright and lively. Good luck to her.

But then she looked across the seat at her, at the way Veronica leaned back hard and spoke straight into the windshield, concentrating even on this trivia, and it broke upon Miriam like a giant wave: This was the baby she had wept for, day after day, night after night, when she was lost to her. This was the same flesh she knew so well, every fold and cranny that she'd swabbed and powdered, kissed and patted, the first she had ever made out of her own body, who had been severed into a stranger and now, miraculously, she had brought her back. And wasn't it a good thing Ronnee hadn't had to live deprived? *She* had lived deprived instead.

Of course, they would all cut themselves loose some day and go off into their various privacies—Evie was beginning already. The boys, even Seth, who was older, was like his anatomy, all on the outside, very little hidden, though it would come to that with him soon enough. But they wouldn't have to account for their lives! My God, my God, she had been robbed. And not only did she lose this child but she deformed her life because of her, because of the loss of her. She had been struck dumb with remorse, and her muteness had become her voice.

What took her breath away was the memory of those feelings, not the feelings themselves. Of being the person who suffered them, for whom she had such pity her stomach knotted at the thought of her. She saw herself in a room with the blinds drawn, incapable of swallowing. She saw herself like a madwoman or a criminal, stalking the house where she knew her baby was. She saw herself sitting one day—though she hadn't allowed herself to think of it in all these years, how could she ever forget this?—sitting in the bus station in Memphis, she couldn't remember why it was Memphis, she must have been changing buses, leaving Mississippi—and she was weeping, doubled over, weeping into her lap, gasping for breath, because she had just done something irrevocable: she had finally stopped fighting for Veronica, exhausted and demoralized. She had given up and she knew she would never see her child again.

But now she was learning that that child had a passion for eating mayonnaise right from the jar; an ex-boyfriend named Thomas Hardy (which didn't seem to amuse her); one weak ankle, for which she'd had an operation; an irregular period (which, Miriam suspected, her daughter inherited from her, and which in fact had made a significant contribution to that daughter's conception); an incapacity to do algebra but near fluency in French; and extra-wide feet, hard to find shoes for.

"By the way, on the subject of shoes," Ronnee said, interrupting herself, "is there some way we might be able to stop along the way and maybe buy me some sneakers? Somebody stole mine."

"Somebody stole your sneakers?"

"In school." A mock-bitter scowl. "Can you imagine, in a place like that? Half those kids could buy—I don't know what. The moon. I left them out of my locker for a couple of minutes because I got called in to see a teacher, and when I got back—psshtt." She snapped her fingers. "Gone."

"Well, okay," Miriam said. "Sure. We're not in any particular hurry. We can stop in Hartford, maybe, or Springfield, and get you some new ones."

Ronnee was looking out the window with what looked like sat-isfaction: If you live in the city and have no occasion to visit the suburbs, this open landscape could look good to you, its clumps of development—pastel wood (no, more likely vinyl siding, for less frequent repair)—and the small huddles of trees left standing, lonely survivors of ancient pine forests and thick woods. She tried to see it through Ronnee's eyes, this blighted scene. Ronnee was taking it in avidly, moving her head left to right and back again. "The names of the towns are all, like, they sound like England, don't they?"

"They do. You're in New England, after all."

She laughed. "Shoo, I never thought where that came from. Wwhh." It wasn't exactly *shoo*, it wasn't exactly *wwhh*, that long slightly disgusted breath. She had a little repertoire of noises, tiny wordless conversations with herself, all wind and teeth. Miriam supposed that last one denoted surprise or maybe derision at herself: *Wwhh.* It was a language.

They found her a pair of K-Swiss that she liked—she grinned like a little kid when she tied them up—and on the way out of the store, Miriam didn't know if it was her look as they passed the juniors' department or if it was her own need, but of course they stopped and fingered a few things, held them up in front of Ronnee, and in a very short time she'd bought her daughter two shirts, a pair of good black jeans, and some overall shorts. (Lightning-fast flash of the SNCC workers, twenty years ago, who affected farmers' clothing, bib overalls especially, so as not to stand out from the people they were organizing. Their affectation, and now, how different, hers.) She put an arm around Ronnee's shoulders, leaving the cashier. It did not feel natural, she was very self-conscious touching her, but she did it anyway. "We've got a lot of lost shopping time to make up for," she told her, and the girl leaned toward her a little.

"Thanks. Oh, thanks," she said, and she seemed to be glowing in her skin. "That's not something I could do with my daddy."

Before they got back in the car they went to get some lunch.

"I suppose you're eager to hear some—I don't know what to call it, an account—of how we ever got separated all those years ago." Miriam realized how abrupt this must sound, but she felt like a child who had waited forever for something she coveted, had fantasized and prayed for, and now, finally, it was happening. Why be constrained? Ronnee must have wondered about this over the years—where had her mother *gone*? Why had she deserted her? If adopted children blame themselves for their abandonment, even if they've been given over—not away!—before they have distinct personalities, how much worse for Veronica, whose mother had a chance to love her for eight months. Deep, deep down, where love of self warms and hatches, what could she have made of that?

She looked into her daughter's eyes, which were not green like the eyes of so many light-skinned girls, that odd compromise of colors, but a golden hazel, a warmth like caramels, with dark spokes in them.

Then, quickly, Ronnee looked away, not at anything, she could tell, but elsewhere, anywhere but at her. "I've got to go to the bathroom," she announced, already rising.

"Well, I was going to say we ought to save it for a better time," Miriam told her, her face burning. "I just thought, you know, if you were anxious . . ."

Ronnee was already turned toward the rear of the pizzeria. "No, it's okay." She shrugged at Miriam's urgency. "I can wait. Do you think you could order me another Coke while I'm in there? Diet?"

"Diet." Big girl, she probably needed to be careful. *How can this be a child of mine.* A flutter in the gut, vague as the first kick of the fetus. What she had to guard against, Barry had warned her, was having particular expectations. She had failed, then. Had imagined more tears at their meeting. Had imagined her daughter's curiosity as great as her own. Had planned the way she'd tell her story, Ronnee's story, as carefully as a seduction: lamplight, country quiet, and Ronnee abrim with old questions. (Well, the child was nervous, and who could blame her. She wasn't ready one-two-three. Time, Seth had told her with delight one day—"This isn't original," he admitted. "I heard it, okay? But it's so good. 'Time is what keeps everything from happening all at once!' ") Barry was right and he was wise, Barry who liked things predictable but could make allowances, and sweet of him to be protective: Just let it be. But you, she had thought then and thought again, you who are neither her father nor her mother, can let it be. I can't.

Get me a Diet Coke?

THERE WERE BEAUTIFUL VISTAS along the highway: the long, symmetrical wooden tobacco barns in Connecticut, set in a field like abandoned barracks; the blue hills of Massachusetts opening out ahead, at the end of a bowl of empty space, a succession of gray to blue to purple, hazy as a watercolor, and shadow falling into the bowl in great irregular splotches, each under a ragged piece of cloud.

"Do you want to stop to look?" she asked Ronnee; there was a turnout for sightseers. Don't ask, her old teacher-self insisted—how would she know? She pulled off the road and got out of the car. Ronnee followed warily. Miriam was showing her a foolish proprietary grin as if she had made the scenery herself.

"That is . . ."

Miriam waited and waited. "What?"

"I don't know. I never saw anything so—far away." She looked disappointed by her own explanation, but Miriam was satisfied. Ronnee was rapt, her hands out in front of her as if she expected to receive a piece of it in her arms. "Sometimes I go down to the Promenade, you know, in Brooklyn Heights? It's near where my school is, so I go over in the afternoons some days."

"It's not a place I know. I haven't seen much of Brooklyn, you know."

"Well, it's along the river. You can see New York—I mean, like, Manhattan. The city. And you can look out into the harbor, water

going on a long way. But it isn't—like—that *far*. It's a couple of
miles, I guess. Less. And Alabama where my grandma lives, that's
so near and flat and scrubby. This . . ." She shook her head. "This
makes my legs feel funny. Weak." She laughed. "This makes my
knees itch."

They drove on and Miriam strained to see it through her daughter's eyes. Was there a picture people carried in their heads
that said *New England*? She thought they had one when they
went shopping for their house and came upon Hyland; they
knew it when they saw it, instantly. But "people"—what did she
mean by "people"? Ronnee was a Black girl, if that was the right
word to catch as the wheel of fashion went round—and anyway,
what was she, black, tan, gray? Off-white?—from Brooklyn.
Inland Brooklyn, the Brooklyn without lawns, cheek-by-jowl
Brooklyn, music-all-day-long Brooklyn, Bed-Stuy-girl-borrowing-
Brooklyn-Heights Brooklyn. Everything was qualified, everything
particular: there was no such thing as a Black Girl, let alone a Half-
Black Girl, From Brooklyn. Miriam saw how she was launched
into a new life in which she would pick up every settled thing in
gingerly fingers, turn it over, inspect it, put it down gently, and
wonder what she'd felt, and what she was supposed to.

In Northfield they passed the lovely precincts of a famous
prep school. "This is a school sort of like yours, a place to get a
good solid education," Miriam told her, thinking black-girl-from-
Brooklyn-who-did-not-go-to-a-dreadful-public-high-school—
another category?

"Like mine?!" Ronnee laughed. "Oh, no. *Look* at it!"

"Why, what's yours like?"

She covered her face with her hands, Miriam was so amusing.
"Past tense. Well—no, I guess it's still like it was, only it's just not
mine anymore. Anyway . . . It's just a building, first of all. One big
overstuffed building, with a couple of added-on pieces. I'm not
knocking it, it's pretty much a good school and it *costs* like—
but—"

The green swept up a long hill here, so smooth it seemed to have
been applied by a broad paintbrush, and dotted around were the

old sweet wooden houses with their dark shutters and their shingled roofs, and brick buildings with flowers hunched around their bases, and trees still fluffing out with fresh growth. Far off, a girl and a boy (if she could tell right at that distance) were walking toward them, reduced and unreal, as if they were caught in binoculars held backward. Space. Sky. Green and more green, a dozen subtle greens.

But while Miriam was rhapsodizing to herself about its beauty, Ronnee said, "I don't know if I'd like that kind of place." She was whispering, as if she didn't want to offend anyone. "I think I'd miss—you know. Concrete. Stores and—like—things *happening*. This is so deserted!"

And on they plunged, the simple houses thickening, thinning, as they moved through the towns, heading north and east toward Hyland. There was one purple house right at the roadside that made her laugh and roll her eyes, and the brick factory on the millpond in Harrisville that looked like a postcard captioned TRANQUILITY. She was taking it all in, but who could tell what she was making of it? Her comments were cryptic: "The houses are so far from each other." "Is that the only store?" "There aren't any—like—what do you call them? Billboards." Miriam got the drift.

She was thinking of the town where Ronnee was born. Not the city, where the hospital was, but Rowan, where the college sat like a strange growth beside the road, where once you got past the back fence there were open fields and houses dotted in the middle of space, as lonely as these. Ronnee would have no reason to remember Mississippi, she was far too young, where the sky was everywhere, overwhelming, isolating. If Miriam didn't think it would undo her, she would take Ronnee back to see it. Maybe she would. Later.

And Hyland. "It isn't real," Ronnee said as they glided down Garden Street. "Those white fences and all, it's so—cute. It looks like the little towns they build so you can run your electric train around them at Christmas."

"Is that good or bad?"

She shrugged. "I don't know, it's just strange." She was looking around as she talked: they were passing the Unitarian church with its rustic fencing and its golden clock tower. Ralph Waldo Emerson spoke there once, the town fathers were happy to tell you. William James had a house in the next town over, and Henry came to visit when he could. "Do you think this is a beautiful place?" Ronnee asked.

And she realized they were not really talking aesthetics: there were no black people here. With the exception of a few recently arrived Cambodians brought by the Good Samaritans of the Unitarian church, there were few variations on Hyland's pleasant, uninflected whiteness—white houses, white fences, white faces, white as the snow that buried it in a different season. But Miriam said, "I do. I certainly do."

"Because?"

She had to think. "Well, it's—calm, I guess. The people know each—"

"No, I mean what it looks like."

She didn't have to hesitate at that. "Oh yes, honey, yes. I love the houses, they're sort of classically simple, their lines are pure, they're like variations on a couple of themes, you know, a few basic plans, but they feel so different depending on where they sit and how they're landscaped. And they have so much history in them."

Ronnee looked at her mother levelly again and nodded, but made no comment. She was probably asking, Whose history? Not hers. Not, in fact, mine either, Miriam objected. When she visited the graveyard down the hill, with its mossy old granite stones inscribed to Lucinda, consort, and Reverend Obadiah Hastings, she remembered how she drank strange waters here, sweet and affecting but not hers, not hers either, yet she could love them.

Then they were in the woods, off the blacktop, where the late afternoon light flashed through the trees like a strobe, dizzying. She had to shake her head to get free of what it did to her. She couldn't believe it was taking so long to get there. The brook ran along beside them, curling and twisting—she always thought of it as a loyal animal that chased their heels but didn't ever catch them.

When Ronnee saw it, she cried out, "Is that—does that *belong* to you?"

Miriam had to explain that, out here, a brook didn't exactly belong to anyone, but that it ran across their property and everyone else's and out again. "It's no one's really. It just—is." She'd never thought about it that way.

"Is it a river? With a name?"

"No, it's just a brook. In the South that would be a creek. In Texas and Louisiana, maybe a bayou. But here it's called Tanager Brook. I love it." They had come to the pond, in which the willows' reflection shimmered. The water was so still they scarcely wavered. It was breathtaking. Ronnee could not believe this belonged to Miriam. "I thought you said you can't own the water."

"Well . . ." Again a new way of looking at what she'd taken for granted. The distinction, she told her, was hard to explain. She hadn't any idea what the difference was, except that the brook was smart enough to keep moving. "Don't worry, in the eyes of God," she reassured her daughter, a little grandiloquently, "nobody really owns any of it. It's borrowed." She was thinking how, in the fall, though not here, Orthodox Jews build their little sukkot, those wooden houses that must have holes in their roofs big enough to see the stars, to remind them of how transient and humble is their shelter on the earth: borrowed, all of it. Theirs was a religion bent on keeping them humble.

"Can we swim in it?"

"Of course."

"Right now?"

"As soon as you get your bathing suit on. You did bring your bathing suit, didn't you?" She had to stop feeling she was speaking to a child.

"You can't just—nobody goes by here, do they? Can't you just, you know, go skinny-dipping?"

She explained that the road wasn't used much but that some people took it as a shortcut from one place to another. It was technically private but in fact you could be seen by someone going by.

"They'd get a shock, wouldn't they?" Ronnee said. The idea seemed to appeal to her.

"It's kind of a shame, but I don't recommend it." Miriam started up the final hill to the house. Oh, she loved that first sight of it every year, the lovely, clean, generous shape of it, those dormers poking out, her kids said, like frog eyes. Beetle brows. The tall barn alongside with its little cupola, and the early evening light making a cool fire in its windows. It had the purity without harshness that New England farmhouses have so gently given to a modest people, the uncluttered shape of habitation without pretense. She always hated Houston to the bottom of her soul when the view of that house broke through the shaggy trees. It was as unflamboyant as everything else up here. It impressed by being only what it was, not by wanting to be something grander, richer, finer. Behind it the mountains spread their haunches with an implausible clarity. She had come two thousand miles for this. Thank heavens Ronnee was rooting around under the front seat looking for her shoes so that she couldn't see her tears.

Apologizing for their mustiness, hoping Ronnee wouldn't notice the piles of mouse droppings along the baseboards (not to mention the chewed cardboard she knew she'd find under the sink, stolen, she assumed, for nest-building), she showed her all the rooms of her beloved house, the long kitchen–dining room with the refectory table at the far end, the bedrooms with their very different moods, the boys' with its rudimentary furnishings and Red Sox pennants, the plastic mesh basket hung above the door, even the single gym sock peeking out from the dust under Seth's bed; the daintier decoration of Evie's with its dried flowers and the mirror around which she'd stuck photos of her friends, on the walls her pictures of fairy-tale characters—Puss in Boots in his huge galoshes and Cinderella weeping on her hearth in an aura of ashes.

Ronnee stood at the door of each room. She didn't venture in. Miriam wondered what stopped her there at the threshold, whether she felt the strong gust of years that blew through the rooms, all those summers they had lived there as a family, whether that was painful for her, or of no consequence at all. That would depend, she supposed, on the kind of love Eljay had given her, and the number of others, loving or otherwise, in her life. Though, in spite of all, she had felt that surge of jealousy at Ronnee's Christmas gifts, laid in her hands by strangers.

"You choose which room you'd like, Ronnee," she said, and showed her the last, which was the anonymous one that they kept for guests. It was big, half empty, unclaimed-looking, though it had its high bed and two white-painted dressers, a chair and two lamps, and above the chair a needlepoint they'd found in an antique shop that said something in Swedish about snowy nights promising the greatest warmth. She knew Ronnee would choose this one, and, without explanation, that was what she did.

Miriam was the one who was almost apologetic. "You can put your own things anywhere you'd like," she told her, though she couldn't quite imagine what those things might be. "And if you want to leave anything here—you know, over the winter—that's okay." She thought her duffel probably held some shorts, some T-shirts, some jeans. Ronnee looked at Miriam with the slightest smile, as if to say, Oh, don't try so hard. I know you want me to feel at home, but it's not that easy. But she said nothing. She hefted her duffel up onto the bed and stood looking (or was Miriam imagining everything?) rather bereft. I am not, Miriam thought, a witness to be trusted.

"I'll leave you to unpack," she told her. She wished she could put her arms around her the way she would her other children, but it was not possible for her. Not possible yet, she insisted to herself, going down the stairs. She wished she were a different kind of person, large spirited and effusive. She had always meant to become one—at that moment she saw how totally she had failed. The best she could do was repeat to herself, Not possible *yet*.

The house felt like a stage set onto which a new character had walked, familiar but utterly changed by her presence. She was the one the butler and the maid were whispering about when the curtain went up: "Did you hear the mistress's daughter is coming?" "So I've heard. The one nobody knows about." This had been a place, for her, where she'd rarely thought about this daughter.

Veronica-proof. It was an island, laboriously made to contain what she used to call her second life, so pervaded with the voices and darting movements of her other children intent on their summer pleasures that she'd never brought her along with her in her imagination. She sat herself down at the scuffed old wooden kitchen table and realized that she was out of breath, as if she'd been running.

THERE WAS NOTHING TO EAT in the kitchen except a few staples that experience had taught her their winter residents, the ants and mice, disdained. It was late, dark already, when they walked into the A&P to do their shopping. Ronnee stayed at her side and Miriam solicited her tastes: she liked the horrible sweet cereals they didn't allow in the house, but she wasn't arguing—not yet, anyway—and she liked lemonade, fake cocoa, peanut butter cut with grape jam. A child's diet. Miriam bought a lot of greens Ronnee swore she would not eat, and a six-pack of diet Coke Miriam would not drink. They were concentrating hard, as if this were a game with rules, played on a court, with an outcome that mattered.

Which is why she didn't notice her old friend Nance when she stopped in front of Miriam and said, "Hey!" She and Nance had played tennis together for years, and taken yoga, and long green walks and trips to the mall three-quarters of an hour away (though, given her forced time in the Galleria, Houston's mother-mall, she had slightly less than no desire to go shopping here. But it was different, she had to suppose, if your neighbors were mostly trees).

"Hey, hey!" Nance said again, until Miriam looked away from the cabbage and noticed her. "Summer's on! Look who's here!" Nance was wearing plaid Bermudas and an old flannel shirt, because this place was as air-conditioned as anything in Houston and you could shrivel and die in front of the freezer chests if you didn't dress defensively. Barry said they turned up the AC when they saw the Veners coming to make them feel at home.

They hugged and, how could it be, Miriam realized for the first time that she would have to introduce this girl—girl taller than she was—waiting patiently at her elbow. Nance and she were truly affectionate, more than conveniences, but they were summer friends who rarely carried that friendship over into the other seasons. Nance was the town children's librarian, married to a veterinarian, mother of two rambunctious boys and a teenage girl. Miriam tried to keep the alarm out of her eyes, and the sharp knowledge that she should have had a conversation with herself long before the first encounter.

"Nancy Forman," she said to Ronnee very slowly, grappling for a foothold. To Nancy, "This is Ronnee Reece—"

"You're visiting?" Nance asked casually. She was just sophisticated enough so that Ronnee's color did not visibly surprise her, even in this place. She herself already had a suntan from her dozen outdoor devotions that made her skin as dark as Ronnee's, especially in contrast to her very, very blue eyes. Her thick, short gray-white hair always made Miriam think that a gull had nested on her head, but comfortably.

"Sort of," Ronnee answered sullenly, and looked away.

"I'll call you, maybe tomorrow, hon," Miriam said to Nance quickly, in her cutest Southern, which, even as it emerged from her mouth, she recognized as a deflection. "We'll make a date." Nance could see she was ready to move on but she didn't look particularly suspicious.

"Well, I hope nothing's eaten your racquet this year!" Last winter one of their more presumptuous mice had unstrung Miriam's brand-new Wilson and digested it (or maybe not; she couldn't have said). "Everything all right? The kids? Is Barry here?"

"Fine. No, they're all at camp and Barry's so busy he hasn't noticed it's summer yet. Eddie and the Pack?" (Her children were the Wolf Pack. They burned energy like kindling.)

"Okay, darlin'. Call me quick with your calendar in your hand or I'll call you." And, with a flick of a look at Ronnee, she was gone, around a column of Tuna Helper boxes.

Dear Lord, she was stricken. She had nothing to say for herself; pure self-loathing rose in her like a belch. She thought she might be sick with it. Her daughter had walked down the aisle ahead of her, showing her purple-shirted back, and Miriam didn't blame her. A wave of shame dragged her under and the hard thing was, she knew that she deserved to drown in it. She thought she had drowned already.

When she found her Ronnee was leaning against the locked car, looking off into the distance where there was nothing to see. The river ran over there but the parking lot was falsely bright and the water was dark, invisible beneath steep, tangled banks.

"Ronnee, I'm sorry." She couldn't get her to turn her head. "I need—I guess I need a little time to figure out how—"

"How what?" Ronnee asked her in the voice of a child with her bottom lip thrust out.

How so many things. Her daughter couldn't have begun to comprehend the intimacy her presence dragged out of the shadows. It wasn't really surprising. "It isn't one thing," she told her. "And it isn't what you're thinking."

When Ronnee turned her eyes on her mother, her lovely, hurt eyes, Miriam thought, You always wonder how you'll manage in a crisis. And who said a crisis couldn't overtake you in the A & P, under the cold fluorescence, in front of the vegetables? You wondered if you'd measure up when that time came, be a hero, greathearted and competent, or be a goat, a fraud, a washout. Everybody wondered.

Now she knew.

THEY MADE A QUICK DINNER, spaghetti and bottled sauce. Miriam did. Like a balloon that had lost its air, Ronnee sat slumped in front of their snowy TV, her legs out in front of her, just asking Miriam to trip over them, sending her anger in waves of silence.

But, given a little time and the fortification of a few sips of cabernet, Miriam had begun to mount her defense: You do not want a simple response from me, she was going to say to her. If I am to have a place in your life we will have to build a relationship around a lot of important things, and race is only one of them. Must it be the first? Well, then—well then, how can you expect me to react without layers of complexity to your sudden appearance in my life. If you have needs, so do I. Adults know this kind of thing, she would say to her; children do not. She was working up a righteous anger, slicing tomatoes so hard their pieces bounced across the cutting board, tearing up the lettuce as if she had a bone to pick with it, laying down the dishes with a defensive thump.

Ronnee heaped her plate with pasta and salad, and returned to the couch in front of the television set. Miriam stood at the far end of the room, the kitchen end, in consternation: Did she dare trot out her maternal rules ("In this house we don't watch TV while we eat")? Who is *we*? Was this child hers to discipline? Would you call yourself punitive? she wanted to ask her. Maybe just a little too quick to judge? She didn't recognize herself, this indecisive woman who picked at her own dinner at the kitchen counter, too self-conscious to cross the room, stepping delicately across her daughter's legs, to sit at her own table alone.

Ronnee returned her plate to her mother hardly touched, put it on the counter without a word, and turned and left the room, not having met her eyes for an instant. This was a game she had learned from her father, this passive-aggressive sulk. Alone with him for nearly eighteen years, she had learned to draw blood without having to say a single word.

Miriam stood in the doorway for a few minutes behind the screen door, then went out to sit in the pure, inhuman dark. It was a perfect temperature out there, not smarmy like Houston, not chilly the way it would be in August. The stars' cold shimmer suited her mood: they asked nothing, they gave back nothing but a speck of bluish light that might, you could never forget, already be dead. But humans—humans were tiny, she thought bitterly, sitting in their heat, their recklessness, their moods, in the pain they exacted from each other; they were laughable in their caring. The brook sounded like wind soughing in the trees, endless and unchanging. A patient sound that said, We can wear away anything, we are in no hurry.

Here she was without a compass, without a clue, and they were supposed to go on some kind of journey together.

Sometimes, looking up, you think you see a falling star or a meteor, but it's only a firefly. Imagine confusing them, the cool zillion-pound sun and the tiny hopeful mite with phosphorus on its belly. Whichever it was, one of them slashed across the northern sky as she got up to go inside. She stopped and fixed the empty place where it had passed. Let her love me at least a little, she prayed, as if it were a star. Let me love her. Let time pass faster—that always seemed a sin against life, to want to hurry it, but they had so much to *get* through!

And then it was dark, and only dark, again.

6 WHEN RONNEE REECE GRADUATED from St. Helen's School in Brooklyn Heights, she surprised none of her classmates by being elected, in addition to Best Actress, Girl on the Go: Most Likely to Get What She Wants. (This was not the same as Most Likely to Succeed.)

The award had a slightly nasty edge to it, but then so did a few of the students at St. Helen's, who had made themselves adept over the years at giving and taking away at the same time. Ronnee understood that it was a badge of belonging to be the object of their casual cattiness. If they'd been too unequivocally nice to her, she'd have known she was an outcast.

In spite of her ambiguous award, Ronnee was never sure how well she was liked by her classmates. The thing was, did she care? Seretha Charr she was sure of; each was so happy to find another black face (Seretha darker, but no way black) belonging to someone reasonably smart, reasonably decent, that their friendship was born assured. There were a few other students of color in her class—one Korean; one Taiwanese, who so sternly instructed them in the distinction between mainland Chinese and Taiwanese that it was a lesson they would not forget; one Filipino; an Iranian, however one should classify her; and an assortment of the Hispanically oriented: Dominicans, one Honduran, one Panamanian, a very well-to-do Mexican who came to school with her chauffeur and brought him into the kitchen behind the cafeteria each day for a snack before she sent him home. Plus—could this be, in New York?—only one Puerto Rican. And not off the streets, that one, either.

None of these non-Europeans, Ronnee knew, was in quite the same position she and Seretha occupied: people did not claim, or even expect, to know much about who they were or where they came from. (Korea? Honduras? Did anyone really know exactly where they *were*?) In her case and her friend's, and those of the seven other black kids distributed through the other grades, shaken on the bland student body like a little pepper, everyone knew every damn thing they had to: their poor out-of-work fatherless families, their grubby, druggy neighborhoods, the dead-end lives they'd be preparing for without the succor of St. Helen's. Forget the surgeon, the professor, the magazine editor. Her father's book, *Ujamaa: The African Roots of Jazz*, was a classic, a textbook. She had snuck a copy out of his box of first editions, forged his autograph, and given it to the St. Helen's library. (He'd have killed her if he'd known.) It made Ronnee sick to be patronized, but she lived with it like a chronic low-grade illness that sometimes flared up. It was the price she paid for the sharp girls and boys, the genius teachers, the absence of chaos, the navy-and-green plaid uniforms that left a little room for serious concentration, and an ambitiousness they drank with their lunchtime diet Coke. As long as she could see it coming, she thought, no ambushes, it was still a good deal.

She had stayed at the public high school through her freshman year, angrier by the day when they laughed at her for taking her books home, for trying to please her teachers, for deriding the passivity her fellow students indulged about their futures. Angry at them for calling her white. She tried every tack before she gave up: ignored them and felt lonelier and lonelier. Turned on them, cursing, warning them that they'd end up flipping hamburgers at McDonald's (feeling dirty for that—it was her own too-easy stereotype) while they called her a snob and a house nigger. Why had her father discouraged her from going into Manhattan to one of the special schools, Stuyvesant, Hunter, La Guardia? Why had she listened? She suspected some kind of jealousy of her opportunities. She suspected angers of various kinds.

But then, she had her own angers. The day three boys cornered her in a stairwell and managed to get her on her back, her legs flung up like some tripped cow's, before the vice principal discovered them and marched them away to their futile punishment, she went home and consulted the Yellow Pages under SCHOOLS. There, perhaps the first of its students ever to find it so democratically, she came upon St. Helen's and wrote them a letter, which the admissions director quoted frequently, with great self-satisfaction, over the next three years: *Please help me*, Ronnee had written. *I am drowning.*

And it was true: she *was* drowning. She had always had "a touch of asthma"—that was what her father called it, as if it were the delicate feathering of a hand across her brow instead of the frightening breathlessness and wheeze she couldn't stop. But in the late winter of that first year of high school she felt it coming on her more and more often, felt as if the waves were closing over her head, and she landed in the hospital again and again, more lonely and afraid with every visit. Her father couldn't follow where she was going, nobody could.

Ronnee had always thought of herself as strong, her body (thicker than she'd have liked) at least vigorous and forceful if not delicate. Now it was running out on her. She felt as if her chest had been hollowed out, and a thick, sticky, poisonous liquid had filled its concave chambers. One of these days she would die of it.

But one morning a doctor (young, black, gorgeous, a man whose name she'd have written in her notebook beside her own, twined in a heart, if she'd had any strength to spare) said to her sternly, "Now listen, girl, something's wrong in your life and you've got to think about it and figure out how to change it."

"I don't smoke. I use my nebulizer—" Bad enough that her father was on her case; the guys were ganging up on her.

"I don't mean the physical stuff, I'm sure you do all that. Although if you're depressed you might be getting sloppy about it. I mean your life. The rest of your life." He actually sat down on the bed beside her. "Would you say—see, I'm not a psychiatrist, but I come up against plenty of this kind of thing—is everything else okay with you? Because sometimes, not always, but sometimes you can have a kind of—collapse that shows up in whatever your weak organ happens to be."

She looked hard at him and considered. He had close-together eyes, intense, and maybe a little Mohawk in his sharp, thin nose. He seemed very eager to be right; she wanted to oblige him by agreeing.

"Everybody has a weak organ system, just about everybody, you know. There's nothing shameful about it. Circulation. Respiration, like you. Skin, even, most people don't realize that's an organ. It's the thing that feels the stress. Whatever that system is just sort of craters, you know what I mean?"

Funny that he said it just that way: *Craters* was the word that convinced her. It described the feeling in her chest, the ominous dug-out place that had taken a blow, that kept filling up and choking off her breath. She closed her eyes and tried to let what he had dignified by calling it *her life* flow in on her the way the thick and putrid mucus did, and what she saw was the wire cage around the stairwell at school where those boys had flung her down like a dirty rag. She saw the false glint of care that made the hall floors shiny as ice, and smelled the cafeteria, tomato soup and rancid cheese like sweaty feet. Bodies everywhere, bobbing up the steps into the locker room, moving like spilled molasses down the hall, slow and dark. Making a ruckus everywhere they surged.

She kept repeating the doctor's words, "nothing shameful, nothing shameful, nothing shameful," and it was as clear as anything had ever been what she had to do, even if it meant a massive argument with her father; if it meant the threat that she would leave his house if he did not give his blessing, or at least remove his curse.

She was as tall as he was, large for a girl who wasn't an athlete. There were stage roles she couldn't play because of it. *Strapping* was the word she had heard, though what it meant, exactly, was never clear. She tried to loom when they argued, but she quailed inside because this was her sweet daddy, and this was the first time she had opposed him, no compromise, no going back. "I don't care if it's white folks," she had said to him. "I don't care if it's green folks, you want me to be able to breathe I'm getting out of that school. Somebody ought to close it down before it kills somebody."

Her father had barely gone to high school, but he almost had a Ph.D. No wonder he thought people could survive anything and be strengthened. He believed she was learning something different from French and algebra: class, not classes. Everything with him was about "the underclass, held under. You think *you're* drowning," he liked to say, and shrug off her choking asthma one more time, as if it were playacting. "A whole people held under, and you're ready to bolt, you want to escape, you want to run off and let your enemies take care of it all for you." They were in the kitchen. She had cooked his dinner like the good wife she was.

She drew in a long breath, terrified that it would rasp and shudder and collapse and in would flow the foul waters. But it was a clean one. "Easy for you to forget, but half of me is those enemies," she had said very quietly and evenly, and put his plate of ham, yams, and greens before him, but not gently.

SHE HAD A DISTURBING EXPERIENCE in the fall of her senior year at St. Helen's, and she didn't know quite what to do with it.

A student from Zimbabwe had taken a distinct interest in her. Not only was he large and good-looking—finished-looking, somehow, more like a teacher than a student, with a broad shield-shaped chest and a neck that rose from his tweed jacket and achingly white shirt collar like a tree trunk—but he was far more mature than her sappy classmates. The usual unfounded rumors went around: he was a prince's son, or a tribal chief's, or a head of government's, always something exotic and unverified. If anyone had asked, he'd have volunteered that his father worked for the U.N., but perhaps that was insufficiently glamorous for anyone to want to hear it: No one at St. Helen's was allowed to be ordinary.

But Nkoma Ndgeoulu was exceptionally interesting, whatever

the occupation of his father, and Ronnee let herself be courted, if
that was the word for what he seemed to be doing, sitting beside her whenever he could, compelling her to hear his com-
pliments with an embarrassed smile. She had just broken up
with Thom Hardy, who was too jealous and who couldn't keep a
dime in his pocket for half a minute, and she would have been free
to see Nkoma outside of school, but he made no move in that direction.

One day at lunch her table launched a discussion of interracial
dating. They knew each other well; some had—she shuddered at
the thought of the cumulative bill—been in school together since
kindergarten. Ronnee would have said they were about 50 percent
honest with each other, which wasn't bad, considering the way
white kids lied to themselves, and black kids in a place like this
thought they had to be polite. Nkoma, who was always earnest,
though not without an amused shimmer in his eye, told them he
had promised his parents—"like a girl who will stay a virgin," he
said, smiling—that they should not worry about him during what
he called his "sojourn" in America, that he would never put himself in danger of falling in love with a white girl. "Therefore I will
not even go so far as to invite her on a date. People are so naïve
about the outcome of the casual."

Having said this, astonishingly, he turned his handsome,
smooth-planed face toward Ronnee, that face so dark it was like
lustrous polished wood, and said, "Sometimes this is difficult. It
takes sacrifice. And discipline. Which are not words I have heard
often since I am here."

"Yeah," said a dorky boy named Aaron, "my parents say the
same thing about going out with shiksas." He turned pointedly to
Nkoma. "You know what a shiksa is? That's a girl who gives your
mother nightmares and your father wet dreams." He giggled into
his sandwich and his friend Scott hit him in his arm muscle. "I
don't know this guy," Scott said loudly. "I never saw him before."

But the way Nkoma had smiled at her, Ronnee understood that
he meant she had been chosen to be—a biblical word might fit—
forsworn. And that she was meant to be flattered by that.

She knew, from the testimony of many (her father resisted it
but it was true), that American blacks in Africa are more often
than not relegated to feeling themselves American first, however
regretfully. How many times had she heard that, even in their living room, from friends who had eagerly flown to Senegal or Kenya
looking for their home place. It *was* one, in some ways, a place to
be proud of; in others, a thousand details, it was not theirs and
they knew it. It wasn't only a matter of how they were perceived.
It was, they testified, internal: they had been formed by their
American experience—McDonald's, for better or worse, and TV;
politics, even if they didn't like the way things came out—even a
certain set of expectations of what you'd have to call racism. They
were like trees that had done their growing canted in a particular
direction and could not be bent in another direction, even a more
comfortable direction, at will. She was waiting for her father to admit that about his own trip, the year she had been sent to live with
his mother in Alabama. He told her he had found his spirit home
in Dakar. But then, she noticed, he had come home again. "You
were here, darlin'," he always told her. "So? If I'm African, too,
why don't we both go live there?" "It's complicated," he would
say. "It's a cop-out," she would reply. This had become a ritual argument like so many, unchanging.

But to be seen by this sophisticated young man, Nkoma, as
white! She wanted to take it up with him right there, but—just to
prove how unwhite she was, she thought angrily—she was embarrassed. She waited until they were side by side, another day, in the
library. "I have to talk to you," she whispered at him urgently.

He took her hand and pulled her gently until they could hide
themselves in a corner against the oversized shelves. Her legs got
spongy when she stood so close to him.

"What was that the other day about me being white? What's the
matter with you, brother, you need glasses?"

Nkoma smiled his benign, adult smile. His eyes, his teeth,
whiter than shell, looked like gaudy ornaments against the deep
velvet of his skin. God, she thought, what would it be like to kiss
that mouth? It would make the other kisses of her life seem like

baby bites. "But, darling, you don't call yourself black, I hope! Look at you."

"Black is a culture, Nkoma, it isn't how dark you are. Everybody in America has been, you know—diluted. More or less."

He was keeping her hand in his. Everything inside her stirred. "Maybe that isn't something you have to recognize back home because you all share that culture. Simple for *you*."

He seemed to enjoy standing very close to her, even if she was forbidden. "Say I were to bring you to my village and take you to my father and my mother, what would they say?"

She loved the song his accent made. But she tried to protest. "I thought your father worked for the U.N."

"My theoretical father, then. And my real mother. My mother wears pounds of fabric on her head. She bears tribal scars. You would not believe it."

She tried to picture herself brought before them like a piece of meat for inspection. They'd sit in front of a round straw house, or maybe a long one made of mud, or none at all, out under the stars, in the harsh African veldt. She did her best, but it was all cliché, and she was ashamed. But she was, after all, as her father's friends had insisted, an American, a New Yorker, Brooklyn bred. "I can't imagine what they'd say. 'Take her away, she's a stringy white chicken'?"

"No, it wouldn't have to do with you. You should not be angry. They would surely say, 'But your children will be impure. You will bring half of a foreign heritage into our blood.' Not to offend, but you must know they would be correct. It isn't a matter for choice."

" 'So?' " She felt as if she had to defend herself, though she wasn't quite sure against what.

" 'So?' is a different question. I am not speaking of 'so,' I'm only speaking of the fact of blood, do with it whatever you will."

" 'The fact of blood.' That seems . . . cruel. Hard. Don't you think?" And why, she wanted to ask, are you standing so close to me that if I leaned up against you a little, I would feel that same blood rising in you, making you hard?

Nkoma sighed. "This is a story as old as the world, I think, and people have always suffered for it personally. We want what we want, in the—what do you call it—the short running."

"Run."

"Run. But dynasties"—he said "dinasties" in his British English—"have an interest in absolute purity that goes beyond individuals."

She had ceased to feel the hand he held in his, in self-defense, as if it had been lopped right off. But the rest of her was weak, liquid, helpless.

"Some people don't have to care, or at least don't want to. In my own case, well . . ." He was too modest to continue.

He *is* a prince, she thought, or the son of a chief. No reason a chief—his real, not his theoretical, father—couldn't wear a suit, she supposed, and show up for work in a building with elevators and a coffee shop. Yet it was absurd to think of the chief's son accommodating himself to the life she had grown up with in Brooklyn.

She hadn't given up. "How is it different from, like, when they beat up someone who doesn't belong in their neighborhood? Black or white? You know, 'My turf, keep out.' "

"But no one is beating up anyone, darling. They are simply keeping their, ah, heritage, the heritage of their genes—uncompromised." A big word for a high-school boy, Ronnee thought, jealous. She tried to imagine him at her old high school. The kids would have fallen away on all sides as he walked through the halls. He'd have been a freak or a god, one or the other. But he would never have seemed to be their relative.

"So I'm tainted," she said, trying to keep her voice light, "by my mongrel half."

He had the calmest brow she'd ever seen. What would it take to upset him? What if she fell upon him right here, in the corner where no one could see them? Would he resist?

"Oh, Veronica, I don't want you to be insulted. Please. I only mean you are—ineligible. That's no taint. It's just a fact. Like a hybrid flower." He picked her chin up with a hand that would make mahogany pale. "A rose bred of two histories. Those are the strongest kind in the end, you know. Speak to any gardener and he'll tell you so."

The rose made her angry; she dismissed it as the courtliness of an old-style young man bred to pretty lies and flattery: the lightly patronizing finger under her chin, bucking her up, was foreign to any American girl, black or white. Black and white.

But she kept hearing something like an echo: *Ineligible.* What would be the catalog of her ineligibilities? Barred from some, would she then be eligible for another kind of wisdom? This was the first time the whole thing had been made to sound simple and—natural. Nkoma seemed to attach no moral value to what one was or was not; it was nearly scientific: There is the allowed-to-me and then there is all the rest. What, she wondered (and she had not wondered often), was the rest of her made of? Usually black people like her father thought of white as a nothing, an absence, a ghostliness. She might, because of it, be slightly incomplete in her blackness, flawed, but that didn't suggest the *presence* of something else. But her whiteness seemed finally to have a solid shape. It might even cast a shadow.

There was nothing to do, exactly, but to watch and wait and listen a little bit differently. She tried to keep this curiosity separate from the way she viewed her white classmates and some of her teachers in all their clumsiness—no one said you had to be like them at their dumbest or most insensitive. There were plenty of— she had to stop thinking "my own"—who were equally dumb and insensitive: she knew quite a few. After all, she had fled her high school so as not to live out her life with them. She had to believe, like Nkoma, that decency was a neutral category. She had a vested interest in learning to think that.

RONNEE HAD CALCULATED once and for all that she was going to have to work more hours than actually existed to be able to meet tuition and board at Stanford. She had known that, without the infuriating particulars, the day her acceptance arrived with its generous but not-generous-enough scholarship because she was "the caliber of student we are dedicated to assisting." The problem was that her father would have nothing to do with the enterprise. He called Stanford White Folks' Heaven, black folks step around to the rear, please. "They *do* say please," he conceded. "They have the rest of their say behind your back." The financial aid he called a "Pity the Poor Nigger Scholarship." "You're there, darlin', so their brochures will look good."

She rolled her eyes.

"You know, I've been out there. It looks like a goddamn hacienda, all low, and these tile roofs? Very cute. But if it's supposed to be Mexico, how come everybody's blond? You come home blond, girl, you're out of my will."

"Your will. I'll probably *owe* money when you kick off."

That was the way they tweaked each other, roughly, as though tenderness would soften them too much for the daily fight. But she was angrier than he was this time. She'd have to get a blond wig to come home in, her first vacation. Anyway, she was not consulting him, nor asking a penny of him. It wasn't worth it to have to hear the diatribe it would cost her.

The college applications had marked a place for parents' income, very technical all of it, and, desperate, she had remembered suddenly that she had another parent. Half the kids in her class seemed to be listing their parents' assets separately because they were divorced. "It's very good for college if your parents are split," one boy had said earnestly. "If the custody agreement has you with the poorer parent, you might be able to get the college to dole out some more." Her other parent, her father had told her, finally, when she pressed, not for the first time, was very wealthy. He seemed to be telling that to spite her, like holding candy out in front of her where she couldn't reach it. "Took the silver spoon back out of your mouth and retired to Texas."

"Where is she now?" Her breath had quickened. If this was the real story for once, maybe help was on the way.

"I wouldn't know. I've got more important things on my mind."

"Do you know how I could find her?"

"Use your head, Ree. You've got a brain. It's worth it though. If you can find her I bet you can probably get her on accumulated guilt." He considered, smiling to himself. " 'Gelt' is the Jewish word for money. Guilt gelt is what you want. It's probably better than interest."

"*Jewish?*"

"Jewish."

She had the feeling he was embarrassed even to think, now, of having been involved with a white woman. All he had told her (when he finally stopped saying she was dead) was that the woman packed up one day suddenly and left, right in the middle of the semester, walked out on them, on her students, on her contract. In fact, he made her sound like a disappearing father.

Ronnee bent to the task of tracing this Texan—she had taken to thinking of her as a cash cow, a big woman with big hair, horselike if not cowlike, responsible for *her* size, wearing a white cowboy hat and boots and something made of denim with a fringe. (She knew it was absurd, but she considered it the shorthand version.) All she could think to do, feeling again like the little girl who'd loved to play detective, who'd even had a Sherlock Holmes kit once with a magnifying glass and a set of disguises, was to write to Parnassus College in Mississippi, where her father and this woman had been teachers, where the dirty deed was done. "Around 1967," she would tell them. Year of her birth. "I think she taught history." And then she'd see if she could gather her in.

If that didn't work, she'd have to find another plan to get that tuition paid. She was too big to model. She was a terrible typist and no way would she flip hamburgers for minimum wage. She was, her father said as if with satisfaction, as skill-less as a cat. He promised he'd fix her up with a publisher he knew, but he jinxed that on purpose by telling the man—she'd been prepared to lie— that she was saving for college and would be leaving in August. Some father. He knew how to give with one hand and take away with the other.

She came home from the scuffed offices of the State Employment Agency one day, tired, grubby, and hopeless about finding any kind of paycheck she could endure. The mail was bills, as usual, one of her father's music magazines, an invitation to join the Record of the Month Club which she could no way afford, job or no job, and an envelope from that Parnassus College, where she'd been ready to inquire into the whereabouts of the Runaway Woman. But odd, odd—inside it was another letter, and it was addressed to her.

THE DAY BEFORE her mother came, Ronnee sat down yet again to run through her calculations: They were giving her plenty, but she'd be paying it back forever. An actress could never manage that! Twelve thousand a year would probably do it. More would of course be better. Or a lump sum for all four years, but that seemed doubtful. She could wait as long as possible to broach the subject, until they were some kind of friends. She was curious about the woman, but dispassionately. Seeing her mother's name when it arrived from that college, recognizing (but slowly, because it was too weird) who this was who seemed to be trying to find her, after the blood rose again from her feet where it seemed to puddle, her stomach and her knees gone soft, she felt a strange power that made her clap her hands and laugh out loud. Had she called her mother to her? She must have made this happen.

When she stopped being amused she thought, I know what I want from her, okay, got that, but what does she want with me now? She thought, What gives her the right, taking off and reappearing at her own good time? She knew these stories, she'd heard about them. It was what fathers did: Disappear, conveniently. Reappear when ready. She thought, Daddy will *die*!

That letter had been so sure she would want to meet. The woman walks out and thinks she can walk back in again, it ought to cost her something. Aside from the fact that she was probably imagining the wrong person entirely, she prided herself, Ronnee did, on having no illusions about the difference it would make to her at eighteen to suddenly have a mother. It would have been something else at eight when she envied her friends their mothers' attention to their hair—her father had a thousand thick fingers that made a mess, though he did try, and that was why, though her hair wasn't as bad as some, she had gotten herself shorn like a lamb, early, and kept herself that way, her trademark. Their mothers murmured over their skinned knees, their skinned feelings, and told stories of their own, from when they were children. Her friend Electa's mother went to Mets games with her, and showed her how to do her nails, and they sang duets together like two-thirds of the Supremes. Once she had made the mistake of telling Electa that she wanted to be just like her mother when she grew up—wear her rosy perfume (which she sometimes let Electa use), speak soft and Southern, teach second grade—and Electa had laughed and said "You can have her!" and told all her friends. She had spent part of one lovely year in Alabama with her grandma, Ma Thelmie, but that came to an end before she'd had her fill of nestling against a soft body, kneading dough beside her on the same board, humming her way to church. Her daddy did lots of good things, but only lots, not all. He made sure to keep women around, friends who could pay attention to her, but it wasn't the same. She hoped he didn't think it was.

But somebody can be *not there* only so long before she's forgotten, she tended to say if and when the subject came up: out of the picture, dead gone. She had been through longing, anger, and finally forgetting. Now, she told herself, and told her father, crowing, she was strictly into money. "It's like a joke from heaven," she said, "having her show up right now. Somebody up there's looking out for me!"

"Some joke," he answered her grimly. "White woman's money, white woman's power. You watch yourself or you're going to be bought sure as your slave great-great-grandma was bought."

"Nobody's buying me, but if she wants to, hey, remember, half of all that's mine." *All that* was the part he never understood, though she couldn't claim to understand it entirely herself. Still, there was a part of her that knew—and maybe, on second thought, he did too, maybe that was what he feared, that made him such a pain in the butt—she was a mite or two different from him. How-

ever much she'd objected, Nkoma saw it. Money was the least of
it. *All that* was half her inheritance.

WHEN THE BELL RANG she seized up for a minute: stood in the
living room paralyzed, suddenly incapable of remembering she
couldn't buzz back—the buzzer, like a lot of other things here, had
been broken forever. She'd have to go downstairs to claim her. The
top of her head seemed to have flown off somewhere. She recognized these nerves from opening nights, which seemed only appropriate; she was about to launch the performance of her lifetime,
writing the script as she went along.

And what a shock she was, this Ms. Miriam S. Vener. Of course,
Ronnee thought, when she had time to reconsider, of course, how
could her big-haired Texas woman in denim fringe ever have been
the hippie civil-rights chick who came to teach at that college,
probably got arrested for demonstrating, lured her father into an
affair? That dude ranch ho in her wide belt with silver buckle,
maybe even a cowboy hat punched in on the sides, had never made
sense. She was a character in a sitcom. It was time to get serious.

But the small, well-exercised, carefully manicured woman who
strode out of the dark of the hall in classy sandals, really good
clothes, that pricey hairdo—that wasn't a woman who looked
right for the part either. Ronnee was confused. At the very least,
though, she could see the money on her back. Three years at St.
Helen's had taught her the look of quality, which was usually un-
derstated. You found it in details: subtle stitching that didn't call
attention to itself, good fit. Ooh yes, she thought avidly. Ooh yes.
Like he said.

The woman—all right, her mother, for what it was worth—
looked more nervous than even she felt, and if she knew what
Ronnee wanted of her she'd really have reason to tremble. Ronnee
showed off her room, gave in and found a picture of her father,
watched her mother laugh at the sight of him. She described a real
tight-ass, worse sounding than the one Ronnee was putting up
with. Her mother looked around his bedroom and said, "Well, I

don't know if it's an improvement or not—he used to be incredibly neat. I mean, rigidly. Like a soldier." She pointed to a T-shirt flung across the rucked-up blanket. Books lay scattered, easy to step on. The dresser was as littered as a teenager's. "What an extraordinary . . . lightening up." Ronnee, who had to clean up after him, could not imagine her father's possessions in any order she had not placed them in.

Just before they left, Ronnee's duffel and backpack in hand— she thought it was going well, she could do the charming innocent without too much strain—her father called. He just had to know if it was happening, couldn't stay away, needed to taunt her one more time, to show who was in control. They were more like a bickering couple, she thought, than a father and daughter. "Do you think she's pretty?" he dared ask her.

"I haven't thought about—it—that way." Was he asking if she approved? There was something sick about that. Or if she could understand and forgive? The man was so nervy she couldn't wait to put him behind her.

Then he said a stranger thing. He asked what she was going to call her.

"Are you jealous?" Ronnee wanted to ask but did not, because her mother, her so-called mother, was standing right there. "I don't know," she said impatiently. "I'll figure that out later." Had he been walking around somewhere, or sitting coolly staring at the phone, wherever in the world he was just then, and wondering what share this ex-lover would have of her affection? This seditty white lady? Get real, she wished she could say. Take it easy. You may be a pain in the butt, but who is this woman (who keeps staring at everything, who is making me nervous with her curiosity) to me?

IF SHE HAD A CHIP ON HER SHOULDER Ronnee couldn't see it. She liked to describe herself as a loving woman, a critical woman, with a low tolerance for stupidity and insensitivity (learned from her father) and a kind of street-smart capacity to take care of herself. One of her teachers told her that she was exactly like the daughter of an alcoholic. "My father doesn't drink," she objected, but Mr. Hill said no, drinking had nothing to do with it. It was a syndrome, though, and she had a good case of it in all its particulars: She was extremely competent, capable of taking care of herself and this other person (read: father) in her care. She was easily disdainful, and did not suffer fools patiently. In addition, she was secretive, and a little chilly out of suspiciousness and the fear of being hurt.

"So is there any hope for me?" she asked him when he finished his description of someone she didn't think she'd like to know.

"It'll depend on what you let happen to you," he had said.

"Let? Don't a lot of things just happen?"

Like her father, he was another man who smiled as if he knew all about her when he had no reason to flatter himself. "Depends. Some things happen, some you're responsible for. It's like your genes, Veronica. It isn't over till it's over, and the hardest thing is to know which part's up to you."

My genes, she thought a little bitterly. *My* genes were born fighting. But she couldn't argue. She didn't know what he meant. Another mystery which, she understood with all the resentment of youth, she'd have to age and suffer and get on the other side of. Only then—if then—would she have any way to know what she'd been handed and what it was up to her to take.

AND SO THEY DROVE (in the version she told herself) into the sunset. This wasn't going to be so hard. Her mother seemed timid. She had such small white hands, like a girl's, that looked as if they'd never done any work. People like this have maids to do the scrubbing, she reminded herself. The servants even look old for them. Ronnee had the feeling she could lead her where she wanted to. She asked, experimentally, if she could have a new pair of K-Swiss; told her a story about how hers had been stolen—as if anyone in her school needed her grubby sneaks. More likely somebody's father owned the damn K-Swiss factory.

Her mother bit. She also bit for a couple of cool shirts, some bib shorts and a pair of Guess so tight her friend Seretha called them "yeast jeans." For these she had to accept a little hug for letting her mother buy them. There was something so eager about the way she listened to what Ronnee said she needed that Ronnee almost felt she was doing her a favor asking for it. Which was peculiar, actually: She acted like a woman who had no other children. It was hard to understand why that should be, but there it was, desperation on toast. Who would object? she thought. If anything, she felt a little guilty, but not enough to discourage her from proceeding according to plan. You do owe me, she thought. You owe me eighteen years' worth. I'll tell you when it's enough.

SHE HAD NEVER SEEN SO MANY TREES. They came in every color, when you actually looked at them: bluish, brownish, yellowish, endless variations, and there were tight ones and loose ones, they were more varied, even, than people: Some looked inhibited, like they were holding themselves in, very neat, very pared. But then there were the shaggy ones, wide and loose and sloppy, their branches hanging low to the ground, a place to hide. You could probably spend a lifetime cataloging the differences. Bergen Street and Brooklyn Heights, where her school stood behind a few narrow, polite-looking trees, might seem like the world, but it was hard to picture it while you were looking into this green shade.

Actually, it made her nervous to feel so far from people, from the possibility of something happening except—did animals run through these forests? Could you be jumped by something with fur and claws? She apologized for what might sound silly but she had to ask. Oh, her mother said, there was nothing dangerous to people out there except for the occasional moose—very occasional—that would charge if it felt endangered but would probably split and run first. Her mother told her that she wouldn't want to meet up with an owl if she were a small animal, but not to worry, that's not what she looked like, even in the dark. And there were

minky kinds of things called fishers—related to rats? she wondered—that seemed to survive by stealing and eating the family
cats. Porcupines, but you didn't have to lose any sleep over them
either because they were more afraid of people than vice versa.
"And they're so slow, they're real lardy-asses, they waddle around
like fat people. You can't hurry them." Her mother thought a
minute. "Then again, I guess if *you* had quills you wouldn't have
to hurry."

"No bears?"

"Oh, not really. Not many. I think I saw a bear's shoulders once,
but he took off so fast I wasn't even sure I'd seen him."

Bears! Ronnee thought about Prospect Park, how far from civi-
lization and safety she used to feel when she was little and ventured far from her daddy across an open field, toward one of the
stony bridges that seemed so exotic, and there might meet up with
an unleashed dog and come running back in tears. In Alabama she
had seen woods near Ma Thelmie's, but they were skimpy and dry,
like a garden that no one watered. All these New England woods
were thick and healthy. Endless.

And everything seemed to be made of wood from all those
trees. The outside of her mother's farmhouse (where was the
farm?) with its dark shutters, the creaky sloping floors, old
dressers with sticky drawers. From a distance, these New England
houses were very pretty, like the pictures on Christmas cards—not
beautiful, they weren't grand enough to be that—but up close it
was all just old splintery wood, painted over again and again till
the layers were what she knew was called "crazed," like the fine
cracks under the surface of old china. She lay in bed thinking
about the word *crazed*. Paint gone nuts? Cups and saucers running
around like wild men?

They had already had their first argument. They had met a
friend of her mother's at the store and she wouldn't introduce her,
just stood there like a piece of wood and let her friend think Ronnee was no one special, any old visitor. So this mother of hers, surprise, was just another white woman who couldn't face unpleasant
facts. But it was one thing not to need anything of this *mother*, she

thought, seething, playing the word *mother* around in her mouth, all its street ironies sour on her tongue. It was another to let herself be insulted. That she did not need. She would have to figure out how to punish her without making her and her bank account so mad they turned on their heel and walked away. She didn't want her little Texan thinking, Why am I putting up with this?

Her father had trained her like a bear cub, had knocked her around enough to toughen her up: pushed her with his paws tucked so that he didn't hurt her, but definitely taught timing, feinting, jabbing, and—most important (Mr. Hill at school got this right)—wariness. "Somebody hurts your feelings," he would say, "you either go on the offensive before it happens again or you get out of their way. What you don't do is stand there and take a face-ful of abuse. No way." He had said to her, when she was old enough to hear it, "Black men have all kinds of shit to put up with and a lot of it is dangerous. They can end up shot in the back easy as spitting. But black women do, too, different shit, but never easy." As for black-white women . . . well, he didn't say. He never thought of that.

She watched him in the world and it was true, you could see how he protected himself. A radio interviewer once asked him if he was a racist. By the time the man had been forced to define his terms, he saw that he had somehow described himself and her fa-ther had demanded (and received) an apology. She watched his contempt for tantrums—any girlfriend who made a scene was out the door before she'd dried her eyes—the strictness of his expecta-tions of friends and colleagues, his refusal to deal with them if he wasn't sure of their loyalty. He had instructed her more than once that he was not at home if so-and-so called. She called him a black mafioso. A hard man produces a hard child. She could be one if she tried.

And here she had this cream puff to eat up, this soft little vanilla pudding, this Mrs. that she had called to her side. She could see the way she had the woman worried, confused. They were circling each other, trying not to make a misstep. She let herself act as sullen as she felt, like a mother disciplining her child instead of the other way around, and then, after an evening of silence, which Ronnee thought quite effective, she went up the noisy steps to bed.

The doors were open to the rooms of those other children. Their ghostly leavings lay scattered around, these kids who could actually leave clothes in the closet here, and sneakers and a soccer ball, which meant they had two, or maybe many, of everything, when it was hard enough in her world to own one. She could see from the hall that the little girl had a tall, fancy dollhouse with a little porch on the top of it, a widow's walk. Floppy hats festooned her mirror, dangling off hooks; a huge stuffed sunflower bent protectively over the top of her bed.

Ronnee had gone to a town on Long Island called East Hampton once with a girl in her class named Mireille, and she recognized how confused the whole thing made her, the greasy mix of envy and contempt. She fingered the objects in the guest room, thinking it was a sin to own things you could afford to abandon for months at a time, whole seasons in which they weren't so much as looked at or thought about, let alone touched: the lamps unlit, the mirrors empty, the lovely flower-bordered dishes gathering dust in the cupboards, wine bottles lying on their sides in little ceramic tunnels of their own, aging in the unaired dark. Mireille's parents told stories about the way local vandals sometimes got into houses and did grotesque damage for the fun of it. But she understood—it wasn't fun, it was fury. It was *wanting,* and doing damage didn't begin to take care of it, only left a severe burning dissatisfaction, like a raw throat after too much smoke, where it seemed something inside should whisper *Enough!* It was wanting what no one should have if everyone couldn't have it. Her mother's house wasn't particularly beautiful, with all these "genuine" antiques that looked rough and graceless to her—more old wood, some of it in dull greens and blues that her mother called "colonial"—but just to have it, to own it, and then to leave it behind seemed like an act of contempt for nine-tenths of the world.

She had been standing in the hallway looking into the room with the dollhouse. A triangular wedge of light spilled in and caught the side of the quilt on the bed, a lot of red and white in it, and pinned down one arm of a Raggedy Ann doll, whose head and body were invisible. The little girl who owned all this—she foraged around in confusion to weigh what this meant to her—was her *sister*. Half sister. Feeling nothing for her, not even knowing what she looked like (why had her mother not shown her pictures? Was she trying to spare her something?) didn't make it any less true. Her name was Evie, she was pretty sure of that. The boys—her half brothers—were Seth and something else from the Bible. Ezra? They were (this was too hard to believe) her family. Like all these possessions that stayed in the country, they were hers whether they were with her or were not. She would meet them sometime. Was a blood tie just a matter of chance? As if she had taken a blow, she was dizzy with what it might mean, might not mean. Whose choice would it be? She had a thousand cousins on her father's side, too many of them, he said, to chase them all down and stay current with them. He didn't get very sentimental over family. She hadn't seen most of them since the last time they were in Alabama, one long time ago, a Christmas, when some of them were visiting from L.A., West Palm Beach, some little place in Louisiana, on and on. One uncle, Ronnie, gimpy-legged, still lived at home with his mother. How could she, a different Ronnee, be the connection between these families? Imagine them in one room, these rich white children whose faces she'd never seen and the dizzying mix of her father's nieces and nephews, all colors, all sizes, D'Netra and Sweet-trick, Krissia and Derrick and a dozen others, and Derrick's and Krissie's daddy in jail in Florida, how's that for something to boast about. Most of them didn't live with both their parents—didn't even, lots of times, know their daddies. Grandmas inherited them. She had turned that one around all right, like a joke, not knowing her mama's name. She turned away from the room where the dollhouse hulked on the floor. She had pleaded for a dollhouse for years, hadn't gotten one, her father apologizing: no money, no room, why do you want that, honey, it's just a lot of tiny little matchstick furniture, breakable, too expensive for what they give you. Then she grew out of wanting it.

    And if she lifted a little of that matchstick furniture, just a couple of small things, that chair upholstered in gold with the elegant lattice back, a dish or two fit for a flea's dinner—they didn't begin to fill her palm, crushable as bird bones—would little Evie (who'd abandoned the house for the winter and, apparently, for the summer, too)—would she even notice?

IN THE MORNING a tumult of birds woke her and she remembered what she'd decided to do the first minute she saw it. Ronnee threw on her clothes and, in spite of the noise of the floorboards that complained with every step, pulled open the sticky kitchen door, got herself out to the road, ran down the hill, whose little stones shifted perilously under her feet, and there, as smoky as the scene of a fire, was the pond; it was invisible until she came right up to its edge. There seemed to be a tireless chorus, water hissing offstage, a _sshhusshh_ that was neither approval nor argument, that just went on and on and on mindlessly, without a shutoff switch. She had never heard something that seemed to live outside of time. What could time mean to falling water?

The pond was tranced. No breeze rippled its brown-gold surface, no frogs or fishes broke its perfect plane, but the mist ruined reflection. The water looked as if it must be on fire deep deep down in some unwet place; it seemed to be steaming. This was the strangest place she had ever been, Ronnee thought, advancing slowly on the little beach. She began with her sneakers; the sand was cold and damp, all sharp edges that glinted up like gratings of precious stone. Then her black T-shirt and the gray athletic bra she had to pull over her head. Last came her shorts and panties—shocking how raw the air felt leaping against her warm skin. No one could see her from anywhere, she knew—even if someone drove by (unlikely at this hour), the mist was so solid it took the world away. And no one could come up that pebbly hill unannounced. Still, she looked over her shoulder. If no men lurked out there, were those owls watching, the ones her mother told her could astonish you, staring down from behind a curtain of leaves? Beavers with cold little eyes, those humps that looked like rocks could be their heads poking out of the water. Naked in the light of day (having only been naked in somebody's bedroom, once in the back of a car, once in an empty storeroom, and not quite naked at that because there was always a rush, the secrecy of stolen time), she would faint at the sight of anything that moved.

Goose pimples stood up on her body like nail heads. How strange, how unreal, that she was the same girl who had awakened a day ago in her bed in Brooklyn, bored and sweating, and here she stood like a goddamn goddess—she saw the curved tops of her breasts, their power, their perfection, her dark nipples stiffened by the chill—on the edge of a forest pool! A goddess. No, an animal. A living thing between the sky and the crust of the earth. She was exactly sixty-eight inches tall. Hearing feet compressed into inches had always seemed to make her (even at her impressive height) sound pathetic. Imagine, a sixty-eight-inch thrust off the face of the earth! Still, she had read about people who knew exactly where they belonged in the whole scheme of things and were satisfied with it—Indians, she thought, out on the plains. But it wasn't easy to feel like an animal (except maybe a hunted one) in the city. Tonight, she thought, she'd go out and look at the sky and see if the Milky Way was up there. Were you huge or were you tiny, standing a few inches off the ground with your head poking up into the universe? It wasn't the kind of thing anyone could answer for you. The waterfall certainly didn't care.

Everything lay ahead. She knew how to take what she needed and, because she had dared, even this pond would be (if not entirely, then partly, legally) hers. No way would she get involved with that woman's neediness because no way could she really believe she had ever lived inside her, made out of her, in debt for her life. No way. This woman was so pale and tense and lightweight, and she was trying so hard to *connect*, it was embarrassing. Her own kind of trying was different: if she acted it well enough it would buy her a future, since it was too late for a past.

THE KITCHEN WAS FREEZING when Miriam came into it to make breakfast—odd—but then she saw that the front door was open. The frosty white beard of dew was still on the grass in places and the sun was frail slanting across the trees. No Ronnee on the lawn. No Ronnee in her room—Oh, Jesus, she thought, have I driven her away? Is she punishing me? Trying to scare me?

Up in the guest room her clothes were still there, her hair pick, even her sandals splayed two ways on the floor near the bed. Her asthma paraphernalia was on the bureau, the nebulizer and some bottles of spray. Maybe, she told herself, panic subsiding, she's just curious to see what's outside. Maybe—and then she knew exactly where to look for her.

The road down the hill was a million pebbles, like the bottom of an old riverbed—dirt soft as flour pocked with hard little stones in a dozen colors. The kids used to love to collect them, big and little, and range them in rows, edges touching, from white through many shades of brown and maroon and mica-shiny all the way to black, and ask how they got that way and Miriam couldn't really say.

She tried not to make too much noise walking, but the waterfall, she knew, would cover every sound with its tranced shushing. And one more turn brought her to the pond, so unreal and beautiful in the morning that it made her ache. If she hadn't known what she was seeing she'd have thought the earth had been consumed in fire, smoke caught above it. Every day the pond was erased for a while.

It would come clearer and clearer as the mist rose and the trees would throw their perfect likeness on its surface. She was there, off in the distance on the edge of the dock, and Miriam thought without certainty that she must be naked, just standing still looking down at the unruffled water.

Closer, she saw that Ronnee had shucked her clothes, which were lying in a little heap of color at the near end of the splintery old dock. She was a rich, delicious light brown, her flesh shiny with water, her wet hair tighter to her head than any bathing cap, and she was not looking around anxiously to see if anyone was spying on her. Probably she didn't care. Miriam was used to Evie, she realized, who was just beginning to bud, not even quite, but giving promise of changing shape, her little hips barely starting to bow, her breasts not even as swelled as plumped raisins yet, all eager expectation. But Ronnee's breasts were larger than her own, they had real weight to them, mature. They cast shadows against her rib cage. She had a little stomach, just the beginning of one, softly rounded, and below it a lush deep tangle more substantial than the shorn hair of her shapely head.

To look at his daughter, naked, and think of Eljay seemed nearly illicit, seemed incestuous, but there was no getting past it. She was stirred as nothing had stirred her since this girl's father had laid a finger on her arm, no more than that, the very first time he'd touched her. Understatement, always: "Let the song sing itself." She thought of what she had brought to him, her mingy, underused, luminous white body, come to him out of a different, distant life. If women were like fruit, sweet and ripe for a short time only, all that sugar perfectly poised, then she had had her moment; what was left was more than pit and rind but never exactly succulent again. Here was a woman, more of a woman than she had been— not a girl but a woman—at the peak of perfection. Miriam felt herself blown back as if by a gust of wind or a shock of bright light, watching her—that this large, smooth-limbed, commanding, *finished* woman had begun inside her. No, she objected, no, that is no way possible, as if her legs had to open again to let this being slide out of her as she was this minute. She saw her daughter's tiny shoulders as she had, jubilant, for the first time, felt the slick slide of a body out of her own, the little fish, remembered the swoop of her release, the doctor holding her up for Miriam to enjoy the solid fact she had delivered—her sturdy shoulders and chest—and then, to ruin the moment, the look on his face when it registered that he was holding a tan child with knotty hair still attached to the pale straight-haired white woman who made her, who was crying tears of joy, not horror, not disgust.

Ronnee would be embarrassed if she approached her while she was naked. She waited until the girl had, slowly and dreamily, pulled on her iridescent pink-white underpants and lowered a plain gray stretch bra over her head, stepped into her shorts and, arms up, flailing like starfish limbs, after she'd put it on backward and shrugged it off again to start over, her black T-shirt. She looked serene, the light of all that sex, thank God, extinguished.

I ought to go down there, Miriam told herself, and stand beside her, naked myself, and force some mystical mother-daughter moment. "Look, we are women together, and surely your father could not have given you *this*." But the sight of her womanliness—would that be the word?—really her un-child-ness—had drawn a sudden firm line for Miriam, and perhaps she should be grateful for seeing it so soon: Her child was no child. She had missed Ronnee's little girlhood entirely, irrevocably. There was no paying her back, filling it in; she could only come as a stranger to it. She would have to figure out how to get on, now, with her daughter's adulthood. Miriam stopped short to work this out, her feet in the long grass, which itched like stubble. What could she do but *earn* her?

She listened for a while to the endless, causeless applause of the waterfall—it would sound like an approving audience no matter what transpired between them—and then got herself into motion. "Hey, Ronnee!" She kept her voice innocent, surprised, as if she'd been casually strolling past. "You found the pond." Dumb. As if it was hard to find.

"I went skinny-dipping!" Such jubilation, because her mother had forbidden it. "I don't think anybody went by, but if they did—" Ronnee did a little stripper's bump with her hip. "Looking's free Monday, Wednesday, and Friday."

Miriam skirted the sandy shore, trying to keep her sandals out of the water, and sat down on the dock. "It's always nicer than I remember. It's terrible, I tend to think of the rocky bottom and the mosquitoes—"

"Pessimist."

"Depressive. True."

Ronnee ignored that, or assumed she was exaggerating. "It's pretty far from Texas, I guess."

Miriam sighed. "You can't imagine. So many ways." Every image that leaped up behind her eyes was static, heat-stunned, bled of color. "You just cannot begin to imagine what a gift this is." Then fairness kicked in. "Of course, see me in January."

Ronnee was looking across the pond, whose steam seemed to be vanishing even as they watched it. "Is that a cemetery over there?" She was craning toward the slope on the other side of the water, where skinny third-growth pine and lush blueberry bushes hunkered up the hillside. Rhododendrons glowed like headlights out of the dark.

No one, Miriam told Ronnee, even at the Historical Society, knew why this centuries-old burying ground was there—whether it was an adjunct to the major cemetery closer to town, an overflow, or a few families' show of independence. Had there been a feud or a falling-out that sent the Hastingses and Trotters and Weatherbys and a few-odd unaffiliated people—friends? servants? random relations passing through?—up here, far from the church and from their neighbors? Their history had gone into the ground with them.

"Isn't it spooky?" Ronnee asked, still squinting because it was easy to lose sight of the stones between the trees. "Isn't it scary to have all those dead people right up there when you're, like, fooling around in the water?"

"Oh, you'll see. Come on, I'll take you up there. It's very peaceful and lovely, you won't feel the least bit morbid. Unless you have an overactive imagination. Do you have one?"

Ronnee laughed. She strapped on her sandals and rose to follow her mother, but slowly, to show her reluctance. "Overactive? How can you tell what's normal and what's, you know, double time?"

"Well. I guess if we get there and you see ghosts or hands reaching out of the graves to grab you. But I doubt you will. People used to visit cemeteries all the time, and the children would run around and everybody would think about the people they loved who were buried there. Things are only creepy if you let them be." They were headed up the pebbly road. She had to look hard for the half-cleared path into the woods.

Ronnee regarded her carefully. Miriam felt herself being looked at, assessed, perhaps for peculiarity. She still had no idea how conventional this daughter of hers would turn out to be. Ronnee's mood had improved since last night. Maybe the solitary early morning swim had cleared her head.

"When I stayed with my Ma Thelmie in Alabama?" she began. "She used to go to the graveyard all the time, visiting? And there was a grave one time, I almost stepped in it, it was falling in, vines all around, it was so overgrown my ankles got all caught and that saved me from ending up down there! Everybody thought it was a scandal to walk away from a grave like that, just let it go. But I guess the family must have died or left town or something. So Ma and some other ladies got together after I almost fell into it, and they cleaned it up. Like, you know, 'Honor the dead.' I remember it was a little boy buried there, and I was just, like, eight or nine, around how old he was. I had a lot of nightmares after that." She shuddered delicately.

Miriam felt a kind of jealousy brush her cheek, like a wing, that she hadn't been there to lift her daughter out of her bed when she was frightened. That was one of the privileges of parenthood, that helpless comfort you were called upon to give. Eljay had had the nightmare beat.

The graveyard, inside a low stone wall, broke on their sight like a mirage. Its gate was off, lying up against a corner of the wall. But inside the grass was always, mysteriously, mowed and there were live flowers, bright little impatiens and a scrap of blue something she couldn't identify planted around a few of the graves, ancient though they were, that someone must be tending. So much of the year Miriam wasn't here.

Ronnee walked with great deliberation down the aisles facing the dark old stones; she could hardly get herself to step close enough to read the small print, the letters obscured by gray-green lichen. Occasionally she exclaimed over an inscription—"Look. This one says 'Third and best wife of Henry Carstairs'!" "Oh, the babies have these little lambs. 'Our darling, gone before us to prepare the way.' " She had a funny, disbelieving smile in her eye, as if it were all unreal, a kind of joke Miriam had arranged to amuse and befuddle her.

"So this is, like, home," Ronnee said, hostile or not depending on how challenged Miriam wanted to feel. The implication was somehow that it was strange to feel at home here.

"Oh, good God, no, not the way you say that. I don't feel like this is really my place. This history—their history—oh no, Ronnee! I can love it but that doesn't make it mine." She gestured to a deeply shaded circle beneath a very large oak. "Let's sit here a little, okay?"

Ronnee sat and circled her knees with her arms. "So why do you love it then?"

She thought for a minute. The blank block of Scimitar, where she lived, shimmered in imaginary heat; it was always deserted. Her neighbors darted their heads out to pick up the newspaper from the grass; they walked quickly between their air-conditioned houses and their air-conditioned cars; yard boys touched the living plants for them. The quiet here was deeply different. "Hard to say. Just because it's old, maybe. I can see where these people lived, I can sort of imagine what things were like, though of course I can't really. No electricity, no telephone, you know—so much that we can't even reconstruct. But still, if they looked up—see that big tree over there?—if we happened to look at the same tree, we'd be seeing the exact same thing they did a hundred and fifty years ago, around the time that house of ours was new. And, I don't know, that thrills me somehow."

"Wow." Ronnee shook her head in wonder. "Can you imagine life without a telephone!"

Wow. So much for the blandishments of history.

"Well, you know, I used to teach history. I was teaching it when I had you." She said that casually. Ronnee couldn't possibly hear the way the bone of the words caught in her throat. "Maybe that's where I got my curiosity. But these people—they're surely not my people. Very fine maybe, who knows, probably some were and some weren't, but not mine any more than they're yours."

"Mine!" Ronnee snorted the idea away. "So, your people. Where are they? Houston?"

"I guess. Sure. And before Houston, back in Russia and Poland, in lost graves, all those villages that don't even exist anymore. No one could ever track those down. Between Stalin and Hitler and all the miseries of this century over there. And then, later, rows of them in this Jewish cemetery along the bayou—Houston has these waterways, you know, sort of half ditch, half river? And there's a very pretty cemetery up on the banks of one, Buffalo Bayou, and it's full of—" She paused in amazement. "Honey, it's full of *your* relatives." She couldn't help it; she laughed a little at the surprise of the idea.

Ronnee stared back wide-eyed.

Miriam was flushed, trying to gather up all the pieces of the past that had brought them here to this anonymous graveyard. "You have your Ma Thelmie on one side, your father's side—Roker was your father's father's name, wasn't it? I think I remember that. Roker Reece? So you might have his people there, or not. Depending. And on your other—" She was careful not to say *but*, not to set them in opposition "—you have Starogins, Merwitzes, Bronsteins, Waxes. My mother was a Merwitz. Your other grandmother." She was warming to this. "You have cousins named Jennifer and Sarah, and my brother's kids, Holly and Christopher." Those little half-Catholic darlings who would end up pagan, her mother believed, if Alan didn't choose one religion or the other and stop trying to placate everybody. (And if he chose Catholic, she threatened to die of it. It was funny, but it was no joke.)

Ronnee was still silent, her mouth open slightly, as if she needed more breath than she could find.

"Haven't you thought about that? That you have a whole other family, a whole other history that's real, that's—" She took a very deep breath that didn't seem to fill her up, either; the air out here was suddenly inadequate. "There's as much of it on one side as there is on the other. Veronica?"

Ronnee was looking away, into the trees at the far end of the burying ground where Miriam had told her the dead and buried might have looked and seen the same thing, those hundred shades of green that quaked slightly in the breeze. The woods, too, seemed full of breath. "Yeah, I've thought about it, of course I have, or I wouldn't be sitting here like this. I know it isn't just, like, why my skin is, you know—light. But I don't really know *how* to think about it, actually, when you get right down to it. What does it mean to just—like"—she snapped her fingers to illustrate the absurdity of the effort—"think about it?"

Miriam pressed on, pushing at what suddenly felt like a powerful force, like water bearing down on her, against her. "You're like the—what's it called?—the fulcrum, I guess it is, in the middle of a seesaw. Weight on one side, weight on the other, and they balance. I never thought of it quite this way. They balance on you."

When Ronnee turned back to her, finally, her eyes were huge with tears. "My father would—if he heard that, I don't know what he'd do. He'd never admit—he thinks—" She stopped abruptly.

"Oh, Ronnee, you don't have to tell me what he thinks. Why do you think he had you all those years."

Something skittered in the dry leaves not so far away. The tiniest living things—birds, chipmunks, light and quick—made the most boisterous sounds, magnified far beyond their force, in last year's brittle leaf piles. They watched for a while, trying to see what was scaring up all that noise. Finally the stripes of a chipmunk, many kinds of brown, streaked out and away, like something in a cartoon.

"Oh, I thought it was a snake in there!" Ronnee breathed out.

"No poisonous snakes up here. They seem to stop at the Massachusetts border, I don't know why. You'd think they can read the highway signs or something."

Ronnee had covered her mouth with her hand. It was hard to tell if she was holding back words or if she was thinking of being sick at the very thought.

"You've spent time in Alabama, didn't you ever run into a copperhead when you were out playing?"

"If I did it was a long time ago. But I'd probably remember. Ooch."

Miriam took a breath so deep and held it so long she thought she could easily pass out. It would be easier not to do this, but it had to be done, and this might as well be the time. "Now why don't you sit on back against that tree and get comfortable. I have some things to tell you."

THE THINGS SHE SAID. The things she could not say.

PARNASSUS COLLEGE of Rowan, Mississippi, twenty years ago, was random, a scatter of buildings born in every architectural generation, vaguely Victorian dark brick, the new optimistic tan stone of the science quad, the student center a bright turquoise plastic-sided remnant of the fifties. The president lived—will always live—in the Big House, pillars and all, left from plantation days; the landscape man, thrilled to control the landscape of such a palace, watered the bushes and flowers so zealously he could have been reclaiming them from Death Valley. What a lovely irony to walk and eat and sleep where The Man did, the wheel turned all the way around, the world on its head. Campus tours featured this triumph proudly, without coyness or subtlety. Why not? It was just desserts.

The students swarmed over the paths and the green, they sat on the benches under the hanging moss, they ran around the track and tackled each other with big football shoulders. Miriam taught history. She was taking a break from graduate school to come south for her generation's Spanish Civil War, her Lincoln Brigade. It had been startling to look down from the airplane window and confront Mississippi, terra incognita, the notorious beastly Other she'd been gearing herself up for, fighting the conservatism of parents and professors: lush tufts of trees, broccoli forests, far greener than she'd expected. (What *had* she expected, she wondered later, paved parking lots?)

IN SPITE OF THE URGINGS of the zeitgeist, when push came to shove, how conservative and self-protective Miriam's professors and even her friends had become when she proposed to go south. She wasn't surprised that her parents didn't want her to go, that's what parents were for, to think of Schwerner-Chaney-Goodman and see themselves weeping at her funeral (even though she kept telling them things were a little safer now, maybe, sadly, *because* of Schwerner-Chaney-Goodman). And she was going to teach, not to march. She'd be safe in her classroom.

But her adviser, her teachers, her friends, were all very protective, though not exactly of her, that was the surprise. It was professional, most of it, and disillusioning. When she told them people were dying, people were starving and being abused, her adviser murmured, as if affronted at her negligence of a clear duty, "Your dissertation!" When she said that she wanted to be part of the history she was learning to chronicle or what was this whole enterprise for, he suggested, lowering his voice confidentially, "Aren't you concerned that you're going to lose your place in line? It's competitive out there." So she found herself learning something quite unexpected about what social movements really felt like. Her dissertation was to be called "Power and People in Conflict: Unionizing Texas." And because of this push-pull, she'd begun, even in her little way, to feel what the pressures might have been like on the workers she was seeing so abstractly. Think what they must have had to resist when their "loved ones" butted in, always, always for their sake. It was not pleasant.

Just before she left, she had an argument with her roommate's boyfriend. He was doing a residency in psychiatry at the University of Michigan hospital and when he heard where Miriam was going he put on his most professional face. (He was practicing jowls.) "Ah, yes. Well." (A real Dickensian harumph.) "Of course we know about the problems in the South among those people." (Those people.) "First, there's a lot of under-stimulation—nobody talks to them when they're little, in their crucial language-acquisition period, and of course they don't know much about culture. Then there's a lot of *over*-stimulation: People bathe together, if in fact they have access to anything like showers. The children witness the primal scene in those little houses. Fathers routinely sleep with their daughters. *You* know. And then there's all the rest . . ." And he waved "all the rest" away. "No jobs, bad diet, bad housing, bad education. All that." Miriam couldn't imagine how Judy could be planning to marry this caricature of an over-educated cretin who would eventually, unstoppably, make more in a week of talking than "those people" could earn in a year of chopping cotton. She knew such conversations brought out the self-righteousness in her, but at least that stiffened her backbone whenever she thought she was about to lose her courage.

Behind glass, now, a safe thirty thousand feet beneath her, the occasional lackadaisical curve of a river snaked through. Suddenly, for the first time, she suspected it might be beautiful down there—no, "oh, the horror," no, she was not about to admit that, simplifying child that she was (and knew that she was) and so well-intentioned, because those were the rivers, those wild ticklish syllables—Pelahatchie, Oktibeha, Tishomingo—from beneath whose brown skin the torsos of brown-skinned men were dredged up daily. Daily, she breathed to herself, and flushed at the strangeness of the thought that she'd be down soon on that ground, near those smarmy rivers.

RONNEE WAS WATCHING her intently while she spoke, as if she had lapsed into a language that took extraordinary concentration to penetrate. "We're getting there, don't despair," Miriam assured her. "But you need to know where we were or none of it'll make sense." No response. "You with me?"

Ronnee nodded. "I'm trying," she said earnestly. "I'm pretending it's a movie. I'm, like, trying to see it."

"Good idea," Miriam said. " 'The Birth of Veronica: The Movie.' "

SHE HAD BEEN MET at the plane, like all the rest of the new faculty, by the wife of the dean, Nettie Oliver. Nettie was called the Lioness at the Gates; she thought that if she didn't discourage the poor fledglings from continuing on their journey to the campus then they would surely be intrepid enough to succeed here. This formidable woman, sent to do the dean's dirty work, looked to Miriam as if she'd been painted into her clothes and then sprayed with—she remembered it from art class—fixative. She wore hubcap-size pearl earrings framed in glinty gold, and high heels that made crossing the campus on foot so laborious that she rarely attempted it. Nettie had the look of someone forever awaiting the arrival of her sedan chair. She was a grim woman, worthy of sympathy but not easy to grant it to if you were new and frightened and she was going out of her way not to be helpful.

Having been claimed at the airport, Miriam tooled along in the Olivers' very good car, a maroon Lincoln whose prow seemed to breast the waves of the highway, and every few minutes Mrs. O. quite visibly stifled a serious bout of yawning, meant to offend. Partly this was hostility to her husband for foisting this menial ferrying job on her, and partly it was to put these little hotshots in their place, to hint that their arrival here was less extraordinary than had been their departure from the safe clutch of their northern friends and terrified parents. It would be hard to determine whether she was harder on the white ones, whom she hated approximately the way a lawyer picking a jury may peremptorily overrule whole categories without the need to explain, or the black ones, who came with degrees from "good" colleges, thus throwing her into silent fits of jealousy and spite too unseemly to admit. Rather democratically, then, she threw every possible snare at every foot and smiled congenially, hostilely, nonstop.

Miriam was nearly the dozenth rookie she'd been sent to re-
trieve and drag home along the highway and then, after a hard
right, through the raggedy all-black town of Rowan, where sad
houses leaned in every direction, some little tract-style places and a
few of discolored brick that looked palatial beside them, where
weedy lots and a lone gas pump/grocery/motel stood at the
turnoff to the college, then through the impressive black wrought-
iron gate (PARNASSUS COLLEGE, FOUNDED 1883 · AD ASTRA PER AS-
PERA), and down the broad allée of live oaks, sun flashing through
them, a drowsing afternoon. Finally Mrs. Oliver unceremoniously
turned Miriam out a hundred yards from her assigned house—the
faculty lived on the campus to avoid the dangerous attentions of a
local white populace that hated them—and handed her a key.
"Watch out for copperheads in that field across the way," she told
her, told everyone, "and if anyone shoots through the chain link or
throws a firebomb, report it to Campus Security."

So there stood Miriam on the rickety wooden porch of a rickety
wooden house sloppily white-washed, wondering which predators
to fear more, the human or the reptilian. A dark green vine with
huge hand-shaped leaves—squash, cantaloupe, some more exotic
melon?—grew haphazardly alongside, most likely a sport sprouted
from floating seed or seed from the rinse water of a garbage pail
the last tenant had tossed over the side. The little bungalow,
flanked on both sides by identical houses, made her think of the
old motels on the outskirts of Houston, up near the airport, too
modest to have been replaced by the new-style one-piece brick
jobs that look like apartment complexes, with brand names and
swimming pools: pathetic, mildewy, slumping. It was a distinctly
"What am I doing here?" moment, orchestrated by the dean's wife
for maximum discomfort. For that reason alone she'd be damned if
she'd ask it. She knew what she was doing here. It would take
whatever it took.

WHEN SHE HAD BEEN AT PARNASSUS just under a month,
Miriam could see that her students didn't much like her (she who

had been voted Best Teaching Assistant in her department at the University of Michigan). She worked them too hard, she was new, she was white, they seemed to assume she was Northern—she had no accent to suggest otherwise. And she was pretty sure they laughed at the way she dressed down, which they undoubtedly took as an act of disrespect but which actually meant that, like many a graduate student, she rarely thought about what she put on her back. Nor could they be expected to appreciate the considerable victory this represented over her mother's zeal for fashion correctness, to the point where, horrified that Miriam had refused a girdle and cast aside white gloves, she had even written Miriam a letter to this effect: I don't understand, she had said, what *studying* has to do with this rejection of everything you've grown up with. How can you so dishonor your heritage? What will people think of you, especially, a Jewish girl, who lives in jeans and an army jacket, and your hair as wild as the fur around the collar, like a *wilde chayeh*? A wild thing? A *wolf*??

To make matters worse: One time, new to the campus, she desecrated a Parnassus tradition without realizing it, and those who saw or heard were not about to forgive whichever sin it was, ignorance or contempt. On this day, Miriam was on her way to lunch, coming from a dismal American history class, knee-deep in thought: Her kids were beyond help, whatever the particulars: They didn't know the difference between Martin Luther and Martin Luther King, or they thought the Civil War ended (yes) in 1945. She knew very well that you can't send a child to wretched schools, taught by teachers who hardly had any education themselves, and expect them to be ready for a college that isn't a cruel joke. She knew, she knew, but it hardly helped.

There were brilliant students on the campus doing high-level work, winning fellowships to graduate school; there was even a Yale Ph.D. on the faculty who had graduated from Parnassus years ago. She hadn't had much occasion to meet them yet, but even if she had, they wouldn't have redeemed their agonizingly unprepared classmates, or settled the constantly roiling tension between those, like herself, who insisted on holding them to some kind of departmental standards for graduation and those who didn't want them to feel bad about themselves or their subject and so applied an elastic measuring stick that collapsed when anyone leaned on it. Parnassus *looked* like a college: it had dormitories and a library of a sort, it had a gym and a track, though no football field because it wasn't big enough for inter-collegiate football. Everything about it could lead one to believe it an institution of higher learning. And yet, and yet, day after day she ended in tears or a depressed slog of sleep. If she had a morning class, she crawled into bed before lunch; if she met her charges in the afternoon, she went home and pulled her shade on the light and sacrificed the early evening to her sense of failure, that soporific. She was so full of despair she was thinking of quitting, except that she couldn't give her parents and teachers the satisfaction.

Worse, these kids did not even try to perform for her, they sat slumped in silence, or (better or worse?) let loose arrogant denunciations of her stupid assignments. When she mentioned something, in passing, about the myth of Jesus—this in the service of her idea that a little cultural relativism never hurt anyone—the churchy ones, the ones who understood, at least, glowered at her from where they sat disrespectfully, way down on their tailbones, and hated her, she could see it, in their stone-rigid indoctrinated little hearts.

The day of the Jesus episode, dragging herself toward the student center where the cafeteria put out the enticing perfume of chitlins au gratin, head down, she walked straight into a daunting, black-shirted, high-stepping line, a line as orderly as the Rockettes at Parris Island, and she came face to chest with one of the fraternity kings who was leading the stepping, her chin right up in the important red bandanna knotted around his thick athletic neck. "Hey lady! You blind or just stupid?" he shouted rhetorically into her face, and grabbed her by the arm.

"What is this?" she shouted back, recoiling, trying to twist her arm out of his grip, failing. She was seeing, apparently for the very first time, this phalanx of black-shirted, red-slashed, heavy-booted young men strutting with something tucked under their arms that seemed to be a cross between a baton and a walking stick. "It's a *line*, can't you see that?" The boy was actually suppressing some vivid epithets that could, if he let them, have fouled the air right into the adjacent county. Who is this l'il white thang with a briefcase anyway? (He'd finished his history requirement last year, so he didn't have to know her.) Couldn't she hear their chant, see the precision of the unison march, their dip, their pivot? They were beautiful and full of disciplined, honed, riveting power.

There must have been fifty students, a ragged mirroring line, the men envious, the women admiring, watching the show, thinking "The Kappas are too *much*, they really got their shit together." And this dumb professor walks right—splat—into the middle of the line like there's nobody there. How stupid can a white bitch be? Or is it sabotage? A lot of the teachers here didn't like them, thought fraternities were dangerous to your health and shriveled your brain, and the students were on the defensive. But Miriam looked so shocked and scared, she didn't seem like someone on a mission of destruction. She looked lost, and her briefcase gaped open on the cement, papers flying out, a green apple rolling away, the whole scene like a cartoon involving a banana peel. A girl from her nine o'clock class, who thought she was too serious by half, laughed out loud, delighted to see her up-ended, her dignity challenged. She yelled encouragement at the boy in black, who looked like an avenging crow in his long sleeves, his glossy, perfectly pleated pants.

She had one new friend, Jewel Proctor, black, local, beloved, who was on her way to lunch, full too of her own despairing thoughts about her introductory classes, though by now she understood that it was mostly at the beginning of the semester when she saw them plain, and then at the end when she had to measure them, that they showed up most wanting. (In the middle there was a little delusionary hillock of hope.) But at least she had her eyes open. She grabbed Miriam by the shoulder, wrested her out of the grip of the furious young man, apologizing for her newness, her innocence, and pulled her through the glass doors toward the cafeteria.

"What was *that*?" All Miriam's blood had plummeted to her feet; she sagged against Jewel. "Is there a campus army?"

"Oh, darlin', that's the finest fruit of college-educated black manhood," her friend told her. "I guess they could look pretty scary if you end up in the middle of all that. That's a bunch of manpower we could use in demonstrations and sit-ins that would rather piss away its time being frivolous and ganging up on each other. You ought to see what they make each other do when they're hazing. One of these days somebody's going to get hurt."

Miriam had smoothed herself out, straightened her hair (which was rowdy at best, a mane of it), regained a little dignity. "It looks pretty stupid, but I guess there's a lot of discipline that goes into it."

Jewel agreed.

"Of course, there are always those drill teams, isn't that what they call them? The ones who run around with the flags? White kids from Iowa are good at that, I guess. Kids from Houston go to camp to learn how to march in squares with sharp corners."

"True, true. Everybody seems to like *order*." Jewel shook her head; she had a long thick braid down her back, and got away with overalls, like a field hand. "You know, baby, this Greek business is different where black people are concerned. When a brother or a sister shows up in your town anywhere, here in this country where we never know if we'll find a hotel or motel that will let us through the door, see, there's always a friend to call to find a bed, no questions asked except 'You're a Delt?' 'You're an Alpha?' Aliens need passwords. I just wish they weren't so stupid in a crowd. I wish they'd spend as much time studying as they spend learning how to step like the backup chorus for the Supremes."

"There's a lot I don't know about where I am," said Miriam quietly. "And who these kids are." She had already learned a lot. She kept being humbled, day after day after day.

"Well, if you like understatement. But you're trying."

They sat together with a trayful of something in a glob slathered in white-flour gravy. Jewel wanted to be helpful, but she came from a very different place: Her real home was just outside the

grand gate of the college and across the road. It was, she had told
Miriam, without being coy, the largest and nicest house in Rowan
Village, which, in contrast to the campus, was a series of fairly pathetic living places and garbagey lots on unpaved streets that gave
off dust like fumes except when they were pacified by a winter
freeze. Here and there, especially far from the town proper, stood
shacks that couldn't keep the cold out, or the heat either. But
Jewel's father, a Parnassus graduate, in fact valedictorian of his
class, was principal of the consolidated colored high school and
her mother, a school nurse who had even worked for a while in the
Parnassus infirmary, constituted what little aristocracy the town
possessed. And so their house had a garden and a garage more
sound than many of their neighbors' houses. They had, Jewel told
her, a mailbox with a pink wooden flamingo standing atop it on
one elegant leg, looking superior. Her parents were, not surprisingly, dear friends of Parnassus's president, Harry Storm, and his
wife, Maxie, for all the years of her girlhood, and she, Jewel, had
spent an extraordinary amount of time sitting, in her lace-trimmed
anklets and her little pearl choker ("Never too early to practice being a lady," the mothers agreed), being seen and approved but not
heard, and subject to shushing.

"My God, Jewel," Miriam said, fanning herself with her hand as
if to dispel a miasma of perfume. "That sounds like my mother!
They must have gone to the same finishing school."

"Huh! I'll bet."

"You laugh. Your mother went to school longer than mine, you
know. My mother couldn't finish high school before she had to go
to work. Yours has a nursing degree."

"Now, I wouldn't have guessed that, child."

"Lot of things we don't know, aren't there?" She was happy to
gain a little ground.

Jewel was busy, like Miriam, repenting her privilege. She had
been to Mount Holyoke and then to Columbia for her master's—
plenty of snow in her veins, a little socialism, and a lot of anger at
earnest Northern white obtuseness—and only up there had taken
to wearing those overalls and jabbing her finger in the air in the

self-righteous manner of the real civil-rights leaders. "I don't want to mock them or myself—this is serious business, not fashion, hon, you know it can get you killed—but I can't help saying it. I can see what I'm doing, you know, sort of épatéeing my parents and their complacency. They have comfy jobs, they're wedged inside the status quo. I can't blame them. I always see them sort of like aged palace retainers, you know? The first to go, come the Revolution. They're good people, giving people, who want change but, you know, they want to keep it modest, inoffensive, polite. So every time I get arrested (and let me tell you, baby, I get arrested as often as I can), they have to apologize to somebody for my rashness. I don't mean somebody white, either. I mean some aunt, some neighbor's got the heebie-jeebies, think they're going to get in trouble somehow because of me. Everybody covers their asses, like anything else. But I absolutely believe, maybe I'm crazy but I can't help it, even though I've never heard it from them, I go on believing way deep inside they're proud of me."

Of course Miriam's upper-middle-classness, she assured her, was very different from her own, founded as it was on considerably more actual money. "A lot of black middle-class life is what you might call undercapitalized. It has to do with how clean your work is—how you dress when you go to your job and how dirty your hands get doing it—not with owning stocks or even having savings." Still, Jewel said, she knew she was luckier than most, and so was Miriam. They had something they could kick around and it would still love them. How could they not become friends?

MIRIAM WAS OBSESSED with her teaching because it was in her nature to be serious about everything she did. (Her sister had always called her humorless; she thought her sister brainless. Did that make them even?) She had little time for friends and she saw nothing of Mississippi, but rather considered it her contribution to the cause of general enlightenment to work long into the night on lesson plans and paper grading. These she did in such fine detail that, with a few exceptions for the remarkable ones and the diligent ones and the ones on probation who had to concentrate harder than they ever had, she terrified her students. Jewel told her to look around hard: Some of the least stringent teachers here, who grew up as their students did, badly educated but hungry nonetheless, were a lot more effective as models, as friends, as gentle leaders into accomplishment. There's all kinds of ways to get an education, Jewel insisted, though of course the new set of young teachers with whom Miriam had been hired were here for another purpose entirely: Had she noticed, Jewel asked, how they were always introduced by the names of their colleges and graduate schools as if they were basketball players in the draft? Every degree was another dollar's worth of prestige in a strained economy. If they taught well, so much the better.

If she wasn't humorless, Miriam had begun to wonder if she was inflexible. (But I'm *here*, she thought, in this unlikely place, and then worried about her tendency toward self-congratulation.)

Well, nothing she could do about that. She felt condescending, harsh and legalistic, distinctly unloved. She had a sneaking feeling, which rooted around in her like a worm, that she would never be comfortable here. The night the president had the faculty over for drinks and she'd stood in the golden light of the oversized lamps, on the plush carpet, drinking white wine no different from the kind she'd have at any party, she realized with a little bump that, however theoretically she felt for them, she had never been in the presence of so many colored people at one time. It wasn't only Texas, it was Smith, it was Michigan, how could this be? And how could she not have thought of it before? She had never known enough of them to be comfortable giving honest evaluation to their merits: black people had come into her life one by one at most. The vice president of her class, the class of '61, at Smith, Nuriya Washington, had played volleyball beside her, but all they did was croak "Mine!" or "Yours!" to each other as the ball approached. One graduate student in the history department at Michigan was black, though barely. She remembered he had beautifully sculpted eyebrows and carried a briefcase in admirably lush leather. Where, she had wondered, had he acquired such a luxurious accessory? She had never actually spoken to him, aside from the housekeeping inquiries graduate students live among: Do you know if that book is on reserve? When did he say that paper is due?

Having had a maid all her life not only didn't count, here it was surely a demerit. Flukie, narrow-bosomed and imperious, co-conspirator in Miriam's childhood and adolescence, calm, critical, and coolly affectionate. Flukie could not be so much as mentioned now. Suddenly it was as though Miriam's family had owned slaves. Fervently she had thought to herself as Mrs. Dean Oliver drove her through the gate to the campus, "Flukie, I'm here for you," and her eyes had filled with embarrassing tears. With the back of her balled fist she had wiped them away like a sleepy child, but since Mrs. Oliver had no interest in looking at her one way or the other, no one had noticed. Flukie herself, whose sense of irony was necessarily well developed, would have laughed, quick and derisive: "For *me*, sugar? Huh. For *me*? All the difference it make, don't you bother none for me." But her presence would make a difference, Miriam knew. Or knew when she signed on for this. If it didn't repair the world, she had thought, it would go a way toward repairing her own repentant upper-middle-class Southern soul. And where souls were concerned, every one who went on record would represent thousands who kept silent. Surrogacy. Testifying.

SHE HAD PROMISED her parents—it was the least she could do to pacify them—that she wouldn't take part in demonstrations or anything that threatened to be physically dangerous. But it began to seem, in ways she couldn't even try to explain to them, that her psychological health was in imminent danger if she forbade herself the rites of passage her friends and students had undertaken. Otherwise shouldn't she have stayed at home? How could she not ride into town in what was called, absurdly, a "mixed" car? Say to a black student, No, I will not sit beside you because we might irritate someone looking in the window? Refuse to eat in a restaurant with her "colored" colleagues?

One time she had gone to dinner with the History Department.

They weren't agitating: grading departmental exams had made
them hungry. They were led by Henry Hamby, a tall, slender black
man as dignified as a diplomat in his carefully pressed striped suit
and mirror-shiny shoes, who had been teaching American history
longer than Miriam had been alive. Dinner had passed uneventfully; they had argued out standards and grades and, over dessert,
were making plans to hold a History Fair just before Thanksgiving. Henry got up to go the men's room and, with a restrained exclamation of surprise, took a flying ball of something slimy—a
handful of okra, it might have been, or a mess of string beans—
right at the back of his neck. The missile had been lobbed slowly,
like a softball, as contemptuous as a gob of spit. Miriam watched
him reach around to wipe it from the white collar of his shirt, regard it in his hand and move slowly, decorously, to pluck a dark
green cloth napkin from an empty table, clean his palm, and pass
the napkin carefully between his long fingers. His expression had
not changed.

Miriam leaped from her seat and stood with her hands on her
hips, searching out the perpetrator. Faces, some smiling, looked
back at her silently from every booth, every square table. Such
cowardice apparently did not need to boast. But her own party
was hissing at her to sit down. "Come away, girl," Henry himself
prodded, sotto voce. "Sit yourself down here and eat your cobbler
before it gets cold." Reluctantly, she pushed her way back into the
slippery leather of the booth. "You don't have to respond, little
miss," he said to her soothingly. "That's kind of you, but it's not a
good idea."

"But it's not only disgusting, it's illegal now, Henry!" she
quailed. This was what she was here to refuse, here to reverse.

"It'll come around of its own weight, Miriam. Just leave it alone
now. It doesn't need us to make it happen."

"Well, who, then? How's it going to change if you don't *use* the
right— How did the law get changed anyway? It was—"

Henry looked at her a long time, smiling an old wily-animal
smile, leaving her to imagine the scars he bore hidden beneath his
careful gentleman's clothing. "We're here, aren't we? We're eating
their food, drinking their very bad coffee. Tell you the hard truth,

I think there ought to be a law against their _coffee_, while the lawyers are at it guaranteeing us our _rights_!" He was so inured, he sounded almost cheerful.

Arlene Mowbry, a ginger-colored woman with a high-stacked hairdo who, Miriam suspected, spent more time on her coiffure than on planning her classes, nodded sadly. "Let it be, dear. You're still so new. We've seen this kind of thing too long to be surprised by it."

When Miriam brought the story back to Jewel, she heard the response she wanted. "Old goats!" Jewel loved to fume at them. Sometimes she said they'd come around slower than the bastards outside the gates. "They think they deserve a medal just for going to eat in some integrated place, but they're throwbacks. I'm telling you, honey, it's like the Jews in the desert, moping around behind Moses. At this rate it's gonna take another forty damn years to get them to remember they're not slaves anymore."

Miriam was ready to go to jail; she yearned for it the way a warrior longs for his initiation scars, put herself in harm's way, followed Jewel to every potential confrontation, but spared her parents the news. They were the Young Turks, along with a handful of faculty, white and black, and a dozen or so students. A few years before, there had been an army of them, but they'd fallen back out of weariness and satisfaction at their partial successes. She was a year or two too late. Now they were outnumbered on the campus by the Henry Hambys and Arlene Mowbrys, who thought them incendiary and impatient. "Patience is for the grave," Jewel muttered when one of the old guard lobbied the administration to prohibit their "provocations." "They'll have to plant flowers on me to stop me from sitting in. You with me, girl?"

SHE CAME MARCHING, on a Tuesday in late October, out of her classroom into the pale sunlight, livid. She had given them a quiz; they had objected. A few docile ones submitted, the others were sullen or complained that they hadn't been warned. "No, you were warned. You weren't listening."

"Who needs this shit anyway?" a boy named Carlos had asked,

kicking the seat in front of him. "What this Napoleon ever done for me?"

Southern Negroes, everyone knew, were all too docile, all too cowed in the face of white authority. Should she have applauded him his insolence, congratulated him on his independence, or put a black mark in her attendance book and dealt with him when the grades came due?

She was out of her depth here, she was drowning.

So when she met Jewel in the hall and Jewel said, "Lunch, girl, you need a little energy to get you through," Miriam told her, "Oh, I just want to go home and get under the covers and sleep the rest of the day. I don't know what I'm doing, Jewel. I might as well go home."

"You're scared of these kids, Miriam. I don't know if it's growing up a little ol' cracker that did it or just what." She held up her hand like a traffic cop; they had their routines down already. "And don't tell me a Jewish cracker's different, it's all the same right here. You don't really like them, I mean that's clear from way across the room. You're giving off fumes, it's like this sour smell—hostile—only you don't know it, and they must be catching a whiff."

She didn't want to see herself that way. She refused, in fact, to believe it. All she wanted was some—some reach, some evidence of an attempt to learn a few things and be serious. She was not prejudiced, she only had standards. She walked beside her friend with misty eyes, in danger of bumping into things.

They passed the side of the building where the campus theater's door was propped open, a modest door with a brick as a doorstop, and a great wave of song, a duet, wafted out and across the grass—two implausible voices, a man's and a woman's, in sweet accord. She had to listen hard to decipher it—could that be *Italian*?

"Well now," said Miriam, "what is *this*?" They walked in out of the sun and, when their eyes adjusted to the black-box darkness, they saw two students standing in an island of light in the middle of the room, their music on stands in front of them. Eljay Reece, a man Jewel knew fairly well and didn't much like, whom Miriam had never really fixed on before, was at the piano, shouting a complicated assortment of directions, corrections, encouragements. It was astonishing to hear these singers, who, crossing the campus, would look like any ordinary pair. *"Caro mio ben,"* the young man sang, his eyes closed, swaying just a little. *"Credi io mio men."* He was tall and husky, very dark, with a complicated face— sleepy eyes, incipient jowls—not the stuff, certainly, that matinee idols are made of. But when he sang, his baritone swooping out into every corner of the room—"Not kidding," it seemed to say. "I am not a schoolboy and I am not playing, this is for real"—everything about him lightened: his eyes opened, his face organized itself.

As for the girl, she was so stick thin she could have been taken for a basketball player, not a soprano. She had a shy, abashed expression until the gorgeous syllables filled her mouth, her cheeks filled out. Then she attained a kind of stature, as if she had put a cloak around her scrawny little shoulders. Miriam did not believe that what she was watching was quite real; it had the feel of mirage.

Jewel had seen Eljay Reece do his number before, and he wearied her, she was exhausted just watching the way he danced around, like a boxer, but a very theatrical one. Maybe he was too much like her—she sometimes thought that—a kind of bully for a good cause. A little overdramatic, a little fake-earnest. Not that he didn't mean what he was doing, only that from the minute she met him, she always thought he was one of those people with invisible mirrors out in front of them: they do enjoy the view. Part of their power is how seriously they take themselves, without irony. And others gladly follow along.

But Miriam was mesmerized, watching Eljay. He moved so much and so fast he could have been teaching dance; in fact, he was wearing white sneakers that picked up the light in all that dimness, dressed for his athletic agility. He tugged at their faces, rearranged their cheeks as if they were putty, he gave them vocal exercises that made them laugh, great sweeps up to the top of their registers and down again, leaping and swinging, then tiny little mincing syllables that forced them to sound like chickens pecking. Possibly these were as standard to singing teachers as the givens of history were to her, but she had never seen anything quite like the intensity with which he worked his charges, and the speed with which he moved. "Don't worry about looking silly," he chided them. "Nobody's looking." Then he talked to them about the characters they were playing: Why does Don Alfonso want to betray the infidelity of women? Does he have motives you can't see? Is there a difference between the reactions of Ferrando and Guglielmo or are they identical? How about the women? Is Fiordiligi as sweet as she is made to look? Under the bombast and the posturing, what is going on? At first the students gave him shy silence, but he prodded and rephrased and would not accept nothing for an answer. He was teaching them how to think about character and plot. Miriam suspected he was doing it better than that bunch of literature teachers out there in Staggers Hall, pulling teeth.

Miriam, in the dark at the rear of the rehearsal room, seemed to be alarmingly near tears. She couldn't quite sort it out, she tried to say to Jewel—joy at the music, awe at the talent hidden in these ordinary children whom she herself could not reach (who were not so much younger than they were, if the truth be known), pleasure at their discovery of a culture entirely alien to them and their dusty little towns—anything is possible, she told her friend—what a flight! Sublimity, sophistication, and this man was a genius for finding a way to transport them to such unlikely heights. They slipped out before anyone saw them. "Oh, honey, look at you, you're missing *art*," Jewel told her. "Rowan, Mississippi, was not the place to come to if you need to be transported by high art. Ain't no branch of the Metropolitan Museum anywhere *near* here."

"But yes it is," she answered back. "Art. You saw. That man has music flowing in his bloodstream." She was sweating with pleasure. "Look what's *possible* here!"

"Baby, you don't need to tell me that." Jewel pretended to be insulted. "If I'm here, anything's possible."

The next time they looked in on the rehearsal, which came right after her most benighted class of dozing seniors—Jewel came along to guard her in case she swooned all alone back there—they watched a girl named Latitia (one of her own students, who could not seem to learn that the French Revolution preceded the Depression, likely because she didn't care) fingering the deep green gown she was to wear in *Così fan tutte.* Part of its bodice was overlaid with beige lace, and a hoop had been sewn in to make it round and floaty at the bottom. She stood inside it gingerly; she leaned over and touched the hem like a child in a bridal shop, the way she'd prod this strange beautiful thing with a single finger. Eljay, watching her, said gently, "You're going to have to get comfortable in that, Latitia. You're going to have to act like you wear that kind of thing all the time."

Latitia giggled. She had a toothy smile with a little gold in it and, probably from a habit of embarrassment, she kept her hand in front of her mouth.

"You know what I want you to do?"

"No, sir."

Eljay laughed. "First I want you to take your hand away from your mouth. You've got a pretty mouth, why do you want to hide it like that?"

She lowered her hand but didn't quite know what to do with it; the best she could do was clutch her elbow to restrain it, as if her arm were broken. "Yes, sir."

"Then, I want you to go over there to that Coke machine, you know the one out back?"

"Sir?" Latitia could hardly look at him. Her eyes darted everywhere.

He shook some coins into her palm. "Go buy yourself a Coke and walk around with it back there. I don't want you to come back until you finish it. Just keep on moving, though. I don't want you hiding. Get used to the way that thing feels. Stand up, sit down, turn around. I know it's heavy, but it's not a space suit. You want to live in it awhile. It's got to take your creases, yours and nobody else's. Know what I mean?"

She finally got it. "Yes sir." She giggled again and took off across the creaky wooden floor, her taffeta dress sweeping it with a soft brushing sound.

Eljay spotted the two women where they stood—Miriam stood—transfixed. He nodded brusquely at Jewel; he didn't seem to approve of her any more than she of him. Or maybe he could tell already what she hadn't quite admitted to herself, that no man would ever have much power over her—no resonance there, and someone like Eljay would sniff that out.

"Whoever thought college would be like this?" Miriam said shyly.

"You been peeking back there? Eavesdropping?"

"Well, sort of." She laughed, a fetching, flirty little laugh no woman friend ever heard from another in the ordinary course of things. Maybe he really meant it when he promised his singers that nobody could see them; maybe it really mattered. "I hope you don't mind. This is the first thing I've seen in a long time that made me feel really good."

"It's a stretch for them," he told her soberly, "but you come to the production next week and you won't believe where you are. You just will not recognize anybody." Eljay had an aura that no one else on this campus had: a kind of real-world authority, a certainty about what he was doing that cut across the hyperbolic pride and, beneath it, the lethargy of discouragement, like a cool breeze on a hot day. He was a professional; the rest of them, even the good ones, seemed like fumbling amateurs. "This is like sports, you know," he said. "No faking. You don't win games pretending you can do things you can't do, and you don't sing Mozart either."

Miriam took a deep breath as if the exertion had been hers. "You think any of these kids have any kind of career out there?"

Eljay looked at her, full in the face. Fine-boned and clean-shaven, except for a restrained tuft of goatee, he was a rich, vivid medium brown, like something polished with care. She thought his face very pleasant to look at. His eyes, slightly close together under a permanently worried brow, had the innocence of enthusiasm in them. "I've got to proceed as if they could make it. Yeah, I think so. Edgar and Charita, the two you saw there, and there's a new little freshman coming up, girl named Patty. Going to be a contralto if I can rearrange her a little." He laughed. "You can try to play God like that, but in the end it's all theirs. If they've got the will for it. The will is the hard part. I'm never going to figure out how to teach that."

She was standing in the shadows with him, close enough almost to touch. Jewel was out in the light. She could actually see it, though, a little charge, electric, that seemed to leap from his arm to hers, from the cotton of his plaid shirt to her bare skin.

"Hey, look at Latitia," he said, stepping away, clapping. The girl was whirling around in the middle of the floor in her fine shiny dress, holding a Coke bottle high, her shoulders shaking one way, her skirt the other, and singing out "My Man" like Diana Ross.

"Oh baby," Jewel said to her when they hit the path. "I think you're in trouble."

"You call that trouble?" She knew she was pink as a brine shrimp; it was embarrassing.

"I call that trouble," was what Jewel said, but she didn't fill in the details because it was clear Miriam either didn't believe her or didn't care.

THEY BEGAN TO ENGAGE one another's glance. Something about these exchanges was, from the very first, unchaste. This might simply be what others called flirting—Miriam hadn't had a great deal of experience with that—but if it was, if this was what her sister excelled at, she wished she had not been so snobbish, that she'd managed it years ago. Eljay's eyes widened just the slightest bit, immeasurably, when they touched hers. (And it was a touch that, the first few times, almost made her flinch in surprise.) Each locked gaze was an event: there were words in the infinitesimal movement of his pupils, his eyebrows, at some nearly subliminal level, but she found herself thinking there was more intelligence and curiosity, and surely more sex, in the tiny movement of Eljay Reece's eyes than in the whole rocking, thrusting, shuddering

body of her fellow history student Andy Solowey, who thought
she was in love with him, old-fashioned boy, because she let him
excite himself against her body in the dark stairwell outside her
apartment. Or in the Waspy Yalie who had unburdened her of her
virginity—she was doing her senior thesis and thought she could
concentrate better on her work if she got it over with once and for
all—who bought her a good roast beef dinner at Wiggins Tavern,
the best inn in Northampton, then took her upstairs and per-
formed so dispassionately (the kind of lover who hung his pants
neatly over a chair, then swallowed back the eruption of sound at
his climax like a man stifling his sneeze at church) that she felt as if
she'd undergone not sex but outpatient surgery. Next time, she'd
thought, she'd find herself a longhaired poet who would coax her
into bed with long draughts of Yeats, but she was pressed for time
and energy and this was sufficient to meet what she took to be the
minimal graduation requirements of one of the Seven Sister Colleges.

Eljay, though, right now. Eljay passed her one late afternoon
when she was rapt in conversation with one of her better students,
a boy with original ideas and execrable spelling. They were searching for a solution to his problems: a friend who could edit his papers, a chance to correct and resubmit. She was earnestly looking
at the young man as they spoke, sitting shoulder-to-shoulder with
his blue Parnassus track jacket on one of the benches along the
main path, when Eljay came hustling past—he was always bent
double, cramming in more work than he could ask of himself and
his students—and when he turned his very clear, very avid eyes on
her and, slowing just a little bit, flicked them open a jot, a tiny flare
at their center, as if to say "Well?," as if to say "See?," she felt an
unholy flush suffuse her face all to the way to her hairline, and the
very follicles of her hair prickled. This, she knew, was not an accidental glance, not informational. It was not politeness either, it was
nothing but the touch of his finger on some forbidden never-
before-touched spot she could never locate if she had to. She tried
to send a signal back, a receptive warmth, without actually moving
a single muscle, and the way he almost smiled—almost, like a

shadow of a smile that had already happened—she thought, Eureka! Message received.

AS SOON AS MIRIAM WALKED into the cast party after the opening—*Così fan tutte* in the chapel on a makeshift stage sacrilegiously spread out where the podium/altar usually stood—the most extraordinary music swept across it in gusts like clean air, fresh cool water: *Felice al tuo seno il spero tornar!* Passion, separation, despair, reunion, passion again—it was clear where they were headed. Miriam picked up a cracker spread with spicy cheese and watched Eljay, the impresario, trainer, conductor. He was like a politician who's won an election, the erotic heat rolling off him in waves, every gesture exuberant and charged, though the worry-creases between his eyes seemed to be indelible. The admiration of everyone (especially the women) circled him like a string of little flashing lights. He stood with one arm paternally around Charita, the other around Edgar, his stars, eyes dazzling in the glare of flashbulbs. Their friends were cowed with respect, as if they had barely been introduced; they circled the singers, asking if they could bring them anything to drink, to eat. Who would imagine a Mozart opera could produce such awe?

No sooner had she turned away than Eljay came up behind her and leaned against her, he who had never so much as touched her hand before. It was as if he were drunk, his inhibitions down, and maybe his better judgment; or maybe this *was* his better judgment, and it needed only this triumphant high to consolidate his daring. He didn't even care who was watching. His hand was on her arm, urgently. He wanted to detain her. "Did you like it?" he whispered right in her ear, his breath hot and damp. His tweedy jacket rankled against her, she was aware of his body inside it. Every material thing she touched was jangling and full of texture. "Did you love it?"

"I did, I did," she told him earnestly, turning her face just enough so that their undefended cheeks touched, pulled back in surprise and then touched again, far beyond the snare, suddenly too theoretical, of glances. The darkness of his face was shocking, strangely, purely lovely. (I am not prejudiced, she would tell Jewel. Watch, I can prove it to you.) Such rich color, such vigor, she hadn't imagined how he would look up close, like moist earth, like night sky, more substantial by far than any white face she had been close to. His breath was rich with wine and cigarettes, the taste of adult lust. She had a vague memory of how she had been sleeping, sleeping, wishing she were gone from here, obliterating herself; suddenly it seemed unimaginable to be anywhere but here. His mouth was dark as an Italian plum, the late summer kind, moist with syllables. She wanted that mouth more than she had ever wanted any thing. "Do you even know my name?" she asked him, whispering. He was more than life size. What eyelashes the man brought close to hers, so enviably, unfairly lush. His goatee was firm as a hairbrush.

"Do I know your name?" He laughed with the pleasure of his outrageousness. "Aren't you Despina, who knows that love is the kingdom and women rule?" Quietly. "You know you have that look that says 'Watch out!' " The corner of his lip was almost on hers; when he said "Watch out!" she felt a little puff of air as if he were blowing out a candle. "Will you let me finish up a little business with my cast here and meet me round the back door of Staggers in about half an hour?"

He was too close to see her eyes widen.

"Please?" She could imagine the heat of his body beneath his jacket. "I need to know more about you than your name."

So I'm a back-door gal, she thought, walking as slowly as she could toward the shadows at the rear of his building. She stood against the tickle of the bushes for a while, imagining the room at the very front where she taught European history around a seminar table scratched with the names of students, scored by decades of indifference. Staggers was a grab bag of miscellaneous spaces: classrooms, offices, single rooms for single faculty. The fraternities did their nefarious business in their club rooms at the back. A lot of people lived on Eljay's hall. She should have asked him to come to her house, where they wouldn't have to worry about being

seen. But he was going to put his seal on her somehow, she understood that. With his deep-dyed flesh he was going to brand her, so
new and frail and colorless, in his own bed.

She was in what Jewel, when she heard of it, would call ten
leagues of trouble, and months later, when Miriam finally lifted her
head to look her friend in the eye, she was going to be in something even deeper, and Veronica—unknown, unnamed, still un-
imagined—would be in her deeper still.

HE HAD THE ROOM—lived in the space—of a purposeful man.
Her own little house, with its square white rooms, was sloppy,
strewn with books she would never get to and papers she should
have graded yesterday, her shoes unfindable under chairs where
they lay on their sides amid dust balls, dishes left forever in the
drying rack, in the bathroom a syrupy stain that persisted on the
sink for days where her shampoo bottle had dripped. It would stay
there, probably, until she washed her hair again. She excused this
disarray as graduate-student habit, attributable to perpetual haste
and the life-denying concentration on intangibles that doctoral
students had to put up with until their real lives began. Though she
was more likely slovenly because Flukie, infinitely patient and
paid for doing it, had walked behind her all those years, making
order.

But it was Eljay's room that looked as if it had been picked up
and kept dusted by an attentive servant. He had towers of books
for which there weren't enough shelves, but instead of flopping in
disarray in the corners, they sat with edges neatly squared against
the walls, orderly as stock waiting to be sold. Clotted schedules
hung like timetables above his desk, clustered beside the postcard-
size faces of his favorite composers: Gounod blessed him where
he worked, and Gluck and Mozart and Handel. Above his hot
plate—as if living in this building were not sufficient indignity, its
unlucky inhabitants were expected to eat regularly in the dining
hall—hung a few modest, shiny-bottomed pots. His bed, sealed
under a navy blue blanket, would have passed muster in the mili-

tary—hospital corners, Miriam speculated. His mama had taught him to run a tight ship.

It was not the house of the poet she had dreamed would murmur "Sailing to Byzantium" in her ear, who would seduce her with his dishevelment, his disdain for conventions of order and parental coercion. But Eljay, she had no doubt, would have his own forms of abandon.

They had tiptoed down the hall of Staggers, whose floorboards seemed to complain at every step. He had turned his key in the lock with great care, to keep it silent. She made note of his slow, unrushed burglar's andante and knew that he would take his time with her; the back of her neck contracted when the tumblers clicked and hit home, and the wooden door, so narrow it might have concealed a closet, opened wide.

She never saw him turn on the music but there was soft jazz somehow, which seemed to fill the space of the room with sweetness, like an inviting smell. He had left a lamp on, just one, and it too warmed every station of the room, those separate domains, with its syrup. She had a dozen questions she was eager to ask, but when she began, "Oh, where did you—" he put his finger to his faceted lips and touched it gently to hers. "I'll whisper," she promised like a rebuked child, but he shook his head and stood even closer, so that her breasts touched his tweed lapels, his hands firmly on her shoulders. "No, I don't mean whisper. We're gonna make a *joyful* noise, but we don't need no words." His grammar had slipped, but it was the only thing out of his control. Even it was probably calculated, that return to the natural. She could feel the way Latitia and Charita must have felt when he molded their faces to call forth from them exactly the right sound, and led them around the stage, placing them where he wanted them and then bidding them sing out in their own voices.

When he was accusing her, later, of her many sins, he told her his deep brown skin—his *flesh*, he called it, which was supposed to make it more elemental, she supposed, more shocking—had excited her. Well, it had, yes, as her pale shoulders and breasts (which he called gardenias the first time he kissed them, called gorgeous stemless flowers) had lured him on. Yes, he was right, she had looked at their smooth intermingled thighs and then up, up to where he had planted the root of himself inside her, around it a lush corona of springy hair, darker than dark, and she was amazed at what she saw: that, no part of them forbidden, they were beautiful together, they were remaking the whole ugly world, and yes, he was right (she told him caustically), she had not failed to notice their differences.

But there was so much more to their coming together that it was one more insult among many to hear them reduced to the prurience of forbidden meat. Worse, it was the prurience of their enemies. "If I wanted black flesh up against me," she said when it had all fallen away, "there were simpler men to get it from than you, Eljay, believe me."

ELJAY'S METICULOUSNESS was the kind that was brought about, though it could as easily have been undone, by his childhood. From his mother he learned that it helps your dignity, at least a little, to keep the outside of your life neat; at worst, she demonstrated, it frees more energy for dealing with the mess at heart. Certainly, living that childhood in Euphrates, Alabama (whose river had run, perhaps, in someone's dream), did not feel to him like a cliché, but it always sounded like one in the telling. His daddy was brutal, a sad scrawny unschooled man for whom very little had ever gone right, and his mama a vigorous, rigorous, ample-hearted woman (though she was tiny in body—all the Reeces were small and strong)—who could only try to redress her husband's demonstrations of power over the helpless. "If we'd had a dog," Eljay told her, "my daddy would have kicked it. Which was why we didn't have one." Eljay had hated him, pure and simple; it was his one uninflected emotion. When he was ready for high school, Roker Reece said no, his son was chopping cotton like the rest of them—there were five (one of them, Ronnie, born gimpy-legged) and why should he be different—and nothing Thelmie could say would sway him. That he was smart, that he was musical seemed only to incite his father against him, as if he were playing tricks, purposely putting everyone less smart at a disadvantage. Eljay employed his friends to bring him work from school, and he would do it wherever he could cadge some privacy; he sat more than once in the outhouse, pants down in case anyone looked in, his books across his skinny knees. He knew he was a darling boy; his mother had taught him that, in spite of Roker, and that was all he had. He borrowed his oldest brother's one white shirt and took that confidence into town to see the principal and used every wile the Lord had given him to convince her to let him try on his own to do what his classmates (his would-be classmates) were struggling with daily. When it came time for graduation, he snuck away to take his exams and when he passed them he snuck away again (his mother right behind him) to walk across the stage to receive his diploma, for which his father rewarded him by throwing him against the wall and breaking his arm. "I never heard how he punished my mama for all that, and just as well or I'd have had a murder on my record before I was eighteen." He had flexed his arm while he told her this. "And I'm not dreaming, this still hurts me when it rains."

And so he was gone at an early age. Diploma in hand, with goodbyes to no one but his friends, those co-conspirators, and the select few of his brothers and sisters who had been sympathetic, he went off to Tulane, which happened to be looking for smart black boys just then. If he ever allowed himself to think back to Euphrates, that chicken-scratch-dry, unlovely town, it was only to worry about Ma Thelmie, and finally to cheer when his father, at work in Birmingham, was felled by a crane that, turning, had taken off the top of his scalp. His mother wrote him—he would not come home for the funeral—that Roker's disposition had sweetened a little when he finally found good work. What an irony, then. He had learned the word *irony* at college. When his father was killed he was in Salzburg studying opera, learning German, learning French, reveling in the distance between the red velvet rope that kept the audience discreetly waiting in the lobby of the opera house and the bare dooryard of their splintery house, which his mother swept clean as if it was the floor. *Irony* was the word

that measured all the hurt in the world, he decided, the distance
between what should have been and what was. It was the word
that made you smile a bitter smile and shrug—his mother's helpless shrug—and keep on going. "Irony," he said, shaking his head
against Miriam's on their pillow, "you know, when you think
about what you've got but you can imagine another way, so you're
not altogether *stuck* in it—that was a luxury none of them over
there ever had."

So now, what he was left with were his habits: diligence enough
to save a life, cleanliness as if he'd been toilet-trained at six months,
a will more adamant than stone, and the tendency to sweet-talk
anyone softer than he. Most people were softer. Miriam, whose
childhood had made her trusting and led her to believe that even if
you gave everything away you wouldn't wind up sleeping under a
bridge, was like a snail without a shell. What she thought was
hunger in him, she learned too slowly, was desperation. In her, far
from home, it was appetite for everything rich and real, thick and
moist, probing and sharp and unadulterated by artifice. If she was
desperate, she didn't know it.

In her school back home she had been ostentatious in her out-
spokenness, which wasn't difficult: the others, the girls, were being
brought up for Texas gentility, where only men and old women,
confirmed matriarchs, tended to speak their minds, unstoppable,
and all the rest learned deviousness. So to say what she meant, simply to open her mouth wide, take a deep breath, and level with
someone, was nearly revolutionary. She was voted Class Mouth in
her high-school yearbook, which she took as a compliment
clothed in an insult. Whenever anyone said, "You ought to be a
lawyer," she knew what they'd been thinking, and it was not good.
One of her team members had said to her after a debate-club meeting, "The reason I like debating is you don't have to actually *believe* anything. In fact, the less you care about the question, the
better you do!" Miriam laughed bitterly and said, "Lucky for you.
I have so many convictions I ought to be in jail." She had thought
of herself, in fact, as Class Conscience, though that would have
been arrogant to say.

But that was boldness of speech. Boldness of body was a differ-

ent story. Perhaps she had been afraid; perhaps she had valued—or
trusted—mind too much and touch too little. (She was the only
girl she knew who didn't "get" Elvis.) Even Eljay had established
himself in her eyes by way of his talent, his energy, his enterprise
and taste, before she had really looked at him. If it hadn't been that
he managed better than she to combine mind and body—what was
voice, after all, what was opera, but a subtle conjunction of
both?—she might never have lain against his chest consoled, nor
opened her legs wider than she thought they could stretch. She
loved the lapping sound, like deep water against a jetty, of the two
of them, belly to belly, at their rawest and deepest, and she let herself believe she had found an alternative to her life as the nearly
virgin Houston good girl, the A student her teachers loved. "Oh,
you're Joy's sister!" they would say, astonished, because Joy had
been all erotic challenge and intellectual laziness in their classes,
her sweater open one button too many, her notebook pages a jun-
gle of boys' faces in indelible ink, and hearts with their initials in
them. "You're Joy's sister!": a combination of surprise, relief, and
amusement, at which of them she could never determine. Now she
wondered if Joy hadn't understood something deeper than what
she'd gotten, behind her barricades reading the proceedings of the
nuclear-disarmament hearings. Joy used to call her crotchless. She
would laugh derisively and call Joy a bitch in heat.

   She and Eljay still locked glances across crowded rooms, when
they passed on the campus roads, when they drove to the movies
in a mixed group and, black and white together, underwent the
routine abuse of hurled Coke cans and epithets. They could not,
after all, appear in public together as a couple; that was worse than
illegal, it was dangerous. Nobody knew. Only Jewel had any idea
what had transformed Miriam into a vibrancy she'd never imagined for herself. The longer things went well between herself and
Eljay, the more Miriam liked to remind Jewel that she'd been too
skeptical. Jewel had no interest in men, as it happened; she was
deeply, and sometimes not so deeply, involved with a series of
women (one an assistant dean, long legged, stylish, and famously
lovely) with whom she shared a secrecy even deeper than Miriam
and Eljay's. She tried not to be contemptuous of men, but in gen-

eral she thought them less sensitive than women, more tempted to be brutal. After a few early skirmishes with possessive and clumsy young worshippers, she acted like someone who had finally found shelter.

It had not been in Miriam's plans, an affair like this, but very quickly she saw how her life had reorganized itself around Eljay's presence in everything she did, from her teaching (which was subtly transformed by her perception of the respect in which he held his students) to her cooking (which now included, gladly, the Southernisms her mother's kitchen had excluded: the okra, the corn bread, the greens boiled, with ham, to a midnight-green welter in the pot).

These were the years—the sensation-seeking sixties, different from the decade she seemed to be living—when a lot of her friends were discovering drugs, not just grass but LSD. She had tried them both, a bit, and backed off after a few ecstatic trips turned menacing, but those friends had described their highs as intensifications of ordinary moments, as the focusing of their attention on the subvisual world. They could finally appreciate the invisible crawling universe that swarmed everywhere, and at the same time see the deep wild colors that swirled around them, numinous, enlarging. No wonder they began to speak with exclamation points.

Eljay's presence was that kind of drug for her, a substance that did not mellow so much as sharpen everything she touched. They sat back against his pillows after they had slaked their body-hunger and she listened nearly tearfully to his stories about the living death of the mind in Euphrates, its indignities, and the happy-enough life of the body, its pleasures (so different from the comforts of her childhood): baptism on a suffocatingly hot, damp day, that sudden dip in water so cold it was like smelling salts; for a few years, his service to Jesus, for whom he sang out in church and wore white at the baptisms of others; learning to pick on his cousin's guitar, and the feeling of power it gave him to pull music up out of its hollow center. He remembered staring down into the hole in the instrument's belly trying to find where the sound came from. Nothing in there but air and darkness, like a well. "Nobody could take my music away from me," he said, "not my daddy, nobody. It was like another element. It didn't have a body, so you couldn't hurt it or forbid it. It was like the air, you know? Just *there*."

And now he could lead her into his music as if he were taking her hand and walking her into a forest identifying trees that had looked identical to her. She began to see a string quartet as a perfect replica of a life, running in parallel to every emotion, every desire or loss or tension. She learned to hear the intake of violin breath, the long withholding rumble of viola and cello, the almost insupportably postponed resolution, and, like a drama in which an action and its consequences finally break upon the characters, the great scatter of emotion as the harmonies find their way home and then—in that half-instant before the torrent of relieved applause— the way they sink back to silence, exhausted.

He had found this rescue himself, as a boy, though he was seventeen before he'd heard a bit of classical music. She thought of Desdemona, how she had loved Othello for the dangers he had passed, loved him because he was so unlike her, yet human, and because, his heroism insufficient, he needed her. (She refused to think about the way their story ended.) Eyes locked with his in a long embrace at the faculty Christmas party, having downed two flutes of champagne, she had stood with her back against a wall, so engorged with pleasure at his diabolical open-eyed stare that she had come, silently, perfectly, her knees buckling a little, but all invisibly. She stayed in the shadows a long time, shivering in the dimming aftershocks of climax, and realized that she loved him now (she couldn't wait to tell him next time he came to her ravenous) even beyond touch.

THEY WERE AS DISCREET AS IT WAS POSSIBLE to be. Still, one night they found hunkered outside their little closet door Eljay's closest neighbor, the math instructor Bruce Ortle (whom Miriam called "Frogbottom" for the color and apparent texture of his skin, though she tried never to get near enough to him to confirm her disgust). He was listening eagerly, ear to the door, while his hand delivered pleasure to himself. But all he could have heard on that particular evening, Miriam laughed when she recounted the event to Jewel, was Mozart's K. 516, all its sadness and bottled-up passion exploding like something sexual, of course, but not exactly what Frogbottom had been hoping for.

Too embarrassed even for revenge, Bruce never mentioned that he knew about Eljay and Miriam; they never knew if others had guessed why she was seen so often in the dark halls of Staggers. A college like Parnassus, moored on its little gated island, was a vicious place when good gossip started up. Nothing could animate its soul so thoroughly as a black-white romance, and not only that but one between a long-timer and a short-timer, like an officer and an enlisted prole, and one whose sexual center was so hot you could catch a whiff of sweet burning halfway across the campus.

Miraculously, nobody blew the whistle on them, though they feared it, out of jealousy or rancor or a literal commitment to truth-telling. Nobody turned them in for moral turpitude or cohabiting with The Other. In fact, there was speculation in some quarters concerning Eljay's lack of interest in the eligible women on campus. "He hate dark meat, you think?" asked one particularly forward librarian who had set her cap for him. Cute, tiny bottomed, her hair assiduously greased and straightened, her defensiveness in the face of white women stayed abstract: the librarian wouldn't have considered Miriam a sexual being, let alone competition. Wasn't she just a badly dressed, stringy-haired, unmade-up history teacher come to preach somebody else's word? If Eljay didn't like a woman as well turned out as she was, and an Alpha at that, there was something wrong with him. "He like guys? Lots of those arty types are—you know—" She bent her hand at the wrist, almost violently "—fruits." She was talking to Jewel.

"I think he's just really busy," Jewel told her innocently, smiling. If she wasn't protective of Eljay, she certainly cared about her friend Miriam. As someone practiced in cunning and deep cover, she enjoyed helping out.

AND THEN—THIS IS THE WAY Miriam told it to Veronica, to Ronnee, to Ree, and remembered distantly that there was a song with that refrain—then there was you.

She had rearranged her classes and taken the train to Chicago to meet Eljay, who had gone before to deliver a paper on recitative in early French opera to a convention of musicologists. They had met in the red-gold-blue extravagance of the Palmer House lobby; she had pulled herself up almost reluctantly from the lush pillows of an ornate couch to greet him for this holiday escape from surveillance. They planned to punctuate with occasional public convention sessions a maximum of private time: For weeks she had dreamed of the huge bed and its deep froth of soft sheets and downy quilts, the lovely large shower, faucets gleaming the way nothing on the Parnassus campus gleamed, room service, strawberries on a dish with a gold rim. How she loved to arrange the symbols of luxury in her mind, not only for herself but because these textures marked Eljay's arrival at yet another point far from Euphrates, Alabama. And if, when they were eating dinner in Greektown or wherever they chose to go, they met anyone Eljay, Professor Reece, knew, he would introduce her without hiding, without fear. No Bruce Ortles here, no sheriffs, no law, as far as they knew, against interracial (not to mention interfaculty) pleasures. They would turn outward the DO NOT DISTURB sign on their doorknob and sleep, sated with freedom.

But no sooner had she arrived in their room and bent to remove from her suitcase her new-for-the-occasion white nightgown, edged in a foam of lace, than Miriam felt a peculiar lightheadedness, disembodied as if she were only half there. Something had its whole hand over her face. She wasn't sick, she insisted when Eljay saw her stand frowning, she was just—odd, she called it. It was the way she felt when she had too much MSG, a slight quivering disturbance she wasn't sure she was feeling, yet couldn't deny.

Eljay sent down for coffee and toast; she'd missed lunch, surely that was the problem. He flourished the cup and saucer—yes, there was the very golden rim she'd imagined, and a shapely pewter carafe for the coffee, weighty and important looking—and as he poured and she inhaled what she had always found so bracing and reassuring, the sharp sour kick that got her through nights

of paper-grading and mornings-after of exhaustion, a high im-
placable wave of nausea swept toward her and over her, tumbling
her to the bottom of some dark place where she couldn't catch her
breath, and when it had passed, though she'd had no such experience in her life before this, she knew. What a stupid old story, she
had to admit that was her first thought: shame, to be caught like a
dumb teenager who didn't know any better. What an embarrassment. But, she swore, her second thought, nearly simultaneous,
was How intriguing. What would a baby be like, look like, that
came of the two of them, made in an instant of joy? What whole
new being would emerge from the joining of their two ancestral
streams? Eljay liked to say, with perverse relish, "We're Klan bait,
baby!" The blacks and the Jews, he insisted with no argument
from her, were the least understood and most passionate and imaginative of all people. They had made American culture vital.
Maybe they could have this child, she thought, and give her, him
or her, to the world as a gift. Hybrid vigor was always a step forward. If it was a girl—she pulled the silky nightgown out of her
bag and slipped it on, though she still felt unreal—if he didn't
think it was too corny, they could call her Hope.

BUT, FIRST OR SECOND THOUGHT, Eljay was not enchanted.
He was nearly finished with his Ph.D. at Tulane, looking all over
for time to write his dissertation, fearing he was going to fall in the
crack between scholarship and practice and never escape to a better job, a more prestigious college. Work with his Opera Theater,
plus his teaching, plus this, plus that—everything in his tight-
wound life had been carefully scripted, timed, projected, willed.
He gave each of them his all, he didn't approve of skimping. A
baby? Say *what?!*

Perhaps at the sound of those words she should have known
where they were going, perhaps even thought again, differently
this time, about where they had been: when Eljay called her "ignorant," which to him was an insult born of his own beginnings, the
worst thing (like "shiftless") he could sentence someone to, no

decent end in sight, perhaps she should have known where they were heading. Had she served a purpose, then, other than the one she'd imagined? Had she been a little relaxing interlude for him, a tension-releaser, a respite from work, like a rest in a piece of music, when you can take a breath? A man as tightly wound as Eljay needed to lie back and be delivered from his demons once in a while. She, with her gardenia breasts and her awe, her soothings, had she (she had to ask) merely been of service, to be dismissed now that things were getting difficult? Again, embarrassment set in, that she should be caught in such an old, predictable story. They had never talked about where they were headed. He called her "ignorant" for not taking care. "Don't get on him for that," she cautioned Jewel, though she did find it necessary to report the word he'd used. "Your family isn't from Euphrates, Alabama." She was grasping at generosity as if it were a branch floating downstream in a flood.

"Apologize for this man at your own risk," Jewel answered her. "I find that patronizing, to tell you the truth. Plenty of people would keep quiet before they'd make fun of whatever it is he's calling ignorance."

When Miriam (more than once) asked him what he wanted her to do, he'd slap his fist into his palm and turn away. It occurred to her, impossibly, that next time it might be her face—did he have a little of his father in him? If they were in his little room, there was no place to go but to the wall. If they were in her cottage, he would walk into the kitchen or erupt onto the little front porch as if from a burning house, breathing hard in anger. He hinted at entrapment. She thought, adopting Jewel's language, He's had his meal and he's wiped his mouth and now he doesn't want to pay for it. This happened all the time, this sudden coldness—she was not so ignorant that she didn't recognize it—but, like dying, it always happened to someone else.

When she mentioned abortion, though—not an easy thing to contemplate, nor inexpensive, but something her Texas friends, even in high school, had availed themselves of quite readily—he was the one who flinched. "Thinning the herd," he called it. Brutality to his people. "We don't hold by that," he said. "You'd better not."

"We? Who's we, all of a sudden?"

"AND HERE," Miriam said to her daughter, "is where everything got complicated." Up until now it had been simple—a love affair, whatever its motives, was more or less private. But here was where the world and history entered, strangers and ideas and a lot of things that didn't have a personal smell on them. "Not every child has her life determined by public events the way yours was," she told Ronnee, and rearranged herself on the knobby ground beneath the cemetery tree, "but nobody lives outside of time. Only what's more invisible than history while you're standing in it and you can't see as far as tomorrow?"

"I don't know what you're talking about," Ronnee said with barely contained impatience. "What do you mean 'determined by public events'? I was a little girl and I didn't have a mother." She didn't look at Miriam, she looked into the trees. "My friend Seretha's mother taught her how to tie her shoes and nobody was around to teach me. What's so public about that?"

"Where was your father?"

"Busy. He was busy a lot. I know he loved me—I mean loves me—but there were some things . . ."

Some things were irrevocably lost, Miriam thought again. She wished she could take him to court and sue him for breach of— whatever it was that he had robbed her of. Hours, days, years. Shoelaces. The bent knee while she showed her end-over-end-and-under. How to make a double knot. How, with her fingertips, to undo it.

BUT ELJAY HAD ALREADY BEGUN to change by then—B.C., Before Chicago—too subtly, at first, for her eyes. It was like a slow melt, or, better, a slow freeze. What she meant to say was that nothing happens in a vacuum; no "movement" overtakes a group or a single person without a world of experiences to justify it, to make use of it—didn't she teach that in her history classes? The French Revolution, the Civil War, and the wars we fight with ourselves and each other—all of them occur at flood tide, when everything spills over.

A few young men in jeans, one in field-hand overalls like Jewel's, only dirtier, had come to a lecture Eljay gave late one afternoon on "Orpheus in His Many Guises," in which he'd traced the changes time and fashion had wrought between Ovid's *Metamorphosis,* Gluck's *Orfeo,* and Stravinsky's *Orpheus.* Miriam sat in the back of the room, tamping down her pride to keep it from showing on her cheeks. Besides these unlikely young men, there were even a few unfamiliar faces in the audience, two professors and a few students who had dared to come out from the white college campus in the city, and afterward they engaged him in lively debate. Maybe, she thought, they'd go so far as to invite him to their school, though that might be premature. What did he look like to them, this energetic, articulate scholar in his deep-dark skin, his following of dark-skinned students bobbing around him like a school of fish? Here in their pure-white world he must seem very peculiar, a new phenomenon, to be esteemed.

After which the young men, also black, who had been hovering impatiently at the edges of the conversation, moved toward him, and she recognized the studied, impassioned, jerky gestures of political challenge. It was easy to tell Movement people, SNCC graduates, by the way they stood, stolidly, legs slightly parted as if to resist being moved. ("We, we shall, we shall not be moved!" went the anthem. "Just like a tree that's planted by the wa-a-ter, We. ShallNot. Be. Moved." They seemed to take it literally.) She recognized the contentious finger-pointing, index finger poking down, without which they apparently could not speak. Jewel spoke like this sometimes, though she could turn it on and off, her more neutral Mount Holyoke–Columbia side dominant when it seemed necessary. Miriam respected and was afraid of them.

What in the world could they be saying to Eljay about opera, though, with such fervor? He'd been talking about a poet with a

lyre, a man who loses his wife for loving her too much to let her
go. When they were finished lecturing him—that was what it
looked like to Miriam, Eljay receiving their words with a surprisingly shy, almost chastened expression and not too many words
back—the man who'd done most of the talking tried to give him a
complicated insider's handshake, but Eljay couldn't manage it. He
fumbled like a child confusing his hands playing patty-cake. "Hey,
bro, you do it this way," the young man said, jolly in his superiority, and like a patient kindergarten teacher, he broke the handshake
down into steps and took this professor through it twice, slowly.
"Now lay it on me," he finally shouted, and, both of them laughing, they bumped palms, grasped fingers, hooked and unhooked.
They seemed to be making a pact.

Jewel was a political creature, Miriam stood thinking, at the
same time that she was a terrific teacher. She loved raising the flag
and leading her little troops into nonviolent combat, and didn't
mind paying the price. But Eljay was so solitary, so apolitical, so
fixed on his music. It was a peculiar moment, out of character. So
was his humility. She would not have called it ominous exactly,
but—one of Eljay's words presented itself, and calling it up, she
felt an odd premonitory loneliness, like a chill—dissonant. She
hung on the side of the little crowd because she could not give him
the tight hug of congratulation he deserved, not here. She stood
smiling beside the chairman of the music department, who was
shaking his gray head, saying to no one in particular, "He's so
good, isn't he. I wish he was a little less good, because one of these
days we're going to lose him."

WHAT HE HAD BEGUN TO HEAR, coincidence or not just then,
was Black Power calling. Shouting out for a manful answer, de-
nouncing friends, agreeing with the Klan, the Citizens Council,
the just-plain-racist-down-the-road, that what God or state had
put asunder no man ought to so much as try to bring together.
("Of course," Miriam said to Ronnee, "this is my biased opinion. I
admit to severe bias, under the circumstances. Your father would

not tell it this way.") Hate no one wholesale, was what she had believed in, and Jewel too, who now, after trying to hold back the
moronic practitioners of white racism, resented it that she had
to split her time trying to overcome racists of her own color.
("Lordy," she had said, "I'm saying the same things as my *parents*
these days!") If you ever endorse mass vilification, Jewel tried to
say in public, and was shouted down by her old allies, with whom
just a while ago she'd been cuffed on the head at Woolworth's and
gone to jail and posted bond and been freed to demonstrate another day, it can turn around and bite you on the rear. But the moment was ripe for impugning white earnestness, white conscience,
white solicitude. It was time to wash faces like Miriam's in guilt
and pessimism.

Somewhere Eljay had picked up (or been picked up by) these
new friends, who had sat through all that Orfeo business to get to
him. Somehow they had found him, had known he'd be fertile
ground. At the time it seemed unlikely he would go political, he
was so busy with his work. Maybe it was the drums, the African
drums, that bought their way into his attention by the open channel that took music into him. Once she came upon him sitting on
the floor at the foot of his bed slapping his palm against a sort of
bongo with ornate carving on its sides, his head bent near the vi-
brating drumhead to hear it better. He looked as if she'd caught
him at something illicit.

She came close enough to stroke its wild corona of white hair.
Its barrel-shaped side was paved with black-and-white beading.
"Beautiful." She said it tentatively. It was a wild-looking thing.

He seemed to clutch it closer to his body to keep her from admiring it. "It's called a *kpanlogo*. From Ghana." It had handles,
like a pitcher. He hit it sharply and nodded, smiling, at the vibra-
tion against his cheek. "Nothing rare about it. This is pretty garden variety," as though she ought to know that, as though
anybody would know it.

"Does it hurt your hand to slap it that way?" She was speaking
ordinary words, the voice she always used, forcing them out, but
she could feel an invisible wall between them, through which, to

judge by his unanswering face, he couldn't hear her. Didn't want to hear. She felt disembodied—it was like that first instant when her pregnancy announced itself, the sensation of being there and not there. Body-snatched. It makes a tiny, world-shaking alteration in the molecules of the air to speak as if no one is sitting three inches from you. He wanted to be alone here. "Enjoy," she said superfluously, and left him, feeling as she went that he had hardly registered her presence, let alone her absence.

Or maybe it was something that happened just around then, so close in time that Miriam knew it was really, like a first visible symptom of illness, the manifestation of something that had been incubating a long time.

Months into their secrecy, just after the trip to Chicago but before she'd shattered the peace between them by telling him she was pregnant, they had just lain down together in his room when the phone rang. He'd sat up shivering. Miriam whispered, "Don't answer," and tried to hold him there, but he shook his head as if he was expecting the call, had just been waiting for bad news, always bad news. He was naked in the half-dark that they liked so they could see each other, and he'd been halfway to making love to her, so imagine how he looked when he stood up, and how he deflated in a single breath. He didn't reach across for the phone but walked right up to it and picked it up with a kind of intimacy, and yes it was bad news, very bad, she could see how his face registered it, and the way his shoulders stiffened. A long, long time passed while he said nothing at all, just grunted to show he was listening. Once in a while then, she thought she heard him say, or rather ask, "Sir?" and again "Sir," a statement of agreement. Or submission.

But by then he had turned away from her, adamantly away. His back shone with a misting of the finest sweat, but she had the feeling he was cold. She crawled across to pick up an afghan, dozens of colors, his mother (Ronnee's Ma Thelmie!) had made for him that he kept folded across the bottom of the bed, and she threw it across his back and shoulders. He turned to her violently, with a face gnarled with such fury that she gasped out loud. He flung his arm out at her to go away, away, out of his sight. You'd have thought she was the one telling him the awful things he was hearing.

When he finally spoke he had crumpled himself down on the floor next to the wall, his head turned as far from her as he could get it. Accordioned down there he had no body left. "Yes sir, he is, he surely is. I've known him years, sir, never a moment's trouble, no sir. That's right, sir." She barely recognized his voice. She couldn't breathe and she wasn't even the one it was happening to, and she wasn't the one who had the long history it fit into. She figured it out bit by bit—this was the one phone call allowed from jail. He was the one long chance.

It was about Edgar, that joyous rippling bass-baritone, who had been picked up for something he hadn't done, some trouble he hadn't caused. She only learned this later, that he had brought his pregnant girlfriend to the emergency room because she seemed to be losing her baby, in pain and bleeding hard. And he had somehow fallen afoul of an irritable cop who arrested him and left the poor girl there alone, nearly hysterical. And now, somehow, Eljay was being called upon to vouch for Edgar to keep them from booking him. Who knows how Edgar had managed to convince them to call (he was an eminently presentable young man who always wore oxford shirts buttoned tight to the neck under Shetland sweaters, though such a display might just as easily have been what set off the cop), but Eljay had done his dance. He was a good actor—maybe Ronnee got her talent from him—and he could jump higher than most. When it came time to say thank you he went all out, bowing and heaving with poisonous gratitude. You'd think someone had saved his life instead of dishonored it.

Tinder, it was nothing less. Tinder for his fire. And Miriam made it worse: she tried to comfort him. Still naked, there in her goose-pimpled skin, she reached out to him and he seemed to be growling like some animal, some undomesticated cat. She said, "Please, Eljay, let me—" but what could he do but hate her for seeing him so humbled, so effaced. She knew and she believed *he* knew exactly how little the scene had subtracted from his true substance, but, not believing, he reached behind him to his desk and picked up a heavy bust and heaved it at her. She ducked. It hit the door frame beside her, gouged a hunk from it, and Gounod lost his chin. But it was so ridiculous—the serene statue, white as a gravestone, with its flat blind gaze—that she laughed. She had plenty of time later to wonder how she could have laughed.

She told herself, dressed and shamed and out on the dark of the campus path half running home, that she loved him more than he loved himself, that anyone would have laughed at the absurdity of the alabaster statue hurtling across space, but she supposed all El-jay saw, how could he not, was the way that cracker judge snapped his whip and made him, in all his brilliance, jump over it. The callousness of racists (North and South, so vicious, so rudimentary in their ugliness, she couldn't believe they could do the things they did) was too stupid for words, too humiliating to the people who didn't know enough to be shamed by it, did he think she didn't understand that? She was here at Parnassus *because* there were hideous men like that judge, not in spite of it, how could he not see that? But that didn't mean, no matter how nervous she was, or what sense of cosmic absurdity she felt, that it was a good idea to laugh at that particular blood-red moment. She was quite sure he never forgave her. When his new friends came calling, that was the kind of insensitivity they could accuse her of: thinking she understood but, white-skin privilege between them like a scrim, not understanding at all.

"We weren't just—individual people, Ronnee, that's what I meant before when I said there were other forces at work on us. I thought we were ordinary lovers, with some obvious differences between us. I don't know, maybe nobody's ever completely independent of when they're living, where they're living. But I couldn't quite grasp it back then." She said this wearily. "I think we were more vulnerable to the way the political winds blew than a lot of people. And you were in the middle of all that."

These new friends were old disillusioned Movement people who had decided to look at the glass that was beginning to fill and to see the part that was still, and perhaps always would be, empty. If they were sinister, it was because they were young and righteously furious and impatient, she could appreciate that, and their despair had dragged them overboard. "See, I thought black folks were already joined at the hand, the hip, the head," she told her daughter, who was digging in the grass now with a stick, uncomfortable, not looking at her. "But no, they said, you people come between us, and therefore they were advocating hounding all white folks out of their struggle. Time's up, they were saying: You did your little bit but we haven't been saved. So I had to watch Eljay listening to them while they poured their poison into his ear. I wanted to see if this was what he needed. The way it looked, that phone call from the judge was the last straw, you know, from this burden he had never shown me."

Miriam closed her eyes, took a long shaky breath. Maybe she'd been, somehow, partly to blame. She realized that the confidences he'd whispered to her, constant as a ground bass—frustration with how much catching-up he had to do to start where middle-class men began, how alien he felt in so many places, how hurt he'd been at the hands of this one or that one—had thrilled her. His openness, his willingness to unburden himself to her was a triumph of trust. So honored was she that he was telling her all this, she saw she hadn't been listening to what he was actually saying. Maybe that hadn't even been trust; maybe he had been beating her with it, first his victimization, and then his victory over it. Maybe he had made himself lovable by reminding her to feel guilty, and to be awed by how heroic he was. And then when that judge called and shamed him, he was caught at his least heroic, for which she had to pay. Maybe.

Now she could see in his friends' eyes their disgust at her presence. She could sympathize with their anger, but there was no way to forgive them for their disgust.

"Ghosts," Eljay's new friend Sonny Skeen called white people. He was the leader of the pack. He would not so much as shake a white person's hand. "Let them take their carpetbags and go on back north, we don't need their help, and we will issue no thanks for what they've done 'for' us. We are our own men." He said this one day sprawled on Miriam's couch like a sultan in a harem. Eljay had taken to inviting them over to Miriam's, where there was room for a crowd.

"Well, thanks for including us sisters, honey," Jewel said to him in her most contemptuous drawl.

Sonny was a very skinny young man with broad high Indian cheekbones, good-looking, with a long hangdog pockmarked face and a baseball cap that he kept on all the time to hide a bald spot that was spreading like mange. When Miriam brought the coffee around he snapped his fingers at her. She wanted him to call her "Bitch" so she'd have an excuse for pouring the pot down his back, but he enjoyed ignoring her.

Miriam had made up a batch of chicken stew, trying to be hospitable, and Sonny and his friends sat picking at the bones, sopping up the gravy while they lit out after those "ghosts" and their frail white asses. Jewel, tired of taking them on and being called an "Oreo," mocked for being hincty, high class, went into the kitchen and hissed at her, "Why don't you tell them to leave. Why don't you turn the chicken and dumplings over on them?"

Sonny Skeen, when he passed her in the narrow hallway, twanged the straps of Jewel's overalls like guitar strings. He leaned his boniness into her and felt around until she used her knee on him. "Bull dyke," he muttered, but he was doubled over when he said it. She didn't have to play helpless like Miriam, who worried that she *was* a ghost, that, crude as they were, they were right, that she was irrelevant, was dangerous to their enterprise (whatever it was). "Show them the goddamn door," Jewel repeated, breathless.

"They're Eljay's friends," Miriam answered grimly. She was stacking the dishes, taking note that whatever they thought of her ghostly hands, they had eaten heartily of what she'd put in front of them, like the ungrateful children of a mother mocked and ignored.

Jewel was disgusted. "You know something, girl? You look like that fool who walked into the fraternity line when you first got here. 'Oh pardon me, pardon me for breathing.' I can say this, darlin', because they're supposed to be my brothers. Even if you can't, *I* can call them self-righteous assholes."

Miriam crept among them conciliating, silently bringing them pound cake, Cokes, and iced tea. All right, she said to herself, what would it feel like to be Flukie, picking up other people's messes? What had she found it convenient not to know? Once one of Sonny's sidekicks, a drummer named Bo McAllister, muttered as if he'd overheard her thinking, "Let her feel what it's like to be the servant nobody sees."

He's right, Miriam told herself, it's terrible for the souls of all the black women who put food on the table while their employers go right on maligning their brothers, their fathers, as if they weren't there. In a small voice she asked, "But does that make it right? Do you have to repeat it?"

"Sure do," Bo had told her serenely. He wouldn't even look at her, he was inspecting the calluses on his drumming hands. "Payback time. I'm loving every minute of it."

When Miriam tipped some more iced tea in his glass he didn't look up, didn't say thank you.

And Eljay, she knew, would never defend her. Vigorous as he was, he sat and watched them humiliate her. Was it a coincidence, she wondered, that she had told him about the baby around the time this pack of vandals had begun to surface? He was trying out this meanness just at the moment when he needed an excuse for turning his back on her and on this baby. That interpretation did a dishonor to politics, she knew. It trivialized centuries of shame. It reduced him to a frightened man looking for a way to duck out. It did all that and more, but she couldn't pretend it was coincidence that while she was beginning to thicken and bloom, he seemed to love her less and less, and had fallen in love with the power salute instead. The salute was a fist. She watched Eljay shake that fist triumphantly, out on the little front porch, as his guests went down the stairs. He moved it back and forth like somebody knocking on a door. Let me in, he seemed to be saying. Take me with you.

But fists were not being raised in Rowan, Mississippi, Miriam took comfort from that. All things were as they had been, the town was black and poor, black and powerless. People were friendly to white folks from "up-the-college" because they knew whose side they were on and sides, to them, were simple—you were safe or you were in danger. People wanted to help you or hurt you. They knew that lives like hers, white and reviled, were in danger for working at the college—like them, not because of anything they did, just because they were there. Not danger like their own, which was a constant, like the sun coming up and going down, but a thing they didn't have to do. Local folks knew that and were grateful.

Eventually, though, she knew that living in a state of gratitude has its problems, it exacts a cost, and that was part of what Eljay's friends were so upset about. She sympathized: They didn't want these people to have to be grateful to anybody. To them, that kept folks on their knees, humble and beholden. Eljay had even begun to love his father, now that he saw what a victim he'd been, how helpless as long as white folks had kept him on his knees, begging for work, for respect; they had broken his capacity to love his own family. It didn't seem possible to forgive him without blaming someone else. But all that would have been news to the open-hearted people of Rowan, who could make distinctions, who were always kind to white people who came in friendship. They were not ideological, not theoretical, just humanly, simply decent.

Miriam couldn't pretend they were as comfortable with her in their church, say, as they'd have been if she were black. Of course they weren't. But they were so generous and friendly and *civil*— was that coerced? Was it a habit of submission? Miriam and Jewel and a few others would come to the door to share their fellowship and these wide women in marvelous, inventive hats and men in their best shirts, clean and beaming, would show them to good seats, smile on them, invite them for fried chicken and dumplings, grits and greens after the service. What would have been the point of staying away so as not to put pressure on their goodness, which Eljay and his friends saw as accommodation and they saw as— well, it sounded naïve. She knew what he meant, but it didn't seem to her to play to anyone's best possibilities: Yes, they could stay separate. The white folks who hated the lot of them *wanted* them to stay separate. But what would be the point? Who would grow from that, who would prosper?

She could argue from the other side, though. She could understand what had happened to her dear sweet lover, some of it, and she could justify it; it was the recoil after great pain. She could, she could. She hated to, but she had to.

ALSO: SHE COULD HAVE STOPPED that baby if she'd wanted to, since his talk about his black baby, his people and what they allowed, was enough to inflame her and make her spiteful. She could have walked away and called the whole thing her crazy Mississippi experience, barely survived.

One evening after dinner, though, she and Jewel were ambling on down the road in Rowan, outside the gates of the college; they were going into town to get away, to leave the miasma that hung over her life like a gray cloud, boredom, anger, the feeling that her house had been taken over by uninvited aliens—schoolyard bullies, really— who were there to mock her because she let herself be mocked.

They couldn't think of anything they needed that they could find in the little village store with its dusty, disarranged stock of cheap items and sagging out-of-date magazines, so they bought stale Tootsie Rolls and even though they'd just stood up from the table, ate them hungrily, like food. And on the road outside, a young town girl came walking toward them and passed them, keeping to the shoulder carefully, a very dark child no more than fourteen or fifteen, and very pregnant, inching along as carefully as if she were walking on ice. She had on a blue cotton dress with a big white collar that made her look like a child at a birthday party, a dress so thin and limp you could see it must have been handed down through a dozen pregnancies. Her stomach was such a finished melon that her little pushed-out belly button was like the stem of the fruit where it fell from the vine.

Jewel said, "Lordy, that girl just walked off one of Faulkner's pages. Lena, remember? Could that be *real*?"

Miriam turned to her very sharply. "You sound like I'm supposed to sound, if you ask those friends of Eljay's."

"What? I just meant, that's the kind of scene you came to Mississippi for, that kind of—"

"Like you never saw any girls like that, you're—so distant. So safe and far away. God, Jewel, you're as white as I am. More. Wouldn't Sonny love to hear you."

"Oh, spare me, girl. This child could be any color. Lena wasn't black. You're talking class. Class, not race. Just because I'm black I'm supposed to identify with every poor barefoot—"

"Ignorant—"

"I didn't say that. That's Eljay you've got me confused with."

They were both on the near edge of tears. Miriam didn't know who they were, who they wanted to be just then. She saw how much their pasts were waiting to take them back again, hers the easy Houston life: a house, a good-looking neighborhood all hers, a maid to keep things neat, a car to drive, and shopping and going to parties, every harsh thing kept to the edges, her parents smiling and a husband waiting where she couldn't see his face yet, let alone feel his hands. Why had she come here, anyway? To dare herself and her fate? And Jewel in the outgrown pink bedroom her mother still kept for her across from the campus, where she was the smart girl with a stiff little pageboy, headed for a fine life, presentable man, a modest pile of possessions, a sorority pin, her closets full and neat, her parents smiling the same smile as Miriam's. The flamingo on guard atop the mailbox and all of decrepit Rowan kept back at the door. All they had rejected waited for them to come to their senses—the default setting, the comfort zone. Waited for a single moment of weakness when it would loom up, the sensible "bourgie" solution, and reclaim them.

But Miriam was thinking something else too, which she heard herself saying. "Just look at her, Jewel. She's having that baby whether she wants to or not."

"Well, she didn't have any choice, did she."

"Right, she couldn't go to Mexico or Jamaica or pay the price I could rustle up if I finally decided to. It doesn't seem fair." If her solidarity was real, deeper than those goony boys could ever understand—wouldn't she preserve *her* baby if it wanted to be born, a brother or sister, a half sibling really, to that young girl's child? If it survived, it survived. And she would survive. Enough of this passivity, which was not her natural habit. What had become of the Class Mouth? Oh, little mama, she wished she could have shouted to the girl in the blue dress, who had disappeared down the highway like an apparition—maybe she'd been sent to them out of some kindly god's desire to provide an angel of clarity. Little girl, look what you've done without doing a thing. Your people didn't enter into it, she would tell Eljay, and let him announce to those pathetic, muscle-flexing, separatist fools he had ceded his will to that he was going to be a father. Like it or not, *our* people did.

"so," she told Ronnee, her cheeks hot, the worst still to come, "you were saved."

But at a price. After so much passivity, so much trying to understand and sympathize with Eljay, all of it repulsed, she made a bargain with herself: If she was going to go on and have this baby, she would do it without him. Jewel told her that was a mistake. "But he wants me to keep this child like it's some abstract thing," Miriam said, "and then he wants nothing to do with what's actually happening to me. When I asked him what he expected me to do, he didn't have any answer. You've seen him—when I press him on it, he leaves the room. Then I believe him, Jewel. He has no answer. So—he is *dismissed*."

It was a sign of how unbending she could be that Miriam actually made Jewel feel sorry for the man. She was tired of abuse, she told Jewel. Jewel was unimpressed. What she was planning seemed like abuse of its own kind.

"If he and his friends want to hate white folks," Miriam insisted, "the least they can do is take their opinions out of my living room. You know by now they only hang out here to hurt me. Every time that guy with the drums, that Bo, hits those skins it's like he's slapping me. And Eljay's learning them. Dahomeyan music, Senegalese, whatever it's called. The hell with Verdi. Fine. Good. It's his choice."

"Everything important in this life has to be negotiated," Jewel said. "That's all the little wisdom I've got, hon. You begin with absolutes, you get nothing. Begin with some compromises, you might get a little something you want."

"God, you sound like LBJ. I don't know how to compromise with a man who had a place for me in his bed, but who can sit there now and let me be insulted by a bunch of—"

"You can tell him to keep his friends away. But why don't you help him out, sugar. He doesn't know what's good for him."

Miriam was learning to sit with her hands on her stomach calmly, as if it were a medicine ball. Its hardness was astonishing, more stone than flesh, nothing like she'd expected. "Then let him learn," she said, and the baby rippled under her fingers as if it had an opinion too, but wordless, unreadable.

WHEN HER CONDITION BECAME OBVIOUS she told her friends and fellow faculty that she had secretly gotten married back home in Houston over Christmas break, and that her husband was finishing a doctorate in economics for which he had to spend the first eight months of their marriage in—she fished it out of the air—Moscow! She planned her subterfuge carefully. She would remove herself from an assembled group by announcing ostentatiously that she was off to phone him. "It's so hard to find the proper time," she would laugh. She named him John Freund after her first high-school boyfriend, whom she had refused to sleep with, terrified she'd become pregnant, in spite of the spirited offense he'd mounted. It amused her to recall this. His honorary fatherhood was a memorial to his persistence. She had every detail worked out, full of secretly sustaining little jokes and ironies, as if it were a game. What a pity, people said, that your husband has to be so far away for this great event. Were they not suspicious? She had no idea. When one of her almost-friends offered to make a baby shower for her, wanting to be inconspicuous she shook her head gravely and declined, saying she hated fuss, she hated show. But they did it anyway; she had a box of blankets and clothing small enough for a doll, and an album in which to paste photos and locks of hair to send to her husband so that he wouldn't miss out.

Whenever she saw Eljay coming toward her, she turned away and hoped to God a fetus was not affected by its mother's poisonous emotions. I will be a ghost, self-appointed, in honor of Sonny Skeen, she thought, who would not shake my hand.

Miriam planned to deliver the baby right in her own house, with a midwife who wouldn't be too shocked when the emerging infant came out something other than lily white. "But, oh, honey," Miriam said, laughing, "you surprised us." She watched Ronnee hear for the first time, wide-eyed as a small child, the details of her own birth. This was something Eljay could not give her. In spite of what was to come, she felt happier than she had in years.

She and Jewel were downtown shopping for whichever parts of the layette she hadn't been given. It was about ten o'clock at night; the storekeepers were mounting something they called "Midnight Madness," when they put out tables full of goods and kept their stores open till very late. There they were, fingering little shirts, dickering over price and color, Miriam thinking from time to time, This could not be me! How could I be standing here doing this? when all of a sudden, stopped in a very theatrical light in front of Goldenblatt's Department Store, she felt herself stricken, her face like the Munch painting of that girl with her mouth in an O. When she looked down in the direction of a strange slippy feeling, there was a huge transparent puddle at her feet, and the next moment Jewel was driving her through the dark, breaking every speed limit, toward Rowan, fifteen miles of straightaway. But the midwife lived way out past the village and Jewel was muttering, What if she's not there, I've called and she hasn't answered, what if we get you out there and she's off delivering somebody else's baby? Miriam's pains, with no preliminary warning, were coming like one of those lightning storms where there is no rest between bolts, flash after flash almost before the last one was done. That is not supposed to happen with a first baby, but try to argue when it does. So they swung around and came back into the city. Now, Jewel said, since everything she thought seemed to bubble forth from her when she was was panicked, would be a perfect time for one of those highwaymen to pick us up for speeding, after all the bogus arrests, this time when we really deserve it.

And so Veronica was born at the city hospital, just as Miriam hadn't wanted her to be, and she did silence them all in the delivery room. They had no time to sedate her, and she had to watch the doctor's face, his eyes over his mask, and the nurses', when the baby made her hasty appearance telling secrets she'd just as soon not have had them know. Little girl the color of a bruise, with her big nappy head, attached by the cord to this weeping white woman with her long, thick hair sweated against her neck. She wasn't very dark—babies darken—but inside her elbows, the folds of her tiny neck, all the giveaway places, she was not, to put it delicately, exactly what they were expecting. There was no curious buzz, and no congratulations, just a hollow silence. Jewel was outside, sitting, standing, pacing like a papa in her overalls under a big clock that clucked as it hit its minutes. Midnight Madness would still be going on. After the baby's first affronted cry, it was as if someone had pulled the plug on the sound. Utterly, utterly silent, and no one cared how cruel that was. Miriam thought of how the midwife would have taken her tenderly, and the cheering and the hugging. No one here called this child miraculous. "May I see her," she had to ask three times, and the nurse plunked the baby down, not delicately, on the rough blue hospital gown that covered Miriam's chest. The whole crew worked silently, as if she'd done something offensive or embarrassing—"Well, I had, I suppose. I was probably lucky they didn't do one or the other of us damage."

"It's hard to imagine that now," Ronnee murmured humbly. "I guess that's good, that it seems so—extreme." This was the first time Miriam thought she could see through Ronnee's tough skin. Finally, at the moment of her emergence, she seemed to be seeing Miriam as her mother.

"God," Miriam said, there in the sweet anonymous graveyard where her daughter sat perfectly silent, unsmiling, listening. "God, you were glorious."

RELUCTANTLY, she went on telling it.

Maybe Eljay's friends were right, Miriam had thought, and I'm just a fool. No one had been very nice to her for quite a while then, not even Jewel, who called her stiff-necked, that Biblical accusation. Maybe there was no place for these races side by side, let alone in a mixture like this gorgeous sturdy child with her perfect bow mouth, her infinitesimal little hands opening and closing like her brand-new heart expanding and contracting. But the judgments came from elsewhere, too.

When she had slept and eaten and gathered her strength, she called her parents.

"Well, Mom," she said right out, "I guess I'm a mother now, too." They had known about the pregnancy and managed—she hoped it took an effort—not to comment, which was comment in itself. Now her mother made a small, unrecoverable sound, as if she'd been hit from behind.

"I have a girl. A beautiful little girl."

"A girl." Like an echo. "And?"

"And what? And then? And who else? What do you mean, 'and'?"

"A *momser*."

Momser was a Yiddish *bastard*. She had always heard the word in affectionate jest—"little *momser*"—naughty adorable child. A grandmother word. It was no joke in law, though, in Jewish or Southern or any other kind; only in the flesh it was not a legal concept.

"That's right, Ma. I never thought of it that way, but I suppose so."

"Am I remembering that this child's—father—is not Jewish?"

She laughed helplessly. "To say the least."

"Oh, Miriam." Her mother sounded weary. "Miriam. How could you do this to us?"

She had really said that. *To you.*

"Oh, darling, to all of us. *Everyone.*" It was a plea, too late by far. "I knew you shouldn't have gone to that place. Didn't we warn you?" Her mother, as was her way in many situations, began to cry. That seemed to be all she could do, in her vanity, her disappointment, her anger. Wait just a minute, Miriam wanted to say. I think I'm the one who should be crying here.

But she had her lovely baby, who gave off warmth like a small thrumming motor, whose arms and legs had a tensile resistance that astonished her: you pushed on them, they held firm against your hand; sometimes they actually pushed back! She wouldn't cry because it might sour her milk. Instead, she turned her sadness into fury, that her mother could care so little about her daughter's accomplishment. How can the details matter, she wanted to shout, but didn't because her mother, yelled at, tended to dig in her heels like a scolded child. Color, religion, circumstances, how could they even begin to matter when she had created this extraordinary new being, this brand-new healthy animal that carried the past and the future in her cells?

Eljay came to the hospital—left his friends home and came alone. She had been dozing when he came striding into her room with a broad smile on his face, the smile of any new father who'd happened to have missed the birth but had come as soon as ever he could.

"Miriam! I couldn't really see her because she was turned away, her head was—"

She had sat up, alarmed. "So what? What do you care whether you can see her or not?" Her neighbor had been dismissed that morning; thank God this was like a private room.

He had dared to stop short and stare at her openmouthed. He was wearing a long-sleeved striped T-shirt; he held his green-and-purple-striped arms protectively in front of his chest as if he'd absorbed a blow. She had never seen him do that and—she would have time to regret this—she exulted to think she could hurt him so. "I don't know what you're here for," she said to him as frostily as she could. "Your relation to that baby was over with nine months ago."

He stepped close to her bed. "Bitch," he whispered, as if it were an intimate word. "You can't do that."

"I guess I can. I'd like you to leave, please."

"Miriam, that's my daughter out there. I'm pleading with you."

Could anything be this hard? "Listen, Eljay. You hardened your heart against me all these months. You wanted out, you wanted to

humiliate me, you and those thuggy friends of yours, your freedom fighters? Well, fine. So take the consequences. You had no
compassion for me and now I don't have any for you."

He ran his hand over his face, rubbing hard, as if he might un-
cover another face under the one she reviled. "This is my child
you're keeping from me."

She was glad Jewel wasn't there to hear her commit this atrocity.
"Please get out of this room, Eljay, before I call somebody to help
put you out." Her milk had just begun to come in that morning;
she had awakened to find her gown soaked and chilly. The baby
had seized her breast with incredible vigor, as if to say, "Finally.
Where has this been?" But talk like that, she thought, horrified at
herself, would surely stop the flow, would poison the body that
spoke the words of banishment.

"You would really call somebody to put me out." She had never
seen him so incredulous.

She closed her eyes so that she wouldn't have to see his face.
"You put me out of your life, Eljay. This child was in me and you
kicked me around in my own living room. You threw us out on
my own doorstep. Are you telling me now you didn't mean it?
Why should you expect to share her with me?" She was astonished
at how level she could sound when everything inside her was leaping and shrieking. She thought she must look like a gargoyle as she
gave him his orders.

"All right then, baby," he said, backing slowly toward the door.
"I'm not going to fight with you now. But you think I'm just
walking away you've got another think coming. You haven't seen
the last of me, and neither has she."

It sounded like a witch's curse. "We can save some time later,"
she said. "The name is Rumpelstiltskin."

It was warfare, the way soldiers become unrecognizable to
themselves. She turned away from him to mash her face into her
pillow, and it was true about her milk. She cried so hard and so
long that when they brought the baby to be fed she had nothing to
give, her milk had seized up along with her goodwill, and Veronica
shrieked until the nurse took her away, purple in the face, to give
her sugar water for relief.

"How can you humanly keep a man from his child?" Jewel de-manded when she came to visit. "Maybe he saw that baby and became—began to become—a different man. You know that hap-pens. If I can believe that, why can't you?"

Miriam kept her head bent over her child. The baby's hair clung to her sweet scalp like moss. When she ran her finger over it, Veronica puckered up her forehead. She did it every time.

"Why not give him a little credit? Everybody's got a kind of a moral bank account, you know? So his is overdrawn. Okay. So ad-vance him a little and see how he uses it."

"I thought you hated him, Jewel."

"I didn't hate him. I hated the way he and his dumb-ass friends carried on with you. All right, they were trifling with some deep feelings. No argument. But that's not him, that's just his pathetic behavior, letting himself get led around by the nose by a bunch of opportunists. Who knows how long that would have gone on, anyway, maybe he'd have gotten tired of acting stupid. Lambie, you got to *fight* for peace talks in war and sex and race and all of it out on the table. None of it's ever easy." She stood up, impatient. "You're not listening to me."

She was right. Miriam was paying attention only to the littlest sounds, the way sucking made such funny lubricated clicks and rubbery noises, the way the baby sighed like an adult, resigning herself to sleep after a heavy feed and, alarmingly, hiccuped with a sharp bounce as she had done before she was out in the light of day. It was a narcissism Miriam had never heard described, quite, this animal contentment with the product of her own body and soul, this capacity to stare into the compact little face, those rounding cheeks, as if into a mirror.

When she went home with Veronica in a yellow blanket they had bought at Midnight Madness the night of her birth, Jewel kept her distance. When she came around she admitted the baby was beautiful. Still angry, though, she insisted on calling Miriam the Mother Superior and her daughter the Virgin Birth.

And her other friends were furious. Lord only knew what the black ones thought when Eljay angrily trumpeted his fatherhood around the campus—she didn't even want to wonder. The white ones felt lied to—those phone calls to Moscow! The pity they'd spilled over her loneliness! She'd made fools of them all; they might be sympathetic in the abstract but the truth betrayed the thinness of their friendship.

Mary Ann Noble, who taught languages and had been knitting a navy blue afghan with a U.S. passport logo in gold yarn to start the baby early on the trail of good travels, appeared in Miriam's kitchen without knocking. She was a wiry little woman with penny-bright red hair that stood out around her head like a skater's skirt, and a capacity for outrage that outdid Jewel's. In a red jumper that clashed with her hair, she stood like a furious child, hands out to show their emptiness. "And who," she demanded, "was John Freund, then? A ghost? A mere figment?"

Miriam sat in her nursing rocker afraid to look at her. She said nothing; there was nothing to say. The baby slept across her lap, satiated on her evening meal. Miriam's nipples tingled from their exertions; it was a lovely feeling.

"Were you laughing at us all this time? That's what they're saying, you know. You were having a good joke at how trusting we were. We barely asked a question!"

At that, Miriam laughed herself. "Sure. A good joke."

"All right," Mary Ann insisted on continuing, though Miriam felt disinclined to be scolded. "All right, we thought it a little odd, one might say, that the baby was obviously—that your alleged—I say, alleged—husband—was clearly not white. But all right, none of us knew him and we even took ourselves to task for automatically, you know, *assuming*. So fine. Freund? Well—I once knew a black man named Engeleiter."

Miriam blinked at her, bewildered by this need to rage at someone so clearly a victim. But Mary Ann had brought the whole deluded community along with her by proxy. "And now that Eljay has gone public, and so noisily! To discover that right here under our noses—"

At last Miriam roused herself. "Mary Ann, don't shout at me, please? I'm not a teenager." She took a deep, hopeless breath. "Can't anybody get past—"

"Being duped? That wonderful gift that he sent, that gorgeous blanket! Your *John*."

"Okay. Fine, if you want to keep saying that, duped. Can't you recognize that none of this had anything to do with wanting to trick anybody, or make you look foolish. I was just trying to stay alive."

Mary Ann looked skeptical. "We were so pleased for you."

"Forgive me, then," Miriam said finally, without conviction. "Tell them all I'm sorry. But do me a favor? Tell them there isn't any less reason to be pleased. Look at this child, Mary Ann." Veronica, in spite of all, had given her new confidence in her powers, though they weren't the ones she could control. "Are you really so angry at me that you can't appreciate her?" She hefted the baby in her terry-cloth sleeper, who moaned once and then delicately burped.

MIRIAM TOOK THE BABY on a trip when she was a few months old, took her, though with some bitter misgivings, to Chicago, where she had felt the first flickerings of her existence. The American Historical Association was having its convention and she went with Veronica attached to her chest like a baby kangaroo in her pouch, prepared to carry her into conference rooms and leave if she woke up in full voice. She needed a break from the difficulties of teaching, nursing, rushing like a demon bent at the waist, and she was going to get as much of one as she could, with nobody's help. She was joyous; she thought, Look, I'm still independent, I can come and go as freely as I ever did, and the baby will sleep and wake and we'll be wonderful together, nothing lost, everything gained. When the school year ends, maybe we'll move to Chicago!

Everyone at the conference was kind to them, and the baby slept like a little bear in hibernation. Something about all those people, maybe, the warm buzz of voices and lights—she was hypnotized. The only trouble she made for her mother was when she woke up in an audience singing, making happy syllables, and everyone laughed, but Miriam took her out anyway and walked her through the lobby smiling.

But this wasn't Rowan, they were up north in a rumbling angry city, and outside, in winter, everywhere she turned in the street, she felt it: the Weathermen were in town. There were even confrontations at the conference; a couple of young black historians were challenging the whiteness of what they tediously called the whole damn racist thing. Well, she conceded, you'd have to be blind to deny it, they were right: How many black faces were in attendance, let alone in positions of authority? And it was afro time—there were some beautiful bountiful creations of mammoth proportions, nests big enough to hold eagles, so grand a stowaway could hide in them, and the dashikis that blazed through the halls (they weren't many of them, but they surely were visible) made the suits look pathetic, wan and unchanging and undynamic. Women were wearing red, black, green, the colors of liberation— slashes of vividness, the way cardinals look flashing through the woods. They raised their fists and beat the air with them. Miriam turned on the radio and heard a kind of poetry that was meant to make her quake, and obediently she did quake: blood in the streets, honkies in full flight, words she had never heard before except from Eljay's new friends, and, though she should have, she hadn't realized there were so many of them so far from Rowan. It was the way rabid white folks threatened blacks. They were rioting in Watts, burning down Detroit. It was a shaky time.

She went to a concert one evening, a group of singers from black colleges like Parnassus; in fact, a few Parnassians were in the chorus, singers who worked with Eljay, and she was planning to go backstage afterward to greet them. She had the baby with her, slung against her chest in her bright blue Snugli. Miriam unlaced the carrier and sat Veronica on her lap facing front in her yellow terry-cloth suit, which usually brought forth little "ahhs" of pleasure, the way babies soften people, the pure protective animal gesture they'd been drawing at the conference.

But these were Northern college students, and maybe others as well, all colors, and she learned quickly enough that some of them were not enthusiastic about a fake colonializing friendship like hers. They were from a harsher, more forthright part of the world, and they wasted no effort on being charmed or charming. Maybe she imagined it all, she was so tense by then. But she was primed. And a young man—boy, really—with a tumultuous afro that was dense in the middle and spidery at the edges, wearing a FIGHT BACK! T-shirt, said to her through a twisted lip, "Hhmp, where'd you find the little nigger child?" His T-shirt, she noticed, had a bandolier of bullets painted diagonally across it, shoulder to waist. She sat staring at the empty stage, trying not to react, because if she'd let herself speak she'd have shouted, "Don't you nigger me, nigger!" She would not flinch.

Of course, she understood what he was doing, tearing into someone he knew it was safe to maim, someone with soft flesh who wouldn't attack him, wouldn't call for help. She was there to take it, she and her little half-breed papoose. She thought of Eljay crouching naked on the floor, shuffling for the judge, and how she bled for him and how the last thing he wanted was to need her blood. And how she had laughed, she couldn't leave that out of an honest accounting. But the kinder her intentions, the more she was despised and the more self-congratulatory she sounded. No way to win when the harder you tried, the deeper you dug yourself. And her heart sank with love for Eljay, and with helplessness.

Away from the genteel, controlled, easily shocked majority at the conference, everything felt menacing to her. Maybe it was the squeamishness of her Houston past, or the leisurely pace of Mississippi, where the horizon was uncrowded and the houses were pale and low, but suddenly everything seemed furious, dirty, threatening. Chicago is not a gentle city. She was uncomfortable under the grinding noise of the el, she had never seen or heard an el before the trip she'd made with Eljay, and the crowds on Wabash and State Street flowed around like angry waves breaking over her, heaving and splashing. When she saw the lake, which was an ugly roiled-up brown, it was doing the same thing, raging against the shore as if it were the ocean. She had heard that it could be pacific, aqua as the Mediterranean, but she didn't believe it.

Another day Miriam made herself get on the train and ride down to the South Side, thinking, Let me see what this feels like, this is where I might have to be to raise this child. Probably I should take her to some liberal white community like the one around the university, where she'll find children just like herself, some "biological," some adopted, and very little shock. But she was drowning in defensiveness. Even without Eljay to coach her, although she didn't intend to cede the baby over entirely, to cut her off from her own whiteness, she thought Veronica would need every bit of blackness she could find for her; she thought she'd worry about herself after she'd settled her daughter into her own life.

She was walking along, her hands and feet cold, looking into store windows, seeing their reflection, when two young men came, making good time, down the block toward her, one, coatless, in a yellow-and-brown-and-blue dashiki, one in a gorgeous voluminous robe that looked like some painter's palette, where he'd wiped all the color off his brushes. They neared her, hair all electrified, they were focused on something—God knows what—but she was so self-absorbed and self-conscious with her little black-white baby strapped to her chest that she could only think it had to be herself they were coming for. And she was knocked to the ground in her imagination, that was where she saw herself, sprawling, cushioning the child. In her mind she must have thought she *should* be, for having something that wasn't hers, her baby snatched and carried away under the extravagant robe, and there she was stranded in enemy territory, stock-still, wide-eyed. And the two of them ran right on by. Maybe they were running for a bus. Miriam held her baby close against her, hands clutching at the little diapered bottom, Veronica's fat legs dangling down, and she watched them go. *Look at the Liberal Spokesman for the jews clutch his throat & puke himself into eternity. . . . Another bad poem cracking steel knuckles in a jewlady's mouth Poem scream poison gas on beasts in green berets. . . . We want a black poem. And a Black world. Let the world be a black Poem and Let All Black People Speak This Poem Silently or LOUD*

That's what she had happened across on the hotel radio that morning, on a station that called itself Liberation News. Steel knuckles, how could she not feel them? She was the jewlady Miriam, she was not being thanked for her dedication, let alone her love, and fury would not help her. Retribution was upon them, and repentance. No one had laid a hand on her, but she barely had strength to get herself back to the train. Downtown she sat cradling her child in the big flowered armchair in a corner of her room, tracing a finger over Veronica's delicate eyebrow that was shaped just like her own (bow with the slightest point at the top) and shivered and was warmed by the baby's slow, even breathing, entirely alone.

HE GAVE HER EIGHT MONTHS. Eight months she had Veronica, and everybody finally knew because Eljay trumpeted it about, raging, that she was his. She was the one who suffered humiliation because Parnassus, if it was a jury, would have voted black; if it was a judge, would have ruled black. And why not? She was the mother here, but fathers had their rights, black fathers who wanted their children, and she, to boot, she was the splinter in the hide and the fly in the ointment, and they knew she had wings and could fly away, if it came to that. Remember the librarian suspicious of Eljay for not liking dark meat? No surprise Miriam was the one to suffer—*she* must have seduced *him*—and he was the one forgiven.

She would never know if the student baby-sitter colluded. But one day she left Veronica the way she always did, and went off to teach her ten o'clock, her eleven o'clock, in spite of a light social freeze she was feeling very good, she had her classes working hard, they were learning some history, they had formed a debate team and were hacking their way through the dropping of the atomic bomb—and she came home for lunch, her breasts still letting down milk for a few feedings a day but her schedule working smoothly, the baby growing and laughing and thriving. And when she came into her little house there was a note from the baby-sitter propped on the table against the sugar bowl: PROF. REECE CAME TO GET

YOUR BABY TO BRING YOU SO I LEFT. HOPE THAT'S OKAY. HE PAID
ME. And when she looked around, not only had he taken Veronica
but he had removed everything that belonged to her except a
ripped terry-cloth suit lying like a rag on the floor, a couple of
frayed pastel blankets without much life left in them, and a little
brimmed blue hat Miriam's parents had grudgingly sent her. The
crib was there but the carriage wasn't. The picture of Veronica
stood on her dresser, the baby sitting in her mother's lap wearing a
plaid sunsuit with her arms up in something like a victory sign. He
had left no note. Give or take a rag or two, and an empty bottle of
baby oil, the baby was as gone as if she had never been. Miriam
had been knocked down and left for dead.

She ran out of her house as if it were burning, straight to Eljay's.
He had moved out of Staggers into a little pinkish place in town
with a wooden pink-yellow-pink pinwheel out front, cute, and a
collapsing carport, dead yellow grass, shadeless windows hung
with sheets—he must have been getting himself ready for this bur-
glary, preparing a nest. And of course he wasn't there. She should
have figured he wouldn't be sitting around in the living room waiting for her to come kill him or fall on his mercy or bring the police. She was entirely wild and entirely helpless. She ran around his
house trying to see in the windows, saw nothing but blank white
sheets, and went home.

The first night Veronica was gone she didn't sleep. She sat up in
the wooden rocker where she had nursed her and she didn't even
cry. Her breasts throbbed, milk soaked the front of her shirt, hardened against her raw nipples, wet her again. She was in the kind of
shock that shuts you down, the kind after an accident. Preserves
you, if you don't die. Just before dawn she watched the sky shift a
little and it seemed possible to imagine light. Probably she drifted
off, or maybe she was in that hypnogogic state between waking
and sleeping. She kept thinking her baby was a mouse scampering
away from her. She heard the rustling and she'd jump, she was
ready to try to catch her between her hands, a lunge, a grab, a slap
of the palms together. She thought she had gone crazy.

But she stayed in the house, the little white wooden bungalow on the campus, and let them come to her, anyone who was curious. Her classes were on their own, abandoned. She didn't wash, barely ate. Finally she had to give her engorged breasts some relief and prodded the blueish milk out, splashing, into a bowl, then sat looking at it blankly, as if, its use gone, she couldn't remember what it had ever been for.

She kept the windows and doors closed, the shades pulled. Jewel came and rattled the door and shouted at her, but by then Miriam was head-to-knees; she looked ready for Whitfield State. Jewel came in through the unlocked back door and picked her up by the shoulders. "You're going to have to fight like hell," she shouted, as if Miriam was the cause of her anger, but Miriam said, "I'd rather die now and get it over with." Jewel told her that didn't sound like her and she was right, but Miriam knew, that was the thing, she knew already, that she wasn't going to win this battle: A man who would kidnap a child was not going to sit down and reason. Why should he bargain? He had what he wanted. Power was what it was about, and she had none. She could not go to the law—a black man and a white woman? She did not want to get him killed, though she'd have liked to kill him herself. She could not ask Harry Storm, the college president, to intervene: it was none of his business and anyway, technically speaking, "faculty cohabitation" was all moral turpitude to him. Eljay's friends despised her; they would say, the way they goaded him, "This is a black child, let her be." There was Jewel, who was angry at her and was probably thinking I told you so, and very few others because she had been locked in her secret life so long it had been hard to cultivate a multitude. And they had never quite forgiven her the John Freund fiction; it was as if she'd proved that she lived apart, that she needed no one, disclosing nothing to them but a lie.

As for the black faculty—well, she thought, was there a bond? Was there a feeling of responsibility? Maybe somebody went to speak to Eljay on her behalf, but she doubted it. Why would they? Custody messes were private business. Everyone was faintly embarrassed, or outraged for one side or the other, but not inclined to make a fuss. What they were calling Black Power was only a crude exaggeration of what already existed, an unspoken brotherhood that held, said, Look out, we will watch out for our own. She had been naïve.

HE WAITED a little while, till she subsided, and then he invited her over to his turf for a talk. As if this were international diplomacy, reason was suggested (in the passive voice, the way, a few years later, Nixon would admit that "mistakes were made"). The note he sent, via a student, said, "I hope we can discuss this matter"—this matter!—"calmly, without heat." She thought of bringing Jewel, like her second in a duel, but she dismissed the idea as a sign of weakness, as if she couldn't deal with this herself.

She scared herself, those days without her baby. (Veronica was still "the baby," too young for her heavy name.) When Miriam was a child she had had a cat named Lansing who—they always thought it must have been because she had kittens by her brother, who lived next door—gave birth to a litter that died within a day in the most awful way: their stomachs split open so that, one after another but one at a time, the tiny little things, small as newborn hamsters, looked as if they'd been torn up by a car. The way Miriam discovered this was that she found Lansing running wildly around the house trying to hide them—she'd pick them up in her mouth and move them every few minutes, from closet to garage to the pitch-darkness under the bed—all in some heartbreaking, futile maternal instinct that told her she could do something to save them. She couldn't. Miriam's brother, Alan, waited for the cat to run off to rescue another one and, while she was away, he picked up the last two by their ratty little tails, pushed them into a pillow-case that instantly bloomed with their blood, and threw them into the murky sort-of-creek, an offshoot of the bayou, that ran near their house. He let Miriam come but she hung back, she couldn't watch, even though he said he was doing it to spare them. For days, back at the house, Lansing kept searching, searching for them, crying in her thin voice as she poked her head into every place she'd stashed them, in the exact order of her stashing. She was unapproachable for comforting. "That was me," Miriam said to Ronnee now. "Eljay did that to me."

A small wind had started up in the trees, whose leaves seemed to flicker with a nervous busyness. Miriam put her head back and felt the breeze cool her face.

SHE HAD GONE to his awful pink house that looked like dried-up Pepto-Bismol. She stood on the little cement slab of a porch thinking, *I am coming like a stranger to visit my own baby.* Her cells, her blood, nourished in her amniotic waters, this real and solid being made of her so literally that she used to squint at the very idea, as if such unlikeliness could be made into something visible. The baby torn free, she'd swabbed the little blackened stem that had attached them until it fell off in her hand, and here she was now, standing outside the door ringing the goddamn bell so she could get a look at her, maybe touch her, if he didn't prevent it. *How could she have come without a weapon in her hand?* The bell was one of those cheerful bing-bongs that made her want to put her fist through the door.

But Jewel, who cared about her, had tried to convince her that some of this was her own fault. It hurt her to say that, but she said it anyway. You wouldn't let him near you before she was born, she nattered at Miriam, you wouldn't let him see how she was half his, half yours. You made him desperate. Maybe you were too angry too soon.

Maybe. But she still thought, the minute he had heard she was pregnant, he was already stealing this child. And now they'd gotten to this point where he opened the door looking like a host, with the blandest, pleasantest expression on his face. It was so insincere, so vague and unspecific, it looked like a kind of dismissal: She didn't matter, she was something to be gotten through. The baby was in the playpen he had removed from her living room. She reached for Miriam when she saw her. Miriam would remember that. And then the soft soap began.

Eljay looked like a man in a hurry to get somewhere, like a doctor at the end of a long day. He sat her down and brought her iced tea, which she hadn't asked for. He took the baby with him on his arm, very comfortably, because if he'd left her sitting in her playpen Miriam might have seized her and run and he'd have had to tackle her on the lawn, that terrible straw lawn, which he would have done.

He argued, in a quiet voice, the way a logician argues: "Begin with the premise that we both want the best for the child." (The child!) "Do you agree?"

"Of course I agree. Don't insult me."

"All right then. Let's proceed to the impediments to your giving her what she'll need—consider what it will be like to bring this girl back to Houston, a closed society like that. What do you expect would happen? Be honest now—how will your parents react to this little black cat?" His smile was so smug she nearly screamed. "What will your friends say? No wishful thinking, Miriam. Have you told them, have you sent everybody word that you've had this baby, you know, celebrate the birth, come see the child? This un-theoretical child who's getting darker by the day." He jiggled the baby on his arm as if to enlist Miriam's attention. "Come on now, concentrate and tell me what you can see ahead of you."

"Concentrate?!" She was afraid she would howl like some wild creature. "You know I've told them." "Them," she knew, was no one but her parents. They had sent the baby a little blue hat, a pa-thetic little present but an opening, a tiny hint that they weren't reading her out of the family. Her mother must have done that; it was a secret signal, so small her father wouldn't have noticed. But she could see Eljay thinking this child would be greeted in Miriam's world the way she'd been greeted at the moment of her birth, fallen into alien hands who could never love her. Eljay had never heard from her lips about that harsh beginning because they never spoke, but he could probably imagine that and worse.

She was so flustered it didn't occur to her to say, Why assume I'll bring her back to Houston, I can go anywhere I want to. She didn't say that.

"Consider how black folks' lives have room for all colors, all kinds," he said back. "We've been raped and our women violated, so look around, by now every combination in the world exists for us, for better or for worse, and we take good care of them. We honor those children, whatever their color."

How simple did he think she was? "Did your friends write your script for you? I think I recognize the voice."

And yet, on balance, what he said was truer than not.

"Sweetheart, remember the judgment of Solomon. The way we know who was the true mother, how we celebrate her unselfishness." He was using his seducer's voice, soft, brushy. "Consider, Miriam. Please. Consider your child."

She was in one of those unhinged states in which she kept snagging on words: *consider, consider,* thinking about how strange it sounded, how little it had to do with the combination of hard and soft that was her baby's skin, the layer of dusky rose petal over such firmness, little twiggy bones, such funny knees sunk in folds of fat so deep it looked like there were rubber bands around her thighs. Miriam used to fold up those knees, bend the infant arms and legs to music, dance with her where she lay looking up at her mother laughing. "If she's going to be treated like a black person," he asked, intruding, "how do you expect to make that fact a positive experience for her, not an impediment?" How would you this and wouldn't you that and look at her, he said, just look, innocent and ready to be imprinted with attitudes, with self-disgust or self-respect, depending.

There was not an ounce of emotion in his voice, so that her own objections sounded like the bleating of a sheep caught under a gate. He made her whole life seem dependent on the family that was waiting for her back home, though the other thing it never occurred to her to say was You're not going back to Euphrates with this girl, are you? Then how do you know what our lives will be like?

"If you stay here with her," he said, "you're doomed. You don't want a mixed-race child out on the streets of Mississippi, believe me you don't. You are so blind, you are so willful, you just confuse what you want with what's going to happen." The baby, in a light green terry-cloth suit the color of saltwater taffy, had been lying across his thighs. He shifted her to his shoulder; she seemed all too happy with him. "Have you ever seen a person *stoned*? I saw a little boy, same color she is, running down Capitol Street one time with a bunch of grown men coming up behind him, they were going to catch him, God knows what they were going to do to him. They got him by the shirt-tail and he was screaming like a banshee, wriggling and kicking."

What a crock, she thought, but only later. Why didn't she say it? It wasn't so unusual to see a little light-skinned kid, half of Creole Louisiana was whiter than she was, so what was the story here? Was he with a white parent? A black parent? And he's wandering all alone in the mean white city, set upon by the dogs of bigotry? You saw this and what did you do? You let the child be martyred for some reason I didn't catch? And what did stoning have to do with it? He lied, he exaggerated, nothing was beneath him. She thought he could have strained harder for a more likely story, but he spun this sophistry, and then he stood up with Miriam's baby, and held her cuddled to his chest and neck, and she did look contented there, arms around his neck. She looked at home.

"You've done something, Miriam, people won't forgive. She's the evidence of it. I don't know if that's fair or not, I mean, I know I did it too. But it's you people are going to be looking hard at. And you can make that thing you did into a gift, you can—"

Which was when she leaped up and screamed at him to stop, to shut his mouth, stop the slogans that belong on posters, to quit the line he was handing her, smooth as a seduction, and give her baby back. She stood and shrieked at him, she was ready to lunge and pull Veronica away, but it would have meant a physical fight with her baby in the middle, it would have meant tearing her away with her bare hands, and he stood his ground, cooler than cool, and then said, very quietly, "Do you hear how you sound? Do you see how unreliable you are? This child will have community. This child will look in the mirror and there will be the same kind of face she sees around her. How selfish can you be, Miriam? How can you put yourself before her? Look at her—look at her—you are different from her. And, like it or not, it's out of your hands, she and I are the same."

She closed her eyes and saw herself in Chicago, standing on the South Side street watching those men in dashikis racing toward her, and remembered the way she clung to Veronica because she expected herself to be knocked to the ground and her baby stolen. And now she had been taken with no violence, but stolen just the same.

Still, she tried to defend herself. Eljay had said he and his daughter were alike. His deep-brown face, hers diluted by milk, Miriam's milk, to the color of honey. And she so ashamed you'd think she had forced herself on him like a white owner on a reluctant slave.

"Nonsense, look at you," she hissed at him. "You're not at all the same."

"But people will treat us the same, and don't be such a fool you deny it. One drop is all it takes. Only one drop! You've lived here long enough to see that everything's not in your hands. That's the kind of arrogant white-girl thing you were brought up believing, isn't it: You think it, you want it, you can have it. Well, not so fast, Miriam. Not so fast."

She couldn't say to him, I can give her advantages. That was the one thing she could not use: The arrogant white girl has comforts to offer her. Shame on me for my advantages, she thought. My Flukie. Solidarity this morning lay with the have-nots, not the haves. "You want a neurotic?" he was saying. "You want confusion? A child in danger of being *stoned*?"

"Oh, stoned. Really, Eljay. Don't overdo it." But an enormous weariness had begun to overtake her, like a pillow coming down over her face, stifling her breath. He was a wall she couldn't scale. She had caused this thing to happen, and, after her hysteria in Chicago, this time she had better believe it was real. She sat back down again out of sheer exhaustion. It was true: She blinked before he did, she and her *advantages*, her belief that she could have what she wanted. He was trying to make her see this as a kind of racial redemption, impersonal, bigger than both of them. It was

appropriate that they were confronting each other in a room no
one really lived in: There was the spring-dead chair she sat in, a little low table littered with coffee cups and ashtrays. She supposed
he'd been sitting and thinking, talking, wondering, himself. She
didn't want to make him seem like a demon. He had changed so
much in less than a year, in the hands of his militant friends who
could play his bitterness like one of their drums, that he was like a
teenager who grows a foot and still doesn't know where his body
begins and ends.

She tried another gambit. "I don't trust sudden changes." She
could hear how depleted her voice sounded. "Your music, what
about your music."

"You haven't heard," he said quietly, as if he'd been reluctant to
tell her. "I'm leaving. This isn't my bag anymore, this French, this
Italian, getting these kids to pretend they're in the eighteenth-
century court, you know? Walking with books on their heads,
wearing knickers." He gave a contemptuous little laugh. "I've got
to tell you, that's all pretty embarrassing now. I feel like I made
these kids look like monkeys doing all that."

She swallowed hard. If he left, Veronica left.

"We're all giving up something we love." He shrugged as if all
things were interchangeable. "That music's done for me. Mozart
and his court, Rossini, Frescobaldi, the powdered wigs and short
pants, the money, all that gold leaf, the fake grandeur, what's all
that to me? It's just been an escape. A denial. But I told you, we're
all giving up something, and that's what I'm walking away from,
years of it." Was this possible? His life until this moment? "I'll finish out the semester, but I'm learning a whole new tune and they're
not going to like it here."

He didn't elaborate, but she saw his nasty friend Bo's drums
propped in the corner, gracefully shaped, unless Eljay had his own
by now, and a couple of objects that must have been instruments,
exotic, African, utterly new. To him as well, she suspected. Would
she hear, one of these days, that he and the baby had gone to live in
Dar es Salaam or Dakar?

"Then you're telling me the revolution has come?" she prodded.
"It's come to Rowan? That's the way people talk when they're

picking up their guns and lining up their families and their old friends against the wall."

His face almost softened for a second. "I'll try to spare you," he said, smiling. "For old times' sake. I'm not doing this to *hurt* you, Miriam. But you have to make your sacrifice. If you ever wanted the best for us, like you said—"

"I didn't mean I was volunteering my flesh and blood." Spoiled, all of it spoiled, is what she was thinking, the way you'd feel after an accident that smashes up a healthy body.

"But my people give their flesh and blood every day. All the time. Nobody asks us nicely. And for nothing in return."

This was a ridiculous conversation, carried on in full seriousness. He was not good at this yet, and, she thought, might never get good at it: he was a musician and teacher, and though he might have acted the thug to get Veronica here, he was not a warrior and he was not naturally unkind, so this wasn't easy. His sloganeering was a pose that couldn't last and, sincere or not, the words sounded badly rehearsed. She wondered how she'd have felt if he'd simply said he needed his child. Said she made him more human or more forgiving or more anything at all, not less. Just a man learning tenderness, not a spokesman. Would she have been more reconciled?

"And how—" This suddenly struck her like a harsh light flashed in her eyes— "How do you expect to take *care* of her? Eljay. What do you know about *babies*?" She narrowed her eyes to look hard at him. "Are you taking her home to your mother?"

"You can spare your contempt for my mother. There are worse things that could happen to her. But listen." He gave her a helpless shrug of a smile. "I'm not pretending anything here. I'll learn. In an emergency you do what you've got to do. And no, I promise you, nobody's raising her but me."

SO SHE WAS AN EMERGENCY. Thanks, Eljay.

The baby was asleep on her side in the playpen, her legs drawn up, her little petal cheek showing. When (with his kind permission) she picked up Veronica to hold her and say goodbye, he was discreet enough to leave them alone together. But he went out on the front step to wait for her, which meant she couldn't steal away with her prize. He didn't trust her and he was right. If the back of the house hadn't had high, stingy tract-house windows, she'd have been out and gone, with her baby tucked up against her.

She could not tell Ronnee what it was like to pull her up out of her sleep and feel that head against her shoulder and know she was leaving her there. She still could not see it, could not put herself through remembering that ever again, even to let her know how impossible it was. How she had felt every bit of blood drain out of her, as if she'd been chopped in two by a sword. She seemed to feel it flow right down and disappear. Once she was in an Etruscan cave, in Italy with Barry, and the guide said, "Lady, right where you're standing, just there, that was the altar and the prince would stand exactly where you are. And right above, on a little platform, they would slay a bull and the blood would wash down over the prince, bathe him, his arms, all of him, and run into that gutter, you see it? And it would flow out, and the prince would be blessed and everyone would bow down."

So there she was, but she was unblessed. She put Veronica back on the clean floor of her playpen, and the baby cried for her. But Miriam couldn't give her over into Eljay's hands, he had made himself a principle and not a man and she owed it no honor but to withdraw before she slew all of them in her fury. She actually thought for a minute that even if he was guarding the door, he had not removed the knives from the kitchen—assuming it was a real kitchen, not just the rented prop against which they were playing this scene.

But that much sacrifice was beyond her. She couldn't look at her child again. She put her down and walked out the front door without saying goodbye or good luck and walked, more or less, give or take a ride or two, until she got to Mexico, all the way to San Cristobal de las Casas, near the Guatemalan border, where she wouldn't have to speak. The Mouth, humbled, had nothing to say. She took a lot of mescaline—mushrooms—until she started having bad trips, far worse than anything she had been prey to in the safe haven of Ann Arbor, very scary dreams, crypts and falling airplanes, tidal waves and once a pond with deep leaf-black muck in it and she rising out of it naked, her face and body as dark as Eljay's, clawing and searching, and she knew she was searching for Veronica, her tiny brown face, her fat arms, her ears like winkleshells, to show her how they matched now. And she let herself be fingered by as many strangers as wanted her for a while, waiting to see if she'd ever feel anything again. For a long time, months and months, almost a year, she wouldn't have known it if someone had set fire to her. But she was so cold, so removed, her skin so clammy, she didn't think a match would have caught. She was metal, she was stone, not wood, not anything that had ever breathed or grown or leafed out. No matter what anyone did to her she let it happen, because now in addition to loss, she had guilt to chill her, she had the failure of her instincts and her nerve. They thought she was very amiable, the Mexicans, the Americans who huddled down there each for their own hidden reasons. She didn't know whether Eljay had saved his daughter. Maybe Ronnee could reassure her about that, once and for all.

"But I'll tell you," Miriam said to her now, looking straight into her noncommittal eyes, "I'll tell you, for one long season I was indestructible, you could even say I was safe, because there was nothing left of me to destroy."

8 RONNEE LISTENED to the very end, impassive, yielding nothing, not so much as a raised eyebrow or an indrawn breath. How could she not react? But if she was able to sit there without expression, Miriam thought she should be able to do the same. "No questions?" she asked, the same irritable coda she'd had to append to her history lectures at Parnassus, at the beginning, before she found her groove. This was the humiliating silence out of which she'd been reduced to pleading, "Do I see any hands?" while her students waited for the bell to ring.

Ronnee shrugged impartially, looking hard at her, combing her face for—she had no idea what. Confirmation that the story was true? A hint of how her father could have loved this woman in the first place, or why, or if?

"Then I have some questions for you." She admired her daughter's sangfroid the way she admired anything she couldn't achieve herself, but it worried her: was the girl entirely *sane*? "Did you know any of that? What's your father been telling you all these years?"

The shrug again, the impatient twitch of her shoulder. "Mostly nothing. As far as I knew you were dead for a long time." Ronnee shook her head as if to clear it. "No, wait, that doesn't sound right. I mean, for a long time I thought you were dead. Then he said he only told me that to spare me knowing you walked out on me because that would hurt me. To know it."

Miriam nodded. The worst. She wondered why he had decided to fess up. Her mouth was so dry she thought it might burst into flames.

"He said you were feeding me, you had this silver spoon you used? And I threw something over the side of my high chair, I don't know what, some food, I guess. Or a cup, maybe a cup. And I kept doing it, I wouldn't stop. And you got so mad you put the spoon down and just got up and put everything you owned in a paper bag and walked out."

Miriam's stomach hurt, cut across by a sharp ache that made her want to bend over double. But she had to laugh in spite of it. "Well, that's pretty imaginative, isn't it? Not exactly subtle, the silver spoon—but I like that, along with the paper bag, they really go together. I wonder if I got mad because you were throwing all that caviar over the side."

Ronnee wasn't laughing.

"Well, God, Ronnee, you can't honestly believe that anymore. I hope. You don't think I made up that whole story." Her voice was rising in spite of herself.

The girl was sullen. "Don't get mad at me. You just asked what he said and I told you. What was I supposed to think?"

All right, she told herself, trying for compassion. It must be bewildering to hear a story like that and to be told your father's made a career of lying. "You might be mad at both of us," Miriam suggested. "I could understand that. We didn't exactly—"

"I don't want to talk about it yet, okay?" Ronnee got up slowly, unbending, stretching her sturdy legs like a calf getting to her feet for the first time. "Give me a little time to think about it. It's a lot of—a lot to just . . ." She dwindled off, her eyes on the trees.

Miriam cheered silently for every sign of strain. "Okay. I can understand that."

"My father never—" Ronnee shook her head.

"I understand." But she felt farther from Ronnee than ever, distanced, somehow, by the whole truth. There was that baby, hers, and now there is this silent young woman. What did one have to do with the other? She had made a spectacle of herself.

"Thanks for showing me this place," Ronnee said, unsmiling, as if they had done a little simple sightseeing. "It's cool, the way it's hidden in here."

Miriam took that for a benediction.

OH, HER STUPIDITY! The way pain puddled up each time they ventured downtown. She had dropped Ronnee, credit card in hand, at the end of the row of shops on Main Street to amuse herself while she did some business, reopening her bank account, visiting the town clerk to discuss property taxes. "Just keep it reasonable," she said. "I trust you."

And, finished, having peered fruitlessly into the dark of the Well-Dressed Mare and Ruthie's Juniors, she finally saw her jiggling from foot to foot in front of the jewelry store. As she got closer she could see Ronnee seething like a volcano ready to spew. "Ronnee?" How easily the girl intimidated her. "What's—"

"I want to get out of this place! I want to go home!"

"Why? What happened?"

"Every time I meet anybody here—"

"Every time what?" She cringed at the memory of Nance at the A&P.

"I was buying something—it was something for you, if you want to know—"

On my credit card, Miriam thought dryly.

"So I give it to the guy behind the counter and he says, 'What are you doing with this?' so I say, 'I'm her daughter. She gave me the card just now—'" Ronnee's face was blotchy with anger, little islands of red mottling her cheeks. Eljay's angers had no chance to show on his darker skin, he had to turn them in like knives in his palm, until he got tired of mutilating himself. "He says—*you* know, you can guess—he says"—and she lowered her chin into her chest to do his deep voice—"'*I* know Miriam Vener and *I* know her daughter, and *you're* not her daughter. I'm going to call the police.' He's, like, holding the card up in the air, he thinks I'm going to jump across the counter and grab it from him. They're probably on their way, otherwise he'd have chased me himself. Old bastard, he's probably afraid he'll have a heart attack if he runs after me."

Oh Christ, here we go again. She had been stupid to send Ronnee off like that, the way she gave Seth the card, which no one ever questioned. She had wanted Ronnee to feel trusted. She had wanted to be generous. How could she have been so casual? "Oh, honey, these people know me too well. I mean, they think they know me." I've got a life here, she meant. *We* do. "I just wasn't thinking."

"Well, I'm the one who keeps getting beat up, not you! And don't 'honey' me, I hate that."

She was going to have to stop saying, "I'm sorry," because it didn't ring true. "It isn't really his fault, if you think about it. What's he—"

"What do you mean it isn't his fault! Whose side are you on, anyway?"

"But there aren't any sides, Ronnee. A strange girl comes in—"

"Right, *strange*." She made a gargoyle face, eyes crossed, tongue out. "This just shows you don't know *any*thing about the kind of shit we have to put up with." She stamped her foot on *shit*.

"I mean, you're somebody he's never seen before, and he knows me, he knows my kids, I've bought birthday gifts for them in here, watches, necklaces. I got Seth a Swiss army knife last year. What should he do when somebody he's never seen tells him she's my daughter? With my money in her fist? Actually, I mean, I'm glad he's protecting me. This is how fraud happens."

But she knew the shadow would keep falling between them. Logic was an affront, and ordinary behavior an insult: a lesson in fraud prevention was not what Ronnee needed. She had laughed when Eljay, naked, leaped like a trained dog under the judge's whip. Behavior echoed like rhyme, never exact repetition but close enough. She had felt shamed then. She felt shamed now.

Worse, there was no one to talk to about it. She didn't have to run her finger down a list to know that her friends were useless— it would take a while gaining their trust back again if and when

they learned about Ronnee. Her husband would be eager and irrelevant. Her mother was disqualified for more than one reason. She
could sit in the dark and brood if she wanted to, but that wouldn't
help much. What a deep deep hole she'd dug herself. Eighteen
years since she'd sat alone in the same hole at Parnassus, friendless,
heaping dirt on her head. She saw herself back in her kitchen, collapsed in her nursing rocker, Jewel like an avenging angel standing
guard at her shoulder as though she could stop what had already
happened. Responsible but not guilty, was there such a thing? To
blame but not to blame?

Jewel stood up straight and plain as a post in the middle of her
mind, her thin back divided by that paintbrush of a braid. She used
to keep her hands in her overalls pockets, dragging at them like a
teenage boy, when she wasn't gesturing like a Sicilian. Her voice
was so emphatic it sometimes cracked with passion, and her accent was variable, depending on her audience—flexibility, she'd
insisted, was the first sign of an effective speaker. Miriam remembered it as well as her own mother's. Fleeing, she had abandoned
Jewel, who would never have abandoned her.

And then she thought, so suddenly it was like a blow to the
head, If Parnassus could find Eljay, they could surely find Jewel.

Better yet, she'd call her. Surely the statute of limitations had
run out on her anger. She would have an opinion, but about *what*?
It wouldn't matter. Jewel was the only one who knew her, after all.
She would figure out what the question was.

WHEN SHE TOLD THE VOICE in the alumni-relations office that
she needed an address and, if possible, a phone number and gave
Jewel's name, the operator said without hesitation, "Please stay on
the line and I'll put you through."

Put you through? She'd imagined Jewel anywhere but there.

"Dean Proctor's office." A very local accent. Tentatively she
asked for Ms. Proctor. She gave her name and, waiting, felt her
heart thudding as if she were afraid.

"This is Miriam Just-Who did she tell me?"

"Jewel? Is that you?"

"That Miriam! Well, listen to you! You're not still mad at me."

"An eighteen-year funk? Even I'm not that stubborn, girl."

"Hey girl, yourself! What in this world full of wonders are you doing talking to me today?"

"Oh Lord, Jewel. It's a very long story. I found her—Veronica?—just when she was looking for me. Just—God, only a few weeks ago. It feels like forever."

"You haven't had any word before?" She didn't wait for an answer. "That jive son of a bitch."

"It's complicated."

"Everything interesting's complicated, sugar. Want to talk about complicated, did you know I'm a lawyer now?"

"I don't know one thing. How would I know anything?"

"And the vice president of this place—"

"Parnassus? You really are still there?!"

"Well, I escaped, you could say, but then I came back. It's my fate, this hellhole, I'm never going anywhere, I've just accepted that. I'm gone be buried up in that graveyard next to the chapel, no doubt about it, so I might as well relax and enjoy it. My father's up there, you know. All tucked in under a big stone, befitting his position. Honey, we've both got long stories stretching out behind us. My daddy used to say that's why they call them tales. We've got to do something about all this. But in the meantime—"

"I'm just so—"

"Stop. I know. Me too. We both need to take some long deep breaths, get our pulse down a little."

"I feel like I can see you!" Her loneliness was like something solid in her hands. "I just want to look at you." She could feel it beginning to crack.

Jewel snorted. "Wait a minute, hon. You didn't call to tell me that. You're having a problem? You've fished this girl out and you want to throw her back?"

"No. I mean, I've met her and—I don't know what the problem is. I didn't know what to expect but—Jewel?"

"I'm listening, sugar."

"I think it's my—I need to talk to you."

"About what?"

"About my life." That was a surprise. She let it stand.

"Your life."

"I mean, with or without Veronica in it. She's called Ronnee now, by the way."

"A pity. Such a beautiful name."

"Well—I guess that's the least of our problems."

"She mean to you?"

It was too much to explain. Ronnee was pacing up and down the creaky steps looking for afternoon snacks and turning on and off the TV in the other room. Nor was she going to talk about the waste of years, the pathetic, ignoble crouch in which she'd been living since, practically, the last time she and Jewel had been together. "Tell me about you. I think it's simpler."

"Here? Well, let's see. I'm dean of students now, and unless something unexpectedly occurs to jumble the line of succession, I'm going to be their first-ever woman president. One hundred twenty years of white men and black men but no wi-men!" Her laugh hadn't changed. It was still full throated, a little rich for dignity. "Honey, I got framed pictures in my office you'd have trouble believing—yours truly shaking hands with this mess of state leaders, ex–confirmed racists all semi-sincere and smiley now over one kind of agreement or another. Thank God for realpolitik," she said with satisfaction. "They don't have to like me to shake my hand these days. They just have to like getting elected." She was, she declared, shepherd and goad and occasional prophet, loud-voiced believer in every kind of possibility for her graduates and oh, she said fervently, they were awfully good these days. "You could teach them things now you never dreamed of getting them to listen to in the old days."

"You! Jewel! You were arguing all the time, you were forever reforming the faculty, cursing out the administration. You were a professional overtime thorn in everybody's side."

"You mean a pain in the butt," Jewel said cheerfully. "Yeah, well, you can call me the LBJ of the Negro College circuit now.

Break bread with bankers. We need scholarships, we need a new gym, you've got money, we'll name it after you. Course, only friendly types tend to apply. I really don't think we have to worry about the Senator Stennis Student Center. But anybody who can help us, fine. I'll deal." She stopped for half a breath. "Even at that I'm probably a little too vigorous for everybody's comfort. You know, I always step a little too heavy, come down too hard. But I try to be good, I ask about their little towheaded children, I compliment their wives for losing a couple pounds, highlighting their hair. *You* know. But I'll tell you, a girl comes along now like the one I used to be, who couldn't compromise, I'd put her on probation and throw her out if she couldn't cool down."

"Oh, Jewel, we're getting old."

"I don't know. How do you tell what's old and what's wise?"

"I'm not one bit wiser than I was last time you tried to talk some sense into me."

"You ever get married? You ever forgive yourself?"

"I hope those aren't supposed to be the same question. Yes to the first. I've got a very sweet husband, I've got three terrific kids. Two boys and a girl."

"Naturally terrific. Whose aren't? And this one? The one that's giving you fits?"

"I just—I think it's too late. I'm not sure, exactly, what to *do* with her. Or what I *expected*. I'm not sure she thinks she needs a mother anymore."

"Like I said, the jive bastard. Or did I say son of a bitch? They both fit."

Maybe this needed to happen in person. "Can I come see you, Jewel? Or would you come visit? You get any time off in the summer? I'm calling you from New Hampshire."

"Oh, hey now, there's a cool thought on a hellish afternoon down here. You know what it's like, you were born in Texas. It's only half human with a fan *and* the AC."

"Well, you could come and see this godchild of yours. We'll take you swimming."

"Let me check my schedule, sugar. It's a ball and chain, but maybe I can sneak off for a long weekend or something. Call you back quick as a twitch."

"Jewel?" She felt her eyes mist. "I've needed you all these years."

"Honey, I'm sorry to hear that, since you didn't have me." She gave the comment its moment of gravity but it probably embarrassed her. "Hey, picture this, before we go. Picture a crystal vase, my favorite pink and white lilies in the corner of this desk that's big as two rowboats. With a student assistant who changes them twice a week."

"Hey, Jewel." So that was how Jewel's mother was asserting her legacy in her daughter. Surely no other ways but the little ones. Obviously Jewel hadn't needed *her*.

"I have stopped apologizing that I'm a hell of a lot more efficient at my work when I am contented." Miriam could imagine the battle scars that would make her so defensive.

"Good."

"You'll be all right till I get back to you?"

"I guess I've managed for about seventeen years."

"Tell that girl her fairy godmother's coming." Her hoot of a laugh again. "If I was the guy I wish I was, that would be a double entendre."

"Got it. I'll tell her." And hope she cares. She didn't have the heart to say that, even to Jewel, who would pretend to be indifferent. But how much she seemed to care, now, what others thought. Maybe a college vice president had to.

IT WAS A SHAME they had never built a screened-in porch to make late afternoon and early evening tolerable. The sad reality of country life was that, if high sunshine attracted flies, noisy and persistent, the prettiest part of the day—photographer's light— brought out squadrons of mosquitos. Miriam was braving it, seated on a lawn chair under the spreading maple on the front lawn with a book she was too distracted to read. What could she have said, what should she have said there in the graveyard to change

anything at all, her life, her daughter's life? What was all that bitter
history supposed to do except stir her up? So Eljay was indicted,
she was exonerated, and Ronnee seemed hardly to have heard a
word of it, not, at least, the way it was intended. She saw the
planes of her daughter's face when she'd finished the story, the
stubborn flatness of her eyes that warned: Don't ask me to say
anything. Keep your distance. "You said you were looking for me.
Just what," she'd have liked to ask Ronnee, "did you want of me?"

But if Ronnee had leaned toward *her* and demanded "What do
you want of *me*?" Miriam could not have told her. Not shopping.
Not chitchat. Not a stranger's courtesy. How was it possible to
feel so much emotion—like molecules dancing, bubbles of leaping
heat flinging themselves up toward chill air, to cool, to change—
and not know what it was all supposed to mean? Had she, in the
unhealth of her life, in the stasis, opened this wound only to feel
herself bleed?

Was Ronnee bleeding?

She looked up when the screen door slammed. Ronnee was approaching, bland-faced but clearly determined. She thrust a
brown-covered book in Miriam's direction. "Here, I brought you
this. I figured—" She dropped it as though she couldn't wait to be
free of it and backed away, wiping her hands on her shorts.

Good God, a manifesto?

Had Eljay really been sentimental enough to keep this album of
photos? It was clad in stiff fake leather, bordered with a wavery
gold stripe. The glare of the plastic over the pages was like still water.

She couldn't look at Veronica-as-a-baby, she was too familiar,
too close to the child she had said goodbye to. She flipped the
pages, black-and-white, then all those tender pastel-y colors babies
used to be dressed in, Easter Parade pales. As she got older the colors deepened—red, navy, brassy green for the toughened toddler!
So much time and feeling were contained in the book that it felt,
there in her lap, like a living thing, fleshy and mysterious; it was so
full it seemed to move in her grasp. A birthday party, the baby
held up to face the camera by an anonymous woman's arms,

brown and lustrous. Veronica smiling hard, showing teeth tiny as kernels of shoepeg corn. Under a glittery Christmas tree with Santa's hat awry, one hand up to hold it on. School picture—kindergarten? first grade?—sitting extremely straight, yearningly good. So adorable it was hard to look at her, this ur-baby, cheeks like a little squirrel's, stuffed with acorns. The pictures interchangeable with her children's—her other children's—the well-loved, well-turned-out child, product of the parent who got her up and fed and dressed her for the day. The centerpiece. The surrounding cast is voluminous, cheery, none of them white. Oh, one: looks like a teacher, around sixth grade maybe, Veronica—surely Ronnee by now—diligently concentrating on a page of something, a young woman with round glasses and unfancy hair, how could she not be her teacher, looking at the camera with a challenge: You *see?* Grass in the park, Veronica dwarfed by a poster announcing TWO PLAYS BY PIRANDELLO, taller than the two white girls beside her, arms out as though to gather them in. Looking coyly over her shoulder in a prom dress, she's too young for a prom, then just a dance, but she is suddenly full-grown, blooming, a little fleshy around the straps of the dress, a nearly electric cornflower blue. Her shoes match.

They were mostly celebratory: Who takes photographs at ordinary times? Probably somebody other than Eljay was responsible; he never seemed the kind to stalk around with a camera keeping records. Even in his compulsive days he was more a *now* man than a *later* one. Music, he said, is always taking place in the present: Like making love, hon, no past, no future. *Listen. Feel it.*

But she knew how little you could read from pictures. Those smiling children in the newspapers who live and die abused, cigarette burns overlooked by the social workers on their desultory visits, such apparent gaiety dredged up out of boundless hopefulness and politeness it must be hardwired, all for the sake of the camera, which is conscienceless. Who could tell, then, what kind of life she'd been leading?

Enough fantasies: This child was so sound, no one could imagine her mistreated. Buttons, gloves pinned to sleeves, nosebleeds, warm milk, Robitussin, maxipads: on and on the list went for each child, some generic, some unique. Which child loved rutabagas? Which got hives from tomatoes? There was one flute, one clarinet in her family. (Musically recalcitrant, Eli had heard enough. But he was young; she still had hope.) How many grilled-cheese sandwiches did it take to be a good parent? Her mother would have insisted it mattered that the OJ was fresh-squeezed. Has the elastic in the jockey shorts stretched too far for salvation? In the warm parental bed Sunday mornings. Saying no. Saying yes, if Daddy agrees. And if there is no Daddy? No Mommy? Saying yes, period. On and on and on, the flow of it: Was this the sum total of parenthood? Was the bottom line of that inventory the guarantor of her parental rights? Surely there was more, inexpressible, uncaused, like the expression in someone's eyes. Darling, who does she favor? Your genes, your genes are just where in this girl?

"NOW," Miriam said at dinner, against every impulse to keep the subject buried. "Tell me something about your father." Ronnee's ears straightened like a listening cat's. Well . . . He wouldn't get a TV till she was twelve. He was afraid to let her learn to drive. "Stay in New York," he said, "and you won't ever have to learn." She did all the cooking. At least he was an appreciative eater, he made generous noises of appreciation, his tokens of gratitude. He helped her with her homework (very good at math, which was not unusual among musicians). He gave her a curfew. He sent her shopping with his girlfriends. He wouldn't let her get a cat because he thought they were shifty eyed; he really did believe a cousin's child had been smothered by a tabby. She suspected he was afraid of dogs. They had a bird for one season, bright blue like something dyed, that sang to slow jazz, especially brushes on tom-toms, and died mysteriously overnight, and was never replaced.

The details of Eljay's attentiveness fell on Miriam like blows. She probed for weaknesses, heard proofs of his selfishness, but heard, too, how he overcame it sufficiently to make Ronnee a happy enough child. "One time I was really sick, I had this terrible pneumonia, and I thought if I didn't get better soon he was just going to lose it completely. I never saw anything like the way that man paced and prayed and smoothed my forehead, I remember I liked all that stroking, I thought, Wow, I'd better do this more often."

I didn't know! Miriam objected. Her child was sick and she couldn't feel it so far away. She'd have worried, too. That was the privilege of parenthood.

"And another time, he had this girlfriend? Ooh," Ronnee marveled. She narrowed her eyes to look back a long way, through who knew what kinds of rubble of memory. "She was this singer, this big woman, sort of getting famous. *She* said. Well, she did have some LPs, so I guess maybe she was. I don't know. Ormalu, her name was. Did you ever hear of her? Anyway, she was every way big, and she was dark, like this tribal goddess or something—tall, and big all around, with this voice on her, she came out of the choir, you know, she was almost this baritone. A lot of smoke in her throat. Very sexy. And she would walk around, she had this, like, kimono kind of deal, red satin and a belt that liked to sort of fall loose so you could half the time see one of her boobs, like accidentally-on-purpose. These huge, like, jellyfish squishing all around. She thought she was some kind of geisha or something in that outfit, only she didn't bow and mince around, she was more like this marine captain in drag. She vamped my dad, but she was so mean to me. Come here, don't do that, bring me a cup of coffee. I hated her."

Miriam was mesmerized. Was there such a thing as retroactive jealousy? She could imagine the way this woman would loosen that kimono over her mammoth breasts and let it drip from her shoulders and puddle at her feet. There was something kinky about Eljay's daughter talking about her. The apartment must have reeked of sex.

"So one day they have this big fight, and it's over me. She's mad because he couldn't take her someplace, I don't remember what it was—he had to do something with me, maybe some school thing or the doctor or something, I was only ten or eleven—but the

woman basically says, like—she puts it to him—this was so stupid—'Her or me.' Which shows you how little some women understand about the way parents love their children, right?"

Miriam couldn't tell if this was pointed or not. Ronnee looked
at her with innocent eyes. She gave every sign of having forgotten
who it was she was talking to.

"And then she comes to me, she sort of sneaks in when I'm in
bed, and she says, like, in this whisper like she's my best friend,
'Tell me, Ree, is he putting moves on you? You can tell me. You
two doin' the nasty?'" She covered her face with her hands, embarrassed. "'Cause here you are—you know—just him and you,
and you are *so* adorable, who could resist you!'"

I am so naïve, Miriam thought. And she's so matter-of-fact!

"She made me so sick. I didn't tell my daddy, it was too—you
know, gross—but I guess that 'Her or me' made him mad anyway.
So of course he says, 'Woman, are you crazy?' He says, 'You must
have all your brains in your boobs and your butt.' She was so mad
I remember she threw something at the mirror in the bathroom,
the medicine chest, and it splintered all over, glass in the sink and
the tub, I couldn't walk in there barefoot for a month. And Daddy
took her records, these albums with her looking all come-and-get-
me on the cover, and he dropped them in the trash when he was
sure I was looking."

Nothing without making sure he got his credit, she thought, but
stopped herself. Unfair. The child was under threat and he had to
erase it. Miriam watched Ronnee smile over the memory as though
she had vanquished the woman herself. You could see her receding
into the comfort of the long intricate trust Eljay had built for her,
the comfort of their days, thousands and thousands of mornings,
summer, winter, spring, and fall, and evenings and long nights
spent asleep under the same roof.

"So what are the problems you're having with him these days.
Now that you're older. Back at your apartment you made it
seem . . ."

Ronnee hesitated. She took one breath and let it out, then another, larger one, wrestling with this invitation to betrayal. Ronnee

looked at her so hard she felt as though she'd been the one who asked the question. "Oh, it's about—he—forgets I'm not him, sometimes. He thinks his solutions to things ought to be mine, like we're exactly the same. Or if we're not we ought to be."

"The same." Patience. Let her define it.

Ronnee closed her eyes and said—it was strange the way the words emerged, all in one gust as if she had practiced them—"I have two parents, he doesn't like to remember that. I have—I'm two-colored, which he doesn't seem to notice much. He says everybody's got a lot of mixing in their background, but I try to tell him that's, like, *invisible*. Who they were that, what would you call it? Diluted them. How things—" She paused significantly "—happened. They don't have a parent they can see, the one who brings in that difference."

Miriam could hardly speak. She reached out to catch her child's hands and pull them close. Ronnee always smelled sweet, some kind of hair grease, every part of her scented, worried over. But her hands were lemony, their skin slicked with something citrus. Her large, cushiony palms were slack but not resistant. "But you didn't used to be able to see me," Miriam whispered.

Ronnee whispered back. "But I knew you were there."

Where did such fervent belief come from all of a sudden? She had said her father'd lied about her all those years; she had grown up on *not* knowing.

Ronnee, shoveling second helpings of meat loaf onto her plate, told Miriam stories about doing theater at St. Helen's. She had played Desdemona to a white Moor. The children of St. Helen's were proud of themselves for their reverse casting, but her father had called it a triumph of outdated liberal social engineering and an artistic absurdity, and of course he wouldn't come to it.

Then they'd done a sort of ballet-drama-musical of Demeter and Persephone, which she'd loved. First of all, the story. (Miriam strained to remember: The daughter separated from the mother, in the grip of Father Hades? Ah yes, that story. Perfect.) Then, Ronnee went on, myth worked where realism was questionable. Even her father couldn't pretend that color mattered when they were all faceless behind masks, Earth and Death, light-footed Persephone, grief-laden Demeter, their masks huge and high-colored, like warrior's shields. (Eljay's only complaint was to wonder when they'd find it in themselves to do an African myth.) It was hot under the masks, but it was thrilling to be so transformed, so removed from particularity. They wore black capes with bright-colored taffeta linings and ballet slippers, the boys and girls as interchangeable as the races. Anyone could pick up anyone else's cape backstage and wear it, though your shoes were your shoes for obvious reasons.

Slowly, slowly, Miriam assured herself, with time like this they would become acquainted. Ronnee's gusto over her food was reassuring. She would have to assuage her own hunger patiently.

Ronnee insisted on doing the dishes, eager to show off her prowess. "You have a dishwasher at home, right? You probably don't even know how to get a dish clean the old-fashioned way!" This was the cheerful girl she had been back in her own room in Brooklyn. Maybe this was simple bravery, Miriam thought, letting pain and anger flow over her, and then subduing them and getting on with it. She had had that kind of vigor at Ronnee's age and later, when she'd followed what she'd needed, against her parents' outcries, to Parnassus. It was Eljay who had let himself drown, and like a man going under he had dragged Miriam down with him. Now, buoyed up by her daughter, she was rising again toward the water's surface.

While Ronnee stretched out in front of the television set, Miriam sat herself down at the kitchen table to write to Seth and Eli and to Evie. Ronnee had a few books to read for Stanford, but she was resisting them as long as possible. "I do that," she admitted, "but I'm a good girl in the end and I always get everything done. Daddy don't 'low no slackers 'round the house!" She laughed self-consciously at that. Maybe, Miriam thought, it was a sign she was relaxing.

Then she remembered she hadn't called her mother today. It wasn't fair to take advantage of her mother's shaky sense of time. Didn't she tell her children promises were meant to be kept even if no one was watching?

The phone in her mother's apartment rang so long its trilling began to sound unreal, like a word repeated into nonsense. She couldn't have slept through that. It wasn't mealtime. A walk? A visit to Lillian's apartment? Miriam was probably overreacting—guilt would do that—but the hour's time difference meant she could catch Barry at work. She dialed him anxiously.

"Oh, Mrs. Vener," Sallie the receptionist said. "Dr. Vener just left a little while ago, I think he said—is it your mother who's sick? I'm pretty sure that's what he said."

Pretty sure! She was struck cold. Her heart lunged against its cage. Good God, she'd only just turned her back!

An hour passed, blank. She spent it pacing. Of course Barry wasn't home, he wasn't findable, and here she was down a dirt road two thousand miles from where she ought to be, in the other room a laugh track exploding, a stupid flood of noise, every few seconds. She restrained herself from making Ronnee turn it off.

And then it was her phone ringing and it was Barry, distraught, out of breath. "Your mother," he said. "Your mother. I was just there—"

"Where?"

"Memorial Southwest, the ICU. I didn't want to have to call, Mir, but it looks like it's her heart and—it doesn't look very good."

"I talked to her yesterday!" But not today; guilt heated her cheeks. Her mother had thought Miriam was about to drive over to see her. "She sounded so good!" As if it would help to complain.

"She was fine," he agreed. "But she's not fine now." His voice was so apologetic that even in the middle of her panic she was touched.

She had left her mother in Houston, worried only about whether she'd remember Miriam by the end of the summer. But why should she be surprised? She'd seen the way her mother's body had begun its crumbling, accompanying her mind loyally in its collapse. This wasn't ambush; not really.

"You think I need to come? Is that what you're saying?"

"It doesn't look good, hon. They can't get her stable. I don't know—"

"Yes or no, Barry. Please."

He blew out his breath slowly—she knew the way he considered hard subjects, as if he had to empty himself out to give them room to flood him with their implications. "I hate to say it, but yes, I think you probably do. You'd never forgive yourself."

He didn't say if what. "Oh God."

"I know it's lousy timing but I guess you'll just have to bring her back to Brooklyn and get on with all that—you know—later."

She wanted to think about her mother undistracted by the details of her own little life. "God, Barry, I don't know what I should do."

He told her how her mother had been eating dinner in the dining room, waiting for dessert, when she suddenly sank to one side and slipped off her chair. "Like a sweater or a jacket," Aunt Lillian had whispered, as if it had been an indiscretion best kept quiet. "Just crumpled." He told her about the kind of resuscitation she had received. He was trying to give her time.

She looked across at Ronnee, who was paying her no attention, her head back against the flowery couch as if she were sunning herself. "Oh, God, don't you sometimes wish you were a little kid and somebody else could make your decisions for you?" Probably he didn't; Barry was responsible down to his toenails, which he clipped into the palm of his hand on schedule every other Sunday night.

"I can't even give you good advice, Mir. You've got a lot of different obligations going, I know. This one's your call."

"That's what I mean." When she was a child, she'd had the terrifying thought that one day she'd have to go to her mother's funeral but—a thrill of panic—she'd need her advice, her mother's perfect advice, or she wouldn't know what to wear.

"YOUR MOTHER," Ronnee said, perplexed.

"My mother, yes. Why does that seem so strange? Do I look too old to have a living mother?" Ronnee couldn't tell if she was irritated or amused.

It hadn't occurred to her, though, that her mother was someone's daughter. She had spoken about "your family"—"your relatives" buried along the bayou in Houston with names like Horowitz or something with a "witz" and Jewish stars on their headstones, and maybe Jewish writing. It was too weird. She couldn't begin to picture any of it, not the bayou, not the rows of stones. Her grandmother was Ma Thelmie, who used to be thick and strong, built the way she was built only shorter, wirier, never out of her apron unless it was Sunday or midweek church meeting, and now dwindling but still and always herself, her skin the smoothest sanded walnut. Now here was another grandmother, faceless, bodiless, but hers all of a sudden, and technically—"technically" is a serious word, it has implications like justice and fairness that might be invisible to the naked eye—she was as much that woman's granddaughter as she was her father's mother's sweet child. She had two adopted friends who said their parents always reminded them that what made them parents was all the time and care and love, all the walks to the potty, the fevers in the night, the meals on the table, the "Watch me! Look at me!" obeyed. Sometimes their parents said that gratefully, sometimes bitterly, depending on what was in the air, whether their kids were giving them a hard time about their "real" parents or not. What counted, everyone agreed, were the minutes, hours, days of concern.

Not that grandparents didn't have those; she knew plenty who raised their daughters' inopportune children. Sisters raised them, cousins, friends: black people took in whoever they had to. Their openness, their generosity was one of their glories. White people, she knew, did not. Ma Thelmie did a year of that kind of time while her daddy was off in Ghana and Dakar, one of her best years, and would have kept her happily if her daddy'd let her go. Who was this grandma who had been spared? Had she wanted to be spared?

She reached down into her bottomless self and pulled up a question. "Does your mother know about me?" The lamp behind her mother's shoulder seemed suddenly to occupy all her attention.

Her mother's face always looked like she was expecting bad news. It was one of those faces made for perplexed frowning. "She does. I told you that."

That was tight-lipped; it didn't sound encouraging.

"Did she ever want to meet me?" How had her voice gotten so small?

A little cloud of truth passed across her mother's eyes. She was such a bad liar. Ronnee's acting gene must have come from her father's side. "She—asked about you just a little while ago. But remember? You were gone from me before she had a chance to meet you." Now her mother was the one who couldn't look straight at her.

"That's not the same thing as wanting to." She might as well be hard, what was there to lose. Heat from nowhere rising up her cheeks, she began to cough; she realized she had stopped taking ordinary breaths. She felt herself choking a little. Oh, let it not be the asthma, Lord, please let it not. A huge weight of depression came down on her chest, like a roller flattening everything—she called it The Big Zamboni—when she thought she was headed for breathing trouble.

"No, you're right, it's not the same." Her mother was struggling with herself about whether or not to be honest, it was easy to see that. Once you could see that, though, why not give it up—there was no reason to bother answering. Ronnee's feet suddenly felt oppressed. She leaned down and unbuckled her sandals. Her beefy toes disgusted her.

"So are you taking me home with you?" She asked this with her face still at ground level, fussing with her buckles.

"Home? To *Houston*?" She watched her mother's pretty, pale eyes widen with alarm.

"No, to Timbuktu." She knew she should be sweet and pleading but she could not plead. "I'm not going back to Brooklyn, I can tell you that. So you better take me with you or I'll have no place to go." The suggestion stunned her even as it emerged from her mouth. But they hadn't gotten anywhere close to—she didn't know what to call it—the money thing. It had been a while since she'd even thought of it, until tonight, in fact, when her mother grabbed her hands and she'd coughed up the speech she had carefully planned and couldn't wait to use: Oh, I always knew you were there! My father won't let me be me! So what was all that gushing about? Her mother just wanted a look at her, that was all, and then she was going to send her back. Was this lady scamming *her*?

She was so confused, spun around the way she felt when she'd had too much to drink. Nothing mattered more than anything else. Let it happen, whatever wanted to—it was all just beyond her reach, she controlled none of it. Why had she ever *begun* this?

"Oh, Ronnee, this isn't the time for that! How will I—I won't have time to introduce you, get you started—"

"Started? You think I need a coming-out party?" Her mother hadn't even planned to take her home into her life, she could hear that, her pauses were guilty little gaps in her poise. She was like a man who has a mistress and a wife and won't let anyone meet the woman he keeps. *Kept* meant *kept away*! Why hadn't she thought of that before? Why hadn't she seen that was why they were up here in the woods in Nowheresville, in Whitefolks' heaven? It was a good place to keep her a secret. She had been dumb enough to think it was a gift.

"Ronnee, think about it. I'm going to be totally unavailable to you. I am going to be—" Her mother's eyes teared up for her own mother. Her lashes stuck together in damp little clumps. "I'm going to be entirely involved with my mother, who may be dying. This is no joke. Do you *get* this picture?" Affronted, her voice was deadly quiet.

Ronnee was not pleased to be thought to be joking at a time like this. "Got it," she said, nodding in big mocking dips of her head. "Definitely got it. Lucky you, you get to be with your mother. Even if she's dying." Really dying, not dead like you, dead for my father's convenience, then alive again.

"Really, Ronnee."

"You don't want to introduce me to all your friends and your family. You're embarrassed. It'll be like that woman in the A&P and the jeweler all over again. 'Who's this *strange girl*? Where did all this *blackness* come from?'"

"You know that's ridiculous. It's only a question of timing. This is not the time—" She lowered her voice confidentially. "I won't be able to concentrate on anything but—"

"You weren't ever thinking of taking me down there before this happened to your mother." It would have been better not to be right. She knew she was not being ingratiating. Though maybe guilt would make the check bigger. *That guilt gelt.* "Does your *husband* even know about me?"

Caught. It was hard to keep your embarrassment to yourself with skin like that: Ronnee watched the color drain from her mother's face and then flow back into those petal cheeks the color of watermelon. "How can you ask such a question," Miriam said. It was a comment, not a question. "That's offensive."

"Well, how should I know?" She was pushing too hard. "And what would I know about mothers? At least you had a life together."

Her mother was quiet awhile. "Ronnee, you know, you're very self-absorbed. I had no idea you were such a petulant child."

She had an answer ready. "You had no idea about anything, so why should this be any different? Anyway, that's what happens when you've got to be your own mother and take care of yourself and your father too. You have to be self-absorbed or who else is going to do it for you? You have to protect yourself." Oh, stupid, stupid, all this bitchiness and self-pity was not the way she should be sounding. Where were these tears coming from that she had to swallow back down? None of this was in her script.

Her mother was inspecting her icily. "I guess I would have liked to see you take a step back while I was having to deal with this. I'd have learned something very important about you."

Her father told her she was too mouthy by half but she was proud of that; she didn't respect wimps. She respected honesty. "Well, you did learn something, I guess. You just don't like what you learned." She had one more turn of the knife in her. "When you call the airlines, see if you can get me a window seat, okay? I want to see everything down there. Especially when we cross the Mississippi, seeing as I was born right near there." She managed to make her voice daringly innocent.

Her mother was a weak and obedient woman—no wonder she left her baby behind. Probably Ronnee would only have learned bad habits from her. She pinned Ronnee with a long unaffectionate glance and said, "You are going to regret this, and when the time comes I want you to remember just whose decision it was." But the only thing that mattered was that she went to the phone, as if Ronnee held a gun or a knife on her, and dialed. She made two reservations from Boston for early the next morning, one of them at the window.

THE MISSISSIPPI was all right, but life kept surprising you: there were other rivers, nameless, more achingly beautiful, that curved in great coiling crescents, silver where the light hit them the right way. She was spellbound. Her father got to fly around a lot, lecturing, but he never took her along: *You stay in school and get your work done.* Very convenient, so he could travel light. Well, goodbye New York. And what would California be like? She had seen it in movies but that was never the same, she knew that from seeing Manhattan (they never did Brooklyn) reduced to flatness, buildings just containers for whatever story they were telling, crowds with no crunch to them, no smell, no noise, no jangle. And when you saw them in the movies you were distracted, wondering how they could get all those people to ignore the camera. But now she'd have to work her way through Houston (for which she had no pictures, correct or not—who made movies about Houston?) to get to California. Your job, girl, she told herself. Your summer job. Sweeten your attitude. Dig and find some fucking gratitude. She couldn't remember why she had cared so much, yesterday, what this woman thought. Don't screw up now.

Her little white pillow felt like it was covered with a Handi Wipe. She pressed it to the window and put her head against it. Closed her eyes trying to imagine the Texas she was going to and got it wrong, from cactus to palomino to cottonwood tree.

THEY EMERGED into a crowd of black faces, dozens of families, it looked like, carrying silver balloons and flowers and a huge banner welcoming home REV. HOTELING from the Homeland. The reverend, dark as creosote, walked out just in front of them, a broad man whose black minister's jacket was stretched perilously across his wide shoulders. His dark striated neck was sweating. He erupted from the pleated corridor into a tumult of joy, his parishioners cheering, crowding around him as if he'd won the marathon. Ronnee and her mother came just behind, so that before they had taken in the scene it sounded as if the clamor was for them. It was humiliating to have been caught imagining such a thing, as if they were the heroines of something, even for half a minute.

A good-looking white man in a business suit and an open shirt collar, smiling wanly—anything would look wan beside the grinning reverend—was coming toward them, weaving through the clot of fans. She thought she saw him hesitate a split-second at the sight of them walking one behind the other, taking an instant to figure out that they were together. His head bobbed once and then he put on the look of someone eager to please, his smile so forced and fixed you could tell he'd decided on it, like an obligation. He gathered up her mother in a large embrace, making comforting noises as if she were a baby, patting her back. Ronnee heard him saying, "She's okay, she's better, she's much better."

When her mother removed her face from his shoulder it was shocked-looking, washed in tears. She smoothed his dark hair back from his forehead as if he needed comforting. He had one of those faces with perfect small features, too good to be true. There was a little gray starting up in the hair over his ears, but it was like his smile: just right.

"Ronnee, this is Barry. Vener. Barry—" And her mother gestured unnecessarily, because who else could she have been? "—Ronnee." Not "my daughter," just bare-bones Ronnee, shift-for-yourself. She was swamped with loneliness; it poured through her chest like one of those shining rivers they'd just flown over, damp and cold. She made herself breathe evenly, in, out, in, out. A little tight but not too bad. In—a little catch—out. You did this to yourself, girl. No complaints now.

He shook her hand as if she were a client or a patient or whatever. Bedside manner. "Oh," he said, blinking. "I didn't—this is—a nice surprise." So she hadn't dared to tell him when she called to give him her flight information. She never dared a damn thing.

The reverend's friends were bobbing around him like protective fish around the master swimmer, blocking him from view. But she could hear a rich phlegmy "Praise Jesus!" rise from the inside of his circle, echoed by a chorusful as they began to move as a phalanx toward the terminal, bearing along their precious cargo. The minister looked out over the shoulders that were hurrying him along, nipping a glance as if he were sneaking something forbidden. Ronnee was surprised by how old his eyes were, thickly lidded as a turtle's. Maybe it *was* miraculous that he had gone across the world and come back again whole. He saw Ronnee staring and, the heavy mechanism of his whole face widening sympathetically, he winked at her. Just then, stepping off the precipice, she found that look, which made no judgments, supremely comforting.

"WE'RE GOING straight to the hospital," her mother told her on the way down the escalator to Baggage. The way she said it, Ronnee could sense the little shift: No consultation, no apology, just an order, as threatened. A couple of days of good behavior, a couple of crises, and they were falling back into their real selves already. She was going to crawl home empty-handed.

Her first step outside the terminal was like nothing she had ever felt—no, wait: Mireille, when she took her to East Hampton, had a sauna, a little wooden house like a large wood-lined closet with benches and a door that closed with ominous finality. It was staggeringly, relentlessly, stomach-turningly hot and wet. You need snow to jump in when you're through, Mireille had said. Sorry, she'd laughed, the best we can do is a cold shower or a fast run down to the beach.

They lived with this, Houstonians? They *survived*? In that interval when, stepping off the plane, the out-of-doors penetrated the space before the jetway, she had felt as if someone were wrapping a damp towel around her. But then, instantly, there was the well-tempered terminal, which obliterated the memory of weather. Now, shouldering through the doors to the parking lot, the air was bright with heat; it was like a lightbulb, evenly glowing, and they were trapped inside it. She had to concentrate on her breathing for fear she'd choke on the dampness, the heaviness. In the two minutes or so that it took them to reach the car she could feel the sweat break out on her forehead, where her elbows bent, behind her knees. "Does it stay like this?" she asked her mother. Barry was fitting their luggage into the trunk of a BMW.

"Like—?"

"This—I don't know—it's like a furnace." She knew she sounded outraged, but that only seemed appropriate. Anyway, you couldn't insult weather or it would have died of shame long ago.

"Oh, it does, indeed it does. Till maybe late October." Was she gloating? "It'll probably rain late this afternoon, but it won't cool anything off. And then it'll be dry in about ten minutes."

Ronnee stared. Her eyeballs itched with sweat.

"It starts easing up before that, off and on. It gets beautiful, actually. Seven months of the year it's great here. But basically, darling, yes, you have the good fortune to be discovering summer in

Houston." She tried to remember summers at Ma Thelmie's in Alabama, but she'd been so little, running, swimming, drinking nice cold soda pop, that she probably never noticed the heat. Goddamn, if this woman was going to get that I-told-you-so look every time Ronnee was unhappy with something now that she'd won her way down here, this was going to be hell in more ways than one.

Everything she saw as the highway unwound was low, low and light, not bulky and brick. There were dozens of little businesses with signs that didn't tempt her: WORLD'S FINEST COLD WELD! GOD'S BLESSED FORGIVENESS PENTECOSTAL CHAPEL. She'd seen *The Last Picture Show,* but there did not appear to be any stores around the town square with sagging metal awnings or pickup trucks parked on the diagonal. No men spitting tobacco juice either, or cur dogs at their heels. The Pizza Extravaganza, Finger's Furniture Outlet, Video Exchange, nothing particularly Texan about it.

Her mother and her husband sat in the front seat talking quietly about the hospital, the fact that the dying woman didn't seem to be dying this morning. Ronnee supposed that was good, but then what were they doing here? They could have stayed in that nice cool house and taken their time trying to figure each other out and maybe she could have worked her way around to getting her hands on the keys to the safe.

They walked her mother to the swinging doors of the ICU, she and—what was she going to call him, Dr. Vener? Barry? Mom's guy?—and watched her go through them high-speed. They swung like the barroom doors in a western. She knew what it looked like on the other side, she'd been there twice when they'd nearly lost her to her stupid, stubborn lungs. It was like entering another planet, impossible to believe it was just a few steps away from the ordinary world, high-tension, that wild blue-white fluorescence, the machines that ticked or gave off, so modestly, a high outer-space wired sound, or beeped, or, strangest, were as silent as the glass tanks in the aquarium, and inside swam somebody's heart, their guts, their brain, reduced to lines and dots, spikes and terrible horizontals. The horizontals horizons, really. No-horizons. End-of-the-line lines. Dead ends. Urgent news up there on the screen, nothing you could touch or change by wishing, but there it was, a report of skin and blood and all those fluids coursing around, and oxygen, the one thing she never seemed to have enough of, reduced to some TV show, the old kind, black-and-white. All those victims flat in their beds while everybody walked around out here joking, eating potato chips from the machine, in the waiting room trying to read *Newsweek, Field and Stream.* Nobody concentrating.

She was terrified of all of it, she shivered at the memory of laboring on the other side of those doors just for the privilege of breathing. Instead of getting used to it, she was more and more afraid to think of herself in there. And who was the grandmother of hers hooked up in there, wavering? Her link (said to be, alleged) to the centuries. This old white lady who didn't want to meet her. Out of the blue like this, was she really supposed to care?

"So," said Dr. Barry to her, as though they were finally someplace they had tried to get to.

"So," she answered. They sat themselves side by side in the little waiting room, an alcove really, adjacent to the hall, on pink and purple leather chairs, Life Saver colors. Tropical fruit. The worse the news people were waiting for, the brighter the colors. Subtle. "You weren't expecting me to come."

He smiled and shrugged. "Well, these last-minute arrangements. You know. I guess I didn't have all the details." She had the feeling his politeness was a scrim, it was called backing and filling. He was not happy to see her. "So, uh, Ronnee. Have you spent any time in hospitals?"

Oh sheee, she thought, surprise me. This was going to be an interview. Or a blind date, the way some people sit down and work to get to know each other, or at least know the parts that are left visible to the naked eye. When her mother came at her that way in the car going to New Hampshire she had tried to disappear, pretended sleep. How do people get to know each other, anyway? How could that be something you forgot how to do? Forcing it was the bad joke. She thought of her father—how could she ever have learned him this way when their lives were made up of—how many minutes? She would do the math on it: eighteen years, four months, twenty-two days, how many hours times sixty minutes in an hour. Wait, divide or multiply? Math was not her strong suit. The point was, she saw him at seven in the morning when he needed his coffee. Saw him sick with flu. Joyous when Aretha did four encores at the Apollo. Shaking his head Yes! over her chocolate cake. Just looking out the window at nothing, a man alone. Trying to teach her some things and unteach her others.

She told this stranger about her asthma, the minimum, without emotion. He was remarkably unintimidating, one of those people who perpetually look slightly amused, even—maybe especially—when they're uncomfortable. What her friends would call a Clean Machine. And very hard to read, that good-looking face swept clean, no particularities to it—a sort of general white guy's presentable face, narrow-nosed, his lips almost carved in their precision, his eyes the exact blue of a vase she kept cattails in, fake Chinese, given her by an ex-girlfriend of her father's. His women patients probably fell in love with him—he had the slightly superior look of that guy who played Superman.

He was afraid of her, that was pretty clear. Something—a millimeter's worth—about the way he held his body. Unconfidingly. Self-protective. The angle of his head that kept some privacy, the look in his eye, ready to be alarmed. Maybe it was acting that had taught her how to be attentive to the cant of a shoulder, the way the eyelid sagged or pulled up into a stare. You learned, when you acted, that everything meant something, and left visible hints everywhere. Her acting teacher had shown them the work of an artist, she couldn't remember his name, but he painted portraits made up of little tiny boxes, grids, he called them, full of secret squiggles like another alphabet. The world, her teacher Ms. Dexter said, was like that: each inch was filled with information, ready to be deciphered. If she'd been playing *wariness*, it would have come out the way Dr. Barry looked. She was so sure she could trust her instincts that sometimes she thought that if acting didn't work out she should be a psychologist.

"So—am I going to like Houston?" At least if she asked the questions she might control the boredom factor a little.

"That'd depend on what you like to do, I suppose. How do you like to spend your time?" He pulled farther away from her, not closer, his hands in front of him like This-is-the-church-this-is-the-steeple. It gave him a kind of uninvolved look.

Shopping, she wanted to answer. Spending your money double-time. "Oh," she said, and waved her hand vaguely. "Museums. You know. Theater."

"You act, I understand." Poor boy, so stiff. Was it *who* she was or *what* she was that had him scared?

She was going to scream. I'm acting now! She bit it back. The best acting is invisible. But then he was too, acting, in his way. He was being polite but he didn't want her here. She was making him nervous. (Maybe, actually, it was *whose* she was?) Careful, she told herself as they sat shoulder to shoulder waiting for that other stranger to come through the double doors and save them. Don't blow this now. She had screwed up everything since she'd met her mother, or almost—she had had a plan that needed steadiness but she'd been inconsistent and unlovable, all those angers bursting to the surface against her will like this Houston sweat, and now where in the world was she?

Why had she thought this would be easy?

HER MOTHER CAME around the corner into their alcove looking haggard and relieved at the same time. It doesn't take long to age. Ronnee could see how hard times took permanent chips out of a face, scratched out roads that would never be smoothed. Her mother's mother was awake. She couldn't say much, what with tubes and electrical wires and the effects of general terror, but she was still here, her eyes focused and grateful, and her tests were encouraging. Maybe it was all a false alarm, or an exaggerated warning of things yet to come. "But I'm so glad I'm here!" her mother kept saying, elated. "I'm so relieved I could see her conscious."

RONNEE SAT against the oily-smooth upholstery of the backseat of the car, invisible. Lucky man, she thought about Dr. Barry, that he can just take time off from work to drive his wife around. She wished she were sitting in her little blue-and-yellow kitchen with her father, elbows on wood, chattering over a plate of something spicy, crumbling her own very superior corn bread between her fingers. He was a good listener unless you were fighting with him, when he could only hear himself. He tilted his head and got a curious look on his face, a funny quizzical narrow-eyed squint, fixed on the distance where he must think the answers were coming from, that kept you going forward saying more, trying harder to make things clear. He asked questions, sometimes surprising, sharp ones, till he *got* it, and then his satisfaction just bloomed and took you inside it. Everything this mother of hers had said up there in the graveyard might be true, that whole righteous story, but wasn't it clear it was all because of how much he loved her, Ronnee? How angry could you get at a man who just wants his child with him?

She didn't know about her mother's excuses. People in books, in the little history she knew—mothers—throw themselves in front of lions, of steaming trains, of armies and rapists with knives and every other danger, fire and flood, to protect their children, and her mother was saying *politics* was to blame? A social movement? A bunch of guys sitting in the living room beating on a drum and making fun of her? A nasty poem she heard on the radio?

But not politics, really. Be fair, she cautioned herself, it won't help to be simpleminded. (They were speeding past more uninterrupted shopping centers than she had ever seen, low and bright and modern, sign upon sign, letter upon letter, in the blinding light. Didn't they do anything down here besides spend money?) Be fair, it was confusion, it was not knowing what was best for *her*, and that must be a kind of love, too, when you know what you want, but you're not sure it's the right thing to want: like her father had said, that Solomon story. She had always thought it would be cool to have two guys fighting over you, but look, these two did nothing but suffer and make the other suffer until one of them let go. If it had been a physical fight and she'd been in the middle, they'd have pulled her arms right out of their sockets. What do you say to the one who tells you, "I have to let her go or I'll hurt her"? What do you say to the one who says, "I can't let her go"?

The back of her mother's head was glossy, her hair almost mirrory. She didn't envy white folks anything but, once in a while, their hair. A lot of girls with a white parent got their hair, or at least a little of it, but that straight gene had surely passed her by. What would it be like to have a fine wispy cap of it that didn't need ironing to get it straight, and didn't end up stiff as a board? No one she knew would admit to such envy, but they'd lye themselves to a crisp to get halfway there. She let hers be, wouldn't fuss with it; whatever its grade, it was what it was, her trademark, securely hugging her head, the world of the Jheri Curl be damned, but still. It was like all the other things white folks didn't have to think twice about. Her mother's hair bobbed as she talked to her husband about levels of test readings, medicines, nursing care.

Ronnee knew her mother was right, it was stupid for her to be here just now, and this husband surely didn't want to see her—not now and maybe not ever—but she couldn't let her peaceful memories of her father blind her to the way she left him; she could not go back defeated. He didn't know she was here and she wasn't telling him, either—he didn't need to know how close she was getting to the gold. But he would gloat if she came home empty-handed: *See, Ree, your white family doesn't give a good goddamn.* She was tired of the way he left her on her own—finding St. Helen's all by herself. Of how he simplified her. She was tired of bearing the whole burden of reminding him she had another side to her, however weak and unexercised and maybe purely physical, genetic, whatever you called it, with no one to help her represent it. She was tired of being intimidated by his defensiveness, the guilt trip he liked to lay on her that accused her of not honoring him and his blackness: Whiteness didn't need her, that's what he thought. Blackness did, as if they were talking about a winning ball club: *Yo, the Yankees win too many games, they have too many fans already, so come on over here with us!* She sagged for a minute, exhausted, at the memory of his contempt for the part of her that was not his. Well then, wasn't that how her mother must have felt? Badgered? Taunts from strangers in the living room, from him (you'd better believe it) in the bedroom? The best and worst thing about him was the way he wouldn't ease up, wouldn't give in. Maybe he'd still be back in Euphrates if he didn't have that iron grip, but cotton-chopping wasn't *her* history. It wasn't fair.

The more powerful Eljay, the harder they had to fight their way out of his shadow, both of them.

She wished she could reach out and touch her mother's dark head, stroke it for just a second, make it familiar.

UNREAL! She had been in an apartment once, up on Madison Avenue, that looked a little like her mother's house; it belonged to some big recording executive her father had had dealings with. Their coats were taken by a black man, their drinks served by a black man who was nearly tripping over his dignity, their dinner prepared by Hispanic women she could just glimpse hustling around the kitchen in their green uniforms with white collars and cuffs like restaurant workers. She wished she could go sit in the kitchen with them, the scene with the scurrying, fake-elegant servants made her so uncomfortable. (Did they hate the people they were pouring drinks for or was it just a job and happy to have it, thank you?) Instead, she had spent most of the evening inspecting every bought object on the tables, on the walls, pushing at the atomizer on the dresser in the bedroom hoping it was perfume, not cologne, petting the leaves of the live lilies in the bathroom, peeking into the closets and fingering slippery sleeves in the dark. (She had a fantasy that she'd reach in and a hand would grab her, a strong hand attached to a gorgeous body. Yesss!) If you owned all this, did you still see it? What did it feel like not to need anything you couldn't get?

But this house (without the bought faces, thank God) was in her family! After an elaborate winding through neat, flat streets—she was going to have to revise her expectations of Texas, she could see that—the house was long and low, white edging toward a silvery gray, it seemed to go in a few directions, set back amid complicated greenery, bushy, sleek, a dozen kinds of trees and shrubs, and flowers in neat swoops and circles, planted by the dozens—the hundreds—like something in a park. Certainly you'd need a gardener for all that. She couldn't see her mother on her hands and knees poking all those pink and red flowers—whatever they were, some giant kind of impatiens?—into the black soil.

She could feel her pulse race. Everything surprised her: The massive wooden door, so casually opened, like something on a damned Italian church. That gray pocked tile in the front hall as if they were still outside, the silver-framed photographs (she would have to study their subjects), the colossal vase of flowers, an urn really, iridescent as mother-of-pearl but nubbly and rough as stone, in the middle of the dining-room table, which itself was amazing, a sort of puzzle of metal slabs fitted in odd shapes like a mosaic, silver, brass, copper.

It was a museum. You didn't tell me! she wanted to shout, as if she'd been cheated. Or ganged up on. You didn't say you had all this! She stood in the doorway to the blindingly white-and-metallic kitchen and, though she had no idea why, felt tears rise thick in her throat.

"Ronnee?" her mother said from behind her, and dared to take her gently by the shoulders and hold them while she turned her around and combed her stricken face. She had barely ever touched her before. "What's the matter, dear? Are you all right?"

But Ronnee couldn't say. It struck her vaguely that she was in this deeper than she'd intended. The grandeur of the house made her feel like a thief in earnest, because there was so much to steal. An extortionist wouldn't even have to feel guilty taking this on, like robbing a big powerful bank. It didn't make sense, but it fueled her with shame, her shabby need, her hunger. She wasn't poor, she wasn't hurting, she loved the colorful, worn, honorable apartment she and her daddy lived in. This was so beautiful she didn't want to want it. None of it made sense to her, she only knew all this was another life, a different kingdom. There must be some other way to get what she needed. She wished she could creep away, murmuring, "Excuse me, I was mistaken, I didn't mean to intrude."

And then her mother said the strangest thing, her face desperate, gone pale, as if she were sneaking a word out to a rescuer. "Well, child," she said softly, just to her. "Welcome to my dungeon." When the words were finished, like a flash of light after which the silence was a kind of darkness, Ronnee wondered if she had dreamed them.

IN FAIRY TALES, the princess is tranced sometimes—becomes a swan or a scullery maid until she is discovered and returned to her rightful place. Far out in the "guest wing," Ronnee, sitting on the bed (abstract red-and-purple quilt she could not imagine needing unless the air-conditioning got out of hand), felt just the reverse: She was the scullery maid bewitched into a princess. Everything shimmered. There was no dust, there were surely no scuff marks. There was no age. The house in the country seemed eternities away, its knocked-around furniture suddenly an affectation, a kind of slumming. These pale wooden floors, shiny as the country pond, were covered by small rugs with whole worlds in their patterns. She and her father owned one worn Oriental, whose light had dimmed as it faded. It had lost clumps of white fringe like something going bald.

There was a great deal of clean white space broken by pen drawings and small discreet paintings in narrow wooden frames that matched. On the wall across from where she sat hung three Indonesian shadow puppets on invisible strings, elaborate, delicate, their limbs bent in angular impossible positions, their costumes lush with red and silver. Their eyes were huge and fixed, looking straight ahead as if they might stumble if they didn't concentrate.

If this was the guest room—one of the guest rooms—what did the real rooms look like? Did the children own whole toy stores of goods, closetsful of Lord & Taylor outfits? What did her mother's bedroom contain? Jesus, her dungeon? What did it not contain?

This could have been her life.

Of course, it was hard to keep track of whether the life would even have existed, the opulence, the ornament, the rooms large enough to feel like the sets of sitcoms, if she had stayed with her mother. That was a little like the old game of "I could have been another man's—another woman's—child." It wouldn't have been *you*, then, so you couldn't ask the question. You'd be somebody else. This was headache territory, like looking at the stars up there in New Hampshire: a truckload of pebbles strewn too thick to count, too dizzying, too threatening to her own warm dear familiar self. *What if* and *if only* were unkind, impossible, meaningless, but so tempting. They only confused you.

Still . . . Let's just say, because her mother did have money of her own even before she met this Very Successful Doctor, they had gone off together, she and this Miriam Starogin. First off, Veronica Starogin. Reece-Starogin? Maybe just Reece. Maybe Miss Miriam would have given him that much.

Would she, Veronica Whoever, have been white, then? Not to look at, not to *be*, deep down where the nub of her lay like a small jewel somewhere (she always imagined it) inside her chest. Nothing to picture, but still it was there like the medieval red jewel of a heart, ruby probably, up at the Cloisters, held close in a velvet-lined "cask," open to view in its glass case. Apparently they really believed they had stony hearts that you could hold in your hands, those beautiful men and women who lay, yes, stone themselves now, on top of their long gray sarcophaguses. Sarcopha*gi*.

But this mother would have kept her black. Neatly, exactly half black. As much as she could. Bought her the records, taught her to love her nappy hair, to revere the Heroes and Heroines. And she'd have had a Bar—no, Bat, wasn't it?—Mitzvah. Her mother was so responsible—brave, clean, radiant—wait, reverent—(she always forgot the others) that she'd have lived up to every obligation like something in an instruction booklet. They'd have had an apartment in some enlightened integrated neighborhood where a lot of other nut-brown mongrels like herself would have, starting in preschool, had safe private-school educations and played diversity games. Which was the way it worked out anyway—funny—only she was on the other side of . . . something. What would have been different, what would she have had besides a closetful of better clothes, probably, and trips to cities she'd never seen?

But growing up rich was only one part. It was probably like being tall. Her short friend Seretha told her she had to realize she saw completely differently from up there, from a kind of limitlessness, that short people were looking at a whole different world. The faces she saw when she went to sleep would have been white. That was much more important. The sound of voices, the words, the music of their speech would have been white, black forced in around the edges. It wasn't a question of good or bad, angry or reconciled. She would just be made of something else, cell by cell. In one of her classes—at St. Helen's they had a little psychology, a little philosophy—they had talked about essence and existence, which came first. Had argued, had diagrammed, even shouted. It was her essence she was trying to grab at, then, the one that precedes existence. A bubble, a rainbow, that red heart in the cask that wasn't really a heart.

Daddy, she called inside, help me say. How could it have worked out any other way and she be here to ask the question? Could she see the back of her head without a mirror?

RONNEE VENTURED OUT of her room late in the afternoon. She had fallen asleep for a while on the red-and-purple quilt, whose pattern stamped her cheek like a stencil, and when she pushed open the door she found the house quiet. Since her mother didn't seem intent on giving her a tour she felt entitled to poke around herself. Her bare feet made small sticky noises lifting off the stony floor. Kitchen first, then—she could see if there was something to snack on.

A young woman (browner than she, her round face smooth, her eyes faintly Asian) was pushing plastic bags into a bottom drawer, humming tunelessly. She wore a straight blue skirt, too long, and a sleeveless lavender blouse swarming with huge carnivorous-looking flowers: distinctly Kmart. She had ferociously glossy hair that looked as if it weighed a ton. It was pulled back hard, cinched with a green plastic barrette shaped like some kind of dog, from which it spilled down her back in a straight sluice.

Ronnee stood in the doorway trying to figure out who she was.

But "Who?" the young woman asked her first, straightening up all of a sudden, in the peremptory tone of someone delegated to be a protector. The vowel was full of complicated angles.

This would be the first time she had said it to anyone except that nasty jeweler in New Hampshire who wouldn't believe her. "Her daughter. Mrs. Vener's." She poked her head in the general direction of the bedrooms.

The young woman was not too proud to stare. "Daughter," she repeated frowning. She was computing, silently, alone in the thickets of a language that disclosed its secrets reluctantly. *"Hermana?"*

"No. Daughter. *Hijo?* No, wait." Panicked, Ronnee flipped through her Spanish flash cards. *"Hija.* Right. *La hija de Señora Vener."*

The woman closed the drawer with her knee. She had been holding a bulging plastic grocery bag and, on a long thin strap, a tiny elegant patent leather purse that had probably lived its first life in the señora's closet. She lowered them to the floor with a little thunk so that she could stare harder.

"Ronnee Reece. Who are you?"

The young woman was a long time answering. "Elpidia," she finally said solemnly. *"Trabajo*—working here." She waved her arms to take in the room, or perhaps the whole house. "For Mrs."

"Ah." So there were servants here. Of course: gardeners for starters. And indoor help, was that really a surprise? There was probably a whole cast of characters: drink-servers, cooks, door-openers, ass-wipers. Keeping houses like this was not within the capabilities of the people who could afford to live in them.

Elpidia was a sturdy young woman. She held her ground confidently in her worn-down huaraches, each toe distinct as a filbert. "The daughter—" She gestured as if there were possibly someone hiding in the wings "—Evie."

"Yeah. Well—right, there's Evie. But there's me, too."

Elpidia nodded acceptingly, as if she had been given an order.

"Okay if you say." She picked up her bags again without taking her eyes off Ronnee, in case she might try to get away. "Houston?"

"What?"

"You live Houston?"

It was painful to talk this way. She hated it that this woman sounded amusing trapped in the wrong language. Her life was not likely to be so entertaining if you could see it up close. "No," she answered slowly, enunciating carefully. "New York. Brooklyn."

A silent nod. The lives of employers were probably not expected to make much sense viewed from the kitchen or from behind the towels that made their way into the closets in their clean stacks. Elpidia walked to the door; there was something about her that Ronnee liked, some dignity in spite of all, though she was suspicious of her tendency toward sentimentality in the presence of—what was the word? Not inferiors, not underlings. The disadvantaged? (Elpidia had yielded no advantage.) The—what? Her father had been very strict about this: *Thou shalt not condescend, except to damn fools.*

"See you next time," Ronnee said encouragingly. "When do you—"

"Tomorrow I come." Elpidia turned decisively, then at the rear door swiveled back toward her. "Rooney? Say again."

"Oh, I like Rooney! *Ronnee.* Ah."

"Rah-nee. Ah. Okay." Elpidia nodded crisply, filing it away. She had, Ronnee decided on second look, an exceedingly lovely clear-featured face, like one of the saronged tropical goddesses in a Gauguin that had hung on her art-classroom wall last year. They all bent toward their master like servants, now that she thought of it. She was ashamed not to have noticed Elpidia's looks at first glance when all she could see before her was Hispanic Maid. (*Strange* girl, she thought. Strange girl like herself.) Maybe her father was right, going to that school had corroded the values he'd worked so hard to build into her. God only knew, this place could finish them off.

ONE DOOR off the major hall was closed: she assumed it was her mother and Barry's. Everything else was as she had imagined it, so cool and composed it seemed sealed. What was the word? Laminated. (What if the air-conditioning was really a gas, and everyone was dead? She alone, clever enough to wake herself up, had escaped. And Elpidia, innocent of the disaster, was on her way to the bus stop.) Maybe when her—she said it to herself deliberately—her brothers and sister were here the house got lively. Sloppy. You couldn't—shouldn't—do without mess. It probably seemed quiet to her mother, too, without them. Was she asleep behind that door? Had Dr. Barry stayed home to make love to her? Not likely, straight from the ICU. Whatever she was doing, her mother wasn't out here with her making her feel at home. She was being punished. Iced out. This was one vindictive lady, and not as weak as she looked. Like her mother's friend, what was her name, the one in Mississippi? Jewel—like she said: When she decided on something, this mother of hers could be a real ball-breaker.

SHE HAD TO LEAVE the door slightly ajar for fear she'd be locked out when she came back—better not be any thieves keeping tabs. Instead of cooling off, the heat had intensified as the day went on, like something ripening. There was lots of horizon. She discovered that her mother's block and the surrounding streets were more or less interchangeable, low and stylish and bereft of human presence, though maybe cars would soon begin to deliver husbands home from work, disgorging them—but oh, they would exit right into their garages and remain invisible, so you might conceivably live here forever and never meet your neighbors! No one would willingly walk where she was walking.

A hoarse-voiced dog was barking urgently in a back yard—how could you keep up that frantic noise all day?—but he probably bothered no one because every window was closed. The dog's owners lived in a preposterous house, a sort of ranch with pillars. Somebody's dream of a plantation must have had a violent encounter with his bank account, revising the scale of his dreams but not the dreams themselves. Here and there, though, someone had gotten carried away who *could* afford it: Who could live in that many rooms? Rich people, she supposed, weren't supposed to ask

What do we do with it? Having it, paying for it, making people
look at it and calculate what you'd sunk into it, all that was good
enough. A huge new building, rectangular stone, loomed on too
small a corner plot, its lawn still unhealed from the surgery. It
looked like some European villa; she'd seen pictures of that sort of
house with dukes' and earls' names attached, places called Eweton
Pemberton, Wambleigh-pronounced-Wambley, Egging, all that
English la-di-da. Her mother and Barry lived in a doll's house like
Evie's compared to this.

Maybe these people thought they were living in an episode of
Dallas. Dallas in Houston! People like that killed for their inheri-
tances. She paused beside the scarred lot. She wasn't planning to
kill anyone, but then how would you describe what she was doing,
actually? Extortion? If it was all in the family, did that make it different? Reparations? Blood money?

She stood waiting to cross the one busy street she had encountered, along which an unsettling number of fabulous cars sped by.
One dark green shiny something—was that a Jaguar?—slowed
well before the light, inched toward the curb. The window rolled
down and a man leaned across the passenger seat. Ronnee could
see his dark suit, his yellow-and-blue-striped tie. He was middle-
aged, serious-looking, like a banker or a school principal. He
called out to her, but she couldn't hear him with the other cars
hissing past. She moved closer with her hand at her ear. "What's
that?"

His voice was husky. "Half hour of your time?" Later she
wished she'd had the presence of mind to spit on his high-shine,
but she still wasn't sure she had heard right. Why would you pull
over to ask the time? "Say what?" Could it be she really leaned
down to hear him?

He wriggled himself over to the window. "Honey, I had a real
hard day. You come sit on my face a little, I'll—"

She didn't hear what he had in mind. She stumbled backward a
few steps and then ran as fast as her sandals would carry her down
the perfectly tended street with its nursery-perfected greenery, its
leaf-blower-clean driveways. Her chest was heavy with the effort

of breathing, and with disgust and a desperate wish for the broken glass and chained-on garbage-can lids and the idle, good-natured, protective leering of her neighbors. Be careful what you wish for, she'd heard that somewhere. Not that night, but off in the future when, finally, she hadn't thought of it for a while, she would dream of the man's prosperous face, its comfortable shine. It would break on her memory fat and soft as a balloon and there she'd be, arranging her thighs above him, over his cheeks, which would shrivel and collapse under her weight and, like a blister that you push down on, rise somewhere else until it burst.

THEY WOULDN'T LET HER spend as much time with her mother as she wanted—needed—while she was in the anonymous, brightly lit ICU, but once she was taken to a private room Miriam could sit beside her bed for as long as she chose to. She had no idea what the usual response to dire danger ought to be; it was as if her memory of the actions of others had been blasted away by the heat of her fear for her mother. Sipping cold coffee the color of an army uniform, she reached for anything useful, which didn't turn out to be worth much: vague memories of her mother's collapse at her father's death; how, under the influence of far too much Valium, which was new to her system, she survived the wake-like shiva with a frozen face and an unintelligible voice Miriam had found alarming in its little-girl helplessness. It was the only time she could remember seeing her mother disheveled in public, her hair uncombed, lips unpainted, the vague smell of sweat gusting up from under her blouse. Shiva, after the prayers, was an endless week of absent greeting, limp thanks, her mother thinning before her eyes, refusing the ritually proffered food their friends and relatives arranged on the dining-room table to enjoy themselves: Nobody starves at shiva except the widow.

Not that she hadn't known he was dying—that was the thing that had astonished Miriam, her mother's unpreparedness. His pancreatic cancer had invaded every space of her house even as it rampaged through his body, but his death had fallen on her nonetheless as if he'd been ambushed, and she with him. You'd think he'd died in a plane crash or a head-on collision. Miriam hadn't known what to make of the spectacle of so much—was it love? Anger? Panic for herself? When the season of mourning passed and her mother was back to herself, social and smiling, she had disclosed nothing. She was single-minded, devoted, many fine things, but she was not introspective, nor generous when it came to speculating about why she felt what she felt or did what she did. Later, when Miriam was up east, she met people who were surprised to hear there were Jews in Texas. "Oh, listen, I have a cousin Bubba," she told them. "And some of them can do the belle thing as well as Amanda Wingfield. They even sound like Texans. When my mother hangs up the phone she says 'Ba-ba.' Believe me." Some, she thought, eat their hearts out in secret like ladies.

Her mother had told very few stories from her own childhood, though maybe they'd be flooding back now that she couldn't remember what she'd had for breakfast. Miriam's grandfather had worked very hard as an insurance salesman in difficult times and made bad wages. Before her grandmother married him—this always seemed so unlikely, which was the very point; she and Miriam's mother, with effort, obliterated its memory—she ran a little general store out in the wildcatting oil fields of East Texas. Who could believe there had been Jews out there with those men in the hard, bare, flatland camps surrounded by the swamps and the Big Thicket? But maybe this was just some extension of their old habit of running dry-goods stores in small towns. Miriam grew up hungry for stories, but she never got any. This much she knew, though: This grandmother was cold and withholding (for her own sad reasons, she supposed). Maybe that harsh place made her that way: She imagined barroom fights, imagined dirt and extremes of heat and cold, the cry of panthers in the woods at night—there are still panthers in the Big Thicket that are said to sound like women howling—and the sour smell of oil heavy on the air. Her grandmother was a young woman who had grown up in Zhitomir, in Russia, where she'd lived a delicate life but was hungry all the time, and suddenly she was here with these awful, rough goyim, who were probably starved for women and dangerous. But she was all through with that when Miriam's mother was born, she was back in the city in ordinary circumstances, a member of a synagogue, married to that insurance-man grandfather, and living up in Woodland Heights, near the bayou, in a neat little house Miriam had seen, with at least a little lacy decoration over the porch. Her mother kept a framed picture of *her* mother wearing a suit cinched at the waist and one of those terrible foxes women used to wear around their necks, with the head hanging down, and the little feet with shiny black nails on them. She could not imagine how one woman could live through such changes. It made the dangers of Mississippi seem incidental, if only because she had willfully borrowed them. She had chosen. No wonder her mother, who had escaped extremity by only half a generation, always said she had gone looking for trouble.

Miriam's mother, Esther, was considered an ugly child, which was impossible to imagine, but it was what she loved to say about herself. It made Miriam marginally sympathetic to think how overcoming her wretched looks seemed to have been the great drama of her life. "I looked like a little cat when I was a baby. I looked all gnarled up, my spine curved, you can't imagine, my hair was limp as weeds out of water until I was about sixteen. My mother said I was the runt who wasn't supposed to survive." *Looked, looked, looked.* But—her *hair* was limp? Miriam, in her self-righteous period, thought her standards were too high, or maybe a little too specific.

That was all she got as a teenager, no warm cuddly stories, no extravagant family myths about pogroms survived, the Holocaust averted. Just getting some *body* into that hair. No wonder she had gone looking for trouble and found more than she'd expected, she thought, and for a while attached blame where she knew, now, she should not have. Every generation's task seemed to be to wipe away the path the last generation had made. And then, she thought, when enough mistakes had been made, to slowly begin to discern it, grateful for a wisp, a spoor, a ghost of a footstep or two to follow.

SHE REHEARSED responses to illness and dying—her friend Jenny's dignity at her parents' obliteration on a highway near

Austin, where they had retired; her cousin Ben's devotion to his mother during the long slow seepage of her personality as Alzheimer's took her away cell by failing cell. None of them had taught her how to behave right now. She thought her panic somehow unseemly—her mother would have suppressed it until the very end—but it had seized her in spite of all, and would not yield. It occurred to her that it was guilt that had drawn her home, but wasn't it idle to wonder? Here she was, and things could be worse by far. It was time for gratitude and the reduction of her heartbeat to a normal rhythm. She had, since Barry's phone call, seen a huge wall-like tidal wave rearing up before her. Slowly, now, it began to shrink and recede.

She sat very quietly, relieved at her mother's waking but happy not to have to talk. Her mother was going to be all right: her cheeks had regained their color, her hands were warm, though they moved nervously, suspiciously, over the dull beige blanket as if she were searching for something lost. Her body was already less flaccid than it had been when Miriam first saw her. The doctors weren't convinced now that she had had a heart attack at all. The tests were inconclusive, but they said with some certainty that there had been no damage. At first Miriam was outraged that with all their fancy machinery they had no definitive name for what had overtaken her mother, but Barry smiled indulgently and reminded her that he had always warned her that more often than they had answers, doctors were adrift among probabilities, possibilities, and utter unassailable ignorance. "They spend more time ruling out than ruling in," he told her as if he weren't one of them himself. (Ophthalmologists lived with fewer mysteries, he insisted, a situation not of their own making. They lived among delicate procedures but not too many imponderables.)

Miriam sat in a kind of euphoria—her mother had not disappeared into oblivion as soon as she'd turned her back on her. For however long, she was still here. Nor had she really noticed Miriam's absence—her always-derelict daughter seemed neither more nor less than usually missing. And *her* daughter was found. There was an intimate satisfaction in these symmetrical facts that had nothing to do with the world outside the door. Exonerations, they came at her from both sides; they seemed to concern her survival, to present it to her as a gift: Here, you can still be a good daughter, though you ran out on your mother, a good mother, though you ran out on your daughter. We live. You will live. Motives, she realized with surprise, did not even enter in, nor how she and her blow-hot, blow-cold daughter were faring at any given instant. For once, finding her, she had done the right thing. She didn't expect anyone to understand this, how suddenly she sat, head back against the cracking gray pretend-leather of the chair in her mother's room, feeling the gaping, broken circle of her life heal closed.

AFTER A SUFFICIENT NUMBER of hours had passed, and a rudimentary conversation with her mother in which she had mostly murmured to her without words and her mother had shown her an unfamiliar beatific smile, Miriam sat in her car. She sat and sat, staring out the windshield at a thousand cars in the hospital lot. So many white cars, like ambulances, to bounce the heat back into the sky.

She certainly knew what it was to be depressed, but what did it feel like to be manic? Was this it, slow though her thoughts seemed to be coming, the way certainty had poured over her? Though she knew it was washing away prudence and regard for a few of the people she most loved, how she burned, a bright hot flame, with the necessity of doing this. And if it was mania, would she regret it when the flame of certainty subsided, as it surely would, into depression? So be it. She was going to announce her daughter publicly, joyously. Ronnee had prevailed, she was here in the flesh as she deserved to be. She was not going to hide her daughter. If she hid her now, wouldn't she have hidden her, as Eljay told her she would, back at the beginning?

But it was practical, really. She couldn't bear to imagine the slow drip of discovery if she didn't make a great sweeping disclosure, a preemptive strike against all those words whispered behind well-manicured hands. No one, for example, had called her brother and sister about her mother's crisis yet, which, she supposed, meant that she was assumed to be uncontested nurse, daily attendant, and, if need be, next of kin. It was just as well they hadn't been unnecessarily alarmed; now she could give them a tempered report and keep them from rushing to Houston, which they would surely appreciate. But she was going to have to work Ronnee into the conversation, too. She was their niece.

ALAN WAS EASY WITH THE NEWS. He tended to make a joke out of too many things—so Miriam thought, most of the time—but today she was grateful for his jocularity. "How'd you find her, Mim? Advertise in the want ads?" He didn't ask what she was like or how long she was going to stay: he tended to leave the emotions to his wife, who wasn't home today to shoulder the burden. But at least he had never been shocked or rancorous about Eljay. If her psyche wasn't his business, neither were the events of her distant life, which included her lovers. Whom did they hurt except for herself, he seemed to be saying. If she had been asking his help, she'd have had it in an instant. But she wasn't asking.

Joy was another story. Their ancient rivalries, which had simplified them into opposing types so early and unfairly, had become an unending rain of petty rebuke, not hostile—affectionate, really, in its implied concern. Still, it was faintly patronizing on both sides, as though neither quite believed the other capable of making a sound decision. "Oh, you didn't!" they would cry in mock astonishment at some insignificant action. ("I cut my hair." "I've decided to take an economics course and learn all about the stock market once and for all.") Folly, all of it, to hear the way their voices rose and fell.

But this time, when Miriam told Joy that her daughter had "re-joined" her—that seemed so neutral it almost sounded like a lie—Joy went perfectly quiet. Perhaps this development was too important to warrant her usual gentle hectoring. "Miriam!" she whispered, returning Ronnee to her status as embarrassing secret. For all her precocious interest in boys, Joy, married at twenty-one, had lived as conventional a life as Miriam's had seemed. How peculiarly things could turn out! Miriam tried to picture Eljay and Joy's Kenny side by side, as if for a snapshot, Kenny in his golfing plaids, Eljay in his dashiki. (These days, even Eljay might smile at that picture, but when she'd last seen him, wasn't that what he was showing to the world?) Joy was selling real estate now; she was so good at it that last year she'd won her family a trip to Orlando for highest sales in her territory.

Miriam decided to be candid and unironic with her sister, whose shock had opened her to an uncharacteristic show of sympathetic interest. "You'll meet her, Joy. She's an interesting girl."

Joy's curiosity was not to be slaked so easily. "Interesting, Mim? Remember when we were dating? Well—I mean, *I* do, anyway. 'Interesting' was a euphemism for every kind of dog."

"Joy!"

"Well, for heaven's sake, Miriam, what does 'interesting' mean?"

THEN, WHEN SHE UNVEILED RONNEE, there would be Barry to placate—Barry who, born a generation earlier, would have opposed fluoridation and daylight saving time. What, she was prepared to ask him, is reputation but the guarantee that you can preserve the life you are living? People are sorted into batches according to past and present behavior—acceptable, unacceptable, with a few mysteries allowed at the edges, people taken in provisionally whose papers, in a manner of speaking, are not quite in order. But if you don't care about that life—she could imagine his affronted eyes, his anxiously bitten lower lip if she were to say such a thing—how far should you go to protect it?

The problem, of course, was that he *did* care about that life, while she only cared for the people she shared it with. And he was furious at her. "I didn't know you were planning on bringing her home," he had whispered after their first visit to the hospital.

"You know I didn't expect it to happen this way, with no preliminaries. But I never—I hadn't decided anything about that."

"A lot of people never—"

She had cut off the discussion then and there. "A lot of people do a lot of things." And they had not dared go back to it. But she was obsessed with it.

Her friend Mona would call, or Debbie Pinsky, or maybe her cousin Amy. Whoever phoned first (had already called, probably, while she was drowsing beside her mother's bed) would search her out and ask, "Mir, what was—I have—a girl, it sounded like a youngish girl? answered your phone this morning, and she said—I asked who I was talking to, I thought, Oh no, poor Elpidia messed up another message and Miriam finally sacked her and got an English-speaker—but she said, I mean casually, like I wouldn't be surprised, 'Oh, this is her daughter. Can I have her call you back?' Just like that." Outrage. Affront. As if she owed them something.

To which she would reply "Mm-hmm" while her chest plummeted to her feet.

"So just what's the story, darling? Are you thinking of telling me?" A pause. "Is this some kind of a joke?" If it was Amy, she would make the angry supposition that Miriam was being victimized somehow, Ronnee a con artist out to bilk her and her relatives as well because (not recognizing depression when she saw it) she'd always known that Miriam was such an incompetent dreamer. "Who the hell is over there in your house, Miriam? This New York woman said she was—it's a good thing I was sitting down, I was at work but I wanted to know about your mom—so she said she was, listen to this, your daughter? Your *daughter*? What in the hell is going on over there? Does Barry have some kind of bastard child he's just let out of the woodwork?"

Amy was Miriam's least favorite, most demanding relative; what she demanded in her peremptory way was that Miriam be her girl-friend when, except for their shared family—Amy's mother was her late father's baby sister—they had almost nothing in common. Amy, like Joy, sold real estate. She seemed to lay personal claim to every grand house she had walked through for professional purposes, as if its owners were her good friends and her visits among them personal, even intimate, in nature. Her gossip was urgent: The mayor's wife was thinking of taking up her gold carpeting and

putting down an interesting sort of lavender, with a deep purple
for the stairs. The opera director who had a stunning view of Her-
mann Park from his condo was in the middle of an awful job, taking down the wall to another apartment—she spoke of it as if he
were tearing it down himself in his tuxedo shirtsleeves, getting
plaster under his nails—so that he'd have room for his—uh—companion, who apparently came with a good many accoutrements.
Miriam found the "uh" too coy by half for a seasoned trouper like
Amy. Imagine, she thought, what she'll do with Ronnee.

Anger seethed in her, suppressed all these years, dangerous to
have dared imagine indulging. These were the innocents she might
as well knock over with full disclosure. She didn't fear their reactions, really. Let them figure out how to adjust their vision of her
or not, she didn't care. She went to their luncheons, she sat lick-
ing envelopes when they volunteered their time for this or that
certified-worthy fund-raiser, the years ticked by in small talk over
diet salads; when they obliterated a "girl" whose behavior they
found inappropriate, she had sat silent. Around Yom Kippur each
year, when sins past and possibly future were being enumerated,
they were reminded that the soul of the person who listens to gossip is in worse danger than that of the tale-bearer, whereupon all of
them laughed and cheerfully consigned themselves to Gehenna.
They were decent women, more or less, who shopped hard, toler-
ated imperfect husbands in return for much that they valued, plus
the right to mock them publicly, protected their children against
every danger they could think of—a few did not allow their family
members to enter a 7-Eleven for fear a robbery might be in
progress—and had no designs to change the world. There was no
one among them she couldn't bear to lose.

It was Barry, who liked to speak of "professional standing" and
"good faith in the community," who worried her. He was *made*,
from boyhood on, to feel betrayed by hard truths. He was de-
fenselessly good, and would never be able to imagine what she felt
like waking from her endless, arduous, tranquilized sleep. Unable
to imagine good magic, he could never imagine bad. Or bewitchment. To be fair, she thought—she was still sitting with the air-

conditioning on, the motor off, daring her battery not to fail her; cars were beginning to empty out of the spaces around her—neither could most people. Those drivers, men and women bending to sit down in their sun-baked cars, would not comprehend any better than Barry what she meant by bewitchment. They had never known she was absent in the first place.

But how could she keep from hurting him? Having a secret, keeping a secret, was so forbidden to Barry when he was a boy that finally possessing one, Miriam understood, had made an almost sexual ripple across the smooth fabric of his life. Of course there were secrets in the grownup lives that abutted his: there are always, he slowly learned—didn't everyone?—drinking and philandering, covert disappointment in what, say, someone's children have made of themselves, or whom they've married; there are petty connivances and large, there is hedging and there is diplomacy, a benign form of lying for the sake of peace and kindness.

But he was taught, primarily by his mother, Darline, that honesty paid dividends, and he tried very hard to practice it. How, Miriam thought, could you not respect such lessons taught and learned? Occasionally, though, he sounded like such a goody-goody! As a teenager, he told her unembarrassed, he had ratted on himself after his first joint. He reported to his parents the names of his friends who drank when they weren't supposed to be drinking. He turned in, albeit anonymously, a cheater in his calculus class. About his amorous activities he was merely silent, a sin, if it was one, of omission that could be excused as protection of his girl-friends' reputations at a time when the hypocrisy of the double standard was a dangerous despoiler of good names.

When he met Miriam, he fell fast. From far, far away, she watched him falling without a sound, as if she were behind glass. She knew he had never encountered anyone like her, unless it was his cousin Sarah, who had tormented her mother by refusing to pledge her sorority at UT and then, as if to turn the knife for reasons no one in Dallas could discern, by transferring to Bennington, where she was reported to have fallen in love with a modern dancer named Harriet. That didn't last long, but she never did come home. She married a playwright (now on Wall Street) and stayed in New York, where she continued to favor long hair, long earrings, a faintly Bohemian commitment. Her parents grieved but were, if not cheerful, always civil, and even grateful that things were not worse: her love of women (or was it only that one woman?) had left no scars visible from Texas.

Even the way he met Miriam was thrilling. It typified everything about her that he would (daringly) come to love: she was a woman of banked fires. He was giving time in the ophthalmology clinic—he was a resident then—and this woman was in the waiting room one day, with twin colored boys, skinny and unhealthy-looking, who needed glasses, maybe even surgery, to correct their flaccid eye muscles. Who were they to her? he wondered, and discovered that she was volunteering in a neighborhood center, which meant that she did a good many things for people without payment, sometimes without thanks. "You're not a social worker?" he asked skeptically. The women he knew had paying jobs, at least until they married, or else stayed home arranging luncheons, arranging furniture.

"No. I'm a person. A social *person*, I guess." He felt rebuked by her matter-of-factness. She watched him flinch: her attitude was as stimulating as a quick pinch. This time she was making sure the power stayed in her hands.

The boys needed that surgery, as it happened—they shared their defect—and no one in sight had any insurance to cover it. "Don't worry," Miriam told Barry when he delivered his verdict on their condition. "We'll figure out a way." Which turned out to be a rather large check she wrote herself, against an inheritance she seemed eager to give away as fast as she could.

When they spoke about their "pasts"—he had none, he acknowledged, shamefaced, none worth calling that, anyway—she glided over a few years she had spent in Mississippi as if they were just an extended visit to another neighborhood social center. The only suspicious thing about the way she told him where she'd been until last June was that she cast her eyes down and away when she spoke of this college where she had taught history. Then she had vacationed in Mexico. She'd been away awhile and now she was living at home like a teenager. He liked her straight-on gaze, it was like her short shorn hair—her straight-on bangs, dark and glossy and unfussed-with, which were so unlike the flirty follow-me-down-the-garden-path looks of the Dallas women with their flipped-up hair and bobbed noses who were being so carefully groomed to be his fate. (She had lopped off her crazy mane, which felt irresponsible; memories snagged in her long hair like smoke. She thought she looked like a boy, which was fine with her. Better than fine.)

But when she mentioned Mississippi and this Parnassus College, she took on a very strange demeanor, like someone about to run away, someone in fear or danger. She seemed to hunch around herself holding her breath. He didn't dare ask, but he wondered if something terrible had overtaken her there. And he realized that when he asked why she had left Mississippi he never really got an answer; he couldn't have told anyone what she had replied.

Which was why she liked him: he knew how safe he seemed. Even his dark hair lay too smoothly on his head, his skin too perfectly on his so-symmetrical bones—he hated his handsomeness because it was so predictable, so uninflected. There was no menace in him. If she was the survivor of something evil, he understood he could be the perfect antidote. He was mildly insulted, mildly titillated. But why not take advantage of his decency, as if (having despised it all his life) it truly was the virtue he'd been raised to think it was?

Not the first but the second time they made love (because it was daytime and the light was better; they were in his apartment near the hospital; he was stealing time at noon and managed to convince her to come home with him), he saw the pale stripe down her sweet flat stomach that he knew was the mysterious flag of childbirth in olive-skinned women. "Miriam," he said, pulling back abruptly, staring down at her. "Miriam," he repeated, catching his breath, running his index finger gently down from her navel into the bed of curls below. "Is there something you maybe haven't bothered to mention about your life? Something—important?"

How calm he managed to sound, although his mouth had gone as dry as if he had a fever, and his heart beat as hard as if he'd been leaped on out of ambush. He felt like someone trying to keep his excited voice level to coax an animal out of hiding.

When she collapsed around herself, hiding her face, he un-wound her arms from her knees and held her to himself, his chest touching her pale small breasts, his forearms against her shaking shoulders, warming her. *All right,* he heard himself think so clearly he might have spoken out loud. *All right, I'll be your safety. That's what I'm good for. I'll never do you harm. Whatever the story, I'll see you as an innocent. I promise. You will not scare me off.*

And that became their bargain: Her secret, his cool cauterizing comfort.

Do you want to talk about it or not?

Not.

Her slight body already used, experienced, stressed beyond his wildest imagining. She was taking advantage of him, she knew. Her soul already handled, dented, scratched. He put his finger to her lips, then to his own. *Silence.* Tears in his eyes, he thanked what-ever nasty star had sent her to him.

FOR HER IT WAS LIKE A SECOND MARRIAGE, not the joyous kind that cancels old mistakes but a grateful accommodation, ex-actly as if she had brought along a child in need of shelter. But the child was invisible, its father canceled. Sometimes she wondered what Barry thought or saw when he imagined Eljay—probably somebody far different from who he was, enlarged along pre-dictable lines: bigger, darker, more ominous. She thought of Eljay's bow ties with their tense little designs all in a row, before the dashiki banished them; his finicky British habits: the nose-hair clipper. The shoe trees. He polished his sneakers, "whitewashed" them, she used to say. Even Barry didn't do that. She knew what he imagined, and it lacked subtlety: Why didn't he know danger could be subversive? It could even flourish alongside kindness like his own, unintended. The first time she'd been stripped of her self had been a shock, but that can't happen more than once: she'd walked into her second life eyes wide open. It was like a solid car, a sedan, with top-of-the-line tires that kicked back, a body that would not rust, that would go the distance purring. Her Volvo life, in which she drove a BMW.

"WHAT DID YOU TWO TALK ABOUT?" Miriam asked him.

"She didn't seem very eager to talk, actually. Her asthma. It sounds like it's under control but I guess it's been something of a problem." He shrugged. "Acting."

"Right. She takes that seriously. She won a prize at graduation. It's what she wants to do."

They were undressing. She'd have liked him to show his gratitude that she was back, cross the room across the distance of their going-to-bed routines, but he was looking preoccupied. "She'd better have a generous benefactor."

"Well—I am, I guess."

Barry looked at her hard. She was slipping her nightgown over her head, the bright light of her body extinguished in a wash of pale green silk.

"You are."

"I'm her *mother*, Barry." She gave him an incredulous half laugh.

"Which means—"

"What's that ominous 'which means'? It means I have some responsibility for—seeing her through. After all this time."

They didn't tend to quibble over money, but it was a subject Barry found more engaging than most. "Have you thought about what you're prepared to do for her?" He squinted as though someone were shining a light in his eyes. He was making her nervous.

"Prepared to do for her? Not really. Barry—"

"Has she mentioned money to you yet? Because I've been wondering if she might have—"

Goddamn. "Might have what?"

He hesitated, for the sake of delicacy. "Might possibly have decided you could be—"

He'd stopped himself; she hadn't interrupted him. "You know, you haven't finished a sentence in quite a while. Why do you suppose that is?"

He breathed out hard, exasperated. "And why are you examining my sentences like somebody reading entrails? Are you afraid she's here to take advantage of me?" This without any breath at all. "Do you think I can't take care of myself?"

"Not necessarily, where she's concerned. You wouldn't be the first mother to go off the deep end for a child."

"The mother. A child. What is the matter with you? Do we need an introduction?"

What he wasn't saying was that the money they were talking about was his, not hers. "We just might, now that you mention it. I thought you already had three children that needed taking care of."

"And you knew I had another when you married me. Who's been putting this in your ear, Barry? Jay?" She despised Jay Waxman, Barry's partner. He was the worst kind of racist, the insidious kind that belongs to the Anti-Defamation League and makes small defamatory jokes half-mockingly, attributing them, shocked, to other people who've forced them upon him. He had "taken advantage" of a patient once, in Barry's courtly language, right there on the office couch—she was, conveniently, the last patient of the day and (Jay had said) more than willing. But his only concern had been that she might decide to take some legal action; he was afraid he'd made himself a little more vulnerable than his brains should have allowed. "But ain't it the truth, Bar"—he'd said this with rueful self-congratulation—"we know this bone has no brain." Barry's repeating the story to her, Miriam thought—telling it to her in bed—was a little like the helplessness Jay affected when he passed on the crude jokes: This isn't mine, I'd never dream such a thing myself, but let me tell you what X said. . . . And Barry, she had always thought, was unduly influenced by Jay because he saw himself as naïve. Saw decency as weakness and honesty as "suckerdom." "Oh, he's a good guy," he'd say gamely. "Leave him alone." Which meant what, a good ol' boy, as in "boys will be"? Jay called her "Miri-Miriana," to the tune of "Oleana," mockingly, as if (though she dressed from Neiman-Marcus) he knew she was just an old-fashioned folky hippie, and goggled his eyes wide whenever he saw her. At the same time she could tell he thought her basically a virgin queen, a ball-breaker who didn't cut Barry any slack. Thus, in defense of his kind of manhood, he was automatically obliged to offend her. Now, having heard about Ronnee—so much for the virgin queen—Jay would have cautioned Barry to meet with a lawyer before he so much as saw the whites of her eyes.

"Why don't we leave Jay out of this and you tell me why you think she's pursuing you just now?"

She was ready for this. "Well, first of all, I was the one who 'pursued' her. Technically. But if she really tried to come looking for me—"

"You sound doubtful."

She waved that away. "My doubts, if I have any, are beside the point. This seems like a perfectly logical time, when she's graduated and she's ready to leave home." Leave her father's house, she wanted to say, but decided not to. "Although pursuit has kind of an ominous sound, doesn't it? Anyway, she's old enough now. She's . . . between lives, sort of. What's so strange about that?"

She could see little flames of concern flare in Barry's eyes, their pupils dilating and shrinking again, the way an animal's nostrils swell with suspicion. How could he have made her his antagonist? This was ridiculous.

"Barry. This is my life you're talking about like a rank stranger. Why are you doing this? Is it—what? Her difference? From you and the rest of us?" She was trying to keep her voice steady. "Because money isn't really worth talking about."

"Money is never not worth talking about."

"There are more important things, is all I mean. And if I'd had her with me all this time, just think of all the money—" She shook her head wildly to get the conversation off her, like something sticky. "God, this is too insulting. You're talking about my child, my baby, as if she's a—" She flailed around in search of something appropriately inhuman. "A property you're investing in. A product."

"Don't patronize me, please. You think I don't know that?" He kept tying and untying the string of his maroon pajamas. If she watched his hands she'd be hypnotized. "Haven't I been tolerant all this time? Haven't I been sufficiently understanding?"

"What did you have to be tolerant of? I haven't mentioned Ronnee in sixteen years. Anyway, do I remember that you had a choice?"

If he were another man, this was when he might have hit her. He had made a fist, which he looked at with alarm. "Did I have a choice? Yes, I had a choice. Nobody said I had to marry you, you know."

She sat down on the bed so that something could support her. "I thought we married each other." His passion on this subject could have been attractive—she thought this even as she cringed—if he hadn't had that petulant quality that made him seem more irritated than aggrieved. She suspected he thought winning the argument would put matters to rest. What could she say that would bridge the chasm: Think about your own children? If Seth or Evie or Eli had been raised by somebody else? But if so, then what? Such a situation was unthinkable. Hypotheticals were good for training lawyers, not for representing missing emotions. Fact, not possibility: Ronnee, who carried half her genes, was asleep down the hall in the guest room. She looked at him across a cruel distance.

And therefore if she leaped, she had nothing to lose.

"I want to give a party for her, Bar. People will be wondering about her, so we might as well introduce her in one fell swoop." Her legs shook as she told him that. Her heart beat as though she were being chased around the neighborhood. Barry opened his mouth, aghast, then shut it.

"We can have Ninfa's cater it, no trouble. They can do margaritas and the whole bit. We can have family, friends, everybody, and get it over with."

He looked at her as if she had brought a terrible smell to bed with her. "Ninfa's," he said, shaking his head hopelessly. As if he cared who catered the demise of their standing in the community, her life as a respectable woman, his marriage as a full and consenting partner. "How about one of those little crop dusters with a banner, while you're at it? Or a skywriter, maybe? I think you can get those pretty cheap."

"Barry."

"Barry. What's that supposed to mean, 'Barry'? Why are you making me the heavy in this? Do you think this doesn't concern me at all? Or the kids, doesn't it concern the kids—your *other* kids—this sudden compulsion for publicity? Do you want a headline in the *Chronicle*?"

She waited him out. He was good at outrage but not at follow-through. When he said nothing more, but sat stiffly beside her wearing his martyr face, she plunged on. "What did you think I was going to do with her, hide her in the closet? The garage?"

He sighed and turned from her, knocked his pillow down with his fist and laid his head on it as if it were a stone. "You never said you were bringing her here. We never discussed it. I don't see what you think you have to gain throwing her, I mean really just tossing her, into your life like this. There's such a thing as discretion, you know."

"I have a question for you."

"I have to get some sleep."

"Please, Barry, don't. Let me ask one question."

He grunted assent but didn't turn toward her.

"Is it her—" How could she ask this without being coy? "If she was just any child I'd had, would you—"

"Jesus, Miriam, what the hell does that mean, 'any child'? You sound like you were in the business of having all kinds of children, take your choice. You already asked me that anyway, talking about her 'difference.' Very quaint. Very roundabout. What can I say? She is who she is, and she's going to come as quite a surprise to a lot of people."

"So? That's their problem, isn't it? If it is a problem. Maybe they'll like her, though. Maybe they'll be intrigued."

He sounded exasperated. "Well, sure it is. Their problem. If it is one. And then it's going to be your problem."

"And yours? Is that what you're afraid of, people gossiping behind our backs? Or do you have a problem of your own with her?"

"Well, you've always been more tolerant than I have, haven't you? Moral questions don't really bother you much."

So finally there it was, stifled since the day they'd met, what she had expected in the very first place from him. But his bluntness took her breath away. "I'm afraid—" She swatted at her tears without dignity "—that's too cruel for a reply."

He twitched one shoulder at her, which she supposed was meant to be a shrug of sudden indifference. "Then don't say anything. You know, this is too heavy for this time of night, Miriam. Let's have a go at it tomorrow, okay? I've got to get up at six for surgery."

If hers had been the sleep of recoil all these years, of regret, of submission to the good girl she ought to have been in the first place, his—she understood now, dousing the light and promising that she'd try harder to sympathize with his bewilderment—had been the sleep of denial.

II

"YOU CAN MEET EVERYBODY AT ONCE," her mother had told her cheerfully, having seated her in the magazine-perfect sunroom, which was all white wicker and red tulips the color of her nails, bent gracefully as dancers over the side of their vase. "Some of them—you're not going to like them any better than I do, Ronnee, honestly. They're, you know, family. Even some friends are family by now, you know what I mean. And some not-so-friendly friends. They can be something of a trial."

Ronnee had made herself laugh. "Yeah, I know that kind."

"Others I love dearly. You'll like them if you get to know them at all. And I know they'll like you."

Well, we'll see, Ronnee thought. It wouldn't be quite that simple. She couldn't decide whether the party was meant to be a kindness to her—she had pleaded to be part of her mother's public life, hadn't she, a fully acknowledged person?—or a cruel and unusual punishment. She had never before felt so far from a clear and simple understanding of motives. This lovely woman, her gorgeous expensive house, her nice-enough husband who was slightly vague, maybe (in spite of being the doctor who could afford all this) even a little bit dense in a way she couldn't put her finger on. The hollow quiet in the halls, the white-hot silent streets on the other side of the tight-shut windows, blank as something that had been blasted away by a bomb—oh Daddy, she wished she could say (but he didn't even know where she was)—Daddy, this is so *unreal.* She was walking through Sleeping Beauty's palace, everything tranced, as if the hands of the clocks stuck in their tracks. She'd give anything to trouble the waters a little, for sanity's sake. But if she scared them off, then what?

BARRY HAD BEGUN giving her driving lessons after dinner in the long receding light. She had to plead for them, which wasn't easy, because she still felt uncomfortable with him. "I'm not going to live in New York City for the rest of my life," she had insisted, half flirty, half whiny. "How can somebody go to California and not know how to drive?"

She followed her mother's glance across the room to where it worked on him complexly, without a word. Wouldn't it be fine to bounce signals off someone and have him listen like that, bowing to your wishes even against his will. She wondered what it was that her mother held over him, or refused, or threatened. It had never occurred to her that one of the things she hadn't grown up seeing was a marriage playing out before her, different from the affairs, the impermanent "arrangements," she'd witnessed one after another, all highs and lows and very few ordinary stretches of negotiation. The first time she followed Barry to the car she could see from his posture that he was more helpless than he was reluctant. Apparently that was what compromise looked like, and maybe—each giving a little, taking a little—it was a good and healthy thing. She had rarely seen it around her father.

The second evening, without an argument, they rose right after dessert, before Barry had even changed from his work clothes, though he had torn his tie off before they ate, and, without a word, made for the driveway. He let her maneuver the car slowly out onto the deserted street, toward the high-school parking lot. They didn't talk much. For someone so well-coordinated on stage, she found that driving took more attention than she'd expected. Barry was very laid back, though, in spite of her choppy starts and stops, not to mention her near misses. When she swerved toward an oncoming car, instead of away, he only smiled as if with resignation and said gently, "Better to stop if you're getting into a tight squeeze. Just brake and let him pass you." Maybe he wanted her to crack up the car so he could say, I told you so. Imagine what her father would have said.

The car stalled when she slowed too suddenly, circling the lamp-post in the center of the parking lot. "Oh, help!" she cried. "I'm sorry. I don't know what's—"

"It's okay," Barry said calmly. "You're doing fine. But anyway, it's good—let's just sit here for a minute, okay? I want to talk to you a little."

He looked vaguely odd, not quite as cool as usual, his eyes tense. You can always tell when someone is more focused than he ought to be because he's about to do something that doesn't come naturally. Christ, she thought, he's not going to put any moves on me! She'd jump out of the car before he laid a hot hand on her.

Instead he said, "I was wondering, Veronica—no, sorry, Ronnee. I've got to get that, excuse me. I just wondered—and please be honest with me, okay? Promise?"

That was always the introduction to something you didn't want to hear. She didn't say anything, only looked at him neutrally.

"Do you really want this party your mother's planning? You yourself, I mean."

She hesitated to think about how honest she wanted to be. "I guess the right answer has to be 'No.'"

Barry smiled, a little sheepish. "Not necessarily. This isn't a trap."

"Well, why else would you ask it?" I'm not that dumb, she wanted to say. Should she be getting angry? "You don't think it's such a good idea."

He raised his hands out of his lap helplessly and lowered them again. She had never noticed how perfectly white and clean and almost manicured they looked—maybe when you spent all day touching people's faces you had to baby them. Maybe he had to rub lotion into them like a woman. Putting his hands back down seemed to indicate that he'd retreat empty-handed if she wanted him to. "I just think it's . . . a strain on everybody. Your mother.

You. It won't be easy for you, you know, suddenly thrown in with all these . . . curious strangers."

"And will it be a strain for you, too?"

He said nothing.

"It would be easier for you if I wasn't here, I know that."

"Well . . . " But he didn't deny it.

"You'd like it if I didn't even exist at all. But since I do and you can't do anything about it, you wish I'd just go home while I'm still sort of a secret. I could see that if I was over there by that lamppost."

"Ronnee, it isn't—"

"I don't care what it is or isn't. My mother keeps saying that, too, it isn't this, it isn't that. You wish I'd leave before too many people know about me, is all. I'm just too nasty for your neighborhood."

Barry's eyes had filled with actual tears. That was something you didn't get to see too often. She couldn't imagine how this could matter to him that much. He was looking out the windshield, squinting.

"What if I told my mother you were saying all this stuff?" She spoke very quietly, there was no reason not to. There was something thrilling, almost sexual, about the power she felt over this man, bargaining over his secret request. Oh, please don't! she expected him to say.

Instead he shook off her threat. "She knows I don't think it's a good idea. No surprise there."

"So why are we talking about it here like it's some dirty secret and not, like, at the dinner table?"

He took a deep breath. "Ronnee, I don't know if you can appreciate this, but this has nothing to do with what I think of you, or whether your mother loves you. But—"

"There always seems to be a but."

"There are a lot of surprises that you sort of represent. A lot of—old history—all confused. Some of it has to do with me and your mother. And your father, I guess, if I want to be honest. Which I'm trying to be. Even if I never knew him, obviously this—you—it's hard for me. You ought to be able to understand that." By now his eyes were dry. "And, to be frank, I worry that it's a lot for some of our friends to take in all at once."

"Because my father is black and your friends are all—"

"No, no. Not that. Not only that. Just the whole idea, they don't—we've got a certain life here, Ronnee. And they may think they're pretty sophisticated, pretty worldly, but up close, I'm not so sure what they're ready to—" He stopped.

"Accept. You ought to say it. Say, 'Ronnee, you're a half-black bastard, that's what you are.'" She could patronize him too. This was almost fun. If you didn't feel like you were the one who was being described, it was delicious to make this man cringe. "And I make you uncomfortable. It's okay, you might as well say it. It's just a fact." Now she had tears in her eyes too, suddenly and against her will. "My mother shouldn't have to be brave to take me out in public like I'm something disgusting, but I guess that's what it takes down here." She sat up straight, rigid as a stop sign, and said this very evenly, with a finality about it. She didn't feel like a teenager, she felt like a more-than-adequate adult. "She didn't want me to come down here, I don't know if she told you that. I made her bring me."

He was looking at her soberly.

"And I guess I'm proud of her, in a way, for doing this party thing. That's a funny thing to say but it's true. If she's going against you and not being embarrassed about me, then I have a lot of respect for her."

He nodded very slowly. "And none for me."

"Right," Ronnee said. "Not even a little bit for you."

"That's cruel," her mother's husband answered, shaking his dark, perfect head. "I can understand that you're disappointed, but maybe a long time from now you'll realize that things aren't quite that simple."

"Yeah, I know. Nothing is black and white. Except me. I'm black and white. And I'm getting tired of everybody not saying what they mean about that. If you think your life's complicated, just think about mine for a minute." She shook her head so hard the tears flew out of her eyes like rain. She turned the ignition key and put her shaking foot on the gas too hard. "Sounds like a motorcycle," she said, and giggled. The giggle broke up something hard and pointy in her chest. "Sorry."

Barry was rearranging himself in his cushiony seat. She could see dark spots where he had sweated through his neatly buttoned-down light blue shirt. "Let's practice U-turns now," he said to her like a paid-by-the-hour driving instructor. "They're not as hard as they look."

She supposed it was more mature to be sad than mad, but that would take some working on. She wouldn't tell her mother, which gave her an advantage over both of them. She had thought she wanted power, but it seemed a slightly dirty currency right now that she couldn't buy anything much with, nothing that she wanted. She swung the car in a perfect circle, the kind that looks, in snow, as if it's been drawn by a compass.

"Good," Barry said, and sighed wearily. "Now let's find a street corner and do that the hard way."

WELL, THERE WERE SOME GOOD PARTS to the party plan: Her mother took her to Neiman Marcus and let her try on a dozen things until she found the perfect "coming out" dress, orange and yellow, clingy above, floaty below, and orange strappy exorbitant nothings for her feet, built on the principle that the more you pay the less you get. When she waltzed out of the dressing room wearing the dress, which she had already decided was perfect, but thought (considering who was picking up the bill) she ought to submit for a second opinion, Ronnee caught a look at her mother that hurt her to the bone: This woman needed her so much for something her eyes were brimming with a moist abject pleasure at seeing her turn and froth the liquidy skirt against her calves. She was like a childless woman looking at someone else's daughter. Her eyes fell on Ronnee as if she thought she was giving her some gift of incalculable value, which Ronnee was innocently accepting. It's a *dress*, she thought. I love it, but it's a lousy *dress*. What am I to you?

Then, of course, she remembered—it wasn't fair of her to forget, and this was what pierced her so—that she had thrust herself into this stranger's life, was hers to coddle and pamper, while only she knew why she was here. The argument they'd had about whether she should come to Houston or go home to her father was like one of those fights in the movies between boys when one of them is new to the block, to see who'll be top dog, who can do the bossing, and she had won. It was guilt, then, that so depressed her as the salesgirl swept away with the wild armful of crepe flowers held out as tenderly before her as any living thing. Either that or her mother's depression was contagious. She shouldn't have won. She shouldn't have subdued Barry so easily, either. She was glad she was here but her mother owed it to her to be stronger than she was, or what was a mother for?

RONNEE LOOKED AROUND and thought about the price of everything, of what was walking through the room on people's backs. This was not generous and she knew it—she had been trapped in such rooms before, she was no ghetto girl—but it must have been her ghostly understanding that this life might have been her life that made her count and recount and calculate the sum. Plus motherlove, she reminded herself. Girl, how cynical can you be? Plus all kinds of affection and its offshoots that didn't have a price tag. She was not proud of her tendency toward snideness and skepticism, but she did value practicality. The money was why she was here, was it not? And a little prod at her white side, too, why not admit it? She had begun to think about this the way she remembered her semester of butterflies, the monarchs they'd studied in biology and nurtured from caterpillar to pupa to the real astonishing thing; how, still holding on to the chrysalis, they pumped their wings before they could fly. Like exercise, because they were born all folded up and powerless. Not that she had been powerless, but she was here to get some blood flowing where it had never been. To the people who'd come to this party she would surely be black; trapped here with them, she would be trying out whiteness, which would probably make her feel more black. What a merry-go-round.

With the sound of a hurtling subway train, a small troop of Hispanic men (Mexican down here?) had rolled in carts of steaming
enchiladas under shiny metal lids, plus oblong pans of slick rice
and beans, tortillas, all the fixings, led by a young woman who
could have been Elpidia's sister, ponytailed, in regulation white
blouse, dark skirt, sneakers, personality left at the back door with
her street shoes. They stood at attention, then, after the line
of guests had formed, and lifted the heavy lids, spooned out the
sauces—not exactly a covered-dish church supper, Ronnee
thought. You could pay for a wedding with a feast like this.

A bartender with a tango dancer's mustache mixed drinks, salted
the rim of the margarita glasses with a flourish, flirted with Ronnee
a little, his knowing smile, the tilt of his head mocking both of
them. When he asked, "And a little squeeze of lime for you?" he
made it sound like a proposition. She laughed and turned from him
with enough speed to make the skirt of her new dress flounce
around her knees. She had picked herself a yellow hibiscus from
one of the bushes out back, which she had trouble keeping clipped
in her nubbly hair.

So what was her mother going to do now, tap on a wineglass
with her spoon and when she had everyone's attention announce,
"Here she is, ladies and gentlemen, my dirty secret! My true con-
fession!"? What had she told them, in fact, when she'd called to
say "Sunday afternoon, two o'clock"? She had had to stand with
her mother, very formal, near the front door so they could greet
people as they came in—"Sandy, my daughter, Ronnee Reece.
Ronnee, Sandy Kaufman." And Sandy whoever-he-was, grayish
hair bristling at the neck of a conservative striped shirt and khakis,
shook her hand, did not look her up and down appraisingly
(which would have made her gag and run, as if she'd been a slave
on the market block. Nobody had better). Dolly and Neil Har-
rington, Norm and Marian Fish, Joanie Derman, they came and
came, friendly enough—an actual astronaut, nothing special about
him; he looked like anybody's plain old father in a navy blazer
with sailors' buttons; a television anchorwoman—and none of
them gawked; they were mostly sort of middle-aged, the lower

end, like her mother, whom people referred to as her mom, a whole other person. It was too late to have a mom. Or, rather, too late to *get* one.

She felt like a puppet, but she was good—"Nice to meet you." "Hi there"—out of her body, not happy, not unhappy, only slightly amused at how distant she felt from the scene, and irritated that it took courage—courage!—for her mother to dare to show her off like this. She must be the object of great curiosity to them—prurient interest (she loved the word, which did not show up, as threatened, on the SAT)—but these decent, comfortable, dullish, well-dressed strangers, who were they to her? Her father's friends tended to take up a lot more air and space: Santha, like one of the witches from *Macbeth* in her dark caftans with the big sleeves, and some of the high-butted women in their little black pants. Holy Joe the bass player who liked to wear jewelry it looked like he stole from some church, clumsy crosses heavy as weapons and a silver ankh on a leather chain. Of course, they were artists, most of them, more funky, difficult, noisy, profane than the majority of people, color beside the point. You'd better believe there wasn't a musician or a painter in this bunch.

One thing she was sure of, she'd be having a better time if white folks only knew that music made a good party, or at least laid down the first layer, before you started dancing. No music here but talk and more talk, the jangle of real silverware and then, if the door to the air-conditioned house happened to be open, as the little kids jumped into the pool, the smashing sound of their bodies against the water. The pool, from in here, looked like a million gallons of Windex.

THREE THINGS worth remembering happened at the party and that was all. The first was that a very sweet old man named Sammy, with bright runny eyes and a crumpled neck, nudged her into the den like a sheepdog prodding his lamb, outside everyone's hearing, and put a runneled hand on her shoulder. Oh no, she thought, not a lecherous son of a bitch, *please*. This was too grotesque. She got ready to take off fast. But instead he leaned toward her, licked his lips a few times to get himself unstuck, and finally said, leaning so close she could smell his staleness, "Darling, listen, you should know this if nobody told you. Every child in the Merwitz family, your mother's family, always has a little something tucked away for them when they're born."

She raised her eyebrows and relaxed. Has a little something? Mr. Hill, her English teacher, would ask why that was in the passive voice. Was he the one who did the tucking away?

"And you didn't happen to be here when you were born. So . . ." He had a bit of a twitch, or maybe it was an effortful wink. One way or the other, his eyes flared at her with something like amusement. "You ask your mother about it, it belongs to you. A nice little bond, it's an Israel bond, good-sized. You could use it, every girl can use a little something on the side, right?" For this intelligence she had to let him squeeze her arm, but he was gentle and seemed happy to have good news for her. (How big was good-sized? What did Israel have to do with it? She knew enough not to ask.) Then, ready to go back into the chatter, he raised his shaky hand, which was so dark with age spots it was browner than her own, cupped her chin tightly and shook it a little, as if he was angry. "Uch, such a *shana maidel*, why didn't we know about you this whole time? What a waste. This is a good family, one of the best, you would have liked us."

She gave him a twisted smile like a grimace, the best she could manage with his fingers around her jaw.

"You were with your father?"

"Mmmp."

"You had a happy childhood? You were all right with him?" He finally let her go. She felt dents where his bony fingers had seized her. There was such a funny innocence about him and his straight-on questions that he didn't seem to know were intimate. Or maybe he did but when you get this old you know you don't have much time to waste.

"I had a very good childhood. I did. Thank you for asking. You're—Sammy?"

"Sammy Merwitz. Your mother's uncle, the last one. End of the line, the caboose. I always said that, I'm the little red caboose bringing up the rear. From there I see everything." His laugh was phlegmy and turned into a cough at the end. "Glad to make your acquaintance before it's too late, young lady. You're a beautiful girl. Your mama should be proud of you."

When she found her mother she asked her two things: What's a *shana maidel*? And who is Sammy, can you tell me about him? A *shana maidel* is a pretty girl—"Okay, got it, Jewish 101." "*Yiddish* 101." "Oh. Right. Sorry." And Sammy had been, until not that long ago, the owner of a very successful lighting business. "Very successful," her mother said pointedly. "Lighting and real estate. *Very* successful." Well, lovely, then, Ronnee thought. Her defensiveness embarrassed her. Assuming he could see her, she thought, through those weary-looking eyes, he had made her feel entirely welcome.

But then came the nastiness. The day, she supposed, would balance out.

She didn't hear the offending comment; she was left with her own imagination, which may have been worse than the fact. What she heard was Barry (who would have expected it? You *simplify* too much, she told herself) raising his voice, which broke like a teenager's, to a woman in a sweep of gray-and-yellow scarf who looked better the farther away from her you stood. She was one of those tense, dissatisfied-looking aging beauties who are always tan no matter what the season, dieted to a sharp point, her hair carefully streaked. The kind of woman who'd have walked down Ronnee's street picking her way like somebody trapped in steaming shit. In spite of her clever scarf, Ronnee could see the braided tendons of her neck from across the room. Barry stood stiff with anger, trembling like a tree in wind, and once he looked over his shoulder, embarrassed to have lost it a little too loudly. Ronnee thought she heard, or something like it, in his little Texas lilt, ". . . to say anything about anybody's life, Amy, so you'd better learn to muzzle it. Keep it to yourself." Everybody heard him, of course— he probably thought the tumult in the room would protect him,

but conversation died as his voice flared up; there was only the
crackle of forks against the rims of the china dishes—and her
mother, coloring from the round neck of her bright blue dress to
her temples, looked suddenly up at the ceiling as if at heaven,
where she would meet no one's eyes. She swept up from the table
a bunch of dreggy wineglasses that the roving waiters would have
gotten to in their next sweep; held them, sloppily, to her chest,
where a pink stain instantly spattered and spread like blood from a
gunshot, and rushed out of the room into the kitchen. She went so
fast, so publicly, it was as good as a shout. "Oh dear, oh dear," she
heard from a dignified bottle-blond woman standing beside her.
"Well, *Amy*," somebody said, which meant that her nastiness was
no surprise, but whether she was exempt from judgment wasn't
clear.

Ronnee stood perfectly still, the way you do on stage, stiller
than real life. She was not embarrassed, only seized with rage, but
she wasn't getting into a catfight, oh no. Let anyone defend her
who wanted to, and defend her mother. How perfect for Barry to
be the one to do it. Maybe he had heard her when she told him
how he sounded. Maybe she should keep a little door open on optimism.

The only thing that moved was her chest, because her breath
had tightened like a knuckly fist. She didn't want to snort, trying
to breathe; she tried to keep it quiet, but her head swam with the
effort or with a need for oxygen. How many of these people
agreed with this Amy, whatever nasty thing she'd said? A lot of
them, probably, secretly, but civility would win. A house like this
was not going to stand for whatever was the opposite of civil. She
wished she could get a good look at the offending Amy, but she
had enough discipline in her to stand gazing blankly at nothing but
the big beige-and-black painting on the wall behind the food carts.

Finally the shocked silence began to break up into sharp little
shards of talk, shuffling feet, returns to the carts for more rice and
beans. Amy was gone. She wanted to thank Barry, but he had followed her mother into the kitchen. Her father would have loved
the scene, she thought, not because he wanted her to suffer humil-

iation, but because he wanted her to understand where she stood, wanted it to the point of pleasure when it happened: *You're a little nigger gal, Ree, and just when you forget it is when they'll remind you. So you might as well stay home with me and stop struggling. Love it, darlin', love it, 'cause it's comin' after you no matter what.*

AND THEN ANOTHER GOOD THING HAPPENED, because of the bad. She had seen a boy who'd come with his parents—a boy and a girl, obviously brother and sister, one charmed, the other distinctly not—and wondered what it took to get them to a party of old folks like this. Surely more than obedience. But he was the coolest: a head of light-colored curls like a pile of wood shavings, the kind of broken-nosed profile that she happened to love, and his jacket sleeves turned up, shiny side out, so that his wrists and lower arms showed tan under a thicket of little blond hairs. A very white boy, scrubbed and snug. Thom Hardy had been brown as dirt.

Wasn't it about time?

What did that mean? If she was half white, should half her boyfriends be white?

He had been standing near that bitch when things broke loose, and because Ronnee had noticed him earlier, she glimpsed, but just for half a second, the way his nostrils had flared with feeling— some kind of feeling—and how he'd bounced impatiently on his toes for a minute or two. Now he walked up to her quite purpose-fully, nudging his way past a parental-looking cluster, and said, "I hope you don't think we're all pigs like that one."

"I just might," she answered, and let herself look him over up close, and let him see her do it. It had been such a long time since she'd flirted (if you didn't count the little shiver with the margarita man), she felt the deadness clear out of her system as if she were a motor revving its sludge away. "You don't think she's, like, your average bigot here?"

He shook his head. "Better not be. I don't know, though. Actu-ally."

"I might regret coming." She tilted her head like a smaller girl than she was. She always tilted it for pictures; it was her signature.

"God, I hope not. You're the first interesting thing to happen in this neighborhood since—I don't know—I think they had a murder once, down the block."

"Oh, thanks. Nice comparison."

He leaned the top of his head toward her. She wished she could run her finger down one of those golden-stubbled arms. He had the look of some statue, what was it? David? Alexander the Great? Didn't David have kind of a bumpy nose, big lips like a brother? "No, listen, I mean it. I didn't want to come, you know—you can imagine—" He flung his glance around the room "—but, Jeez, I have *re*considered. Little did I expect."

Smoother than custard. "And what were you expecting?" She lowered her head too, so that their hairlines almost touched.

"Oh, well . . . Can't say exactly."

"But I wouldn't like it. You've got a little of that Amy in you."

"No, oh, no, no. I didn't think anything. Like—blank. You know. Your mother says, 'Hey, this is going to be interesting,' and you think, Yeah, I'll bet. Like she picks your experiences for you after the age of, what, twelve."

She took a deep breath, thank God, nice and open. "Listen, can I ask you something?"

"Sure."

"You promise to be honest no matter what? Even if you don't think I'll be glad to hear?"

"You're making me nervous. But okay . . ." He grinned at her and then, self-conscious, took down the sleeves of his jacket and refolded them. He did it slowly, carefully, with something that looked like vanity.

"What did she tell you, your mother, when she said you ought to come? I mean, do you know what my mother said when she was inviting her?"

He laughed. "You mean, like, how were you billed?"

"Yes, how was I billed?" She looked at him sharply, like a teacher. "It doesn't happen to be funny."

He was thinking. "Well, she—um—she said Miriam seems to have a little surprise for us, something like that. She wants to introduce us to a long-lost daughter. That's all. Nothing scandalous or anything." He reached out and put his hand on her bare arm. "Nobody really knows much about, like, how you got here. Who you are. Is that, you know, a big secret?"

Ronnee shrugged. Depression was washing over her again like exhaustion. Why did her whole life story have to be so twisted? "Who I am? What do you mean? She said I was Miriam's daughter." Was he going to ask "And who *else's*?" and wink?

"No, but you're—now will *you* promise not to laugh? I feel like you're sort of like some princess, you know, what's her name, Cinderella, who shows up out of nowhere? And then maybe you'll leave the way you came, poof!"

"Well," she answered dryly, "some people obviously wouldn't find that such bad news."

"That bitch isn't worth pissing on, pardon my Portuguese. Everybody knows what she's like. No, I mean—"

"There's nothing like a little mystery to make somebody seem more exciting than she might be. I'm just—" She stopped and looked at him. "I don't even know your name."

"Jordan Pinsky. That's my mom and dad." He indicated them with his head. They looked like everybody else. "And my sister's somewhere—Lisa the troll." He narrowed his eyes as if that helped him see her better. "So you're going to Stanford in the fall. I heard."

"Yeah. You?"

"Princeton. My parents can't talk about anything else these days, it's like, I think they're more thrilled than they were when I was born. They're practically wearing a sandwich board." He laughed derisively, but, she took note, he had managed to tell her what he wanted her to know.

"Huh. You ought to meet my father. He's ready to disown me for going out there." She was going to try him on some truth, but she didn't expect him to understand.

"Jesus, why? You're kidding. *Stanford*?"

"He had in mind something more like, um, Spelman. Or Howard, maybe. Fisk."

"Oh, he's—well, so why didn't you want to do that?"

"You know those schools?"

"Well, I mean, I've heard of them, sort of. Sure."

Sort of. At least he was honest. She shrugged. "I don't have anything against them. But it's a big wide world, and also—my life's kind of complicated, you know?"

She watched him putting on his let's-make-a-move-on-this-chick face, watched his look of interest and curiosity change, just slightly, to an ingratiating, generic near-smile. Conniving, though that might be a little strong. What was personal, though, specifically for her, gone. Oh, men. Boys. She didn't like it that everything was so visible to her since she'd left home—not that she understood it, but that she seemed to be taking in what people did and said and how they stood and how they looked at her (because they were all strangers?) as if they were caught in a too-strong light and outlined with a dark pen, the way her art teacher always told them you weren't supposed to paint unless you were doing cartoons. There was nobody she saw draped in the comfortable shadows of habit. It was exhausting.

"So, do you think we could get a chance to talk about it?" he prodded. "Someplace quieter? In, like, softer light?"

Why not, she thought. If she was here, she was here. And funny he said *light* just then, when she had just thought it. "I've got car keys," he said. "Or, I mean, if you want to be exact, I came with my parents, but I know how to lay my hands on some."

"Can't leave yet. I have to stay to the bitter end. My mother—you know. This whole thing is a big deal for her."

"Yeah," Jordan said, and giggled a little, maybe embarrassed, maybe sympathetic, maybe nothing. "I can see that." They looked at her mother, who was back in the room, flushed, freshly made up as if she'd washed tears off her face, surrounded by comforters as if she'd done something particularly worthy of congratulation. Maybe Amy had done her a favor, then, turning whatever tide of disapproval might have been secretly cresting into a torrent of consolation. Were they hypocrites or just good friends who wanted what was best for her?

"But when we're all done," Ronnee whispered, "maybe you could show me a little of Houston?"

Before he could answer, as if summoned, Jordan's sister materialized at their side. Such graceless earnestness, such bottom-of-the-bottle glasses, such a self-despising little hunch of the shoulders, the poor girl. "You ready to leave?" she asked her brother. "The posse's getting restless."

"Why don't you take a letter, loser," Jordan said, and fixed her with his eyes, as if he could hypnotize her if she didn't blink. "Get lost. Sincerely, your brother."

"Jordan. Dork. It's time."

"I mean it, Lisa. Can't you see I'm busy?"

She looked like she was used to ignoring him. "Okay, fine, stay. Only you don't have any way to get home, and don't call later for a ride. You never care how much you bother the parents."

"Darling, you can always come and get me. I'll make it worth your while." He wiggled his eyebrows like Groucho.

She had such an unfortunate face, Ronnee thought, her features all sort of bunched in the middle, anchored by a considerable nose. Maybe she was very smart, maybe she didn't care what she looked like. The way she kept herself, you'd better hope.

"Yeah. The day you get a soul. All right, you can hitch home if you want. Maybe you'll get abducted and they'll find you in the bayou."

"Sweet, isn't she?" Jordan said, but Lisa had turned to leave them. "That girl's not going anyplace till she stops being her mommy and daddy's errand girl."

"I always wished I had a sister. Or even a brother. Somebody."

"Ha. Lisa would have unloaded me cheap." He gave her that smile laden with innuendo and leaned toward her so that he could lower his voice. "But then, see, us two would have had a problem. We would have been into incest."

"Oh really. I think you've skipped a couple of steps, big brother."

He was nearly standing on her toes. "Let me call in a favor and get us a car. Or wait, I'm sure your parents—your mother, I mean—isn't going anywhere tonight. And anyway, they've got two cars."

His confidence was exhilarating and offensive at the same time.

"I can show you all kinds of good things," he said, and put his smooth warm hand on her wrist and held it there as if he were taking her pulse.

12 THEY WERE REARRANGING the chairs, stuffing crumpled napkins into a black plastic garbage bag.

"What did she say, Barry?"

Barry, the sugar-and-creamer set in his hands, said, "Amy? Who cares?"

"Was it—"

"Listen, there's always somebody who's a beat behind, you know? Why not leave it at that? People have no sympathy for Amy."

"She was—"

"I mean it. Forget it, Miriam. Why don't you concentrate on how decent everybody else was."

"Considering."

He sighed. "Okay, considering. You've got a roomful of people, a couple of generations, with a lot of different viewpoints on almost everything—moral, religious—and for the most part they behaved really well. You said, 'Surprise! No more secrets, here's my flesh and blood,' and they smiled at her and smiled at you, whatever they were thinking. What more are you asking for?"

"I don't know," she said. "You're right. I don't know." The caterers had taken almost everything off the tables; they had washed up and neatly departed. She pressed an armful of tablecloths against her chest.

"They're curious as hell, you can be sure the phone wires are singing right now, and they're speculating, but—"

"Well, but wasn't this better than you expected? You hated this party idea so much."

He shrugged so casually he was asking to be distrusted. "You can take comfort if you want to. Nobody turned over the furniture."

"So why do you look like somebody's pouring cod liver oil down your throat?"

He only looked at her, hard, as though she ought to know the answer. But there were too many possible answers. "It must have been hard on Ronnee." He sounded conciliatory. "Unless she likes to be stared at."

"Actually, I think she does like to be stared at." She welcomed the chance to talk about Ronnee with him. "Well, she wanted so much to be here. I mean, in Houston. She gets what she wants, I think, that girl."

When Barry said, "I'll bet," she knew how stupid she had been to say anything.

"Where did she go?" Barry asked. "She ought to be out here helping put this stuff away."

"Oh, let her be. It's a celebration day. Anyway, she and Jordan Pinsky went out, I think. He came with his parents in their car so I gave him the keys to the Honda."

Barry stopped short. "The keys to the *Honda*. For what?"

"So they could go off someplace. She could use some friends, you know. She's lonely out here. Don't you think she's had enough old geezers for one day?"

"Jordan?"

"Barry. What does that mean, that shocked look? 'Jordan?!' "

She knew, bitterness rising in her throat like the whole day's nourishment coming back up into her mouth. Scratch them, any of them, the best of them, and look what you get. It wasn't just his embarrassment before their friends. Barry was seeing her fitting herself to Eljay, her white-peach softness, cleft, his terrifying alien darkness, prodding. It was more than jealousy, or why would he look so suddenly alarmed? He was feeling—what else could you call it?—retroactively betrayed. *Jordan?* "Are you going to say something?"

Barry put the pewter creamer-and-sugar set gently and precisely on the shelf, in the footprint of where it had been. He was a gentle

person, she reminded herself. He had defended Ronnee when Amy
smirched her. He was no goon, but a tender man with a straitened
Southern soul as primitive as it was proper, that lived by ingrained
platitudes: You earn your own way. (Had he?) Every tub on its
own bottom. You do not ever lie, even for expediency. Pull up your
socks and get it done. People deserve a hand, not a handout. "No,"
he said, and she watched as the effort at self-control stiffened his
shoulders. How could you reassure someone about actions, feelings, sorrows so long in the past? What could you promise?

"No," Barry repeated in the voice of an aggrieved father. "No,
I'm not going to say a thing."

WHEN THEY'D GONE TO BED, Miriam pulled herself close to
Barry, feeling celebratory, the sheets light across her in the perfectly
tempered air. The moon splashed in the window like spilled milk.
"Thanks, pal," she whispered in his ear, blowing his hair up and away
in a little puff. "You're a brick. Isn't that what they say, 'a brick'?"

He was turned away from her—she encountered more shoulder
than anything else—so that his answer disappeared into his pillow.

"Hey." She moved in closer, fitting herself around him, breasts
tight to his back. "Any chance I could get your attention for a couple of minutes?" She inched her hands under his pajama top to feel
his skin, firm under her fingertips, then reached around to work
the buttons—she was good at that—and slid it down to his hips,
trying to ignore the fact that he wasn't helping. She laid her face
against his back then, and ran her hand down his side, enjoying the
jut of his hip, the long smooth thrust of his thigh.

Barry heaved himself over slowly, a little too reluctantly. She
could see his face in the moonlight, a black-and-white photo without definition, his expression invisible.

Now—she was as good at untying as she was at unbuttoning—
she could touch him where she wanted to, gently, visiting her favorite places on the terrain of his body, the tender places that
always stayed warm. She made her touch more insistent, and finally he stirred, and lifted her chin so that he could kiss her. She let
everything else float away, all the talk, the complications, every-

thing but the sweetness of his mouth, the paradox of hard and soft that made her want to go on kissing him forever, with her fiercest concentration, and molding herself to him. He had begun to unlace the fragile ties at the front of her nightgown. When it puddled beside her she came into his arms, eager to take him in, warm and moist to welcome him, wondering at the fine way mind and body so conveniently synchronized.

He played with her a long time, head bent to her breasts, hands everywhere, fingers and palms, and took his time finding his way into her. She drew in her breath at that shock—it was always a lovely surprise, no matter how often she had him there, as though her astonishment was reluctance barely overcome. But just when their rhythm should have changed and languor turned to urgency, she felt him slacken and begin to slip. Then, no matter how he labored, no matter how enthusiastically she attended to him, there was no way back—he had gone cold, gone flat.

"I'm sorry, Miriam, I just don't seem to have it. Not exactly a brick."

She made a comforting noise. "Too much good wine?"

He shrugged—"I don't think so"—and slipped away from her.

She closed her eyes, stranded. Beside her, under the sheet, crumpled in the half-light, her silky discarded nightgown felt like a handful of cool white flour running through her fingers. She twitched it idly between thumb and third finger. "Barry, if you're—" She leaned over his shoulder, breasts hard against his warm skin, to talk quietly into his ear.

"Don't, all right?"

"If it's—"

"*Please.*" He shook her off.

She heard him breathe once, twice, raggedly, like a man fresh from a fight and, so quickly she knew he was running from it all, his breathing evened out into sleep.

THAT MORNING, before the party, Miriam had looked solemn when she knocked on Ronnee's door. "There's a phone call for you," she'd told her, gesturing back toward the kitchen.

"I can take it here," Ronnee said. There was a white phone beside the bed.

"No, wait. Maybe I should have prepared you." Miriam was smiling a little. "Come walk with me. It's your sister. Half-sister."

Ronnee looked perplexed.

"Evie. She's calling from camp. She really wants to speak to you."

"Well—but, I—"

"You're her big sister, Ron. I mean, Ree. She's very excited."

"Oh, God." Ronnee looked considerably less excited. Miriam had never really determined whether Ronnee missed having siblings—her life with her father had seemed quite complete, surprisingly, even carefully, peopled by friends: Eljay had taken seriously the need to provide a noisy, varied, comforting life for Ronnee. She couldn't fault him there.

Telling the children had been easier than she'd expected, though who could know if they'd really heard her? "I wanted to tell you something important before you heard it from somebody else," she had said to each of them, as lightly as she could, hating it that they had to do this by phone, and hiding behind it. For surely one of their friends would have a parent who'd consider such gossip fair fodder. She knew the advice she'd be given if she consulted an expert: Don't answer questions they don't ask, however peculiar it feels to state a fact without an explanation. The boys were interested, but rather remotely—Seth kept saying "What? Weird!" as though such a development were just one more proof of the unpredictability of grownups, and Eli only giggled, probably embarrassed, though he would not have known exactly why. They didn't ask any of those questions, didn't seem quite prepared to go to the trouble of imagining this alleged sister when soon enough they would meet her in the flesh.

Evie, though, was entranced. If she was going to wonder how, not to mention why, this person had so mysteriously come about, she would do that later, in private. Meanwhile she marveled. This would mean shopping advice, someone to fuss with her hair; it would mean somebody in the house to protect her from the boys!

"Well, honey, she's not really going to be living with us, except maybe sometimes. She's going to college in the fall, in California."

"Oh, Mom, can I come home now and *see* her?" Evie pleaded. Miriam wondered what kind of doll she was imagining. Evie had a way of pushing down on the phone cord with impatience; Miriam could see her thumping at it urgently, strumming it, wherever she took calls at her camp, in the office or on the porch of the dining hall on a pay phone, looking out at the lake. "Or I could stay in California till she comes. Ohh, Mom!" She sounded like a child with a stomachache.

Eli's next (required) letter did not mention Ronnee; instead he enclosed, like a cat carrying home a prize pelt, a very tiny snakeskin wrapped in Kleenex. An intricate black and white, it looked like the lanyards he was probably learning to braid, only more delicate. Seth said stiffly, "I hope you and Ronnee are having a good time," and left it at that. Evie, though, enclosed a questionnaire, which she pleaded with her mother to fill out instantly upon receipt.

Will I like Ronnee? she asked. *Do you think she will like me?*

Check one.

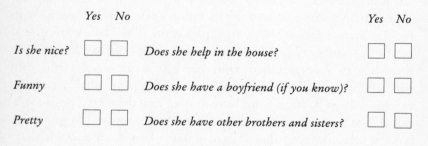

It was Miriam's idea that they should have a conversation, as a compromise. She was sorry she'd forgotten to give Ronnee fair warning. But she made sure to have reason to walk into the kitchen while Ronnee was sitting at the counter holding the phone, looking off at nothing. She was laughing, saying, "Well, no, I never saw Galveston, so we could just go and, like, fool around there. Swim and all. Eat. Do you like to eat?" She talked in her normal tone, not like a big girl humoring a little one. Evie must be beside herself with pleasure, and who cared how this gift of a sister had come about or what she looked like or what she represented. She represented a sister. Evie still had it just right.

Who would have guessed that, at the end of the long, long day, and in spite of Barry's fear for their souls, she'd done her daughter—both her daughters—a favor?

"SO—YOU AND JORDAN—he's a nice boy, isn't he?" Her mother offered her a blue glass darkened halfway to the top with orange juice.

"He showed me a little of Houston. This long strip—Westheimer? It just sort of goes on and on, all those shopping centers. Like something on a roll. Paper toweling." She drank thirstily. "I think that must be what New Jersey looks like."

Her mother laughed. "Don't you want to meet some other kids? We can probably find a few, more or less your age." Her mother stopped to consider. She had a habit of pulling in her cheeks when she was thinking. It made her look weird and gaunt. Then she let them out, pretty again. "Though I suppose almost everybody's working."

"Well, could I get a job, do you think? To keep busy? I could really use the money." She was hoping her mother would leap in and reassure her that she needn't worry about *that* anymore, but she was silent.

"Hard to think what you could get quickly. Most of those are, you know, through connections. The interesting ones. Barry's partner has his niece in the office, that kind of thing."

Ah yes, no surprise there. This would be a cliquey group that took care of its own.

"I'll be thinking, Ronnee." She was so serious about everything. Her mother reminded her of the most earnest kids she'd had in her classes: head down, eyes tightly focused, smiling on demand. Ronnee watched her put the tip of her index finger to her nose while she thought. She'd seen her do it before, amazing, because she did exactly the same thing. It was a comforting gesture that seemed, almost magically, to banish distractions, to let her focus, though she couldn't imagine why. Her father used to kid her about it: "You look like you're sticking your finger in a socket that connects right to your brain!" This fingertip-to-nosetip was too insignificant, maybe even too undignified, to mention, but how strange to think such petty indiosyncracy could come on a gene!

She had been thinking about another apparent trick of the genes. Now she knew why being a hybrid hadn't straightened her hair out one single fraction, one kink, one crinkle. That was usually the gift, if you wanted to call it that: a little relaxation of the curl in return for a lot of inner confusion. But one morning she'd solved the mystery—had caught her mother standing before the mirror in her slip, pressing her hair like any black woman, turning her head with a certain hypnotized gaze. She raked the hot wand slowly down until the steam puffed out around it like breath on a freezing day, then turned her head a little, stared critically, applied the iron again, with extra emphasis at the ends.

"Bad hair?" Ronnee had asked, trying not to laugh. "That's a Jewish thing, too?"

Her mother laughed, too, and shrugged. She blushed so deeply that for just an instant her face was darker than her daughter's.

"MEANWHILE," her mother said earnestly, "I know a couple of kids you might like."

Rich and white, like the girls at St. Helen's. Only Jewish. She missed Seretha, she missed Electa, she missed the few she could get down with. She was like someone in hiding who couldn't let anyone know where she'd gone.

Theater, she was thinking. Are there any kids who act? Even techies would do. Could they find her a stage somewhere? But you probably couldn't drop in just like that, not on a real theater company. It wasn't worth thinking about. She would try to borrow that credit card again, for lack of a better idea, and this time nobody would stop her from using it.

RONNEE REMEMBERED the first time her father took her to somebody's house to play, a couple of kids she had never even heard of, and they glowered at each other for a long time, turf-proud, suspicious. All she had wanted to do was go home. Eventually it was all right, they even sort of became friends, though the details were all washed away. But today she remembered, in the pit of her stomach, that cold defensive feeling: I am who I am and I didn't choose you! What would they know about her? How had they been drafted for the job of keeping her amused? Come keep this poor girl from dying of boredom? This endless calculation exhausted her. Well, let them worry: I am who I am. (She giggled. Wasn't that what God said?)

The first of the girls to arrive was named Polly. She was small, round-bottomed, and blond, with cheeks so fair she blushed like a clown in greasepaint. There was one just like her at St. Helen's. (Not fair, Ronnee scolded herself. Wouldn't you love it if someone thought that way about you.) Polly was clearly under sentence to be friendly: she twinkled, she chattered, she grinned so hard her pointy eyeteeth showed. A little apple tart, sugar on top.

Ronnee, not having figured out her role yet, looked at her blankly, which seemed to propel her, obedient to her orders, into still more furious smiling.

Then Abra arrived, her antidote, scowling. Ronnee's mother was meeting them at the door, hostessing it up. It felt like a tea party. Oh, girl, I can outscowl you any day of the week. In fact, it might be fun. Abra was under the impression she was sultry, the way her black hair hooded her forehead and her eyes, a twilight blue so professionally made up they looked natural. She must see herself in others' faces.

They did sit for tea—iced—and very nice chocolate chip cookies her mother had baked. Ronnee watched her hovering, not very

subtly, trying to look busy. First they talked a little music, a mis-
match from word one, her Smokey Robinson, their John Cougar
Mellencamp, her Nu Shooz, their Van Halen, though the visitors
disagreed genteelly about which albums they liked best.

Then, dutifully, they took up school. Polly admitted, as if
guiltily, that she went to a private school. "It's actually—uh—more
integrated than the public high school."

"Oh, that wouldn't be hard," Abra said sulkily. "My school is
about a hundred and fifty percent white kids and then some
bused-in—" She looked covertly at Ronnee "—others." She
paused. "What do you think of that?"

"Of what?"

"Busing."

"I don't think of it, one way or the other."

Abra looked surprised.

"Do you?" Ronnee said to the other one.

"Well, it doesn't actually affect my school at all. We all get there
on our own."

"Us too," Ronnee said innocently. She saw her father orating—
he did that, sometimes, even at his own parties, got out the little
soapbox, did his thing. Her resistance was a refusal to elaborate.

"You went to a private school?" They were a duet, nearly in
synch.

Don't look shocked now. "St. Helen's. In Brooklyn. New York
State Lacrosse Champions. You wouldn't have heard of it."

"Oh, Brooklyn. Oh. So what's New York like?" the apple tart
asked.

"What's it *like*? Like, how do you mean?"

"Well . . . I've never actually been there. I mean, I've been in the
airport. What is it, JFK?"

"Going to Paris?"

Polly blushed that wild red. "London."

"Ask me an easier one. I can't tell you what New *York's* like."

"Well, then. How do you like Houston?"

Abra, to her credit, rolled her eyes.

"How do you do your eyes, Abra? Abra—is that right?"

"Yeah. Named for my dead great-uncle Abie. We have this thing, it's called Kaddish?"

We meaning Texans? Houstonians? Her particular family?

"It means you have to be named for somebody who's already dead. But you can change it, sort of, if you want, especially if you're the other sex. I was almost Amy, but then my father insisted. But that's why there are no Jewish Juniors. No 'the thirds.' "

"Great beginning." Oh, she meant Jews. Well, she wouldn't want to have a Junior anyway, there were too many cool names to have to repeat one in the same family. She knew a girl with the same exact name as her mother, two Katherines and a lot of confusion when you called on the phone. Why would you do that? Vanity?

"I'll show you my eye stuff," Abra told her and with a snap of the zipper on her makeup bag rolled into her lap an elaborate set of pencils and liners.

"God," Ronnee gasped. "I don't use that much on stage!"

"But i'n' it just perfect?" Abra asked, suddenly coy and Southern. She widened her Liz Taylor eyes and batted her lashes. She was pretty funny if she was trying to be; if not, she was appalling.

THEY WERE GOING to the Galleria, after which, she guessed, they'd be friends for life. They trooped out to Abra's little red car. It was a Beetle convertible, too good to be true. She wasn't too proud to let herself look impressed. The girls' fine hair blew around like in the movies; apparently they'd rather be blinded than wear scarves. Ronnee was amused that the wind couldn't even find hers.

Polly anatomized the malls. Each had its own style, its particular price range: Monkey Ward, Sears, Foley's, Macy's, Marshall Field's, Nieman's. Cartier and Tiffany, though only to look at (although her boyfriend had given her Cartier earrings—"modest ones") and a jewelry store named Fred. "Don't you love it? Fred? That's my cat's name." She had given Ronnee the seat next to the driver so she could see better. "We're taking you to the best. You wouldn't want to go to Almeda or Gulfgate."

"Why's that?" She was thinking of how happily un-malled her life was, how she liked thrift shops and, if she had a little money to spare, the boutiques.

"Oh, it's all Mexicans and—" Polly stopped as if she'd crashed into a wall. Ronnee saw her panicky eyes flick to Abra and then off into the distance. Abra gave off a little sound of disgust like air rushing out of a balloon.

I will not help you out, Ronnee did not say. Go on, blush till your cheeks flake off. She stared as hard as she could at sweet Polly over the seat back that separated them, as harshly, as nakedly, as rudely. There is no rest, she kept learning for the first time, and there never will be in this world. Her daddy, her furious daddy was right again, damn him.

But they all had tears in their eyes from the wind. When they drove down into the Galleria's parking garage, dim and fumy, in silence, they wiped them with their open hands.

"Come on," Polly said, smiling again, hurrying her taut-jeaned bottom along as if a show were about to start without them. "You'll see this is the very best, and then we can eat."

SHE STARTED A CONVERSATION with a very cool boy, dark as she could find, and made sure Abra and Polly could see her. He was giving out the ice skates at the rink; she'd watched him for a while, her so-called friends hanging over the rail where the skaters whirled by, close enough to hear the snicking sound of the blades and feel the chill that rose from the rink. He had one of those sculpted Belafonte-ish faces, faceted in all the right places, cheekbones, lips, chin, only he was a sweet rich brown. She used to make chocolate pudding that color, run her finger around the rim of the pot, lick it luxuriously off.

She flirted with him so desperately it was embarrassing, so heavy-handed she felt pathetic. (Why didn't guys feel that way when they were putting the moves on a girl?) But she could absolutely *feel* what Abra and Polly saw from a distance, suddenly too shy to move up there with her, like this was her business, this pretty brown boy, the other side of an invisible line. Look, they had to be thinking, all that in common instantly, as if they had made an exchange of passwords. The guy, in a dark blue satin jacket open on a muscled chest in a glaring white T-shirt—he looked like he was waiting to be discovered by an agent, modeling or Hollywood, whoever came by first—was appreciating her as he pulled stubs for the little girls in their skating costumes, smiling with a hint of insinuation as he explained their system of skate rental. He asked her if she skated, told her he'd let her have some really good shoes half price if she wanted them. Fine firm new ones. He had eyes like chocolate kisses and the most enviable lashes. At all this she made herself laugh merrily, dipping and tilting her head coquettishly, looking up under her own lashes until— timing was everything—she thought they'd had enough. "See you later!" she called gaily over her shoulder in someone else's voice.

"Be right here!" he shouted back and raised an arm like a victor. "Every day but Sundays!"

Nobody said anything, but she could see their admiration: that she was bold, that she had taste, that they could never—would never, which was different—go there with such a studly character. Maybe (if she could somehow get herself over here without wheels) she'd come back and see if he had a little time for her on one of his breaks.

IT WENT WELL with Ronnee and Jordan. It went very well for a week or two. He managed to get out to Memorial nearly every night, and on a Sunday he drove Ronnee to Galveston to prove to her that even a sleazy beach could be fun if it was in Texas. She didn't understand the Texas part. Maybe you had to be born to it.

The troublesome clarity of her vision did not diminish, though—was this what being a grownup was going to mean, this feeling that she was seeing enough to make her uncomfortable everywhere? Which meant that she saw exactly who Jordan was: a smart, spoiled boy from the suburbs (though in Houston apparently you didn't have to go very far from the center of town to get to neighborhoods that looked as suburban as distant Long Island from Manhattan). He had been stroked, given more of everything than he needed except the perspective to know it, had been groomed for success at anything he decided he wanted, every door wide and effortlessly open, every connection guaranteed by his loving parents. He had a summer job proofreading for a law firm—friend of his father's. ("Of course. How the hell else could I find a job and not have to pretend I was staying on in September?") His father was "an ear-nose-and-throat man," which she found funny—she'd heard of breast men and ass and leg men—and his mother was a Volunteer, bighearted and community minded as long as the community consisted of what Jordan called "MOTs."

"Members of the tribe."

"Got it."

"Maybe a little narrow," he admitted, "but like she says, if we don't look after ourselves nobody else is going to do it. You may not know it but we're the first to be left out."

She hooted. "You've got to be kidding." They fought about this: who had suffered more? Who cares? she asked. Suffering is suffering. Anyway, this isn't a contest I want to win. *And*—she looked triumphant—if you're counting, I get double points for misery. I've got slavery, hey, I've got the concentration camps. Don't fuck with me.

Did her language shock him? She couldn't tell. Maybe it excited him. She wondered, too, what he expected of her. If she was outrageous, would he think, Well, no surprise, I mean—look at who she is. *Look.*

He looked, all right. Stared at her nipples the first time he had her shirt off, fascinated. She kept so much to herself she couldn't believe how open some people could be about their astonishment. "They're like . . . blackberries or something. Whew. Wow. Can I pluck one?"

"What did you expect, rose-petal pink?" He made her want to hide.

"They're beautiful," he said, his lips on her neck, which was dusky, subtly darker than the rest of her. "I'm just—ah—surprised. Somehow. I shouldn't be, but I am."

"Really." She pulled her shirt back on. Was this worth it? Were all white boys this out to lunch?

"Hey, come on, you want me to be honest, don't you? Didn't you tell me that? Anyway . . ." He held her hand around him, hard, having tugged his fly open and then popped the button right off his black jeans. "Anyway—" This was the first time they were getting past their clothes, they were in his too-small car, parked beside the bayou out in a place he called Katy, where there wasn't much light "—anyway, you're probably surprised too." He tugged himself out of the welter of his jockeys, hot to the touch. He reached up suddenly and turned on the dome bulb, which cast tepid light on them the color of dust.

"Bubble-gum pink!" she said, opening her hand, laughing.

"So there. We're even."

She felt like a child, the way she and her girlfriends used to prod and investigate and fall back laughing. "But it works the same way, right?" She tried to ease her way back in the seat. Tight squeeze.

"Pretty much the same," he said to her, his voice already muffled in a kiss that turned so long and intricate she thought she'd pass out for lack of air. "It's blind, though. It's got one eye, but the eye can't see."

They sighed, both of them, at the excruciating comfort of his arrival, even without sight, just where she wanted him.

BUT THEIR TALK, for all Jordan's intelligence, did not amuse her half as much as his body did. What do you know about black people? Life for black people in this country? she asked him, because he had mentioned a local state senator who was under accusation for some kind of bribe-taking and had asked, all too casually, why so many "colored" politicians were dishonest. "So many times they act like they're running some little African dictatorship or something and, you know, their constituents just eat it up. Cadillacs, women, it's all, like, proof that they're men or what?" Those perfect teeth that he showed when he laughed must have put a few dollars in the orthodontist's pocket.

They were at a place called the House of Pies after the drive back from Katy. Jordan told her it was a Houston institution. "Look around you, see, there's a large limp-hand population in here. It's really called the House of Guys."

Jesus, how many people could he insult in three minutes? She felt her heart rate slow, then race, then slow again with disappointment. Her strawberry pie oozed a red too bright to be true, shiny with cornstarch, under a peak of something that looked like whipped shaving cream. All pure ingredients, the menu said. Pure what?

"So what can you tell me?" she asked him again. "About black life in this wonderful country."

"I probably shouldn't be playing this game." He poked with his fork at his Boston cream pie as if the answer might tumble out from between the layers. "I don't know how to tell you anything like that. I don't know—they—you don't really want to hear this."

"I do."

He looked a little frightened of her sternness, but he soldiered on. "There's a lot of poverty, a lot of unemployment, not their fault but there it is. Here in the South, they've had a hideous time. They've had to fight for their rights, though I personally have never seen a 'whites only' or 'colored' water fountain or anything like that. Thank God it's too late for that." He looked at her for reassurance and saw no expression. "The kids in my classes are ninety-nine percent white. Okay. Fact. They don't get into the honors classes, not more than a couple, but I know there are a lot of reasons. I wish there were more of them mixed into our classes. I admit, I believe in having them in school with me but I never go out of my way. Even me, with all I believe in." He tried a smile, then took it away because she didn't return it.

"Okay, more clichés: Um . . . They invented jazz, the blues. Out of their grief. To be honest, don't hate me—though I personally think this is a compliment—I love to watch black people dance, even walk. The way some people swing on down the street. Though not the street I live on, true. Too true." He stopped with a long sigh and thought some more, so serious she wanted to laugh.

This must feel like his college interview. His 800 math score wouldn't help him, either.

"Bill Cosby is a good representative, I think. Athletes, too, though you'd never want to—you wouldn't dare assume some-body was a basketball player just because he was tall, you could insult him. Some black people have plenty of culture, though, and some (like Cosby and, you know, Dr. Huxtable), have as much money as anybody else. I'm sure there are some black people who live in a brownstone like his, but probably not very many." Jor-dan's mouth seemed to be drying out. He took a long sip of his water. "Once when we were watching Cosby and his wife, that, um, Phylicia Ayers Allen—did you know she's from Houston, by the way?—when she swept in with all her style I had this big argu-ment with my mother because she said something not exactly but basically like 'Aren't they lucky, they can straighten out their hair and wear nice clothes, and they can be more like us?' I nearly mu-tilated her with my bare hands."

Ronnee was sitting back against the leather of the booth as if for distance. "You want me to congratulate you?" Her chest was flut-tering.

"Okay, Ronnee, okay. So—more. Langston Hughes was a great poet. A few others too. Toni Morrison. Zora What's-her-name. I read that book and loved it, about Janie and her man and the dog who kills him in the flood? I'll never forget that. Hurston."

Ronnee couldn't say a word for a few minutes. She waited until the static in her mind could clear. You probably had to be from a place like Texas to get into Princeton with a headful of sitcoms. But, she reminded herself, he had an 800 score on his math SAT. You hush up with your 540. "That's it?"

"Well . . . I guess. Unless I have more time to think. This isn't fair, you know. This is—"

"I take back everything we just did out there in your car, boy. Forget it ever happened. It's *canceled*." But the part of her that burned where he had been kept on burning. She should have or-dered cranberry juice.

Jordan looked ready for sunstroke. The tips of his ears were the reddest of all. She pitied blonds when they got emotional. "Ronnee, listen. Sweetheart, please. This isn't my fault. I'm just—look, you've got to teach me. I put myself in your hands." He grinned. "More ways than one." Cute. "How am I supposed to know about people like—"

"Like me? I like the way you kept saying 'they.' Who the hell do you think I am?"

"Well—like you and, you know, double. I mean, like, altogether black—if—"

"You know you're putting your foot in it worse and worse? Can you even hear that? It's up to your knees, if you want to know."

She had him pleading. But who wanted to win this thing, like it was a contest? Like the suffering competition.

"You know what it's like, you grow up with what's around you. I mean, you did too, didn't you? In your own neighborhood and all?"

"And what's around you?" She shuddered to think of it, all those sealed-up houses, those decorator dungeons.

"Well—bitches like that Amy, a few, I can't deny it, and people like my mother who don't know what to think. She doesn't mean any harm. But mostly it's innocent well-intentioned people who just don't have any occasion to spend time, get to know anybody outside their circle." He looked into her impassive face. "Oh come on, Ronnee, help me out here. Don't be so damn holier-than-thou. You know what I mean." He looked away from her as if that was the only way he could think. "You've got your stereotypes, too, I just hope you know that. Nobody gets away without having them." He snagged her gaze with his. "True?"

True, true, she thought, but she knew him better than he knew her. Her prejudices were based on experience—which meant they weren't prejudice? Oh, she'd settle up with herself later. It was better not to yield to this boy-man who always got what he wanted.

Not fair, she knew. Not fair, which made him at least a little bit right.

But not altogether right. "So what do I look like to you? Since I'm not in your circle? Some weird, like, mutant?"

He bumped her knees with his under the table and held his

calves against hers, trying for a little sexual tingle. "Don't." She moved impatiently away.

"I'm convinced," Jordan said, about to make a theory out of it, "that maybe three quarters—no, more—say, ninety percent—of the problems between the races come from unfamiliarity and that's all. Nothing inherent. Nothing, like, irreversible." He was recovering from his long paragraph of self-incrimination, his vulnerability. Like a tire inflating, he rose a little from his slump. "Aren't I right? Don't you have to agree with me so you can go on? You have, see, a vested interest in agreeing. You don't really have any choice."

"Yeah? Why?"

He reached out to stroke her arm. "Because—I mean—you represent, um, the best of both, call them, what? Heritages? *Legacies*. Legacies, all right, in your*self*. So you're under an obligation to see that these halves can be reconciled." He stroked some more, with one finger, slowly back and forth, suggestively. "You are so rare. You make me dizzy."

She blew her breath out dismissively and drank her Coke, looking off into the distance at the tables full of zealous pie-eaters. There was one black couple, young, and one maybe Indian girl, and everybody else was dead-white and prosperous-looking, except for some noisy teenagers who were crammed too many in a booth. She didn't see any of the men Jordan had maligned, not that she could recognize. But who knew what was going on inside anybody, really? The chatter swelled around them. Like every other place she'd been in since she had arrived, it was slightly too cold.

"I'm not rare. I'm not exotic. Just because you don't happen to know anybody like me, that doesn't make me the least bit rare." She couldn't stand that kind of awe in a boy. If he's going to be knocked over, let it be for the right reasons, personal ones.

"I'm planning to double major, did I tell you this?" His confidence was back, full bore. "Sociology and political science, or maybe government, so that I'll have a secure understanding of people and where they're coming from, and I can combine it with, like, a knowledge of policy and how to get things done. I'm going to change things, Ronnee." He told her this quietly as if it was a secret. "I'm going to shake a few things up before I shove off this planet."

"Do tell." She cast her eyes to heaven. This bullshit rose any higher around him, he was going to drown in it with his mouth open.

"You're skeptical."

"Shh, yeah, I'm skeptical." She needed to go pee, but she was afraid it was going to burn. She'd been shut down for so long she'd felt like a virgin again.

"You are *so* cynical."

"Maybe I've got more to be cynical about than you do." She watched his Adam's apple move like a puppet on a string when he spoke. He was *so* young. He was the kind of young who would probably have a beard next time she met him, which would make him look younger still. "You think I'm condescending. But, honey, I'm just realistic. You can keep your politicians and your sociology double major, it's going to take a lot more than familiarity to make white folks comfortable with us. And vice versa."

He was nodding as if he'd proved something he'd suspected. "Comfortable with *us*."

"The part of me you can see. Let's face it, the white part you don't even notice. The white part is not why you're sitting here."

He seized her hand. Very melodramatic. "Not true. Not true. I notice everything about you. Veronica. Ronnee. Just listen. Give me a chance. Please. You don't know what I see, or what you can teach me to see. Trust me. I'm very open." Kiss of death. "And maybe, I'm going to dare to say this although I know you won't like it. But maybe it could even work both ways. There might be a few things you could learn from me."

He was very sweet in his desperation, helplessly arrogant and ignorant, very sure of his good intentions. He was probably the best of them. Her heart sank at the thought.

When was she going to stop saying *them*?

He leaned toward her and half whispered. "I wish we were someplace where I could just stop talking and kiss you and kiss you, all over your gorgeous golden body. And those blackberries . . . Ronnee. You're the most—"

"Jesus, Jordan, cut it out. You're embarrassing me. What is the matter with you?" She looked around to see if anyone could hear. But she could hear and that was worse.

"You don't think you deserve this, you're—"

"Doesn't have anything to do with deserving. I deserve plenty. But, God, boy, get up off your knees. I can't stand that. It's not—" She ground to a halt, suddenly too bored to go looking for the perfect word.

"What?"

"Tasteful. It's not in good taste. Don't be a puppy." That was the thing. And it felt so bogus. It felt like a campaign so that he could be the first on his block to screw a black woman. Half-black. Whatever. She wouldn't be surprised if he tried to steal a pair of her panties—she'd heard of this—so he could take a whiff of her to Princeton with him like a possession to show off. "Baby," she said, mocking herself because she was disgusted with her own weakness for wanting this pretty little boy with his Adam's apple like a hard-on he couldn't hide. Bubble-gum pink, purpling with urgency. "I'll give it to you, chile, if I want to. Do me a favor, though. Don't beg for what you better be man enough to earn."

14

MIRIAM'S MOTHER never answered when she knocked. It had taken her a few visits to realize that this was a statement, a refusal. Ronnee came into the room close on her heels.

"How are you, Mom? How did you sleep?"

"I don't sleep."

A laugh. "Oh, you've given up sleeping."

Miriam waved Ronnee back into the shadows. She shook something up out of a long white box.

"Neiman Marcus, nice enough, is that what it says? I can read those letters even upside down."

"Look, Ma, I brought you a pretty new sweater." It was the color of old blood. Rusty. A color you fight down, Miriam suddenly thought, regretting it.

"I've already got a sweater. A closetful of sweaters. I could sell *them* a sweater."

"But you've got stains on them. And all your prettiest—remember, you traded them away."

"Get me up out of here, will you. Why do you always think you know best? Did I notice that you're the mother around here?"

Miriam laughed again. We all laugh alike; her mother used to laugh that way, too, until she developed this odd leaking noise. Lightly. Southern water must soften the vocal cords.

"So you finally got back. When did you get back?"

"From where? Ma—I was here yesterday." You're the one

who's been away, she wanted to say, if the hospital counted as "away."

"Up east, whatever you thought was worth going off about like that. You'll forget your laugh up there, you know. You know you leave your—Larry—you might come home to a dark house some time, to nothing. No one. Like me."

"Mom . . ."

"Wake up alone. You'll see how you like it. He used to file my nails." She looked around suddenly. "Who's there? Who's out there with you?" What was wrong with her sight? She pulled up the sheet to cover everything. "And my purse is where? It gets away from me."

"Ma, here's—"

"Why do they change the girl all the time? Do they quit? I can never get used to anyone before they send somebody else. I teach them where everything is and then I hope they aren't stealing me blind, plenty of them do, you know, I have to worry about that, how many of them could possibly be honest? The poorer they are, the bigger the temptation. No wonder I don't sleep. Darling, listen—"

"What, Mom?"

"I've been thinking, I should really give you everything I have here that's got any value at all before one of those women makes off with it. Or she might have given it to that little boy of hers, in his pockets. That would be good and clever. And then she'd never come back, so they'd send this other one. You see it doesn't matter who."

"Mother, listen. Please. Look. This is your granddaughter. My daughter. My first daughter, Veronica. Remember, you were asking for her? I brought her to meet you."

"I got a card from her, did I tell you? From her camp, she sent me a pretty card with a butterfly on it."

"No, not Evie. Mom."

"Joy. Don't use that tone with me."

What a long, long breath. "Ma, this is Miriam. Joy is in Hartford. Alan is in Phoenix."

"And just where are we. Where my children are so careful not to be."

"We are in Houston. You are in your apartment. I am one of your children. And this is Veronica, my first child that you asked to meet. And I will not have you insult her."

"Who am I insulting? I am insulting nobody, you are the insulting one here." She pushed off the couch all by herself and stood, swaying. But then she was shouting, "Ah, ah, help! There's this gash all of a sudden, like a slice of red! What is that?"

"What is it, Ma? What's happening?" She was afraid her mother would slide to the ground again.

"Yellow at the edges, frazzly, it's like it's splitting the side of what I see. It's one eye, only one. Like a jagged tear, a gash in a side of meat. Like something you make with a sharp knife. It doesn't move."

"Oh dear." Miriam tried to get close to her. No wonder she couldn't see what was going on.

"Oh, darling, this one's a keeper, Irv used to say that, a keeper." She sank down on the couch. "Some problems move off after a while, you get used to it. The bladder infection, the skin things. Little troubles. But this hole is dancing out there to the side—I saw a tear in a movie screen just like that. Some things, the ruined things, get bigger, never smaller. Something to laugh at, my friends are growing tumors, extra parts of themselves, and I go and get a rip, a hole, subtraction, a less, not a more. Hhmp." She turned her head. "The rip is where that colored girl is." She had to lower her chin to see Ronnee's frowning face. "Do you know how to give a bath? You have such pretty bare arms, strong enough. What are those, grapes on the front of your shirt? Are those grapes or cherries?"

Ronnee opened her mouth and closed it again. *That colored girl.* Miriam waited for her to say something testy, or turn and make for the door.

"A shower, I really mean. The doctor likes me to have a bath but showers wake me up, they're good for circulation. Sometimes I wake up slowly, you know. Ever since my husband went away."

Ronnee still said nothing. Miriam just watched.

"Is your little boy with you today? My help always liked me. Is my daughter saying things about me, keeping you from thinking well of me?"

"Mother."

"Why are we standing in the bedroom? There's a day going on out there."

"Wait, Mom. Please. You wanted to meet your granddaughter. I wanted you to know her, at least a little bit. She wants to know you. Can't you at least *try*?"

"Why do you always plead like that?"

Miriam was holding the reddish sweater in her hands, a sheet of bright color, soft looking. She couldn't stop balling it up like a piece of paper.

"Put that on me then, I need something softer than you."

"My mother used to be a really nice woman, can you believe it?" Miriam said, turning her head toward Ronnee.

"Watch out, you'll stain it. What are you, crying?" She tried to slap the sweater away.

"She was famous for her niceness. Trust me." Miriam was so tense she thought her voice would peel the paint off the walls. She went and put her forehead against the window, light streaming in behind her closed eyes, and breathed. Breathed. It took a while, but when she turned back she was set firm, like a boxer. "Can't you concentrate? Make yourself think about it? I'm telling you this is the child I had way back in Mississippi, you remember that, can't you? We talked about her." I brought her back for you! "Mama, please. It's an old enough memory, God knows. It didn't happen yesterday."

"Oh, really, Miriam," her mother said. "Really, really. Enough." She edged up to Ronnee, who had taken the sweater in her own hands. "You smell of lemon, a little, smell like you come from polishing the furniture." She shook her head gently, experimentally. "The rip still takes the whole side of my eye so I have to move my head if I want the whole scene. But I'm surely not telling another doctor, I'll just have to get used to it. So a little of everything is missing. A little more."

"Here," Ronnee said suddenly. "I'll help you into this. It's so soft. I think it's got lamb's wool in it."

Miriam's mother submitted, her arms raised up, bent, straightened. "You don't talk like you're from here, even for our colored. Where are you from?"

The hands stopped. "New York. Brooklyn. Have you ever been to Brooklyn?"

"I thought she said Mississippi."

Ronnee was smoothing the sweater again, evening up the front where the buttons ran down.

"I can't button anything these days, everything hangs open. Gaping. A gaping life, that's why I get so cold."

"Well, I didn't learn to talk in Mississippi. I was too young." Ronnee spread her hands across the shoulders, chasing out the creases, then held her grandmother out in front to approve, as if she'd made her.

"That happens. True. Oh, this sweater does feel good, I hate to admit it, like another skin, even if it's that dried-blood color. A cardigan this is. Lovely word. Cardigan. Like someone's name."

She leaned in against Ronnee's gold skin in the purple shirt with the grapes on it, made it into a sort of embrace, sneaking it. She stood warm in Ronnee's firm arms looking across at her daughter for spite. "You're always spiny with questions and worries, you never seem to relax," she said to Miriam. "You bring a buzz into the air, demanding, demanding."

Too many years of complicated caring between them to let anything go, just go, Miriam thought. She would always be trying to make it up, pay it back. But the unforgivable *it* was Ronnee. "Just hold me, hon, okay?" her mother whispered to Ronnee, a secret. "Just stay still a minute. If it takes too long I'll pay you overtime. My money's hidden but I'll find it for you. Just stay like that."

And Ronnee did, lemony-cool looking, whispering back in that up-east accent, "Sure, okay, is that good? Nice and soft, huh? Easy."

Okay, Miriam told herself, not sure whether she was relieved or upset. Was it fair that all this woman remembered of her were grievances? Should she have dared to bring Ronnee at all? If they came back tomorrow, would she have to introduce her all over again? Did it matter? If it didn't matter, what *did*?

Her mother looked warm and contented against that solid young chest. "There," Ronnee was saying, like humming. Miriam saw her close her eyes and sway a little. "Is this what you mean?"

15 JORDAN CALLED one morning from work; it was not his usual time. "Hey, can you meet me somewhere tonight? I can't come over to get you."

"You sound funny," Ronnee told him. "What's the matter?"

"I'm pissed is what's the matter. My folks won't let me have the car."

"But it's your car."

"Beside the point. I'm grounded, I guess you could call it. You'd think I was old enough so they wouldn't try this kind of thing."

"Jordan! You're old enough to vote!"

"And get killed for my country, yeah. Well, go tell it to my dad. I felt like telling him when you're old enough to do what I do in that car—you wouldn't think they'd dare."

"What did you *do*?" She was trying to think of how she could get herself somewhere to meet him. There were buses out here, Elpidia took one, along with everybody else brown and black, except for the yard boys—men—who had beat-up pickup trucks to carry their lawn mowers and leaf blowers and all their other noisemakers.

He didn't answer, only breathed furiously into the phone.

"I said, what did you do to make them so mad, Jordan? Did you finally murder your sister?"

"Hey, hey—my sister, now that's an interesting idea."

"You still haven't answered—I want to know if I'm dating a felon or what."

He paused a beat too long. "Only if it's a fucking felony to be seeing you. Or, as my mother puts it—I don't see why I ought to protect her reputation—'the likes of' you. Whatever the hell that's supposed to mean. Jesus, I don't know if I'm going to survive the summer in this place."

She was silent.

"This is bullshit, Ronnee, all right? It's mostly a minor inconvenience. But, I mean, I can't believe they are so uncool with me and my sister bringing them up."

She made her voice very even for fear it would fly away from her. "So how do you think this is supposed to make me feel?"

He didn't answer.

"I think I understand how people can pick up a rifle and shoot up a whole building. I'm beginning to see how you could feel that way. About the likes of your parents, I mean."

"Oh, you'd do better shooting up my mother's elf collection. You never saw all the little gnomes that live on her dresser. Confirmation of her superior intellect. You could come over and do in her whole Hobbit collection with a single ammo clip, probably. Lisa and I would give you a medal."

"Only if I could get your mother at the same time." She said it, but she knew that under a few layers of anger and embarrassment he would find some place that wanted to protect this bigoty-assed mama of his. Of all the targets, in spite of everything, people got killed for insulting mothers. They were the last to be truly abandoned.

"But look, you gave me a great idea for tonight. Lisa goes out to do her patriotic duty, you know, she does this Sanctuary thing? She works to divest South Africa Monday, Wednesday, Friday, and then the other days she's busy saving Salvadorans. Although actually, if you want to know, I think she's in love with this priest who runs the show. But the thing is, if we could, like, hitch a ride with her. I could say I'm going to help out, you know, now that they've, uh, removed me from *harm*, and I have all this time on my hands. Sunday we could swing by and pick you up and we'll just head out."

"But what would we do? You mean, we'd be working with her, whatever she does with them?"

"No, Ronnee. No. She's out by the ship channel, they have this safe house out there. That's a scuzzy part of Houston you haven't had the pleasure of seeing. Full of motels and stuff, a little rough, but, you know—it's okay if you're not a woman walking around alone. It's, like, Greek sailor country, everybody coming off the ships with their pay in their pockets looking for a little entertainment. You can rent your room by the hour."

"Mmm-hmm." Why was she doing this? "Princeton meets Stanford in a roachy motel with gray sheets and mold everywhere? I don't think so."

"Well, hey, what an hour or two we could have. Ron—a real bed. No more stick shift. Think—"

"Jordan, I don't know. Your parents—"

"Screw my parents. They're such hypocrites. All right, listen to this. Out with it. They come back from that party—you know, when you met everybody?—and they're saying, like, Oh, isn't she lovely? What a fine young woman, so this, so that—and then they discover we're—you know—I think your mother told my mother, just, like, casually, it doesn't seem to bother her. Well, it wouldn't, would it?" His laugh was nervous. "And suddenly I get the third degree and then they, like, want me to promise stuff I can't promise, and the next thing you know they're treating me like I'm three years old. They're telling me I'm trying to make a political statement. I asked them just what statement I was making and my mother ends it the way she always ends things when she doesn't like the way they're going."

"Which is?"

"She cries."

"Cries? About *this*?"

"Yeah. Like she's already seeing her little grandchildren and they're, what, octaroons? No, wait. Quadroons."

"Jesus, those words! That's right out of the Reconstruction or something. What are we, in New Orleans, and I'm the Tragic Fucking Mulatto?"

"Believe me. So just screw them."

"Oh, Jordan, is this—is it worth it, really?"

A long hurt pause. "You tell me."

"Political?"

"Political. Shit. Anything that isn't the status quo, there's got to be some kind of paranoid agenda: Is it good for the Jews? And if it isn't—"

She laughed. "Remind them I'm half Jewish. I am, you know. On my mother's side. Isn't that supposed to count double or something?"

"I'm not going to tell them anything. If I said anything it would be 'Kiss my ass.' "

Did everybody have to end up feeling this way about their parents—being owned, being babied? Her father could sit down with Jordan's parents—what an idea!—and they'd all come to the same conclusion about their impossible children.

"Will your sister do this for you?"

"I'll work it out. I've got some stuff to blackmail her with."

"Your sister doesn't look like she ever does anything wrong."

"You'd be surprised. Little Lisa's got a record with me. She's committed—well, not grand larceny exactly, I guess petty, but some pretty serious stuff, moving mucho dineros from my mom's wallet into the hands of this hero priest of hers. She thinks she's Robin Hood. So—"

"So all right. Let's make a joint nonpolitical statement. We'll dedicate it to your mom."

"You wanted to see Houston, right? Wait till you see the Turning Basin."

"The Turning Basin?"

"Where the ships make this one-eighty and head back down the channel again to the Gulf."

"That's not exactly what I had in mind."

"Listen to this, they do more foreign tonnage—"

"Shut up, Jordan. The things that thrill you, you are such a *boy*! I think your parents are right, you're just a little child. You still play with Tonka Toys?"

"No, dear . . ." He thought for a minute. "Now I have an Erector set."

She couldn't help laughing. He wasn't much, but he was better, all pink and gold and eager, than anything else she had discovered down here. (Then again, he didn't have much competition.) Her pathetic stranger of a grandmother with her lights blinking out. Another grade-A bigot under the Alzheimer's. Her bled-dead neighborhood, where even the supermarket, with its so-called music to get you in a buying mood, felt like a gigantic bomb shelter. The girls her age all too busy or too scared to come play. The books for Freshman Comp—Plato's *Republic* on a ninety-seven-degree day, while Elpidia, humming, tiptoed around her dusting "objets" expensive enough to buy a dozen Salvadorans their freedom. She understood what Jordan called larceny, his sister's sin. How long would it be before she could gently broach the question of tuition, bag all this, and go home?

THERE WAS MORE TO LISA than met the eye. For one thing, she was funnier than her brother, because she was more bitter. When Jordan said something about her being in love with "Father Morgan the Sanctuary King," toward whom they were presumably making their innocent way right now, she replied, "Well, do you want to know why I swore off men—I mean accessible men?—at an early age?"

"The laws of cause and effect," Jordan said with a nasty laugh, "force me to ask who swore off who first?"

Lisa had a tendency to sail through his remarks as if they had not been made, though she couldn't resist saying, "Whom. Who swore off whom." Jordan rolled his eyes. Then she told them about her first New Year's date, a monologue that she clearly did not want interrupted. "So when I was thirteen, much too young to be forced to have anything to do with anybody of the opposite sex except maybe a doctor or something, our parents made me and my cousin Scott go out one New Year's Eve. Can you imagine kids that age having to pretend they're dates, all dressed up and carefully combed and trying to look sexy? I barely had any breasts to look sexy with, right?"

"But *now*," her brother interrupted, "now that you've grown into your glorious statuesque body—"

"And because the rule book said you had to, he kissed me at midnight with his lips closed tight, they were like this vise, and his eyes wide open, and it scared me out of five years' growth to look at him that way. Because, you know, I was keeping *my* eyes open, just in case, I don't know what but I didn't trust him. Like, who knew where his slimy hands might end up. And it was like getting up too close to a potato or a rutabaga or something and trying to press your lips into it. It was all, like, spit and hard surfaces." She seemed to be thinking hard. "Not even a vegetable, actually, it was more like kissing a table somebody wiped down with a damp rag. Very unappealing. So ever since, I take off in the other direction when I see him coming. My cousin, God, I'll have to run into him forever. I'll have to go to his wedding some day!"

"Well, he'll never have to come to yours. Has it ever occurred to you you're probably gay?" her brother asked benignly. "That's what that sounds like to me, if you want to know. You're not supposed to be disgusted by sex at thirteen. Not if you're normal."

"What do you know, Jordan. You only know about jumping anything that wears a skirt and can't run fast enough to get away. You've got the discrimination of a billy goat." She turned her head toward Ronnee. "Present company excepted." She began, without a smile, to tell Ronnee how she had discovered what she called— was she being facetious or did she actually dare?—"The Doing of Good." It had audible capital letters. How when she was ten she saved her allowance for a year so that she could send it to some agency that bought goats for villagers in the Sudan. "No, I'm not kidding. They sent me this certificate telling me the goat's name was Bonga—now I wonder if they were all christened Bonga, you know, at the office—and they said the children who drank its milk knew my name and they thanked me with every sip. My mother reacted to the whole thing like I had the damn goat living with me in my room."

"So you figured it was the right path if it irritated Mom enough."

"Pretty much," she said, and tossed her no-colored hair out of her eyes irritably. That hair, Ronnee had noted, was so greasy it looked wet. She was avenging her looks. "Of course, anguish and genocide and starvation and that kind of thing didn't have anything to do with it. Just Mom. The woman's got more power than she realizes. She gets it from going to Jazzercise."

They rode under an overpass. "People drown in these things when it floods," Lisa said, sounding jolly. " 'V'you been here for a toad strangler yet?"

"A what?"

"A big rain, you can get swept away if you're dumb enough to drive into a culvert like that one. People do it all the time. When it floods it isn't funny."

"You really can't get out fast enough?" Ronnee sat forward. Jordan was in front beside his sister.

"No joke. My dad lost a motor once. I mean, he had to have it replaced because it got swamped. And kids are always getting swept away in the bayous. They never believe they could drown."

"Dangerous town," Jordan agreed. "Lot of extremes. My friends and I did that once, we went out into Braes Bayou in a big storm? Scariest thing I ever did. My friend Gordie—Gordie Navasky, Lise?—he got caught in some kind of, I don't know what it was, sort of like a whirlpool, I guess. And we couldn't see him, it was raining so hard—all we hear is this distant shouting, it sounds like somebody up on the bank telling us to stop kidding around out there, but it turns out to be Gordie screaming that he's getting, like, sucked away. And then he bobs up and he's, like, a hundred yards away and he's almost disappearing down this drainpipe. Uch." He shivered. "I still get nervous thinking about it."

They drove slowly and carefully through street after street of battered-looking little wooden houses, dingy white; they were like weeds, accidental looking but somehow durable against bad odds. The few brick exceptions stood out like jewels, glowing, ostentatiously neat. There was nothing about the rest that even vaguely resembled northern poverty, which, however scarred, was never flimsy. It was the wood that did it, Ronnee supposed, and the shingled roofs. The yards were the size of a cigarette pack. But in front of some there grew, in pots and in the patchy grass, the most amaz-

ing flowers and spreads of greenery, and festive decorations—
fences, wooden and iron, and one little house trimmed in bright
blue was protected by a complicated wall of tires stacked like
bricks, with spaces in between. A bright red flamingo stood
queening it over a little yard—bad guess on the paint job, but obviously nobody much cared.

It was so un-depressed! She felt as if there were raucous voices
calling out of those houses, asserting their personalities. Lisa drove
carefully around the children in the street, who seemed undaunted
by the drainage ditches that ran where the curb should have been.
Porch-sitters looked out on the scene, men in undershirts clustered
on steps. Were the other women inside cooking? It was so much
like home, like her block of Bergen Street, her throat thickened
with tears. Memorial, you don't have a clue, so clean and purged
and empty! And so self-righteous. Here you were at ground level
and, better than Bergen Street, you could see the sun come up or
go down over the sagging shoulders of your neighbors' house.
Still, there was something lonely looking about them. She thought
maybe poor people should be able to huddle, even if the hallways
stank. Then again, these were houses. People prayed to have a
house; the idea was magic for them. They didn't want hallways
thick with the smell of other people's cooking. Out on the through
street, most of the signs had been in Spanish. Downtown lay behind them, high crazy shapes and tinted stone, greenish glass,
sticking up into the sky in the middle of nothing, like a bunch of
mushrooms on a lawn.

Now they were heading down a wide street dotted with Mexican restaurants and car-repair shops and gaudy little *iglesias*
behind bright neon crosses. "Almost there," Lisa said. "You'll love
Father Morgan, you guys. You want to see real goodness, not just
some—"

"Lise," Jordan said, not looking at her. Ronnee recognized the
oozy charm of his seducer's voice setting in. "Actually, you could
sort of do us a kind of favor."

"Mm?" She was making a right onto a side street of neat, frail
cottages and fanciful plantings, poised like card houses to fall to

a heavy wind. They were trimmed in harsh pastels, but they were trimmed.

"Um, you could—I should have said it before you turned, but, uh, do you think maybe you could drive us just a little farther down Canal, like—um—to one of those, I think there are some, like, motels about a half a mile or so? More or less?"

The car jerked under Lisa's hands. "Some—like—motels."

"Uh. Right. A little closer to the Turning Basin, actually. You know where I mean."

She snuck a look at him, though she was a driver who tended to stay fixed on the road. "You're not coming to work with me is what you're telling me."

Jesus, Ronnee thought, he lied to her. Goddamn. So much for calling in old debts.

"Well, asshole, if you want to know, no, I will not drive you." She took her eyes off the road long enough to cast Ronnee a very quick, very contemptuous swipe of a glance. "What gave you the idea this was a pimpmobile?"

"Oh, Lise, come on. Where does *this* come from? You're suddenly some kind of one-woman Jewish Legion of Decency?"

Lisa's face looked horsier than ever, her jaw enlarged by anger. She must, Ronnee thought, be just about swallowing her teeth. "Okay, brother, I am letting you guys out at the corner. You can walk to your Quick-Fuck Motel yourself, or you can hitch a ride. Suit yourself." She swung the car around in a noisy U-turn and lurched to a sloppy stop, rear end halfway into the street.

"Oh, come on, what is this? You know, I told you you could help me out of my bind with the parents, and you liked that idea."

"You lied to me, though. You didn't tell me I was—"

"We're consenting adults, Lisa-beth. We are, if you really care about this on your way to do your *illegal* business—which could land you in jail for a *felony*, if you think about it—we are breaking no law, in case that interests you."

Ronnee watched Lisa's jaw begin to quiver and then come back under her control. "I am, for your information, going to take a woman who has just arrived today with a load of eighteen political

refugees in a cantaloupe truck—picture this, all right?—a cantaloupe truck that must have felt like a cattle car on the way to—to
Auschwitz or something—all these terrified people crammed into
the back without air. With barely enough water to drink. Nothing
to eat, nowhere to shit. Total silence." Jordan was looking out the
window trying not to hear her. "She has already been beaten half a
dozen times and the border patrol has a warrant out for her but
she does these deliveries anyway. And I am coming to take her to a
place where she can take a shower and get some sleep before she
gets back in her truck and does it all again. And you want me to
drop you off so you and your—" Now that she had stopped driving she could concentrate her full contempt on Ronnee, who
turned her whole body away. It was too late to tell Lisa she was
mortified. She could only hope that she didn't break and get all
teary.

"You are so fucking sanctimonious," Jordan said. "Can you
only manage to be decent to one set of people at a time? Is that all
the room you've got for compassion? You've got to, like, ration
it?"

"What does compassion have to do with screwing your girlfriend while I'm out there with all these lives in my hands—"

"Oh, please. Hearts and flowers. And I don't think anybody's
lives are in your hands, if you want to know. I think you push papers around in there like a clerk and moon around after the priest.
But whatever you're doing, nobody's making you do it, all right?
And anyway, if you had the chance, who said you wouldn't rather
be screwing somebody yourself?"

"Jordan!" Ronnee objected, and wished he was beside her so
that she could slap him hard. "That's a lousy thing to say."

But her concern for Lisa didn't spare her. "I would have expected you of all people to have more feeling in you for the underdog." Lisa had a large mouth cannily shaped for disgust. Her lips
seemed to have a number of depressed places in them that could
suggest extreme disapproval.

"What does that mean, 'you of all people'? Why should I have
any special feeling for the underdog? Do I look like an underdog
to you?"

Lisa smiled bitterly. "Well . . ."

"Well, what? Did it ever occur to you that I might not be particularly political? Isn't that my right?"

Lisa made a face and looked out her window. She rolled it down and fussed with her sideview mirror, realigning its angle, concentrating very hard. "I guess it's your right. I'm just disappointed, is all. I thought you were a serious person, but I guess I was misinformed."

"It so happens that I *am* a serious person. Whatever that means. Whatever *you're* into, I suppose. But if you want to know, I have never given one single thought in my life to refugees in the back of cantaloupe trucks or anywhere else. So what does that make me?"

Lisa was silent.

"I asked you something." Ronnee felt the hot air push its way in through the open window like a fist.

"Don't bully me," Lisa shouted, her face red. "Who the hell do you think you are that you can talk to me like I'm your servant?"

Ronnee pushed open her door. "Let's go, Jordan. Let her go save the world her own way."

"So long, sister bitch," Jordan said cheerfully, and slammed his door as hard as he could.

Ronnee had a second thought then, and walked around to Lisa's side, where the window was still open. "I just want to say something to you, little sister."

Lisa blinked at her as though she were a bright light.

"You better think a little about what goes into assuming I'm automatically going to love that underdog of yours. That may sound like a compliment to you but it sounds like a condescending little racist something to me, and I don't think you can even begin to understand why."

"Come on, Ron." Jordan was partway down the block without her. "Let it lie."

She ignored him and leaned down close to Lisa so that she could speak quietly. "You don't know who I am or what I'm interested in, you just barely met me, so if you think I have to give a damn about your cantaloupe lady it's only got to be because my skin is darker than yours."

Lisa looked at her with an expression too complex for her to read, but she did not apologize. She dared to look straight into Ronnee's eyes, either sending or receiving a message, and then, after a long silent minute, she turned the key and the car shot away backward. There was a small parking lot beside a shabby, green-shaded house down the block; the car turned in to it and made its way across its broken surface and subsided. Across the street stood a pretty, paint-chipped church with twin steeples, the kind that sits in the center of every small Mexican town.

Ronnee caught up with Jordan, who had stopped and was looking back at the safe house and the car. Lisa had disappeared inside. "Just hang on a minute." He was whispering. "I think we're going to make us a little mischief."

"What are you doing, Jordan?" This whole thing, Ronnee thought, was nothing but embarrassing. Did they have to work out their crude, disrespectful sibling drama right where she was walking?

"Nothing that girl needs that a guy with an unzipped fly couldn't do for her," Jordan was saying. "If she didn't turn him completely off." He had started down the street toward the house.

"Cut it out, okay? I don't appreciate that kind of talk." She was nearing the end of her patience.

Jordan stopped short. "Oh, the Virgin Queen all of a sudden."

"Now why are *you* insulting me this way? You and your sister both—you don't seem to know anything about common decency."

"Hey, *please*. Just you please take it easy. Why don't you let Miss Self-Righteousness take care of herself? I don't think she'd be grateful for your, ah, defense. I don't think she particularly wants your sisterly solidarity."

"You might be surprised. But you really don't get it that she's not the only one you're insulting." What an exhausting afternoon this had turned into, and now she was supposed to walk into some sleazy motel room and melt at this boy's touch? Christ, how was she going to get out of this?

Her father had warned her—how had he known? Was it himself

he knew?—about what he called "taking liberties." A man will talk dirty to you, he told her just around the time she supposed a mother would have been giving instruction in tampons and the pill; he was passing on his best knowledge, her sweet daddy. "But it's a kind of—it's meant to be a little demeaning, you know how I mean that? Honey, it makes you—he wants to drag you into it with him, tear you down, even if it isn't you he's talking about. You don't let him do that. You make him watch his words. That kind of language, that's a weapon of force. You just best be careful." He had his I-really-mean-this-and-it-matters face on. "And if a white man talks rough to you, he's trying to insult your black womanhood and you've got every right in the book to tell him to just watch his step with you. And then you just walk away. You've got more dignity in your little finger than some men have in their whole selves. You know that, don't you?"

She understood, but it was confusing: Did that mean that white men insulted you for different reasons than black men? She knew black men could hurt their women, so what would *their* reason be? She kept silent. She would figure it out as she went along.

Her hand in Jordan's reluctantly, they had walked back to stand on the broken sidewalk beside Lisa's dusty car. "Okay," he said, and flashed that smile of his that was like propaganda for his cause. "Let's see what we can do here. We're going to give the kid a little scare."

"What are you doing? Jordan?"

He was agile, all too practiced. Who said white boys didn't possess criminal gifts? A few minutes of fussing out of sight and the car rumbled to a start. He crawled out from under it without so much as a smudge on his bright blue shirt, with its polo player riding high on his chest. "Let's go. We'll give her a couple of hours and then we can decide if we want to bring it back and keep our little secret or let her come out and find it gone. Ha! She'll shit a brick."

He drove slowly along the desolate street where one motel looked less promising than the last. "Oh, let's just pick one," he finally said. "We're going to have our eyes closed anyway, right?"

It was called La Esmeralda and its sign had a gash through it as if someone had thrown a knife and hit a bull's-eye. A.C.! TV! Welcome to the twentieth century, she thought. There was nothing like a lobby, only a narrow ill-lit office, a counter, really, overseen by an extremely heavy man in a T-shirt who didn't seem to want to move out of range of his fan. They must be saving the AC for the guests. Wind rippled the piece of paper on which Jordan signed them in as Duncan and Linda Albright ("for our brightness," he said. Did he know that "bright" meant light-skinned? How she'd been called, and more than once, "light, bright, damn near white"? Only one of the million things he would never know).

"Car," the man prodded with a Hispanic accent and shoved it back at him.

"Car?" Jordan repeated.

"License number."

"Oh!" He had looked alarmed for a second. "Oh shit, what's the—could you have a look for me? Linda?" He gave Ronnee his payoff smile. "Borrowed car," he told the man, shrugging, as if anybody cared.

She almost bolted. If they'd only been in a civilized place, she'd have walked away from this crude, arrogant, self-absorbed boy— not white boy, she lectured herself. Just *boy*. How far did he think his golden-haired arms and gym-hardened body and fake innocence would get him?

But when she pushed open the door and saw the gravel parking lot, a rusted Dumpster from whose mouth hung a pizza box bloodied with tomato sauce, the broken tide of traffic clattering past, and blue-gray darkness coming down fast over this late Sunday afternoon like a blanket, and smelled chemical toxins, burnt coffee (she had seen the Maxwell House plant down a side street), and the heat—the heat itself seemed to have its own overbearing odor, the way a room smelled when her iron had scorched a piece of cotton—she nearly stumbled with discouragement. It was an ugly moment, standing alone out there in the stinking twilight, the asphalt of the parking lot singeing her feet around the edges of her sandals. There was no way out of this now. None of it was what she had hoped for. She imagined the calm of her mother's house, the way it rose around her, ominous and seductive as cool water. That clean tile floor, so self-possessed under its daily mopping, those perpetual tulips, fingernail red giving over to sunflower yellow to fuchsia almost daily. Elpidia carried the old ones home if they still had enough life in them, their stems wrapped in a wet paper towel held by a baggie and a rubber band. "I put—" she told Ronnee, gesturing, with a shy smile. "I so happy I put these to *my* table!" How quickly it had all become habit.

"Maybe we can take a shower?" she asked Jordan when they were on the way down the stained walkway to their room, which smelled exactly as she knew it would. Mildew was the worst thing for her lungs. She was afraid she'd be sick.

"If they have one," Jordan said humbly, trying for enthusiasm, failing. There was only so much strength he could fake. She appreciated that; it almost made her feel a sliver of tenderness for him. He could do what he wanted with her as long as she was standing under the balm of cool water. She wanted it in her ears, down to the sweaty follicles of her hair, between her scorching toes. She would be saved, she wouldn't even feel him, whatever he did. He was holding her hand so tightly her rings cut into her fingers. "If they have one. If it works."

JORDAN GALLANTLY, with a flourish, pushed open the door for Ronnee. The furrows of her ears still held water from her—their— long shower, their virtuoso shower in which they had so energetically enjoyed each other. Jordan's ideas about how they should celebrate their freedom from the backseat of his car were far more persuasive than anything he'd ever said to her. They'd stood naked side by side, holding hands, before the blotchy mirror that hung above the dresser, straight on, like obedient children summoned for discipline. She had never been able to see, only to feel, that Jordan had the ridgy pecs and flat abs, the tensile strength, of someone with plans for himself; he was working at his perfection. Ronnee was half disgusted, half captivated by her own lushness beside him, the sheen of her skin across soft places and hard, like a piece of sculpture waiting to be stroked by a sensitive finger. They turned, delighted by the picture they made, and untenderly fell together.

Such satisfaction! She felt a druggy exhaustion, half high, half soothed. Nothing was quite like this rush of well-being, though wouldn't it have been better still to lie down in that bed, however spongy, under the frayed sheet, the feeble air-conditioning blowing over them, hip to hip, thigh against thigh, and fall into satiated sleep?

But, "Time to get the car back to the Virgin Queen," Jordan muttered, sibling nastiness beginning to settle over him, inevitable as Houston sweat, as he pulled his jeans back on. Ronnee buckled her sandals as slowly as she could, to stay in the pallid coolness just a little longer. He shouldered the door open onto the furnace-flash of searing air. Such heat around sunset still shocked her; only the glare was gone. He reached for Ronnee's hand, to keep the mood going, and she leaned gently into him. "Told you you wouldn't be sorry," he murmured, and slid his lips up and down her neck as if she were a harmonica. Ronnee twisted herself around to land a light kiss somewhere near his mouth. "Next time I'll listen," she whispered. He was just the right height beside her.

And just then, exactly then, after she'd unwound herself and he had his hand on the car door, they were doused in blue light as if they'd walked into a luridly lit building instead of out into the twilight.

"Stop right there!" a voice called from the other side of the light, harshly. "Don't move."

"Oh, for Christ's sake, what is *this* now," Jordan muttered, as if it were a petty irritation of the expectable kind. He held his hand above his eyes, squinting to see; the light was like a giant wave that heaved in front of them, blocking off the whole world. Then, raising his voice, he repeated, "What the fuck is this?"

"You better watch that language, buddy," said the voice, "or you're in worse trouble than you already are."

Ronnee tried to shrink herself against the car. Oh shit, oh shit, what kind of trouble were they in.

"Walk toward me slowly, away from that vehicle." The voice was addressing Jordan. The policeman it belonged to surfaced through the blue light with his eyes narrowed and his gun—impossible!—held in front of him as if they were criminals. He was big, beefy, like the pictures of Southern sheriffs her father used to show her, the kind of lardy white guy that stayed out of the sun, his hat riding high on what looked like pale red hair. Somewhere Ronnee had read that redheads were the least respected group, at least when they turned up on TV. No wonder they ended up holding guns like the world's biggest erections, like movie cops. He had a small sidekick with him, a wispy, narrow-shouldered guy with a neat mustache, a lover's mustache. They looked like a comedy team, but here they were in this stinking parking lot aiming at teenagers.

They holstered their guns. She hoped they felt stupid for waving them around. The leather pouches that swung at their hips, those holsters weighted by their revolvers, always made her think of well-hung horses.

"Is this your car, sir?"

Sir? That was funny. Jordan, not quite so cool now, looked like he needed the car for support. She could hear his dry lips come apart with the sound of velcro tearing open. "It's . . . borrowed."

"You have permission of the owner?"

Poor Jordan. He threw his head around like a cornered horse trying to escape the bridle.

The bigger, older one, meaner looking by far (though she suspected a small cop might be especially dangerous) bore down on him. Jordan was the one they were after. The cop stood very close and stared into Jordan's face.

"Hey, don't," Jordan objected, shaking his head violently. "I don't need your breath in my face, you know?"

The cop's eyes flared. "License and registration," he demanded, more controlled than Jordan deserved, in that mechanical voice they liked to use.

Jordan fumbled in his back pocket for the wallet that bulged against his hip. His black jeans were so tight it wasn't easy.

"Hurry it up," the cop said, and then looked her all over, twitching his eyes back and forth between the two of them.

Jordan was finally flustered. "I'm trying—just let me—"

"Jeez, boy, looks like you got your prick around back there. You let this gal rearrange you 'fore she was done with you?"

Jordan tugged and lifted a hip. He had to do a little dance to pull it out. His face was as red as the policeman's, which was the color of new sunburn.

The cop looked over Jordan's license without a word. "Registration?" He made an impatient little gimme movement, a flickering of his fingers.

"It's—uh—it's my sister's car."

"And she knows you're driving it."

"Oh, sure," Jordan said. "She gave me the keys, she—"

"Can you show me the keys?"

Jordan stared at him. His mind couldn't possibly work fast enough for this.

"You don't have keys, sir. I happen to know that for a fact. There's a UUMV out on you. You know what a UUMV is? I'll just bet you can guess, can't you."

Ronnee watched Jordan squirm. She had known this was a stupid idea, she had absolutely known. Why had she not just refused?

"Give you a hint, sir. 'S got the word 'unauthorized' in it someplace." He raised his eyebrows as if to say "Get it?"

The other policeman, she realized, had been searching the car. He was bent down, ass in the air, poking around on the floor under the front seats. God, had he seen Lisa? Did she look like she was hiding something? Probably he hadn't, though; probably they got this stolen-car thing off their radio. One look could have saved him some trouble.

"And you, hey." The redheaded cop was talking to her. She turned back to him reluctantly. "You look at me when I'm talking to you." She had been thinking of this as Jordan's problem, a little punishment for his feeling of perpetual white-boy safety. If he'd spent a day in Bed-Stuy he wouldn't have felt so damned exempt.

"You two were in this place here together?" He thrust his chin at the motel.

She hesitated. Were they supposed to have a lawyer or something before they answered questions? Were they in enough trouble for a lawyer? "Leave me out of this, okay? I didn't steal anything," she said, sullen, her heart beating so violently she was sure he could see it. She'd deal with her disloyalty later.

"We have you coming out of there, the two of you. You got any prior arrests, miss?"

Ronnee returned his stare as insolently as she could. She wanted to say something snide, but she calculated the danger; it was worth keeping her mouth shut. She had heard enough of her daddy's stories. Jordan was on his own.

He moved so close to her she could smell his uniform. It wasn't sweat-sour but bitter, like starch, like stiff new fabric, and some other kind of sweetness in a swarm around his head. Was he chewing gum? Or maybe he had something on that crazy pink hair to keep it down. He ought to wear a shower cap like certain people she knew.

"I'm talking to you, Susie," he said. "You deaf?"

"Arrests?" She hated to start this. "You've got to be kidding."

"You can watch your fresh mouth, too, Susie. You ship-channel hookers all think you deserve a free pass cause you go with these perverts, come off the boats like steers out of the pen. You think that gives you permission for any damn thing you please." He tweaked her shirt as if that would show his contempt. They weren't supposed to touch you, she knew that. They weren't supposed to talk that way either.

He was right at her ear. "He pay you extra good for your black pussy, darlin'? You set up on one of these corners here?"

She pulled her breath in hard as if she'd been slapped on the back; she would not look at him. The brick of the motel was mottled and crumbling. There were gaping spots, decayed like bad teeth.

He slid his hand down the top of her arm and back up again. "Let me see your ID, now, darlin'. Come on."

"I don't—" She didn't have anything with her. Her wallet had some cards stuffed between the pictures of her friends—library, student government—but nothing official, and surely nothing with her Houston address on it. "Like what? I don't have—"

"Driver's license'll do."

"I don't drive."

He moved against her again. He came so close he could feel her breasts if he wanted to.

"I don't like your tone, little lady. What can you show me says you belong around here?"

She felt her eyes dim and water. "I don't know what you mean. I don't belong around here. I live in Memorial. I *actually* live in New York. I've got my school—"

In her ear again. "Oh right, Memorial. I'm sure. *And* New York, what do you know. Next thing you know it'll be Paris, France." He took a deep breath. "Tell me, you put your legs around his neck, do you? You got some special tricks you could teach a poor little ignorant white boy like me? 'Cause I don't go with niggers, you know, so maybe I don't have the right experience to know what to do."

If she wasn't careful she was going to use her claws on him. "You can't talk that way, you're not supposed—"

His voice kept getting quieter, more private. "Where did you say your ID was, sugar? I don't think I remember you showed it to me." He winked. Then he turned to the other policeman. "You keep an eye on her, Jimmy. You can take her in back there, check her out, but make sure you keep her hands out of trouble. These dark sisters like to get a little feisty on us when they get mad. It's the African savage in 'em."

Jimmy could do it, too. He bent her arm behind her back while he walked her to the rear of the motel. She let out a yelp of pain.

"You just shut up," he warned her. "He's not the only one can get mean."

"What are you doing? This is ridiculous!" She pulled hard and got her arm back, stinging.

"I'm searching you is what I'm doing." He stood her against the broken cement of the motel's rear wall and ran his hands from her shoulders down every bit of her, slowly, fingers spread, shame-

lessly enjoying himself. His face was impassive, but sweat jeweled
the edges of his mustache. She'd never seen a cop up close before.
"See, I do a real careful job. Can't let nothing get by." Did he want
to be congratulated? His eyes didn't so much as flicker, but when
he passed his open hands over her breasts he gave a little double
squeeze, as if she was a rubber toy that might squawk back at him.
"You got anything on you you're not supposed to have?" he asked
vaguely, as if that justified his palms against her shirt, resting in the
concave dip above her pelvic bone, his fingers fluttering toward
the V between her legs, hesitating, withdrawing, then down her
back to where the slope of her butt began. She could have sworn
he patted her before he took his hands away. "We'll let the matron
do the rest."

"The rest! Who says you're supposed to do what you already
did?" It occurred to her suddenly, through her fear—who said
they were really cops? Maybe this was the way a couple of jerks
got their jollies. Maybe their uniforms were fake. The other one
smelled new because he'd just unfolded it from some box.

Was it always this way, that the realest, scariest things felt like
they couldn't be real? Her friend Santha had told her about an au-
tomobile accident, how everything felt like she'd made it up and so
she could stop it if she wanted to, if only she could figure out how
to. Her little sister had died in that crash. She saw her crumpled
and bleeding, but it was almost all right because she kept waiting,
she said, to simply wake up. That was the kind of thing you only
saw in a nightmare. Or a movie. In a certain way she never did believe any of it, even though her sister was gone, because *nothing*
felt real anymore. She stayed out of school for months because she
couldn't concentrate; everything, she told Ronnee, seemed like
part of a game.

Ronnee looked at the two men in their shades of blue, belts
hung with heavy unpleasant objects, standing, legs apart. They
were pictures of policemen. Here it was, what her father had always told her to expect, and still her heart hammered like it was
going to leap out of her chest. The way they stood you knew they
could do anything they wanted to—rape her in their cruiser, stuff

them in that Dumpster—anything at all, hidden behind those
starched shirts, those complicated unreadable badges, and they
knew it. This wasn't the same as Santha's accident, nobody had
died. But she understood now: some things don't feel real.

"Okay, Jimmy, let's go. Let's move it." And the handcuffs came
off their belts. When Ronnee's closed, all edges, weighting her
hands down in front of her, she thought, Jesus, here we go, are we
in trouble! They were cold and shiny, hard, out of a world she
never had to traffic with, and she knew this was the beginning of
horrible steel surfaces, unsympathetic keepers, till they got free of
this stupid business. Believed or not believed, this was not going to
be fun, but surely they would get out of it in one piece. Just what I
need, she thought bitterly, to impress my mother. And Barry.
Won't straight-arrow Barry just love this. Thanks, Jordan.

Jordan tried to keep from being crammed into his seat in the
cruiser, though Ronnee didn't know why—where did he think he
was going? His cuffed hands useless, he pushed back with his elbows until the redheaded cop, his face an alarming color, pulled his
billy club off his belt and whacked him sharply, almost casually,
across his shoulders. The *whap-whap* sounded like a shoeshine
man polishing somebody's shoes. "Mess with me, you little nigger-
fucker, you're going to be sorry. I can aim this SOB down lower,
you want it where it really smarts, and you won't have nothing left
to diddle these girls with." He gave Jordan a nudge with his knee,
fast and gone. "Or you might not make it downtown at all. You
don't threaten the law like that. You got that?"

Jordan collapsed into his seat, all the way in, coughing, catching
his breath. She didn't say a word. If she'd spoken, her breath
would have singed a layer of his flesh to ash. Dumb arrogant little
child. Little hot shit, you're not so untouchable, are you. He sat
with his shoulders hunched, as if he'd been folded down the middle, his teeth chattering with cold or terror. Once, when the cops
were laughing noisily behind their fence of a barrier, he tried to
apologize to her.

"Keep it," she said as crudely as she could, and turned away to
look at the city speeding by like scenery in a movie. He was
bruised, though, she saw, a wide scrape like a spill of cinnamon

reddening dangerously close to his eye. "What's that on your fore-head?" The handcuffs, heavy as weights, scratched her wrists. She couldn't touch him because they were hard to lift and made her clumsy.

He shrugged. "I don't think he wanted anything to show—he kept poking me with that club, he was sticking it in my side and, like, pushing. But at least I've got this scrape so I can prove he hurt me. Ronnee, these bastards think they can get away with anything they want, but they can't fuck with people this way. They're going to regret that little scene back there."

She laughed bitterly. "They can't, huh? Well, they just did, sweetie. They can do anything they want to. Who's going to be-lieve *you*?"

"Come on, Ronnee. We weren't resisting or anything."

"Oh, please." She turned away in disgust.

"Hey!" It was the big cop yelling. "Shut the fuck up back there! You're not supposed to talk."

Jordan twitched in his seat. "You can't keep us from talking. You ever hear of the Bill of Rights?"

"Can it, faggot. I don't want to hear your debating-club shit."

They were in the dark of that underpass Lisa had tried to scare her with. When they came out into the light she saw a big-eyed white girl about her age staring at her from a car in the next lane. Smile or stick your tongue out? she wondered. God, she was tired and sweaty. Neither.

Jordan breathed out hard. "I'm gonna skin my sister, I'll tell you that." He was whispering. His wrists were red where the cuffs hit them. "She's not gonna recover from what I do to her."

"Jordan! You stole her car. You thought it was funny."

"She knew who it was. She didn't have to call the fucking police on her own brother." He gave her a poisonous look. "I hope you know you're just the same, both of you. Is this a woman thing or what?"

"Is what a woman thing?"

"Loyalty would never occur to you? 'Leave me out of this.' Hey, thanks, Ronnee. A guy can really lean on you."

She took it from him without bothering to search for an answer.

Learn something, asshole, she thought, trying to feel tough for the place they were going to. I hope they teach it to you good.

AND ON THE OTHER SIDE OF IT, it still felt like a terrible joke—after they were pushed inside, fingerprinted, photographed, logged in, their national records searched for, amid the clatter of lockers, the phone that rang so often it was like the hiccups. How could that woman who answered it sound so calm on her three hundredth call of the day, laughing, greeting people gaily between the clashing of bells? There were so many people to admire, Ronnee thought, in the middle of this mess of fools.

But then she listened as well as she could (which was not very well) to the redhead cop listing the atrocities they had committed and she stopped feeling benign. Some of them went by numbers—what were a PSMV and a 402? She gathered that they were accused of all sorts of resistance, provocation, threat, disobedience, crimes that only began with car theft. Against all those letters and numbers, who would hear them if they cried out the names of the crimes against them?

And then they were gone, the men who had made all the trouble. The big gun got a Coke out of a machine and wandered off, uninterested in what came next. She seethed, she had to keep herself from screaming out her list of outrages. They'd put her in a straitjacket before they'd listen. Jordan, beside her for a while, said finally, "Hey, don't we get to call anybody? We're supposed to—"

"Come on, slugger," another cop said, a tall, skinny one, solid and brown as a baseball bat. "We're off to see the Wizard." He took Jordan's arm and swung him around, none too gently, and pushed him toward the very thick door to the back. "Let's not worry about no phone calls just yet, okay? We got some work to do."

She knew she was next. They were going to put her in with whores and women who cut people with razors. She was doomed: either she was one of them and kept their contempt at bay by lying or she wasn't one of them, she was a graduate of St. Helen's, about to go to Stanford, and they'd probably push her face into the toilet. She tried her voice on the comforting woman at the desk. "Can't I call my mother? I want to call and tell her—" How strange it sounded to say that, as if she'd been calling her mother all her life. What a thing to have to tell her, though. The shame of this just might be enough to finish off her chances, get her brought back to the airport and shipped back home. A returned purchase, back to Bloomingdale's. Though no purchase had been made, exactly. What had changed hands?

"Ain't my choice about phone calls, dear," the woman said. Ronnee followed her eyes. A rough-looking white woman with enough keys at her waist to sound like jingle bells was coming toward her. "I'd let you if I could, but I guess they got their own ideas." She winked but she didn't smile. "Good luck in there."

16

BY THE TIME IT WAS ALL OVER it had become unreal for the telling: the holding cell, a dozen details, mostly uncomfortable. The other women, she assumed, were whores or druggies, mildly inconvenienced by yet another arrest. Nobody looked very dangerous, but neither did they look inviting. One white girl in an electric-orange microskirt was probably about her age. She had short, black-striped platinum hair like a zebra, a joke, and as much junk around her neck as Madonna. How she had managed to keep a sweet, vulnerable look around her thickly circled eyes Ronnee couldn't imagine. There was a good bit of sullen complaint in the air, some hearty laughter, and frequent noisy outbursts from the woman who (she heard instantly, as though they were proud of her) had used his own service revolver on her police-sergeant lover, and a good thing she was a lousy shot or she'd be in bad shape: Do you get the automatic death sentence for killing a cop if he's your live-in and you're having a normal fight over who takes out the garbage or who the hell was that woman she saw him standing too close to last night? The outbursts occurred when the other women discussed this legal fine point in the presence of the accused. There was something affectionate in the names she called them, as if they were all complicit, somehow.

She would remember the flurry of curiosity about her, quickly dimmed, which seemed to consist solely of territorial concerns: Where was she set up? Why had no one seen her before? Did she have a pimp or was she an independent, a hot-shit working girl? She wasn't sure how to respond, whether the truth would make her seem haughty or stupid or uncooperative. Being half-white, she suspected, wouldn't help either. She shrugged a lot and muttered answers no one could hear.

But it took a while for these details to surface in her memory because first she had to put a lot of effort into staying alive. She never did figure out what was responsible—the cell was putrid with oniony sweat, foul feet, rancid cologne, and over it all the artificial stink of bathroom deodorizer, a pink smell, knife sharp, hostile to reality. The air was hotter than a fast-food kitchen; the walls on one side of the cell wept, they ran like sores, a thin trickle of something rust brown dribbling down the worn surface until its paint was gone. A stagnant little puddle ringed the half-clogged drain so that it looked like a stuffed toilet.

In one corner, their backs to the bars, two women—one white, as wide as she was tall, the other a long, droopy sister, ashy black like something with mold on it, in jeans held up by hairy twine— were smoking as furiously as they could before the matron came by to threaten them and take their illegal butts away. Not exactly secret, smoke bloomed around them like bus exhaust, impenetrable, foul. And when she tried to list to the other side of the cell there was that intolerable smell of disinfectant so harsh she could feel it clog the air with toxic chemicals. God, you could see the cancer dancing in front of you! She caught a whiff of the vomit that stinkbomb was meant to mask.

But she had begun to feel it, she would tell the doctors, almost as soon as she arrived. Half an hour of that cocktail of odors and mildew and she was out of breath, her lungs tight, and then all too quickly bruised-feeling, sore. She could already feel herself on the brink of hard breathing, starting, want to or not, the labor to pull in clear new air. Then they called her out for questioning and even though she hated them for that, she could almost breathe for a while. But the interrogation room was refrigerated after the dank heat of the cell, and nothing was worse for her than that kind of sudden chill. Why didn't everyone in Houston have pneumonia?

Cold invaded her, lanced her, and made her shiver from someplace deeper than her skin. She had lost her sweater a long time ago.

"Can I have my bag back for a minute? There's something I need in it," she asked the matron as she was led back to the cell. She hoped she sounded young and helpless.

"No, you can't have nothing." The woman looked offended. "Where do you think you are?"

"It's not—my nebulizer's in there. I have asthma." Coffee, she thought, too, maybe if she could get some strong coffee things would open up a little.

The matron, in the drab light blue uniform of a cleaning woman with police connections, looked her up and down contemptuously—automatic denial was probably habit, because these crazy chicks must ask for the moon. Middle-aged, a fine fudge color, she looked Ronnee over with the familiar unforgiving anger of a darker-skinned woman. "I can't give you nothing till you check out of here." Her harshness brought tears to Ronnee's eyes. "Anyway you don't look like you're dying. Big girl like you."

"But I'm—"

"Don't ask me again, girl. You don't like it here, simple, next time don't get picked up." She pushed Ronnee into the cell, clanged the gate shut, and shook it once to be sure the lock had caught. How could you work here if you hated everybody you touched?

So much for the coffee. And it kept getting worse. She coughed and hacked, she searched for a clean space to breathe in, she put her palms against the slimy wall, though it was disgusting to the touch, and leaned down between her raised arms, trolling for good air. But this had happened to her before: once she started, she knew she couldn't stop unless she got away to pure air, and that would be no help either. Even then. She pulled and pulled—it was always lonely right here; a sadness welled in her that she couldn't explain if she had to—but everything was tightening, shriveling; at the same time she could almost feel the swelling, puffing up in there and closing off, all of it untouchable, though she'd have clawed herself open if she could have. She coughed till she thought her throat would burst and blood would come out of her mouth, trying to dislodge the immovable thing. How did she breathe when things were normal? She couldn't remember. When she looked around she was being ignored, except for the young one in the orange skirt who shouted, "Hey, enough, okay? You sound like a goddamn barking dog."

Her fingers stank where they had touched the wall.

By then she was rasping, pursing her lips and breathing small, like mincing baby steps the way her doctor had shown her, until a cough ripped through and big jagged blank spots leaped up in front of her eyes. She didn't know anyone else this happened to, as if, lacking breath, she lacked vision too, those holes that loomed like huge dark featureless flowers, that gaped with nothing on the other side. She was afraid to think of what lay back there waiting for her.

"Please," she begged no one in particular. She had breath for only one word at a time, and then one syllable. "I. Need. Help. Me. Call. Some. One." A long laboring time between words, feeling stupid, hearing herself wheeze, so useless. There was such random inattention, such a tumult of noisy conversation and insult, anger, so much anger, anger under all of it, that no one was going to listen. If the dark holes got any bigger she was going to disappear into one. She could feel the skin of her neck getting sucked back with every breath, didn't have breath enough to shout or power, even, to stamp her foot. Her ribs ached from pulling in, the pain from neck to belly button, none of it working, all that balking effort, her neck so tired, all of it was *in*, none of it *out*, all the bad air puddling. She couldn't do anything but sway, desperate to sit. Finally, just before she hit the scummy damp floor, straight up on her tailbone, like a child she pulled at the puff of dirty shirt on the skinny sick-looking black woman in the roped-up jeans, "Help. Call. Please," and the woman turned on her fast as if she'd been burned. But finally she heard a commotion, a chorus of voices shouting out for the matron, for a doctor. "Somebody choking in here! Move it, man. She don't look good!" A different voice: "Don't people die of this shit? Hurry *up*!" Something, finally, like that. She heard her own desperation, loud and gross as some animal, and it disgusted her. She was drowning. She had drowned.

Still, it was a while. When they got her on the gurney she was swamped and had to sit up or she was done for. She tried to pull herself up and they pushed her back. No mask? Where was the mask to spray the mist that would save her? She had been through this before and knew what she needed. She heard soft cursing, the paramedic looking for the damn thing, turning things over, a lot of useless clanking and tinkling glass, calling out "Albuterol? Al-fucking-buterol?" Not liking the answer. "Jesus H. Fucking Christ," she heard. Jamaican. A good voice, like the women, angry. "Kind of moron loads this wagon anyway?" And then, into and out of the dark empty flowering holes, she couldn't hear anything. "No, not oxygen," and a face over her saying in that music, "Hang in there, girl. We get you there. You be okay. Okay, okay." Or maybe she dreamed that, she was so tired of sucking in on nothing. She heard just enough to know she was still in the world, but barely. Why didn't they cut into her throat, her swollen chest, do that, do that. Maybe she'd stop drowning, her trachea wide open. The tires were hissing like escaping air—rain? She was pulling in so hard she should be inflating like a Macy's parade balloon but she was shrinking instead, her skin sucked back in like she could eat it. Where was her daddy? No, wait, her mother was the one nearby, and she didn't know. How could she not know? If she was her mother she would know this was happening, and how alone she was. Where was everybody? Was anything worth this effort? Where in the world was she?

She only saw when they were close to the flung-open emergency-room doors (yes, it was glistening wet outside, she was glad to know she had heard right, they were pushing her through warm rain but the air was still heavy and thick as stone) that her right wrist was handcuffed to the pole that did not hold what she needed to breathe. Like she was going somewhere. Idiots.

17 SHE DIDN'T COME HOME and didn't come home.

Miriam knew Ronnee was with Jordan and Lisa—when they double-beeped outside, she went running, carrying the sweater she had learned to take along on excursions in this town whose air was equatorial while its air-conditioning was arctic. Miriam had asked why they were going with Lisa, and Ronnee muttered something about Solidarity.

"Solidarity? You mean, like the Polish shipyard workers?"

"No, no! *Sanctuary*. Sorry!" She hit her head with her open hand.

It took Miriam's breath away, sometimes, that Ronnee was so determinedly apolitical. For a smart girl it was almost a joke. Possibly her sense of herself as an actress was too strong to allow distraction by such worldly matters; she liked to call herself a right-brained "feeler" as opposed to a "thinker." But Miriam suspected Eljay behind it, a recoil from his willed hyper-consciousness: Eljay in his first incarnation had been a musician, not a demagogue. She saw him—the image skittered across her mind with subliminal speed—tilting Charita's chin up—up, just slightly to the right—to release her chest voice. So Ronnee would be *damned* . . . But it was her right, after all. It wasn't fair that she couldn't afford to be as airheaded as the next girl. Solidarity!

SHE WENT TO VISIT HER MOTHER. They tried to walk in the garden a little bit, but there was a hot breeze that was no fun. Miriam, her heart seizing, cramped muscle that it was, mentioned Ronnee and had to hear her mother's innocent "Who?" If she were to bring her to visit again, they would do the same mad dance, and the next day and the next. "Who? Mississippi, what Mississippi?" What a pity such forgiveness was useless. She fought with herself to believe this amnesia was not willful. She made herself imagine her mother's brain like an old-fashioned telephone operator's switchboard, every other connection pulled and dangling. It was enough to make you wish for visible damage, something you could cut out with a scalpel, or medicate.

Ronnee was still out when she got home, but there was nothing suspicious about that. By midnight, though, she was too distracted to think of sleep. She paced, could not sit down, asked Barry too many times if he thought she should call the Pinskys. "Call them," he advised. "Anything to get you to relax."

He said this with an edge of impatience that was unlike him. Barry was still in unsympathetic mode, his behavior toward Ronnee exemplary, though distant; she was the one who was feeling the chill. Of course she registered the way he lay at the far edge of the bed and did not approach her, the way he showed her a morose face, unsubtly bitter. Of course she registered his long hours at the office, which signaled his reluctance to sit at the dinner table with them. Now he had a chance to show her how unflapped he could be in the face of crisis. This, she supposed, was the way a gentleman showed his rage. "Call them," he urged again through crimped lips. "They'll understand."

Deb answered before the first ring ended. "Oh, it's you." Her voice was distinctly hostile. Miriam hadn't seen her since Ronnee's party. Did she have a problem?

"Yes, it's me. I'm wondering if you've heard anything from the kids, it's—"

There was a noisy silence. "What do you mean, 'the kids'?" Deb asked like a cat in a crouch. "What do you care about my kids?"

"Well, didn't Ronnee go off with Lisa and Jordan? I thought they were going someplace together."

That peculiar resistant pause again. "Did they? Then I guess I'm the last to know. We thought Lisa was taking Jordan to her Salvadorans, you know she does that crazy Sanctuary thing."

"And Ronnee told me she was going too. Lisa came by for her. With Jordan."

She heard Deb's voice catch as if she'd been hit, hard. With chilling deliberation, she said, "My son had express instructions that he was not to see your . . . daughter." The gap was poisonous. "I'm sorry, Miriam, I know this must sound small of me—us—but we just don't think they're, um, particularly good for each other. Jordan tends to be—well, that doesn't matter right now. The point is, nobody mentioned that she was going with them." She had begun to sound out of breath, like a badly conditioned runner. "This is— we've been on the phone with the police, I thought that's who was calling." Her voice wobbled and got away from her. "It's not good that they're not home."

"Did Lisa say when they'd be back?"

"She said about eight or so. She doesn't like to be down there at night if she can help it—this is near the ship channel. It's so awful there. We hate it, we've tried to get her to stop but, whhh, I think that just incites her. You don't have a teenager, so you don't know."

"Excuse me, Deb. I do have a teenager. She's why I'm calling."

Deb laughed nervously. "Oh, right. It's sort of hard to . . . you know. Remember." She was embarrassed. Good. Let her be. "So, about Lisa, at first we thought maybe having her brother there she might be daring, you know, to stay a little longer. But this—it's almost two o'clock in the morning!" Now she was wailing, as if her appeal might bring some kind of reprieve. "Listen, we shouldn't tie up the phone."

Miriam ignored that; they had call waiting. She ticked off the terrible possibilities, trying for cool. Have you checked the hospitals? Do you know exactly where she goes to, so that you could ride over there? Does she usually call in when she's going to be late? Does she have other friends who go with her? Good God, it felt like Mississippi, the panic over the disappeared. The wild throat-clutching imaginings that were sometimes true, sometimes worse. She put aside, with a vicious thrust, her anger at Deb. Later on that one. Way later.

SHE SAT, stood, walked, called the hospitals herself, called the police, called the highway patrol. She didn't want to hang up. Speaking with someone, anyone, the line open, gave her a surge of hope, though she understood that any news they might have for her would not be good. But the silence, and Barry's bewildered hovering helplessness, were worse. The air hummed, a live sound that was not the air-conditioning—just the force field, maybe, of her wishing—and the walls seemed to break up into abstract patterns, rectangular, square, diced up by the dark shapes of the windows spangled with floaters that came from staring too hard at nothing. There was a feel of unreality about her vigil. She remembered barricading herself in her cottage when Eljay took Ronnee, when she was still Veronica. That kind of waiting was like being sick, how you can't settle into a comfortable position but just want to wake up when it's over.

At a little after six, as dawn began leaking light, the phone cut through the silence. Ernie told her, tonelessly, that Lisa had called, too angry, almost, for sense. She hadn't been allowed near the phone for something like twelve hours. She was in the lockup downtown, not in the precinct house, in trouble over her head. Way over. They were booking her and her whole group on federal charges, *felony* charges, for aiding and abetting aliens, on and on, a lifetime of charges, though her priest had told her that, being under eighteen, she might get off as a juvenile. And, she had added, an afterthought, "Oh yeah, your son is in here too. And his girlfriend. They stole my car."

Ernie delivered this as if it amused him. Miriam knew exactly how his face looked, a bitter smile tugging his mouth down on one side under his shaving-brush mustache: she knew him well. Their families had keys to each other's houses; they went camping together twice a year, in the chilly greenery up at Bastrop, down at Mustang Island on the vast white stretch of beach. They belonged to the same synagogue, they went to all their children's school plays, dance recitals, as if to their own. And there were the boys, now, with their endless free throws. Together she and Deb threw bridal showers, hosted teas for congressional candidates, polite and vaguely useful, coffee in the silver samovar in one house or the other, neat petit fours, decent but not wastefully expensive wine on the sideboard. Ernie and Deb were generous, energetic people of limited seriousness but good intentions. They proceeded from an optimism, a will to see the best in everyone, that Miriam envied, having none of it herself. Their response to Ronnee she would not have predicted, but up close and in the family was obviously not the same as abstract and safely elsewhere. Without discussion. Ask her own mother, she thought, who wouldn't let her say *nigger* when she was growing up, or even *schwartze*. "They stole her *car*?"

"That's what she said. No details. Well, one actually. Are you ready for this? I promise you won't like it." Miriam didn't breathe. "She said, 'Jordan and his whore may have just sealed a dozen death warrants.' I said she was being melodramatic—you know Lisa—but she said she wasn't. She swore she wasn't."

Breathing again did not lift the weight from her chest. "So what do we do now?"

Ernie laughed harshly. "I guess we go get 'em. Storm the station house! Free the prisoners!" He gave her the address of the police station. "Bad neighborhood, Miriam. Take your husband. Take your gun. I am."

He wasn't kidding. But she gave him a chance. "You're not serious."

"Sure I'm serious. Even this neighborhood's changing, kid. You can't afford to be a softhead liberal anymore."

"*Ernie*—"

"People down the block got their door kicked in last week, their kids were in the house. Watching reruns of *Leave It to Beaver*, probably. Rerun Land is the only place you'll find that good ol' life anymore."

It wasn't the time for a diatribe, but she knew she was going to mourn for their friendship after this was over. She kept her mind focused. Did they need a lawyer? It was too soon, maybe this was less serious than it sounded. "Wait a minute. Don't *they* get to make a phone call?"

"Guess not. If we hadn't been phoning all around, who knows when we would have heard from her." His voice changed, sudden as a cold current in the pool. "Who the hell do they think they are is what I want to know. They've got a bunch of children in there. These are children!"

Too much came back to her, in her mouth like putrid food. "They're anybody they want to be, Ernie. Our kids have dirty hands, maybe. Or maybe not. And we're just—you know—folks. Parents. Parents must be the most pathetic."

DEB AND ERNIE PINSKY had arrived at the stationhouse before Miriam and Barry. Deb, looking wrathful, was seated on the kind of molded plastic chair McDonald's uses to discourage long visits at lunch—perpetrators (isn't that what they were called?) were held here only briefly, so perhaps, in turn, visitors were not meant to get too comfortable. Ernie, hands in the pockets of his gray sweatpants, was pacing so hard he made the floor shake.

Miriam went to them prepared for a commiserating embrace in spite of all, because here they were, so familiar in the flesh. But both her friends looked uncomfortable, and guilty about it. Deb touched her chest to Miriam's in the briefest, most grudging split second possible and looked away. And when Miriam asked her anguished "What exactly *happened*? Do you know?" Deb turned away without a word, and Ernie looked at her with the aggrieved frown of a wronged man. "You tell us," he said ominously, chin down, as if he might charge at her. "We've got our whole damn family in here because your little—"

"Ern," said Deb from her chair, and put her finger to her lips like the teacher of small children that she was. "That won't help."

Miriam shook her head and proceeded to the desk to register

their arrival. "My daughter," she began, to a woman with a surprisingly friendly smile, considering where they were.

"Your daughter is—?"

"Veronica Reece." She expected exactly the look she received—amazing how quickly you got used to certain things: the infinitesimal hesitation for surprise, like a connection that takes an extra second, the tiny fragment of dead time. The woman was the rich color of milk chocolate; probably she was trying out possibilities for Miriam: Might she be a Louisiana Creole? Not likely, but not impossible.

"Veronica Reece," she repeated, shuffling papers. "Right." The phone rang. She dispatched the call, put the receiver down, and it rang again.

Finally, "She's a . . . teenager," Miriam told her, partly to be helpful and maybe—this was something she feared she had learned from her mother—to cast out a line of ingratiating complication. Just in case, the humanizing touch, a little something extra, the "See me, help me" of her belle-hood. She hated it in herself, but she did it every time. It was a form of flirting.

"Got it. Here. Yes." The woman smoothed the paper concerning Ronnee with the pink side of her brown hand. She hit some buttons on her intercom and, leaning forward, murmured into it, codes and numbers.

Miriam was amazed at how calm she was being. As long as Ronnee was all right, she could deal with anything.

IT SEEMED TO MIRIAM it was taking a long time for them to find Ronnee (although she had no idea if she was going to see her, let alone be allowed to take her home). She and Barry stood drumming their fingers impatiently at the counter, behind which many people, guarded by the flags of the nation and the state of Texas, were ignoring them. Finally the receptionist answered her intercom, which announced itself with a sound peculiarly like breaking glass. As she nodded, grim-faced, the tiniest flick of a glance at the two of them told Miriam she had news of

Ronnee, and not good news either. She waved them toward her.

"Now, don't panic at this, okay?" She had a broad encouraging face that looked worried, its horizontals turned gravely down. She actually waited for them to promise self-control, which Miriam did, abjectly. "Okay. Your daughter's on her way to the hospital. She's got some asthma, right?"

Miriam was so stunned she couldn't speak. Barry, at her elbow, said, "She does, a little," as if he expected more. But there was nothing forthcoming except the name of the hospital and the woman's best wishes that they find their daughter well. Finally Miriam began to object, "Why haven't we *heard* anything, why didn't anyone—" But Barry was pushing her out, his hands on her waist, as if she had no motor of her own. And there they were, racing back to the car, streaking through the rain, which made it feel like a stupid movie, a crime movie of the kind she hated. Barry was a good speed driver. Calm people can do that without the sloppiness of desperation, which was her way.

"If it's bad enough for them to take her to hospital . . ." Sweat laved her face in spite of the good car's good cold air. "They wouldn't do that unless it was desperate."

"Stop, Miriam, please. Can't you just wait a couple of minutes before you go into high gear? Maybe they play it very safe and take anybody who's in any kind of distress. Don't get worked up before you have to."

At Ben Taub, Barry used his doctor's credentials to get them in where they weren't supposed to be. She watched his face change, and his posture; his mildness and strained indifference turned to command, as if the hard fluorescence had the power to transform him. He led with his shoulder through swinging doors, spoke curt single-syllabled words like an army sergeant, and somehow they were into the cubicle where Ronnee sat partly raised, dark against stiff pillows. She was wheezing, her chest rising and falling furiously. All Miriam could see was a mask, an IV, and a nurse bent over her, holding up her hand, attaching to it a clip of some sort and laying it back down. Ronnee kept trying to make a fist, and when she couldn't, she shook the whole hand from her wrist as if she were trying to dislodge something dirty. "Don't do that, hon," the nurse said briskly, turning to go. "We've got to measure how you're doing. Leave it alone, now."

She was choking, she was smothering. Help her! Miriam cried out silently, afraid to approach her. Help her before she chokes to death! But she didn't want to scare her. She stood still, without new breath herself, and listened to the sound, which was like dry retching. But Barry, who had seen such sights before, bent as close to Ronnee as he could and said quietly, "Okay, Ronnee, you'll be fine now. You'll be okay. Just a little while, the meds'll do it, they're taking care of it. Ssh." He reached for her hand, the one that wasn't clipped, and held it tight. This sweet, sweet man, he smoothed her forehead between her damp hair and her frightened eyes. "Sshh, now."

Miriam bet Ronnee would imprint on his face for life, its unhysterical, reassuring half smile, the concern on his own forehead, the way he focused on her and not on himself. She felt like a bat, her terrible tension made her vile. Her hands were claws, grasping. If she'd picked up anything just then, she'd have dropped and shattered it. Her mother was right: she was not a comforting person to be with when you were in need: she had too much need of her own.

But she could hear the way Ronnee's breathing began to change. There was no place to sit, so they stood quietly by as her wheezing subsided. Her numbers, Barry said, were sliding back toward normal, her carbon dioxide levels getting in synch, her blood gases stabilizing. The nurse, thin-lipped and bony-elbowed, returned to say, barely swallowing back her irritation, "There are a few too many people in here." Miriam was about to announce as ostentatiously as she could, "I am her mother!" when she saw the other person who was cluttering up the little curtained space, standing back in the corner. He was a large, strong-looking man in a blue police shirt, jacketless, his face the blunt shape of an ax head under a marine buzz cut for which he was a little too old, and he wasn't going anywhere: he was there, a whole healthy cop who should have been out on a beat somewhere, just to guard her dangerous daughter. She couldn't resist. "You think she's going to get up and walk away?" It was comforting to think she might; they could still hear the rough noise of Ronnee struggling.

"You never know." The policeman was a literalist. Without smiling, he very slowly and deliberately removed a pack of gum, green as a leaf, from his uniform shirt pocket, slid out a stick, and held the pack toward her. "When you're upset your mouth can get dry," he said, as if he were apologizing for his generosity, in case it seemed partisan. She didn't want any gum—numb as she was, the sweetness would explode in her mouth, it would startle her—but she took it anyhow, by way of thanking him. She crumpled the silver paper in her fist and held on to it, for luck.

IT TOOK A WHILE but finally the tinctures that opened what must be opened and shrank what must be shrunk did their work and Ronnee slept a while. She awakened looking battered.

"Good God, Ronnee, does this happen to you often?" By now, having sent Barry off to work, it was Miriam who had her hand. How many times had she come close to dying? How could this be her daughter and she not know the answer?

"No, not these days. Because I sort of know what to stay away from. But they weren't exactly paying attention, you know? I guess jail's not the place to go for that." She was looking around a little wildly. "So now I've got this adrenaline high. It feels weird, it's like this fake rush. I always come back down and then I have to veg out." She laughed. "So enjoy me while I'm flying."

Miriam gave her hand a little shake of reassurance. "I'll take you any way I can get you."

Ronnee looked at her soberly. "Listen, I'm really sorry. I mean, really, really. This was all, like—"

When Miriam shook her head vigorously, the hair bobbed back and forth over her forehead like something on springs. "No apologies, Ronnee." It would certainly be nice if she ever called her Mother. Mom. Anything. It pained her to feel the careful spaces in Ronnee's sentences. "You've had enough to worry about without—"

"But we shouldn't have done what we did, it was stupid. It's embarrassing."

"What, exactly, did you do?" Miriam blushed. "No, I mean, what happened?"

"You want a blow-by-blow?" Ronnee asked, and, in a voice flat with irony, gave it.

"He put his *hands* on you?"

"And squeezed."

When would such things stop shocking her?

That was an indecent question, this wasn't about *her*. When would such things stop happening? Eljay's bare back, all these years later and still there was his firm brown back, his shivering before she tried to cover him with his afghan, Eljay bowing to that unspeakable judge—Yessir, yessir, he's a good boy, yessir, that beautiful baritone, Edgar—putting survival before honor. The innocent forever torn to pieces casually like that. She didn't know she would always see his back. You never know what you're doomed to see forever.

"Let me just put my head down for a minute," Miriam murmured, and laid her damp forehead beside Ronnee's on the pillow. She tried to breathe slowly, evenly, waiting for her vision to clear.

Ronnee, the clip on her hand making her awkward, patted her gently on the back. "It was disgusting," she said, looking a little chastened, as if she were responsible for this strange collapse, "but it's not worth getting worked up about. I'm not, like, scarred for life."

Miriam stood unsteadily but she felt a nervous energy she didn't recognize. "Who says it's not worth getting worked up about? Ronnee! It's everything you—you can't let something like that just *happen* to you." She looked at her daughter for a sign that she understood. "You can't! Are you the same girl who was ready for murder back in New Hampshire every time somebody insulted you?"

The girl looked unconvinced. This was what it meant, Miriam thought angrily, not to know anything about politics. Sanctuary, Solidarity, Ronnee didn't think it worth knowing the difference. Did she have some invisible personal scale on which she weighed each episode that upset her? Was it *who* was responsible? Was it *how*, being blindsided when she was relaxed? Maybe abuse by cops was no news to a Bed-Stuy girl. Maybe her father told her stories.

"Oh, honey," she said and sat and locked Ronnee's hand in hers. "Let's think about this a little. They're not getting away with it, I promise you. They're going to be very sorry." Her mind had begun to move ahead of itself. There was a "they" now. "Bastards."

"Jordan getting beat up, me getting *felt* up." Ronnee giggled at the symmetry.

"You said he had bruises on him."

"Yeah, and then they swiped him across the shoulders with that club, but you probably can't see anything. If anybody's looking. He was really mad, but pardon me if I doubt anybody else gives a damn, except his mama and daddy."

"His mama and daddy might be enough, if they get mad, too." What were the odds on that? She couldn't guess. "Ronnee?"

Ronnee's eyes were bright with artificial energy.

"What would you think—" This was coming to her quickly, no will involved. "I want to accuse them publicly for what they did to you." She felt like someone else, saying it.

"How do you mean, publicly?"

"I mean I want to make a formal accusation of police brutality, and I want to get it in the papers and make as much noise as we can. I want—"

"Hey, wait! Are you serious?" This was not the sort of thing she expected of her mother, that was clear, not only the aggressiveness of her voice but all those sentences that began *I want*. She wore a very small disbelieving smile.

"Ronnee. You're angry, right? These arrogant bastards told you they knew they could get away with all that because nobody would believe you, isn't that what you said?"

"Yeah, well, they're probably right. How can we prove one single thing? Nobody saw us, it was us and them in a half-dark parking lot behind a scuzzy motel. Everything was, like, shadows." She gave a little spurt of a laugh. "Maybe the rats in the Dumpster saw it."

It turned out that Ronnee's interrogators—they—hadn't cared much about the stolen car, although that was a felony if they felt like pursuing it. As for making a little case against her as a prostitute, that didn't scare Miriam because Ronnee, summoning proof, would embarrass them and have the last laugh. What they wanted was information about the Sanctuary house. And they wouldn't let her tell them *nothing*.

"So I said for the tenth time, I'll tell you every single little tiny thing I know—"

"Wait a minute, didn't you say you wanted a lawyer?"

Ronnee looked sheepish. "I probably should have."

"Did they read you your rights?" My God, she was a child. Of course she was a child, no matter what she looked like, and unprotected.

"I don't know. I guess so." She screwed up her face trying to see the scene. "Maybe not. I don't remember. But I figured I didn't have anything to hide, so I told them how we got there, Jordan and me, and how I didn't really know what Lisa was doing in there, we just got out at the corner. Which was sort of true. Like, I thought I'd better not give anything away, because who knows what matters? So I just said she told us she had an appointment, she had to see somebody, and she dropped us down the block. Period. I mean, they weren't torturing me. But they were pretty nasty."

"How were they nasty?"

"Like, insulting. About girls like me who were—one of them said, 'You're like public toilets, you let these men jam anything they want in you.' He made me want to puke." She shook her head to dislodge the sound of it. "Like that was going to make me want to 'cooperate,' they kept calling it. Like, snitch." She put her hand on her chest, which must still be painful. The little clamp was still locked on her finger, to measure the amount of something—carbon dioxide, was it?—in her blood. "I was only afraid Jordan might be telling them something different. He was so mad at Lisa I thought he might want to see her, you know—practically executed."

"And what did they do when you didn't say what they wanted to hear?"

Ronnee looked exhausted and a little bit fragile, but serious, grave, in spite of her intoxicated air. She had dark circles under her eyes, as though a layer of skin that was usually invisible had broken through. But she had survived a very bad night and she looked relieved. This is how experience grows you up, Miriam consoled her qualmish self. This is how most people get strong: you don't want your children to have a smooth sail all the way through, even while you're knocking yourself out trying to get them one. She did not like to remember herself when she should have been waxing invincible but was being eaten away, instead, by self-doubt. Maybe her childhood had been too soft and she'd gone forth unprepared. Her Mississippi had hollowed her out, had chided her into abandoning her strengths. Her memory was a welter of small and larger and finally overwhelming shames, not the least of which was that she'd come home, after, thinking her mother had been right about everything all along. Or, if not right, at least entitled to exact some punishment, which had been her life since then. Writing checks, then—what an irony—she was just like her parents.

Barry would have an opinion of this idea when they were alone, Miriam knew, and it would not encourage conspicuousness. Maybe his calm, his reason, was building up around his heart like deadly fat; maybe someday it would explode in unquenchable rage. But Miriam felt a kind of liquid joy flooding her veins. This was what she had been overwhelmed by when Jewel took her and a carload of students to demonstrations, when they'd integrated a church one Sunday and had not been chased or even insulted, when they held an anti-war rally, because there was that war too, so far from here, eating up their brothers, waiting to eat them, too, and hundreds of Parnassus kids listened, rapt, to the speeches of resistance: a kind of insurgency of the blood, rising to the challenge. She had never been physically brave, hadn't even relished diving or skiing because she wasn't comfortable in her body, had no instincts to bend or go rigid or fling herself at a goal, let alone an antagonist. But offering herself up at a demonstration was different. It didn't happen often, but when it did it was indelible as a scar.

It had been like running in the rain, being pelted by something she usually hid from, going forward into it, moving through danger for the first time. She knew she could be killed or trampled or spat upon, not relishing it exactly, but, against all the experience of her safe lifetime, expecting it, refusing to be surprised, thinking hard, calling up like a lesson all she'd been taught about falling into a blow, letting herself collapse around it, not fight it, not resist. Later she would think childbirth was like that: you knew where the pain was coming from, and why, and you knew that if it didn't kill you it would be over soon, and in the meantime if you could only relax a little or at least not stiffen with resistance, it would go better. Backs were humped on the ground all around her, recoiling as police boots stamped down on bone but not flinging themselves at their attackers. There was sound, but no words: The snap of the boot-toe connecting, the grunting of the striker and the stricken, it was the most sickening noise she had ever heard, and the crisp crack of a head against the pavement, those were worse than the screams of outrage. She watched a checkered shirt—blue-and-yellow plaid—rip, she heard the tearing as if it were the flaying of the flesh beneath, distracted by the shame of seeing its whole cloth, that nice new-looking shirt, torn like a rag. The wide-open mouth of—that was Ulrike, the German instructor Miriam had disliked for her every finicky habit, wide-eyed now as her arm was yanked around backward, ready to snap—cleansed, washed by rising sentiment, of any irritating quality. Pain ennobles the viewer, if not the sufferer, Miriam learned again and again. There were people who were good at being clobbered, but who were only changed for the worse by it. *Taking it* was a talent, apparently sufficient. Her old antagonist Sonny Skeen, for one, had been peppered with buckshot, his shoulder stomped till it separated, but it hadn't made him decent, only furious and vengeful. But mostly, watching someone brutalized was a strangely intimate, humbling thing: you knew something about that victim, a good many things, actually, about what kind of self-control he had, or she; what kind of commitment worth being beaten to the ground for, how her body or his folded around itself and its weakness; how obedient, really, to the command to be selfless. And *knowing it* was to glimpse some-one's bare-naked character and feel protective, which must be where the forgiveness came in.

One time, standing and watching, she felt herself being pushed backward by knuckles and a nightstick. The worst, the best she could do was reach out and pull the bastard's pointy silver badge off his shirt. She tugged as hard as she could in that half-second and felt it spiny and edged in her hand, a tin star, but it would not give. His police-blue shirt came toward her, caught in the teeth of her palm, elastic, but she didn't have the strength to tear the damn thing off. And the melée of bodies closed over her, hard legs and shoes and limbs hitting the ground all around her, elbows bruised, no air, no light. She lay at the bottom of the welter elated to think she belonged there, in tears of pain and unspent fury.

Another time a police horse's hoof came down on her upper arm—came so close to demolishing the bone, she stood up feeling miraculous luck pour off her like sweat. It had nicked the skin and her watch face had smashed against the sidewalk in a daisy head of cracks. She felt with one exploratory finger how the frail watch hands were left bare as twigs. Small price. The horses gleamed like the polished wood of coffins, hard and repellent. Anger was all she felt, swamping her fear. Contempt, not bravery, had moved her into the center of the sprawl instead of away from it. You couldn't be brave without naming the cause or you were a soldier of fortune. You couldn't run away and live here either, even if no one else noticed. The cops' faces were unspeakably ugly to her. The bastards, the murderous sons of bitches with their mili-tary crew cuts, their beer bellies, their piggy little eyes, was all she could think. Old curses. Inaccurate description, skewed by pas-sion—surely they didn't all have bellies and wristless arms and hands and Marine Corps hair. Shoddy invective, but justified. She had been fortunate to warm herself at this fire before she passed back into safety. She'd hoped she could be forgiven for lov-ing it so.

Her Houston friends would not have recognized her. Good, she thought. Imagine Amy, the bad twin. And now, even if they didn't win—they wouldn't, most likely—just to slow them down a little, embarrass them, those invincible men with their billy clubs banging around like rogue parts of their own bodies. To make them sorry they had to wake up in the middle of a stinking mess of their own making. Barry was going to accuse her of willfulness. He would say she sounded like Mickey Rooney calling out to his friends, "Hey, gang, let's build a—" What was Mickey always concocting? A clubhouse, was it? A theater? He would, he would try to talk sweet reason and she would ignore him and then he would forgive her. She had to be careful, such vengeance was like a drug. She was not supposed to be happy, thinking of filing this grievance. She was not supposed to be, but she was.

"They didn't scare me," Ronnee said, "except I thought you'd be really mad." She was smoothing down her unruffleable hair with her unclipped hand as if she had too much energy in spite of her exhaustion, and had to be touching something usefully. "I was disgusted. They were so rough, everybody there was like—they just had bad manners. I know this was jail, but still. They just didn't think they had to be nice to anybody. I mean, *kind.*" She thought about kindness for a long minute. "Maybe it was because almost everybody inside was, you know, black, so who cares? Though they were, too, some of them, the cops and most of the other people who work there. This one reception lady—I guess she was a cop, too, but all she had to do was answer the phone, so maybe it didn't wear her down or something—she was the only one I saw who even smiled."

"Right. She was nice to us, too." Gratitude for such small favors.

Ronnee was still remembering. "Except that cop when he was feeling me up. He was in hog heaven." That bark of a laugh that had no pleasure in it. "I should have bit him." Then, looking straight at Miriam, "Is there—do you think this is the kind of—I mean, I know it's not the first thing you think of, but is this the kind of thing where you can actually, um, like, sue them for *money?*"

"You mean damages?" Miriam shrugged. "Sure. I guess. I actually don't know if that's part of it. Not just punishment for the cops but something punitive. Yeah, I'll bet. Do you think we'll be able to get Jordan to come along with us on this?"

"Wait, you're serious! You're really going to do this."

"Of course I'm serious."

"But hey, wait. I don't want everybody in the world to know—you know—where I was—like *that*. With Jordan." She looked alarmed. "Anyway, his parents are basically blaming me for, like, corrupting him. You know, the dark seducer. If they only knew." When she shook her head her earrings twinkled like little electric lights. "If only they knew."

"But that's not the slant we'd put on it. We'd—"

"No way!" Ronnee covered her ears like the hear-no-evil monkey. "Oh, *please*." It was not a plea, it was an order. "No way!"

THEY DROVE HOME from the hospital through a morning rain so soft it was invisible; it beaded up on the windshield and hood as if the car were sweating. Ronnee, in the backseat, was silent.

Miriam shadowed her, going into the house. These rooms were so spacious, people got away from you. "Want something to eat? You must be famished."

Ronnee yawned and kept walking. "No, I think it's the stuff I took, the meds? I'm just sleepy."

Miriam took a deep breath and plunged forward to pull the girl toward her. It was the first time she had touched her, except guardedly, in passing. The height and heft of her, the particularity of her skin and smell, partly her own and partly her various perfumes, her hair cream, the vague hospital bitterness—Miriam was shocked by their foreignness. She held Ronnee tight against her, feeling nothing but her will to feel something. "Were you scared back there?" she asked into her daughter's neck.

Something like a whimper escaped from Ronnee, an acknowledgment, maybe, or was she squeezing her too hard? Her voice was small. "I was so scared, you can't imagine. People *die* that way. I know a girl who died. Josephine, her name was. When I got out of the hospital they made us learn all this preventive stuff we should know."

"Good God, Ronnee . . ."

"I guess she didn't pay enough attention or something. I heard she went to a party with a lot of smoke and I don't know what happened, but . . ." She shrugged.

Miriam kept her wrapped close. She wanted Ronnee to know she was precious, that she was irreplaceable. She pictured her stretched out on that hospital bed in the clothes she was wearing now, the blue shorts and yellow top she had put on for her date with Jordan, saw the monitors turned off, listened and heard the awful sound of her breathing silenced. "I can't lose you again, little girl," she whispered, knowing how foolish that sounded since her little girl was a head taller than she was. "Nothing as terrible as that will ever happen to you. It *can't*." It was the kind of thing you said to a child. She wished she believed it.

WHEN SHE TOLD BARRY that she wanted to bring a case against the police, she watched the war in him, so familiar, his sense of decency and justice confronting the pull of the conventional, the peaceful, the unobtrusive. "This isn't fair to the rest of us, Miriam." He looked stern.

"I don't know how to deal with this, Barry, I really don't. I guess I think there are some injuries a marriage has to be able to take and not just . . . shred. This whole—Veronica in my life—is a given, that's all. She came with me, just as if you could see her. If you want me to be whole—I assume that's what you want for me—then you've somehow got to be able to, I don't know. I don't know what you need, since there isn't any going back. I don't want your forgiveness because I don't think I did anything wrong. And I don't want your tolerance, because that's a horrible word that means you're just—barely—putting up with something."

"So what do you want?" She could hear how he was trying not to sound impatient.

She wasn't going to tell him about settling scores. She had made it a point—had thought it a mercy—never to speak of her first life. No way could she have said, "Picture us in bed, Eljay and me," or even "Once I did a thoughtless thing and caused my lover pain." It would have been like bringing Eljay into their bedroom right now, challenging Barry to his right to be there. She kept her men separate; it was hard enough on Barry to have Ronnee here, yet he had shown nothing but grace in her presence. So she talked about abuse of power, about protecting innocent citizens.

"Oh, come on, those aren't really the words anybody hears deep down inside. I'll bet no one ever used the word 'citizens' inside their own head. Ever, in the history of the world."

"Barry, I can still hear her struggling to breathe. I can't stand to think about it."

"What about dragging her through a big public brouhaha? I know I'm being predictable, Miriam, and I know you hate it, but this seems to me a really perverse way to advertise her life, and your life, too, while you're at it. It's like once you decided to go public you've just, I don't know, exploded with this stuff. Can't you do anything that's not extreme? First it's your deep dark secret, then all of a sudden you're grandstanding."

"So it's my life out there, and therefore it's yours too."

"You know this doesn't have much to do with me. I'm just a bystander here."

"A bystander? I thought you were my husband."

"Oh, don't be so damn melodramatic. You're always saying that: 'I thought you were this, I thought you were that.' All I'm asking is, does the whole world have to know this girl snuck off to that roach motel with a guy she hardly knows?"

"She thought she knew him. She's not the first girl to be wrong." She kissed him lightly, the way she always sealed an argument. Barry had accused her, when she was planning Ronnee's "coming-out party," of wanting to have a headline in the *Chronicle*. Well, here it was, quite literally: GIRL ACCUSES POLICE. COUPLE ASSAULTED AFTER ARREST.

She had been living for seventeen years, she thought, without adrenaline. But the signs of change were promising. Auspicious.

She wanted, out of that optimism, to comfort Barry. She went to him and placed his arms around herself as if she were cold. "Don't be jealous, boy." Whispering. "This will all turn out to be good for you. Us." He didn't understand, but she wasn't sure it mattered. "What funny turns things take." That seemed noncommittal enough, but Barry stayed inert, his arms and hands where she had placed them. "We're all attached, love. We're all on a single string."

He pulled back and looked at her harshly. "Does it ever occur to you that I might be tired of being jerked around? Just who pulls this string of yours?"

She shook her head. "Anybody. Whoever has to. Nobody's got the end of it. Or Ronnee does, maybe. Since she's what it's about."

"I'm not good at this kind of game playing, Miriam," Barry said. He shook his head impatiently, like a horse shooing flies. "I can't do this. I can try to be welcoming to her, I can try harder at that, because I know this whole business isn't her fault. I can try to be more open. But I don't know about the heavy-handed way you're making her—it's like you're making her everybody's business."

Miriam put her lips against his warm taut neck. "You don't have to do a thing. Just be here with me." These were amends, too. She had debts everywhere. "There's only one thing you have to forgive me for. Not what you're thinking. Not anything I've done."

He had finally almost begun to smile. "And what do I have to forgive you for that you haven't done?"

She was weary at herself. "Ingratitude." She spoke softly into his collar buttons. "Isn't that considered a sin? I think it says somewhere, Thou shalt not be ungrateful." He still held his body stiffly, refusing her. "Making the past more important than the present."

Pitying you, she thought. Not valuing your dignity.

Wanting to run away from everything he'd bought her—given her—that she was contemptuous of. From how, long ago, before she was ready, he forgave her not what she was thinking but what she had done. Only it had worn away by now. She had used it up.

This was where, her family finally intact, she would have to begin again.

INTO MIRIAM'S HALF-DROWSING EAR Deb poured a bitterly poisoned juice of claims against Ronnee, chief of which seemed to concern her seductive powers. "We all ought to know about girls like that," she dared to say, without defining her terms. "And my daughter Lisa is in jail—*not* bailed out—for a federal crime. A seventeen-year-old girl, this may be the end of her life as a free person for years to come!" It sounded like a slogan, but she began to cry softly. Lisa and a whole houseful of people, a priest included, were accused of aiding, abetting, harboring illegals. "And she wouldn't be there if this hadn't happened."

"But Deb, this, this whole thing you're talking about seems to have been your son's idea."

"You can believe that if you want to," Deb said icily. "I happen to think it was a little more complicated than that."

"Jordan isn't daring to deny that this car-stealing business was his idea!"

"No, he's honorable enough to admit that. But he *is* saying a lot of things you probably don't want to hear. They won't surprise anybody else, I don't think."

"Such as? I don't want to hear any vague accusations."

A sigh. "Such as, that girl is not innocent. She is a very experienced, shameless—If he hadn't been so crazy for her, he never would have taken that car. You have a naïve, impressionable boy who—"

Shameless. The word was comic: *You lily-livered coward. You shameless hussy.* Some people couldn't hear themselves. "Debbie. Really." She leaned her head against the yellow kitchen wall, her eyes closed.

"Really what?"

"You're the naïve one if you buy that picture. Poor helpless boy in the clutches of this vamp. You're selling your son short." But she was beginning to worry. Without much optimism, she told

Debbie about her eagerness to pursue the policemen who had intimidated and roughed up her innocent child.

Debbie was silent a long time. "I have to talk to my husband about that." As though Mirian had never met Ernie. "But I've got to say, just off the top of my head, that I have my doubts, Miriam. I'm not sure I like the sound of that."

"They scraped up Jordan's face—you saw that, didn't you? Ronnee said they hit him across the shoulders with a club. They said terrible things, one of them made—advances, I guess you'd say, indecent ones—to my daughter. They both stepped way over the line. And Ronnee said Jordan was furious, he was talking about making them regret what they did."

"I know. I heard what they did. But—publicity isn't always exactly the best way—"

"Debbie. You don't want people to know Jordan went to a motel with—well, I won't say it, all right? Let me spare your delicate feelings. Is that what you're doing? Protecting his reputation?"

"Ernie will call you back, Miriam." She had begun leaking tears again. "This is too much for me. I'm a schoolteacher, not a lawyer, not a—a rebel. I wish they had never met is all I can say. This boy has his whole life ahead of him."

"Well, he's not exactly going to death row, you know." Mean of her. And when had she become a rebel, she who had spent all these years lying low?

"But Lisa. Lisa could go away for years."

Miriam's eyes had been closed, weary, through all this. She opened them at the sound of Lisa's name. "Lisa's not even an adult yet, legally."

"I don't think that matters. Crimes seem to make kids into adults at the court's convenience, haven't you noticed that?"

"Well, I happen to have a lot of admiration for what she was doing. I'm really sorry she's in this mess. But her brother ought to have thought of the danger he was putting them all in." She didn't mind sounding huffy back. "You know very well he did a stupid thing."

It took Debbie a while to find a way out. "We'll go on with this,

Miriam. I hope you won't do anything rash before Ernie can talk to you. He's trying to get a good lawyer."

"I should think the Sanctuary people would have their lawyers."

"Maybe. I don't know if we want to be involved with any of them. They'll be out to protect their own." She shuddered so hard Miriam could hear it. Another set of dusky-skinned seducers. "Why didn't you just keep your little secret to yourself, Miriam? I have to say, some of us have worked very hard to make nice, steady, sort of—uncomplicated—lives for ourselves and our children out here. We do so much to smooth their way. And then you have to go and drop a—a bit of depravity into the whole thing. You had to be very naïve to think this was going to be simple."

Miriam smiled at that.

"You should have known, you take a little girl, especially a black child—I know you won't like that, but I'm just speaking about reality here—and let her grow up alone with her father, what do you expect? God only knows what she's seen and done. But all this should have stayed your business, and your poor husband's. So now everybody—your children, my children—they all have to get tarred with it."

Miriam felt a knife slash of pain across her gut. "If I didn't have to speak to you ever again after that remark, Debbie, I'd be very happy. But I guess that's not realistic, is it. I suppose we'll have a lot of things to deal with together." Am I really surprised? she asked herself, and hung up the phone with exaggerated gentleness, as though someone were sleeping beside her. But no apologetic tears, she was happy to see. Her anger was building its bonfires on all sides of her, fed by the past, fed by the present, and there was no place in it finally, thank God, for tears.

But she had sounded, herself, like a self-righteous snob. Barry had told her she wasn't trying hard enough to see all this from their point of view, and she knew he meant his own as well. It was Jewel again—another rhyme, today echoing yesterday—Jewel warning her not to close ranks against Eljay before the baby was born, not to get carried away by her own insulted virtue. They had never really talked that through: Jewel had just let her go, when the time came, as if to punish her. Jewel, raising her finger, giving a little lecture. The mama of them all. From here, they both looked stiff-necked and unyielding.

It had been a short time since her friend had said she might be able to come to New Hampshire—back in another, more innocent life. If she could entice Jewel to come down here now and be useful, they would sort this out, and maybe iron out the past while they were at it. The two of them, team reunited, would be unstoppable.

"JEWEL?"

"Hey, sugar. I've been wanting to call you. I think I've cleared a little time to come up and swim in that pond of yours. I could surely use a break."

"Wait, wait! I'm in Houston. The whole agenda's changed. Just tell me, are you allowed to practice law in another state?"

"Sure I can. How do you think those celebrity lawyers do it? Somebody local fronts for you. Why? You in some kind of trouble?"

She told the whole story, or at least a précis, beginning with their rapid departure from New Hampshire—Jewel must think she always stole away from places like a thief!—through the police story in quick summary. She heard her friend breathe out hard, in disgust. "The bastards," she was expecting to hear. "The cretins. The racist thugs."

"You know, darlin', good thing it's summer. Things are a little more fluid around here. Because I think I'm gonna have to come and hear all this direct from the kid herself. Good doctors don't diagnose over the phone."

Miriam was disappointed, but she wasn't going to argue.

"So, honey, I'll be right over. Truly. You know me, half a second between thinking and doing."

"Wait, I've got to—"

"You've got to nothin'. I'm onna be on your doorstep next

plane I can catch, before I change my mind. We've wasted enough damn time. You called before, I hung up and I kept thinking why aren't we sitting in the same room, here we just live a state away. Make me up a bed and get ready to introduce me to that child. Tell her the Lone Ranger's coming."

18

PEOPLE COULD SURPRISE YOU. Ronnee doubted it was as easy as he made it seem—Barry had that way of making everything appear effortless; it went with his unrumpled, lucky look—but yesterday he had invited her to come to work with him. Just like that. She didn't think her mother even knew about it, to judge from the way she stared at him when he suggested it, and chewed her toast very, very slowly. "I want to show you off," he'd said, with a simplicity so transparent she could only feel suspicious—nothing in her could have uttered anything as straightforward as that. The odd thing was that she suspected it was her time in the hospital—the time when he'd helped her—that had made him feel closer to her, as if he'd found his own generosity stimulating. Was that some kinky form of self-love? No, actually, when you thought about it, it was what parents always did: the harder they had to work raising you, the more they had to love you. It was some kind of weird animal payback.

And he was as good as his word. He began the introductions in the elevator on the way up to his office, which was in the professional building of a hospital. She was "Veronica, my stepdaughter," which wasn't exactly accurate. But what, in fact, was she to him? He hadn't consulted her, and it did give her a second of hesitation, as if accepting Barry's shorthand meant somehow betraying her father.

She'd met every receptionist and white-uniformed assistant, including a mahogany-skinned girl whose nametag said TERRYE, who gave her an interminable look she couldn't even try to read. Then Barry, who smiled a lot, like somebody selling something, took her to the office of his partner, Dr. Waxman, who hadn't been at her party. He was a fleshy-looking man with bird-bright eyes behind glasses and the defensively arranged hair of someone whose baldness would defeat his vanity one of these days. He shook her hand with great seriousness and a gallant tip of his head, as if she were a lady and he an old-style gentleman going through their gracious formal dance. "What a terrific pleasure to meet you." He put his other hand over hers and squeezed for extra reassurance; she could feel his college ring, massive as a brass knuckle. "My goodness, this is wonderful." What kind of idiot did he take her for? One who wouldn't see him, as she did, wink at Barry as she turned away en route to a roomful of high-tech diagnostic machines. Wink and grin.

HER MOTHER had gone to take her grandmother to the doctor's. By nine o'clock it was too hot to sit beside the pool. Ronnee was trying to read *The Republic* in the sheer light of the sunporch, which she had muffled by slanting the blinds just right. Mornings, the house gave off its peculiarly restful static aura. Everything in it seemed to invite lounging, torpor even, as if it were some grand tropical hacienda, dozing. One hundred years of solitude, stifling and gorgeous. When the doorbell rang, she ignored it—not her business.

By the time Elpidia got to the door, Jewel's taxi had departed so that she looked as if she'd materialized out of nowhere. Elpidia tried to bar her way but Jewel, smiling, managed to get past her by grasping her just beneath her shoulders and moving her, shifting her decisively, like a chess piece.

"Good God, will you look at this place!" she called out to anyone who might be listening. "I didn't know the Guggenheim had a Texas branch!"

Ronnee looked up, squinting, when the commotion began. A

woman stood in the doorway staring in at her, a buxom black woman in a searing green jacket with smooth round buttons down the front like a row of hard candy. If this was the person who'd been making all that noise, she had gone silent suddenly, as if someone had turned off her sound.

"If you're looking for—" Ronnee began. She refused to stir. What was the matter with Elpidia, letting a stranger in.

But the woman was advancing into the cool white room with an odd kind of reverence in her eyes. She had an amusing face, actually, or rather a face ready to be amused, handsome-featured but rubbery, the kind that registers more than it probably ought to. She was the color of a soft caramel, that buttery tinge of brown. "You're Veronica," she said in a near whisper. "You're Miriam's baby."

Ronnee, her index finger poking into her book, rose from the wicker couch. They were exactly the same height: they could look down on Miriam's head if they wanted to. This must be Pearl—no, Jewel—though, of course, she'd been picturing a long scrawny girl with a braid down her back. (In her mouth when she got nervous, Miriam had said. Which must be now.) But her hair was cut medium length, straightened, tucked, saloned. Middle-aged. Oh God, what would *she* look like in another twenty years? She'd never wondered. So tame, the dozen gold hoops gone from her ears? Would she be all polyester and stockings and heels like bricks, with the waist of a sturdy oak? "Ronnee," she said, unsmiling. "Never Veronica, unless somebody's mad at me."

This looked like a woman you shook hands with. Jewel reached for her hand, in fact—it looked like she took what she wanted, even if it was attached to somebody else—and pumped it heartily, then opened her grip and looked at Ronnee's fingers as if there were something wrong with them. "That tiny little hand," she said, unembarrassed by her own wonder. "About the size of a hedge-leaf, last time I saw it." She shook her head. "I oughtn't to have such a hard time with this, honey, but I don't know, maybe it's because I don't have my own. Plenty of little cousins and friends with babies who go on and grow up on you, but—" That shaking head meant it was too awful. What was so sad about growing up?

Lamely, to put an end to the awe that made her itch, Ronnee said, "You're Jewel. You're here to save us."

Jewel threw back her head to laugh. She had at least half of a second chin. How many black women had ever stood in this pretty little sunroom, laughing or otherwise, not counting maids? Any at all, ever? It was such a relief to see her brown-sugar skin in here. It was home.

"If I end up taking this case, I don't think I'll save you much besides money. Which is no small thing, of course."

"Somehow I don't think money's the big problem around here," Ronnee said. "Except maybe having it. They've got other things to worry about."

"Well, leave those for her to tell me about. I've got a thousand things I'd like to ask you about, hon," Jewel said to her, and Ronnee flinched: This one would look right in your face and know too much about you. Was she suspicious or did she only look that way because she had this bluntness about her?

"Are you thirsty?" Stalling. "You want to sit down and let Elpidia get you something to drink?" She was embarrassed at letting someone else make their drinks, but Jewel didn't say anything. Maybe she had servants too.

Elpidia couldn't take her eyes off Jewel. She smiled slightly, cryptically, all the way out of the room, and delivered a pitcher of iced tea that sweated on the white wicker table like something out in the rain. No tulips today—there was a vase of gerbera daisies, lollipop colors, orange, yellow, a complicated brick red, their stems like stiff little lollipop sticks. They had none of the casual sloppiness of things that grow in dirt.

"First," Jewel said, raising her face from the shiny rim of her glass, "we better get down to the business end of why I'm here. It's nice and quiet, we've got this cool drink to lubricate our brains, so let's go, okay? You tell me everything—every little thing—you can remember about your little party with the noble representatives of the law."

Ronnee made a face and leaned her head back against the

wicker. "Every little thing." She took a deep, untroublesome breath. Praise the Lord for small favors. "Here goes."

WHEN SHE HAD FINISHED, Jewel gave out a long sigh that was either resignation or exasperation. She didn't say which, just shook her head back and forth without interpretation. "So tell me, sugar, what's it like for you here? I can ask you these questions, you know, I'm your godmother."

Ronnee hadn't realized that—smart move of her mother's way back then to tie this crazy Jewel into her life with a binding thread. She could have used her along the way. "It's probably too complicated to explain."

"I'm stubborn when I want to know something. Complicated such as?"

"Oh . . . I sort of begged to come out here, to Houston? I didn't really know how, um . . . boring it was going to be. I was mostly just not wanting my mother to, like, get off easy. With me. You know, leaving me right when she just met me? I thought she was just sort of playing with me if she did that."

"But I thought you were looking for her, too. At the same time." Jewel was studying her. Ronnee tried a little of her speech about needing to find the other half of her identity, the lingering mystery, but it was so false-sounding she dwindled off under Jewel's unsentimental gaze. Could she be suspicious? Was there any way she could guess? Jewel ignored the whole rap, which made her blush with shame. "So you won that point about coming along with her. You're punishing her by being here with her."

"If you can call it winning. At least I wish there were some other kids out here that I liked." Jewel liked to laugh, she would understand what it meant not to be having any fun.

"And your mother?"

Ronnee hesitated, unsure what she owed either of them. "She fixed me up with some kids I could have done without, and she gave me a party. I mean, not exactly for me. For her to, kind of— announce me. The bad news." She wished she could be honest with Jewel, tell her, "This is a business deal," ask her how to close it. Jewel was not going to be patient with her feinting and wobbling. She was like a very clear photograph, every line and hollow clear, while Ronnee was blurry and unfocused. A bad print.

"And your mother?" This woman would outlast her. Well, she was a lawyer. No wonder.

"I—it feels a little . . . late, you know what I mean? To have a mother sort of looking over my shoulder?" This much she could say and not sound conniving. "I hate to say that. I guess I needed her when I was little, but—I feel bad, I sort of messed up her life. Not being with her. She seems, like, permanently sad, somehow. Like she's stuck in this sad position and she can't get out of it." She was surprised at how sympathetic she sounded.

"Well, honey, you ask me, we make our own sad. Somebody wants to trip the switch, there are plenty of ways to do it. Don't you be feeling guilty, none of all that was your fault." She took a long drink. "Tell me about your father, then."

Speaking of fault, Ronnee thought. But she'd be damned if she was going to criticize him much. This woman hated him from way back. "He's really—I miss him, actually. When I left I needed a little rest from how—he can be pretty bullheaded. He has a hard time with me . . ." She shrugged.

"You're half white, babe," Jewel supplied for her. "I know your father. You can say it right out. Don't be ashamed."

"Well . . ."

"And what does it mean, now that you've had a little chance to try it out? Living on the white side?"

She was hard to lie to. "I don't know. Out here it gets mixed up with a lot of other things. But I can't really tell, it's like—maybe everything just stops for the summer, you know, like it's the off season or something. I don't know what it's like when it's not so quiet and sort of—sealed off."

"So were you surprised to find out how—comfortable—your mother is? Financially, I mean. Did you have any idea?"

Oh no, oh no, Ronnee thought, why is she smiling like that? What is she on to? But before she could try to simplify herself into an innocence that would hold up under scrutiny, she heard the car door slam in the driveway.

SHE WATCHED HER MOTHER and Jewel fling themselves into each other's arms like sisters separated by a war. They cooed and cried—it was slightly ridiculous—and then, holding each other at arm's length, they laughed and said all the expectable things about who'd changed how. Both of them, apparently, would have been unrecognizable walking down the city street. It was scary to hear if you were eighteen.

"You going to show me this glamorous home of yours?"

Her mother, finally seated, looked down shyly into her lap. "It's embarrassing, Jewel. I hate this house."

"You hate it! You've got to be certifiable, child! Anything that can keep you this cozy . . ." She laughed at the word *cozy*.

"No—of course I'm grateful for what we can have, I don't mean that. It's just . . . a lot more ostentatious than what I really feel comfortable with."

"Oh, darlin', don't waste your conscience on this kind of stuff. You're not stealing it out of the mouths of the poor. If you didn't have it, you know, it wouldn't change a thing. We're not talking peasant land distribution here."

"Still—"

"Still nothin'. Till the revolution, when they'll line you up against the wall no matter what your square footage, and me with you, you might as well enjoy it."

"*Jewel!* Is that you in there?"

"A seasoned me, sweetheart. I'm long past my inconsistent-socialist period. I think I've learned to separate the youthful excess from the adult—I don't know what to call it. Some sense of what's minimally *necessary* to take care of business."

"Well, this house isn't one of the necessities, believe me. And it's my only business." Her mother looked stern, but it wasn't quite clear who she was scolding.

"Well, you want to talk about self-pity!" Jewel laughed. The thing about her that Ronnee liked was that she could laugh seriously, somehow—she seemed to be seeing around corners so that she could be amused and not-amused at the same time. "People oughtn't to rail against their good fortune. That's the special luxury of somebody who's never been hungry."

Miriam, her face red—she was probably thinking that Jewel had never been hungry either—rose reluctantly and led her into the dining room, commenting caustically as she moved, repenting her furniture. Now there's someone who'd be a fun mother, Ronnee thought. And with God mixed up in it, *godmother* had a nice, permanent sound to it. She wasn't extreme like her daddy or grim like her mother. Why hadn't her father had the good taste to choose Jewel? Maybe together they could teach her mother how to laugh.

19

"YOU DON'T HAVE A CASE, SUGAR."

Miriam was stunned. The jury, returned, had gone its own way.

"What you've got is a lousy shaggy-dog story—nastiness, unbridled hooliganism, power, cowardice, and, God knows, enough racism to turn any charitable person's stomach. In other words, the usual. But what you don't have is a viable legal case."

"Jewel, this can't be you. This is everything you were horrified by twenty years ago. Are you tired or what?" *Tired* was the most generous interpretation she could summon. Is this what it had cost, all the political horse-trading that would make her a college president?

"Well, I *am* tired, now that you mention it, but that's another story. I read too damn many mystery novels at night instead of sleeping. What I am here is realistic, however inconvenient you might find that."

Miriam had begun to pace. She felt as though she'd been granted a moment of new life only to see it withdrawn before she could accustom herself to it.

"Here's the thing." Jewel sat forward in a no-more-kidding position. "You can make a scene, you can get to say some righteous words for the TV cameras about abuse of rights and the violation of dignity and all that, but honey, this is hearsay, your girl's word against theirs, and in the end, they're the cops and your girl will come off as a little black slut who—pardon me, darlin', I'm being harsh, but this'll be the story—you were a *bad*, and I don't mean good, colored girl who helped a white boy steal a car, down in a suspicious part of town, so you could go do—whatever you did, nobody's business, but, you know—" She shook her green polyester shoulders. "Power of innuendo goes a long way. And you put a houseful of felons in their hands, breachers of international law, listen to me, bringing aliens, those *cucarachas*, those stealers of American jobs and welfare and carriers of box cutters in their boot tops, you helped bring 'em across the sealed border. You are implicated, plain and simple. You want to rip her reputation into little tiny shreds for no particular gain, this is the way to do it." She had always done outrage so well, Miriam felt herself lashed with the same whip Jewel had used on their antagonists in the old days. "Even her erstwhile boyfriend—don't you love that word, 'erstwhile'? I never get to use it—her erstwhile boyfriend won't even help out and he's the one who really got whipped. Except for one little scratch that's surely healed over by now, in all those invisible places."

"But Jewel!"

"But Miriam!"

"Don't you believe in making a case even if you can't win it? There's all this brutality in the papers these days. *Time* did a cover story called 'Over-the-Top Cops,' something like that, those cops who knocked around the migrant workers in Colorado and that black woman, wherever she was, who got chased into a culvert and cracked up her car? Can't we at least embarrass them, make them look bad, even if we can't, you know, win damages?" But by the time she got to "damages," she was so deflated her voice was nearly inaudible.

"*Damages?* Spare me, darlin'. You're the one who'll have the damages. Make 'em mad enough and you'll be lucky if this child doesn't go to jail instead of freshman orientation." She sighed theatrically, impatiently. "Listen, Miriam, I'm a pragmatist. I know better than you do what shits those guys can be. I probably hate 'em more than you do, but without apology I am realistic. The law teaches you a lot about the way truth can be twisted and judges can be biased and the cops can be criminals and all the rest. It's a familiar litany. But it also does not tolerate softness or wishful thinking. If you're not careful it can dice you up and feed you to the vultures with their news cameras and microphones, and you haven't advanced your case, you've just taught another lesson to the good students, the ones who are paying attention—against all odds—about cynicism and despair."

"But you've already succumbed to cynicism and despair. Apparently. What would you have said to Rosa Parks? Stand a little longer, you can't win this thing? Or to—" She could see it was futile. Her old friend had made her peace with things as they were, abandoning the light of things as they might be. Miriam could feel the stain of hopelessness climb and spread across her vision like smudged ink. (Hypocrite! she heard without words. You and your pure and useless life. What have you done lately for things as they might be?)

Jewel was beginning to look impatient. She turned and put a hand on Ronnee's arm. "Could you leave us alone for a little, hon? I've got a few things I have to say here."

Ronnee's face was unreadable. She looked, to Miriam, like someone straining to understand a language she wasn't fluent in. Then—it was impossible to predict which mask she would pull up out of her repertoire—she turned sullen. "Why can't I hear? It's *my* life you're talking about, isn't it?"

Jewel seemed surprised. Let her see for herself, Miriam thought with perverse satisfaction. Butter-wouldn't-melt-in-her-mouth Ronnee suddenly breathes fire. Jewel, though, was harder to provoke than she was. "I'll speak with you later, dear," she told the girl, with a downright ministerial aplomb. "Your mother's got a life too, you know."

Meekly, though she rolled her eyes, Ronnee left them.

"That's my vice principal's voice," Jewel told Miriam with a twisted little smile. "Oh my. Well, tell me, how many adolescents does it take to screw in a lightbulb?"

"Oh God, Jewel, let me off the hook. I can never answer those."

"How about two, then. One to screw it in and the other to tear your ticket, give you a program, and show you to your seat."

"You just made that up."

"Of course I did. You make up what you need as you go along. At least I do." She arranged herself carefully, skirt over her knees as if she were there on business. "Look, Miriam, here's what I've got to say." The glass of iced tea sat undisturbed before her on the table. "I don't know what your life's looked like all these years. I know you've been pining for Veronica, who could blame you, but, you know, that's—I hate to tell you this, girl, if you haven't figured it out for yourself, but that's sort of a shaggy-dog thing too. You don't need a lecture from me, I know that. But it's water over the bridge, under the dam, whatever the hell they say." She stood up and walked to the other side of the room and back, as if she had to do something to slow herself down. "There are other things you can probably have with her, friendship, love, I don't know what. You'll figure it out. But honey, she's had her childhood. And give that bastard a little credit while you're wishing you could put him behind bars—it couldn't have been easy to raise this child."

Miriam had closed her eyes as if, blind, she might not have to hear this.

"But okay, you were robbed. True. I hope you don't think you can get those years back."

"No, I don't need a lecture. Not this one, anyway." When she opened them again, Miriam's eyes were swamped with tears. Her face felt swollen, waterlogged, before a single one had fallen. Too many tears had gone into this girl already.

"And you can't go back to 1966, '67 Mississippi either. Those outrages—"

"Yes, those outrages. And these. You didn't used to sit down and just take them. You don't doubt her story. Aren't you angry anymore?" She could see Elpidia staring at her from the kitchen, a dish towel dangling from her hand. "You never answered my question about what pragmatists like you would have told Rosa Parks."

"Different times, girl. Different times. I'm glad to see your blood boil, though. Maybe you'll do something with your anger. Hey, maybe you'll stop moping around your beautiful prison house here. Maybe *you'll* go to law school and then you can pursue whatever the hell you want to! But I figure now we need to put our efforts on things that aren't just symbols. Symbol time's over a long time now. Don't be one of those simplifying fools that confuse what they want with what's *real*." She shook her head in its straightened, greased, ladylike bob. "Tell me something, okay?"

"What."

"Does she want you to do this? Ronnee?"

Miriam shrugged. "Not really." She felt like a sulky teenager, felt how elaboration on an answer meant you were acquiescing.

"And your husband?"

"Good Lord, no. I forgot you haven't met him or you'd never even ask."

"And you—you need your old vendettas, your unfinished business opened up again, to gratify your vanity or what? Jesus, sweetie, we're back to the Solomon business all over again. Think about it: You've got a *family* here. You're her mother. You want your daughter unveiled to the world as a whore?"

"Vanity? What are you talking about? My vanity?"

Jewel shrugged and sighed. "I don't care what you call it, Miriam. Call it Joe if you want. Just don't push it where you don't have any control over where it'll go."

"I haven't pushed anything for so long, Jewel. I was enjoying the movement."

"I know, dear, fighting's good for the circulation. I've dealt with a lot of attorneys who'd be comatose if they didn't have to wake up to litigate. But surely you can find some other way to get your metabolism going." Jewel swirled the ice in her glass, studying it. "You ever think how much Lipton's looks like bourbon? I had a little problem with that—bourbon and her sisters—for a while back there when everything seemed over with. A couple of years after you left? Nobody seemed to need my particular brand of preaching. Or teaching."

"Is that when you went to law school?"

Jewel reached down and pushed her heavy shoes off. "Yup, I went back up to Columbia again. And I had to be sober to do that. Couldn't be cockeyed and read all that fine print."

Miriam was silent. They'd all had their troubles. The recoil. "Sad times."

Jewel nodded. "Sad but done. I've had my bad innings, hon, I want to tell you. So many different kinds of mess you can fall into, you know? It's like a big grab-bag, something for everybody. Some grief just waiting till you pick it up. No two alike."

"Oh, Jewel, what kinds of mess have you been in?" Not like mine, she thought. Not cowardly.

Jewel looked off at the wall, not at her, as if the silvery picture frames held tableaux of her distant past. "Oh, I suppose I had two bad patches, really. Isn't that what the British call them? I love that—bad patches, like they're icy roads or something, minor and inevitable and then, quick—" She snapped her fingers "—over with." She laughed. "The first was—you don't need the details— my one love. Real love. The most superb person. A playwright. You've heard of her." She waved away the idea of a name. "Who lived with me a long time, years, and then, um—found herself a husband."

"A male one."

"A *real* one, she said. Sort of to rub it in. Which left me, I don't know what. Feeling unreal for a long time. Not just lonely and missing her but, you know—severely undermined." She sighed, as if the thought were still exhausting. "So it was a while till I got my feet under me. But I guess I know what it's like to get a nasty shock. Different from yours when Eljay did his nasty business but pretty . . . elemental, I'd say. Basic. Arrow to the heart." She looked down at her hard-shell buttons and polished the bottom one with her finger. "Barbaric, actually. I'm not sure I ever figured out why she had to say it that way, except I guess that was the way she saw it. That our years together were—" She shrugged "—un-natural."

"And the other. You said there were two."

Jewel shook her head slowly, comically, from side to side,

almost to each shoulder, to show her impatience with her own absurd self. "Oh, that was just a little of the usual not-very-surprising career junk. The corporate tease, 'Come work for us, we'll treat you well, we need you.' Big mistake to forget that means 'We'll always see you as a special case. Time to buckle down and take our medicine'—holding their breath and integrating the goddamn office. I don't do too well as a mouthful of cod-liver oil, you know? It was sickening. For all of us."

"You had a corporate job? I can't even imagine."

"Oh, baby. I guess I just wanted to prove I could do it. Or maybe I wanted to prove it couldn't be done, I don't know. Even my shrink didn't know. My parents were thrilled. I had a wardrobe full of real clothes, finally, that's what my mama kept saying. 'Oh, child, you've got *real* suits now!' My low point was when she gave me a set of padded hangers for Christmas."

Miriam put her icy glass to her cheek. Unbelievable.

"I actually used to think of you sometimes, what you'd have said if you'd seen me squeezing myself into this whole scene in these perfect tailored outfits. And the heels! The narrow little shoes with the two-and-a-half-inch heels that got caught in all the subway gratings? Crossing my legs for these guys, these golfer types working their asses off to keep that money tucked up tight in their clients' fists. Oh, help me, Jesus! Talk about unreal."

"So were you pushed or did you jump?"

Jewel finally tucked her feet under her, her green suit skirt over her stockinged knees. It was her first young, untrammeled, familiarly angular move. "Little of both. I just made things, you'd say, untenable. It was like—sort of like the old passive resistance we were so good at. You know, I'd get my work in late. Or I'd lose something really important. Forget things. Kept throwing this monkey wrench into the works. And then my daddy died and I had to come home to deal with all that, and I want to tell you, I have never been so relieved. I probably set back black hiring in that office a hundred years, and maybe just as well. I never thought I'd be so grateful to see that li'l ol' shithole Rowan. Parnassus took me back in a blink, and I thought, Everything I do here is for *my* people. I can be positive, I can be negative, honest, crafty, any damn thing I please, but it's all so we can get over, not those stuffed owls up there feathering their nests. If owls have nests. No more ten-buck cigars I've got to smell, and their genteel bad manners, lower their voices every time I came in the room like I was a spy. God knows what they were saying about me but, shee-it, after a while I'm sure all of it was a hundred percent right." She clicked her teeth with pleasure. "Honey, I wake up every morning now crowing like a rooster."

"Jewel, I tried not to think about you. I tried to pretend none of my—you know—ever happened. Stupid, maybe, but I kept trying."

"Well, I didn't. I wondered a whole hell of a lot about you. Right out loud, sometimes, if there was somebody around to listen. I got to the point where I had a hard time remembering why we gave up on each other without more of a fight. Both of us stubborn as tree stumps, I'll tell you." She shook her head at the spectacle. "But I figured it was up to you to give a signal if you wanted to be found. I would have had a nerve to come messing around in your life."

Miriam got out of her chair to fill another pitcher of tea. "It might have been good for me." She had to shout above the running water. "Might have been terrible."

"No, I was right," Jewel said. "You were healing. Look at the life you made."

"Ah, healing. I was paralyzed." She put the pitcher gently down on the table. Ice cubes nosed each other in the murk like slow translucent fish. "Sleepwalking."

"We had our cocky season, girl."

"And our come-uppance."

"But we're coming through."

"Maybe." Miriam made a bitter face. "You've come through. Me I'm not so sure about."

"Listen. If you can get yourself in step with your particular *times* . . . That's what happened to you, sweetheart, you fell into one of those pits in time between here—" She reached one hand out to the side "—and here—" the other hand. "You got blind-sided and you didn't wait to see what was going to happen. What was going to be needed."

"I wasn't planning on going anywhere." Tears bloomed in Miriam's eyes.

"Now don't start that blame stuff again, I heard it back then. I mean you both. You and that bastard. But if it's any consolation, he suffered for it too, don't worry. Meanwhile, we're both sitting in the here and now. In the air-conditioning. With a gorgeous roof over our heads, what do you call that slanty thing, a cathedral ceiling? Should be counting our blessings. Every student at Parnassus would slay for a house like this, that's what we're trying to aim them towards."

Miriam sniffed. "I hope that's not all." *Ad astra per aspera.* A college founded by ministers with large ideals, though now that she thought about it, the ideals of noblesse oblige were theirs, the hopes for economic independence their students'.

"Easy for you to scoff at, sugar," Jewel said, as if she'd tapped into Miriam's thoughts. "Try coming from some little shit-assed town in the Delta with no running water—you know, this hasn't changed for a lot of folks, and we're still getting some of those children—and putting this down. You or your husband have to steal any money to pay the mortgage?"

"Not that I know of."

"Good enough ideals, then. Let them see what a decent life you can lead if you knuckle down and learn a few things. I talked to a boy last week who never read a whole book in his life. Twelve years of so-called schooling. Not even a kiddie book."

"You sound so much like Barry I can't believe it." Barry and Deb and Ernie, complacent and in love with their security. Securities. "So where does this go, Jewel? What was this whole horrific experience of Ronnee's *for*?"

"For? *For*? You've got to be kidding. You see your life like that? Really? You think there's a divine plan? I thought you were a confirmed agnostic."

"Oh, Jewel, not *divine*. Come on. But haven't you always proceeded out of a sense of purpose? Social purpose?" She wet her lips, which were burning, with a few drops of cool tea. Amazing how hot anger could make you. "Weren't you just saying you went through that bad patch when you lost that purpose?"

"Oh, honey, sure. But you may have noticed by now, it's not all in your control. So you learn when to try to manipulate things and when to leave them alone. It took me a long time to figure that out: You let the wind do some of the steering, 'cause it's gonna blow whether you like it or not." She shook her head. "Which isn't the same as being helpless. Or refusing to pull your load. You *know* all this. I know you do."

"I hate to tell you, Jewel, but you sound like a damned Republican." Jewel laughed, loud, but Miriam wasn't kidding. She got up and went to the door to call Ronnee back in. They were going to like each other, these two; each was apolitical in her own way, one too naïve to care much, the other too sanded down by experience. Barry would love her too. A family of laissez-faire moral capitalists. She was outnumbered.

RONNEE HAD NEVER GIVEN MIRIAM HER PHONE NUMBER in Brooklyn. When she found it without difficulty—"Please hold for the number," Directory Assistance said to her, accentless and dispassionate—she considered the irony that she could have found them any time she'd wanted to. Hidden in plain sight.

His voice did not sit her up straight, it exhausted her. She felt a desperate need to put her head down and, oh, how good it would be to sleep, when Eljay said, "Yeh-up," in something like three distinct syllables.

She would not allow her voice to sound cowed. "Eljay."

"Yes, Eljay. Who's *this*?" He didn't sound curious, he sounded combative.

"This is Miriam." Small talk? That felt absurd after seventeen years of wanting to see him dead. Still. "I hope you're well."

"I'd be better if my girl was here." She could picture how he'd pulled himself close to the phone and was going to make this intimate. "How's she doing?"

"I'm not sure I've seen *your* girl. *Our* girl's doing fine." The more angry she got, the harder she had to fight to keep her eyes open. "But there have been some problems."

"Well, she's a sweetheart, but hooh, she can be a mule. She turning out to be more than you bargained for?"

"I wonder where she gets that from."

"It's a double whammy, babe. She gets at least half from her mother."

"Well, she didn't get much chance to learn it from me." Her lips felt frozen. It took a conscious effort to move them. "Anyway, I don't mean trouble between us exactly. This is very specific, Eljay, and I thought you could help me—us—figure out what to do. We sort of need a tiebreaker. I'd really—" This was hard "—I'd value your opinion. I really would."

Which seemed to warm him considerably. It wasn't cheap of her; she wouldn't have called him if she hadn't meant it. He listened to the story patiently—Jordan, the arrest, the asthma, and finally Miriam's lust for some kind of settling-up—with an occasional grunt of recognition. "This boy black or white."

"Oh, white. She's—uh—I think she's sort of experimenting to see—well, you know. When in Rome." Dear God, she had the backbone of a worm. Why hadn't she simply asked, Why not?

"All too well I know." The streams of warm and cold had always run side by side in him. He dipped you in one or the other with wanton speed.

She was hoping for a little praise for taking care of business, for not just letting them step on his girl. She wanted some gratitude for doing his job of anger, of retribution. Do I or don't I turn over the table? was what she wanted to hear from him.

"And she says she'd be shamed if all this went public?"

"She's less—yes, well, she's a little more self-conscious than I expected somehow. She's so sensitive sometimes—about slights and insults she imagines—that I was sure she'd want to make these guys pay. I mean, this insult was not imaginary."

Eljay was quiet a long time. She heard him breathing. He breathed like a much bigger man. "You won't learn, will you, Miriam. You know, a black girl guarding herself against slights is like a—some animal mother, or a bird mother, protecting her nest. Sometimes what looks imaginary to you feels like a real threat."

She had hoped he'd give her credit for knowing that this time. Her confidence seeped out like blood, a little at a time, like tiny squares through the grid of a Band-Aid. He had trashed her nest, frail white bird that she was, and where had his sympathy been then?

"I know that, Eljay. I'm saying I thought maybe, for that very reason, maybe it was payback time."

"Miriam." He always said *Mir-yum*. "You don't have to do this for her." Or for me, he probably meant, he probably saw. "This little civics lesson isn't going to change anything for her but make her self-conscious about who she's lying down with and where. Another li'l black gal screwing around, just confirms what everybody already thinks, doesn't it. This isn't what she needs from you."

"You think she needs anything from me?"

"Well, now that you mention it, I do know one thing." He cleared his throat as if he was preparing to make a speech. "She hit you up yet?"

"Hit me up?" She had a flash of Ronnee beating her with her fists, angry at last, for her absence. Shrieking. Justified.

"She tell you she's going to Stanford in the fall?"

She had gone cold. "Of course. It's not exactly a secret."

"We had a big knock-down, drag-out about that. I don't think that's the place for her."

"I'll bet you don't, assuming you haven't changed."

"You got it right. I don't need to detail it for you. But she's got her mind made up. She's like a deep-rooted tree when you try to pull her in a direction she doesn't like. She can wear you down."

Hadn't they already done this dance? "I dare say she's had a lot of experience."

He sounded to her like the wolf with Red Riding Hood's grandma still fresh on his tongue. "You think she wouldn't be happy at a college like that fabulous place where her parents met, where all the girls can sit around and worry their nappy hair together?"

What did he want from her. "I don't know this child very well, Eljay, you've made quite sure of that."

"Hey, hey, hang on there a minute! It's not that easy, baby. I don't notice you tired yourself out looking for her all this time. You wait till she's a full-grown woman and then you—"

"*Eljay!* If there was any justice, you'd have been arrested for what you did." She took a deep breath; she was not going to degenerate into fury and blame. "Look, if you want to talk about colleges—which is what we need to be discussing—I just have to say I haven't got a clue about what would be good for her. But if she got in, I'm sure she can manage very well out there."

"That's not the point. Of course she can manage."

"It may not be your point, but apparently it's hers. Anyway, didn't you send her to that very white high school?"

"I sure as hell didn't send her. She had a scholarship there. You know—they get to patronize you for a price. They're hard to pass up."

"For God's sake, Eljay, what kind of thing is that to say about a place that gave her—*gave* her—a wonderful education?"

"That's not what I call giving, all right? They've got her picture all over their brochures. Their pickaninny poster child." He was hissing across the miles. "That kind of advertising's worth at least tuition."

"Well, you know what, Eljay?" she finally summoned up the courage to say. "You know what? This child is half white, can you remember that? And what is she supposed to do with that? She may be black with half of herself, but you just might remember that another part of her is white, and so is her ancestry. Her ancestry is half mine, like it or not. And even if society defines her as black—" Oh, stop, oh stop, enough race business, they had done this already, so long ago. All she wanted was to say, "This is my child, this is my flesh—flesh, that juicy word you love. This is my baby." Maybe the black-white rivalry was only a competition that made use of whatever means lay at hand. Could that be? Maybe it was just a convenient way to accuse each other of soul stealing.

"Listen, this isn't something I want to argue right now. This is something she'll have to figure out for herself, what she is, what she isn't, okay? But meanwhile, this is your daughter, is that what you're saying?"

He must have heard her thinking. "Yes, of course she's my daughter. Exactly."

"She's legally your daughter."

"Yes. Right. So?"

"So I don't want you to say you weren't properly warned what this little reunion is costing you. You may not have heard it but the meter's been ticking."

"What do you mean, is costing me?"

"She's got a little of that blood-money scholarship help out there in her California Eden. A lot of it, actually. But not quite enough to be—you know—comfortable. Like she must think *you* are." He sighed. "What a place that is. Looks like central casting, all those gods and goddesses with the tans against the tennis whites. Of all the places to choose. You think she's spiting me?"

This was too much for her. He could make himself sound like such a naïf. "Will you stop being so goddamn charming and finish this thing?" Now she was up and pacing, the phone to her ear. She had awakened, for sure.

"But, uh, who do you think is going to cover the rest of her toll out there?" Eljay asked. "I guess she doesn't want to be paying back loans forever and working her ass off—she doesn't really like to break too much of a sweat, you know?—if there's some other way. And I can't help her. I can't. I can't and I won't. Even if I could, you better believe I wouldn't, not for that place, and our dear girl knows that. The innocent."

Now she was nothing but silent.

"Well, who in the hell do you think is making up the difference? She wants to go to that rich folks' playground, you tell me who's signing the checks for it. Miriam, she gave your name to them. As her mother. And I think you ought to be informed about it, since she didn't think it was important enough to mention herself."

"Eljay, we've just met! We've barely established anything yet—"

"And she didn't hand you a bill at the door. That was very nice of her, all things considered. But remember, she went out and found you just in time, didn't she, before the first bill comes due."

"Pardon me, my friend. I found her."

"But you gave her a lot of points for looking, didn't you? That swell coincidence? Blood calling to blood?"

"So?"

"So did she tell you she only started searching around for you when she added it up and realized she needed a little squeeze from your juicy Texas bank account?"

She sat down hard, and she was not sure she'd ever be able to get up again. He had had his fun, if fun it had been. It might be that he was jealous. But would he invent this?

"I just thought I'd save you a little more sticker shock than you might be able to take, Mir-yum. Better now than later. So don't say I never did anything for you. Now the two of you can get on with your sentimental reunion out in the clear light of day. Everything's on the table."

"You really did enjoy this, didn't you?" she finally managed.

"No, I didn't. But you may thank me yet, you never know. I want to promise you, I'm not as callous as I seem right now, okay? I'm not Iago, breaking up the furniture just for the hell of it. Trust me. Please trust me on this one."

"Why should I trust you? Look what you just told me! How do I know this is true?"

"I told it to you, doll, but I didn't make it up. Ask her. I just think you might as well know what's really happening, is all. I don't like to see you bumping up against something you can't see in the dark, you know?"

"Eljay, you're as big a bastard as you were the last time I laid eyes on you."

"Oh, baby, it's time to stop the spitting contest. That's one thing besides money I know she could use."

Her mouth was so dry she couldn't even try to speak.

"See, I don't think it's really about the money at all. She does. My theory is she's hung up on what she can get back from you because she never had anything. I think she's looking for—I don't know—a handful of something. Reparations, maybe. Like, you know the way some kids steal out of their mothers' purses? I know you blame me for that, no secret, and I'll always be sorry about that." She closed her eyes as if that way she wouldn't hear him. "Anyway, the fact is, after they're little kids, what's any parent good for?"

"Easy for you to be sorry now, Eljay, you've done the parent part." Her anger was making her light-headed. He couldn't say a single thing that wasn't too ironic to bear. "Are you actually admitting you might've caused her pain? Is that what I'm hearing?"

He gave out a little puff of disdain. "Oh, pain. How the hell do I know? Pain."

"You sound like you've never heard the word before."

"What can I say? Pain is the human condition, I didn't invent it. But can you go back? Mir-yum. Can you do anything about all that except hate me?"

She felt him manipulating her, but the question had been her own ever since she'd told Ronnee their story. It fell on her hard.

"Do I get an answer to that?"

She would have to parse it carefully: Can I do anything about all that except hate him?

Instead, "I have a question for you, then." No snideness. It was no help here. "I'll deal with this money business somehow. I'll figure out what to do about that. But meanwhile, are you willing to let 'your girl' be what she is?"

"Meaning?"

"Meaning a girl with another family. If she wants one." One. Mine. Me. Was this what a child felt who was given up for adoption? Unchosen? Unkept? Whatever the extenuations, unloved? There was something absurd about it—just who was the parent here?

Now Eljay hesitated. "Whatever she wants, doll. She's a big girl, she chooses. I've given her what I could give her. Like I said, it's too late for me to have much influence on her anymore. But I'll tell you, you think she deserves that choice, then she also deserves to say no to going after those cowboys with the guns. Just leave her alone. Hang loose, girl."

"She's very apolitical, Eljay. You must have crammed a little too much down her throat."

He laughed. "You can see she only swallows what she wants. She's very absorbed in herself. Kids are, I guess. Anyway, you never know. Took *me* till I was good and ready. If you remember. So meanwhile it drives you nuts, but you've got to respect it. In the end she isn't my girl or yours, she's nobody's but her own."

Cliché, cliché, cliché. He sounded like a self-help book. Did he believe any of this sentimentality or, having demolished her, was he playing her for a fool? "Do you want to talk to her?"

"Mmmn-mmn. This is your time, Mir-yum. She needs me, she knows where I am. Just tell her I miss her."

He was as hard to hate as he was to love.

"Soft where she's concerned, aren't you."

"Plenty soft. She's been my life." His voice was different. "No joke."

Every sentence burned. "Ill-gotten gains."

"Think about hating, Mir-yum. I know you feel better for it, but it's like a temporary high, you know? Think about what you get back from it when you come down. And listen. She's no simple money-grubber, remember that. Give her some credit. She's a smart girl with some big ambitions."

She discovered she was clutching the phone so hard her hand hurt. "You know how they say the one who wins the war gets to write its history, Eljay? So you get to come up with all these philosophical smiley faces. I never thought I'd hear you sounding like a Hallmark card."

He purled his insinuating laugh in her ear, flirting, always flirting, his words natural and easy, like music. "Think about it, doll. You're right, but think about it anyway."

20 RONNEE AND JEWEL were at play in the pool, being restored to life. Even at midafternoon, sunshine flashed on the water like dozens of flashbulbs popping near, popping far, the way they exploded in the faces of the famous. "It's a bathtub!" Jewel shouted. "We need to throw in some ice cubes!"

But oh, it was good anyway. Not that chill mysterious pond in the country; it was more necessary here.

Then her mother seemed to appear out of nowhere to stand above them, there in her unwrinkled skirt and blouse like somebody in an office. She said in an ominous voice, "I need to talk to you, Veronica." Actually, at this angle, with her arms folded like that, she looked more like a cop.

"Veronica. Uh-oh. Did I leave the top off the peanut butter again?" It wasn't hard to be jolly when you were cool. "Come on in, you'll feel better!"

Jewel looked at her, then at Miriam, her friend, then, fast as a lick, back at her, sympathetically. "Want me, too?" she asked. She was shaking water out of her ears, first on one side, then on the other, as if she'd been doing the crawl.

They pulled themselves up and over the side of the pool and stood dripping. Her mother looked uncomfortable being dry. Ronnee made footprints where she stood. "Where do you want us, massa?"

"It doesn't matter," her mother said, ignoring what would have been called insolence in school. That was the look she had, all thin lips and eyes sparking: punitive teacher, about to read the riot act and keep them in for gym. "I just spoke with your father."

"You called him?" Jewel asked before Ronnee could even register what that might mean.

"I thought he ought to have something to say about the business with the police."

"And did he?" Both of them.

"He thinks you're the one who needs to decide that, Ronnee. You're going to be in the middle of it—the publicity, the questions. I hate to see them get away with it, but he's right, it's got to be your call. I'll just . . . restrain myself. Me and my newfound zeal." She seemed to be smiling at herself.

Ronnee shrugged, relieved.

"But he had a little news for me that . . . surprised me." She hooked her eyes to Ronnee's. Silence except for the rude gurgle of the pool filter that usually went unheard.

Ronnee stood dripping in the sun, the water making dark gray spots on the pale concrete. He couldn't have told her, he couldn't have! "You want me to say something?" God, it was so hot the water spots were sucked up almost instantly, droplets on a frying pan with the heat on high. Why would he have told on her?

"I wouldn't mind hearing something from you." Her mother was a cross between a bad actress doing self-righteous hands-on-hips anger and a small girl trying not to cry. She wasn't made for shocks like this. Shame like a shadow crept up Ronnee's neck, over her ears, and down her face. She had done damage, up close, as if with her bare hands. This Texas cash cow was not supposed to feel real, not supposed to look like she was going to be sick, not supposed to make her feel protective. Her throat ached. There was something without a name at which she was brutally failing.

"Would anybody care to enlighten me about what's going on?" Jewel sounded exasperated.

"I'll be happy to enlighten you. I don't mind if you hear this. In fact, you're probably the most appropriate person to be here right now because you were—" Miriam was too overcome, for a full minute, to finish; she covered her mouth with her fist. "Okay. Let me be sure I've got this right. I wouldn't want to mislead you. I've just learned that my daughter wasn't looking for a mother, she was looking for a sugar daddy." She faced Ronnee again. "Would that be fair, do you think?"

Ronnee blinked back furious tears. She would not justify herself. "You believe everything you hear, no wonder you gave me away."

"Veronica!" That was Jewel, affronted. "Not fair, baby. Not fair at all."

"Who said anything was fair!" Is it fair that you've got all this money, Ronnee didn't dare say, and my father can keep me from doing what I want to because he won't pay for it? Is that fair? She grabbed the beach towel, flags of many nations laid out in stripes, a goddamn educational beach towel, and hid her head in it, swiping at her hair, giving herself another minute of breathing room to think, think how to explain.

"I'm listening if you want to say something." Her mother, quavering, hopeful, hanging onto her dignity. Could she say that out loud—your pool, your house, your *life*? She'd be admitting everything.

She wanted to blame her father—he was endlessly blamable.

Enough lying. It was her fault. She couldn't say a word.

This must be what criminals feel when the police come striding toward them finally or the blue light swings behind the getaway car: this hopelessness, like weariness, an inconsolable sadness, dull, not sharp, somehow, because only surprise is pointed. She had all she could do not to just admit it and sink shamed to the ground and be done with it, like a victim of somebody else's cruelty. Instead she knelt at the side of the pool and leaned over it, scooped up a faceful, trying not to breathe in and choke. Jewel seemed to be saying her name.

She could deny it. Her mother would believe her if she said, "Not true, he's jealous and he's still scamming you!" Do her a favor, she wants it to be a lie. Water dropped between her breasts like sweat. Her mother must love her, to give her such power. If she loved her mother, if she thought she could ever love her, she could rescue her so easily. Mama, you've been *had*. The man is still an SOB.

Just at the side of her vision little wavelets reared up on the surface of the pool and flared like a blown-upon ground fire.

But if her mother really cared about her now, she could reach across all this confusion and pride, all the things you couldn't ask for, and put her arms around her, say her name, Veronica, Ronnee, Ree, it wouldn't matter. Refuse her deceit. Make peace with her father. Ignore the years. Rescue *her*.

THEY STARED AT EACH OTHER for a long time like antagonists setting their feet for combat. Then, without a twitch of warning, Ronnee bolted and ran. Jewel was waving Miriam down, back, away— "Let her go! Poor thing, let her hide herself awhile till she's ready to face you."

So Miriam subsided and went in to the sunporch to sit down knee-to-knee with Jewel. She was red-faced, sweating, which came of not having been in the water.

"Do you mind if I drip on your wicker?" Jewel asked. "I'm not exactly presentable." Jewel was plump as rising dough in a bathing suit wild with green and red and yellow tropical birds. She stenciled damp footprints on the tile, crossing the kitchen floor.

"Drip away. That stuff's not very comfortable against bare flesh, though." Miriam laid her face in her hands, defeated. "Convicted. She could have slid out of that so easily. A little turn and twist and I'd gladly have believed it was Eljay just being . . . diabolical."

"She's honest, then. Give her some credit. For somebody caught in the middle of a lie, she's at least got some conscience."

Miriam smiled grimly. "Boy, you can make the sun shine on midnight, can't you? Wow."

"No, I mean it. Why didn't she just deny it?"

Miriam was still too stunned to think. "I suppose I don't know anything now that I thought I knew twenty minutes ago." She sighed.

"This changes things for her, too, you know. Her golden goose is dead."

"Gee, thanks. I needed that." Miriam made a face. "But you'll pardon me if I'm not burning with sympathy just now. I feel so stupid for letting myself get blindsided. Stupid and—" She scowled at herself. "Unlovable."

"Don't feel stupid, dear. Who can blame you? You weren't exactly asking for something unholy." Jewel shrugged, impatient. "As for the unlovable, come on now. I'll bet the two of you could have a contest for who deserves rejection the most."

"God, Jewel, I thought we were working our way toward a little . . . affection, I guess. Maybe not love, not so soon. I mean, not on *her* side, anyway, I know that's complicated—but some kind of feeling, some sympathy. I didn't have any illusions that I knew her, but now I see I don't have the slightest idea what's *under* there. If anything."

"Oh, I wouldn't doubt there's plenty. A mess of confusion, but plenty."

"The thing is, she's so damn well defended. Eljay would agree with what you said about rejection, he thinks this is all a defense. A way to punish me. Which might be true and might just be his belated little stab at kindness. He sounds like he wants to be forgiven."

Jewel put her head back and closed her eyes, then opened them abruptly. "Meanwhile, down the hall or wherever she's at—Lord, maybe you want to check and make sure she's not dangling from the rafters."

"Jewel."

"I forgot, excuse me, last thing a place like this would have is rafters. Well, you got any razor blades lying around loose in one of your twelve johns?"

"Don't, all right?"

"You don't remember me the way I am, sweetie. This is how I get over. And you'd do better if you loosened your belt a notch or two, you know."

Miriam glared at her.

"But back to Miss Well Defended. This is your time to find out
what's under there. Go on in there while her defenses are down
around her ankles."

"You think now?"

"She's probably had long enough to sulk alone. She's probably
wondering what's left between you now, are you going to put her
out on the street with her suitcase or what?"

But Ronnee's room gave off no sound, distressed or otherwise:
no radio, no music, surely no bereft weeping. Miriam lectured herself not to imagine the worst: People don't kill themselves out of
embarrassment. It was probably more upsetting that she'd lost her
meal ticket. Although teenagers aren't like other people: they flare,
they explode. They implode. Then again, Ronnee had a cat's memory. Surely she had to be as resilient as she was ambitious.

THE MAIL HAD COME. On her way back to the sunporch,
Miriam saw it lying in its usual splay on the tile floor beneath the
slot. She never gathered it anymore without a tiny jolt, this place
where Ronnee had so casually reentered her life. Not casually, she
thought today. Cunningly.

Between a bill for her mother's apartment and a Land's End catalog, a familiar envelope showed its corners, Evie's rainbow of
Magic Markers emblazoned in a burst of arrows, the fattest one,
like a giant red fleur-de-lis, pointed at Ronnee's name: MISS VERON-
ICA REECE, ESQ. Evie was hard on mailmen. She wished she could
open it. Instead, grimly, she carried it down the hall and, bending,
pushed it hard under Ronnee's door and retreated. Jewel was hovering at a distance, watching her.

Her girls, her girls—what a thing to say!—who had been secrets
from each other so recently, seemed to be touching hands with an
avid hunger that took her by surprise. Evie had phoned a second
time; Ronnee had just sent her a silver bracelet, an *E* dangling on
one side of a disk and an *R* on the other. Evie, she knew, felt borne
down upon by her noisy brothers, who, it was true, seemed to
swallow all the available air. But Ronnee—she didn't know, even

now, now less than ever, what Ronnee missed, what she needed. Maybe the two girls, at least, could have had something fresh and clean and untainted. It had thrilled her to think so.

She turned back to Jewel, her face burning. "Suggestions, ma'am?"

Jewel put her hand on Miriam's shoulder and gently turned her around. "My suggestion is, you get into your bathing suit and come out there with me and cool yourself off. You put your face in the water and count to ten, then you lift it out and breathe and dip it in again."

"And what kind of magic will that work?"

"First thing, it'll get you away from this door, 'cause this is one kettle that's not going to boil while you stand here staring at it. Then we make a little something to eat and we sit down dripping and we scarf it down. And I try to convince you that this is going to work out all right."

"Somehow, mysteriously."

"Because most things happen mysteriously, girl. Why do you think I'm here with you and not planning to let you out of my line of vision again." That was not a question. "What have you ever predicted—I mean, important things—that came out exactly the way you expected? Your daughter? Your marriage? Your poor little aborted career, back there when you had something to teach people? I'll bet you can't pick a simple color for your wall and have it come out the way you asked for it. Name me one thing." She waited a beat for that one thing. "You see?"

22 RONNEE SAT ON THE BED and worked her way through it. In the back of her head Smokey Robinson throbbed on, "Mmm-mmmm, hold onto your love." Humiliation, that was what had doubled her over. Shame. That was superficial, though—why care how it looks? What matters is how it feels. No love to hold onto, bro. The heat of it climbed her chest again, darkened her neck, made her face burn as if it had been slapped. She had not intended to hurt anyone. All right, then: She hadn't thought of her mother as anybody real. At the beginning she had been no one. If you're angry—wasn't this so?—you take what you need. Her father called it the Looters' Credo. She could not imagine being in the same room with her ever again. But, goddammit, was it the necessary communion of adults, sending signals above her head, that explained why he had betrayed her?

Well, her traitor father was out of her life. He could spend *his* next eighteen years wondering what had become of her. What did he owe this woman that he didn't owe her first? As for her mother, no matter how embarrassed she was, she could never apologize. She had nothing to apologize for, except for the sneaky way she came to her, like someone in a masquerade: All she had claimed was parental support, past due with interest. She did not want to be comforted, did not want to be touched by her and her greedy needy little hands. It was, all of it, over, done, finished. She was out of here before she could be forgiven for wanting what was only

hers. Cancel all emotional debts, close the accounts, this Are You
My Mother bit had all been a mistake, top to bottom, first to last.
She was going to become a Buddhist like the ones she'd read about
in her Eastern Traditions class, and walk the Eightfold Noble Path,
connecting to nothing, to no one. From now on she was going to
keep clean of all these murks and confusions.

She pulled her duffel out of the closet, where it had sat squashed
in the corner. It opened, blooming like something dried that's im-
mersed in water. She took everything she owned—more than she'd
come with; she considered what else she'd like to own. Nothing.
Nothing from this house, too grand to rob. She would get her
hands on a credit card or some cash, one further shame, the very
last, take it and be gone. Stupid, stupid, all of it stupid.

She happened to be staring at the door when, with a little hiss,
something came poking under. A note from her mother, or from
Jewel, peacemaker to the stars. She picked it up reluctantly and
saw the wild child-colors. Oh, Evie, shit, she'd ruined that, too.
Good work. She'd had a little sister for a day or two. All she could
do was lie down on the quilt and sleep it away, her knees pulled up
to keep her warm, because this was the first time her mother's air-
conditioning felt too strong and she was cold to the core.

WHEN SHE WOKE she knew what to do.

The name of her mother's travel agent was Marian Fish. She had
met her at the coming-out party. She thought she remembered a
tousled, freckled woman who laughed a lot, sort of strawberry
blond, a little heavy, with a neckline low enough to show fat cleav-
age. A softie. That might not be the right woman, but the part that
mattered was that she was everyone's favorite—Barry had said she
cut deals for them, called when there was a special to Costa Rica, a
discounted cruise, a great package. Ronnee thought it was deca-
dent to make your living arranging for people to lie down in the
sun and drink margaritas, but if she let herself judge people that
way she'd end up like Jordan's sister Lisa and her Fun Police.

"Mrs. Fish?" It took effort to steady her voice. "This is Miriam's daughter. Ronnee? Remember—um—the party? Right, it was, right. I loved it."

Marian gushed at her, which meant either that she'd truly enjoyed meeting her or that she'd been outraged, nothing in between. Ronnee got the times to Orange County, wherever that was exactly. "Try to keep it as cheap as possible. You know." Sounding kittenish and confidential. When she hesitated about her return date, Mrs. Fish suggested something called "open return." She hadn't known there was such a thing. On her mother's account. Of course. Sure. Thanks. "It's a little spur-of-the-moment, but—yes, she *is* out there. I really want to meet her, right. I mean, she's my only sister, and—you know—" Breathless, innocent. "It's going to be a surprise." Shock was more like it. And then she'd be gone.

"JORDAN, ARE YOU THERE?"

Of course he wasn't; he had his gift of a job. She wasn't used to answering machines. A few of her friends' parents had them, but she still tended to barrel right in before she realized she was hearing a canned voice. Can you get mad into one of these things? she wondered. If he hears it twelve hours after I say it, does it have any fizz left?

"Look, I just wanted you to know—I mean, you're probably not losing any sleep over it or anything, but—I'm out of here." And no response. Anyone could listen, too—his blessed mother could tune in on this—though the fact that he had his own message meant he had his own machine. "So. Thanks for calling to check up and see how I'm doing, that was really cool of you." Sarcasm didn't work without a response; she needed to see the tips of his ears go red. Well, maybe it was only fair that he had to listen without a chance to butt in and justify himself. But the silence was creepy. "Your mama probably said she'd take your allowance away if you talked to me. So . . ." She couldn't say it all to the empty air. And she couldn't feed him the polite consoling bullshit you were supposed to: Good luck at Princeton, hope it all works out. She didn't hope that. Hope you grow up and understand a little. Hope you wake up some time alone and have to figure out what you really deserve and how mediocre you are. (Beautiful word for something so nasty—it sounded like a kind of dance. *Let's do the me-di-o-cre!*) And how, mediocre or not, even though your parents are less than mediocre, it won't matter a bit. Won't keep you down. You've got your pass in your pocket.

Can you rant quietly, with no one listening? None of it was worth saying.

"And one more thing." This rose up in her and surprised her, but there it was, caught, which made it solid, somehow, and maybe permanent, like a letter. "Remember, I was really mad at your sister back there, and, like, condescending? Because she looked at me and, just like you, I guess, all she saw was 'black girl, gotta be this, gotta be that.' And that made me mad. But you know something?" She took a deep breath to get this done with. "I actually respect her. 'Cause anybody who grows up in your family better have a way out, and at least she's *trying*. She may be obnoxious but she's going her own way. She's so busy saying No, no wonder it makes her ugly—ugly's part of it, too. So tell her good luck from me. I know they'll let her out of jail. I'm sure they will." She had tears in her eyes out of nowhere. "Maybe you'll figure out how to say it some time. Say no. You'd better, Jordan. I mean it." She giggled at how righteous she sounded. "Last words of wisdom before I shut up." She was dwindling down to an embarrassed trickle.

The stupid machine bleeped at her just as she was getting to the end, like a door slammed in her face just when she was trying to make amends. Today it wouldn't surprise her if her whole message got wiped out before Jordan had to hear it. Or he might just push some button and erase her himself. She was the famous tree that falls and falls in the deserted forest. She was ashamed that she cared.

BETWEEN SLEEPING AND WAKING, her head against the window over thirty-five thousand feet of nothing, she thought how long ago it seemed she had come to Houston, and what a short

time it had really been. Those black mountains at the window,
harsh and treeless—imagine being lost down there. She dozed and
woke and dozed. How blasé she was becoming! Next time she
looked, the hills were tan and rounded, like lion hide. While she
had been in Houston, Evie had probably gone swimming a lot,
built some horrible ashtrays out of snakes of mud-colored clay,
made some friendships and lost some. Nothing much—that was
what camp was for. She had been to day camp: same stuff, only
you went home to dinner and played in the street before bedtime.
Her day camp taught "Lift Every Voice and Sing" and taught you
to make African wraps, but it was the same deal: Keep these children busy so they don't bug their parents. She got home in time to
cook that dinner, do her own laundry, she puffed up the couch pillows before she went out to catch the bus, mornings. Sleep-away
would have been a nice rest. Her father acted like he was sending
her to Paris and, trained not to disagree, she'd believed him and
been impressed that she got to go anywhere at all. Some of her
friends had it worse, that was true: all they did was take care of
their little brothers and sisters all summer: nosebleeds, scraped
knees, double dutch till you couldn't jump another minute, and
sometimes an open hydrant for all of them. Then again, they didn't
know what it was to be lonely. Sometimes she felt like Cinderella.

The town nearest the camp was gorgeous—low white buildings,
elegant Spanish tile, a fountain, blankets of flowers everywhere.
She was going to like California, if she hadn't blown her chance to
be here. If her father hadn't blown it for her. It was a shame to
have to throw away so much of her money on a cab to the camp,
but what was she to do? She'd worry about it later, maybe hitch
back to the airport. Evening—Friday—and the day had gotten
longer as she flew west; it had begun to look like it was never going to end. She and a cabdriver who sounded just like Elpidia
bumped along a winding road and suddenly, in a parting of the
trees, a sign loomed up in that Jewish-looking writing that was really English: RUACH MEANS SPIRIT!! Two children danced holding
hands, black silhouettes, under the letters.

The sun was just setting over the fine unrippled lake that sat in a deep bowl in the middle of Camp Ruach, a single tethered rowboat reflected back like something on a postcard. A big bushy brown dog came loping across the cleared area, grassless and dusty under the flagpole—God, why did they all have to salute the country and the state every single day?—that must be a gathering place. Up on the porch of a long wooden building the dog circled and circled and finally, as if he'd made a nest, collapsed with his head on his paws. He knew the schedule, this dog did. Ronnee could hear voices inside, singing. She tiptoed up the stairs and peeked around the open door. So many little white children in white! She craned to hear them, but they were speaking babble—Hebrew, that was. Praying? Up on the stage, her head covered with a blue-and-yellow flowered scarf that was the only spot of color in sight, a girl bent murmuring over two candles as she lit them with a long match, then shook the match out as if it were a thermometer. A huge "Oh-mein" bubbled up when she was finished. Her mother did that Friday nights while she stood by empty-handed. Her mother looked awkward about teaching her what it was all about; she felt awkward asking.

Ronnee's father had told her he had outgrown religion. It was a matter of blood, not reason, and past the point when you longed to be babied by hopeful stories, nobody ought to need it. "That's an unpopular way for you to look at it when you're living with brothers and sisters who love to get stirred up on Sunday morning," he acknowledged, "and half the weekdays too. Keep it to yourself." But he didn't take her to church to keep up appearances. If they ever went it was for the music, where maybe God lived. Just maybe. "My mama's put in enough time for the whole family, baby. You too. You get a pass." Blood, she thought now, looking in at the faces that were as unreal as angels in their white outfits, though there was nothing floaty about their clothing really, their T-shirts and sneakers. Some of them were rapt, just as many fidgety. She was here for blood, not reason. He had missed that point somehow. One of these children shared half her blood, half her genes. None of her memories.

She sat on the broad top step while inside the children seemed to be conducting a whole church service—synagogue, okay—in that strange language. Evie was ten. Could she possibly understand it? They were known to be smart people, but that smart? *They* are *me*. Would she always have to remind herself?

Her mother had planned to take her to their synagogue, which terrified her, but it had never happened. She had the idea that they didn't go that often. "You'll come home for the High Holidays," her mother had suggested. "That will be interesting for you." She didn't really know what that meant, what made them High. A good many of her classmates at St. Helen's had taken off days at a time every September, but she didn't really know what they did during their absence. "Repent," somebody said once, a hint too cryptic to mean anything. They certainly didn't look transformed, or act different when they came back: the offensive ones were still offensive, the good ones good. She didn't think religion entered in.

She saw herself, now, from far away, disembodied, a big cardboard-colored cutout of a girl with a Brillo head and gold-rimmed ears, black jeans and a bright red button-up shirt with a fake hanky like a joke poking out of the pocket. She was stranded somewhere between—where and where? Too many people wanted her. Though not anymore, that was old news. Now she belonged to nobody. Home, her mother had said, for the holidays. *Home?* Till she'd done the unforgivable, landed the ultimate insult, and *pfft!* That home's up in smoke. She was no color, every color, bright and stupid, brave and terrified—they canceled each other out—and, though it would have been easier to be blind, she saw it all. A halfway girl, and only half smart enough for her own good. When she closed her eyes and, tired, leaned her head back against a wooden post, there was almost a kind of relief in the way she'd come loose from everything—wasn't anything possible this way? Later, when she got famous acting, she would tell them, "I did it myself. I'm a do-it-yourself project." It made her motor race, the way her asthma medicine did, on the edge of out of control. True, anything was possible, but that included *nothing*, too: sleeping in the bus station, selling herself like the whore of the Houston ship channel. Somebody was that whore, even if they were wrong about her.

When the screen door sprang back and the kids came banging out of the hall, half orderly, half chaotic, she stood up and studied them to see if she could guess which one was her sister. These girls were far more varied than she'd have expected—her stereotype of a Jewish face and Jewish hair thinned and finally evaporated as the willowy blondes, the freckly redheads, bobbed out alongside the dark ones with swarthy skin, the dark ones with stark white faces, the kind they called black Irish. The ones with the noses, the ones who looked Episcopalian, that St. Helen's ideal. She saw one who looked like the headmistress's snotty daughter. They were as miscellaneous as her own black cousins!

She even discovered a boy darker than she was, with telltale hair, his warm-brown neck lovely against his white Izod shirt. What, she wished she knew, was his story, and how did he like it?

Pick a girl, she urged herself. Pick someone and follow her— was there anyone who looked at least a bit like her? Like her mother? She had seen photographs of Evie and her brothers in the house, of course, but they weren't portraits; they weren't quite straight on, features clear—everyone seemed to be in the middle of some activity, looking back over a shoulder or smiling out of a tree. They certainly weren't useful as mug shots.

One tiny brunette (too young) had a kind of feel about her, something familiar in her tiny face. But she heard a counselor call out "Nicki!" and, hands on her small shoulders, steer the girl off. Another had a certain expression that reminded her of her mother's, an anxious way of shifting her glance as if something was surely wrong somewhere. But this was ridiculous. And it was beginning to get dark.

She was afraid to ask which was the ten-year-old-girls' bunk, let alone where she would find Evie Vener, because you couldn't just come stalking around like this. She had passed another sign that said VISITORS PLEASE REGISTER AT OFFICE. And who are you? she could hear them ask her. And just who might you be, looking her up and down, weighing her for danger. The maid's daughter?

And then somebody shouted, "Evie! Race you!"

"No racing on shabbat, Tammy. *Honestly.*" A little girl in a peasanty blouse turned slightly in her direction with a severe look, and then broke into a fit of giggles. (Not a member of the Fun Police, at least.) She had her shiny dark hair pulled into two tails like little fountains arcing upwards, cinched by transparent bubble-gum balls. She looked like her father, regular-featured, pretty but maybe a bit more fierce. Ronnee stared at her, trying to comprehend, to convince herself: This girl is bound to me, locked, foreordained. That is no stranger. She liked the girl's looks, but she was not ready to believe it.

A woman in a beige wraparound skirt and Birkenstocks, a teacher for sure, was fast approaching, looking a little too official. Ronnee moved out into the crowd of dispersing campers and took off into the nearest verge of trees, not running, but walking discreetly so as not to look like she was escaping. She would have to be sneaky, then—call it an adventure—and wait till night fell in earnest. Let the woman think she'd imagined her, think something about a shadow. Ronnee could easily believe, if she closed her tired eyes, that she had imagined herself.

SHE HAD TO ENDURE a campfire and the sight of many dozens of children in their moth-white outfits advancing on the flames with marshmallows on sticks. The campers who were too impatient to wait for the orderly dispersal of official sticks made brief forays into the trees to pick up loose kindling, onto whose ends they jammed their marshmallows so that they could fence with them and make fiery circles over their heads in the brand-new dark. Ronnee stood hidden behind a thick, sweet-smelling trunk waiting for the miracle of her sister's random arrival, and—it was the first time in her life a prayer seemed to be answered, here in the semi-holy precincts of this camp named for a puff of spirit—sure enough she tracked the little girl in the gauzy peasant blouse as she came near enough to be, with luck and speed and not too much suspicious crackling underfoot, intercepted.

When she heard her name, Evie stood still, nose high like an animal sniffing the air. Ronnee called again, hushed but clear. When the little girl continued to look around, bewildered and a little panicky—it was very hard to see anything in the double-dark of the woods—Ronnee reached out and grabbed her wrist, and, praying Evie wouldn't scream, pulled her behind a tree. "Evie! It's Veronica! Shush!"

Evie opened her mouth and her eyes wide, like a cartoon character. "What are *you* doing here?" She didn't seem to think it peculiar that Ronnee had picked her out of the stampede—she was, after all, who she was, and not much doubt about it. When she thought about it later, Ronnee envied her that certainty.

"I came to see you," Ronnee said. "I took a plane." She wasn't sure that was what Evie really wanted to know, but in any event the question had been replaced by the girl's amusing scrutiny. She was standing on her tiptoes trying to see Ronnee better. Ronnee obligingly squatted, holding both her hands.

"You don't look like I was picturing," Evie finally announced in an urgent whisper, as if it was her fault.

The noise of the campfire swelled around them. Sparks spiraled off it, up into the blackness, with a noisy popping, like toy guns firing. Ronnee could see them tumble, dying, into the night. "What were you picturing?" She had, of course, of course, forgotten yet again that no one would have prepared the child. Maybe her mother had meant to, with time to spare until they met. Maybe she hadn't. Maybe it was too awkward, too odd, too awful. She was so tired of being surprising.

"Are you a—um—black?"

No beating around the bush, anyway. "Half," she said. Bluntness for bluntness. "Guess which of my parents was a—um—black."

Evie giggled. "That's silly—your *dad*. It would have to be!" She said this as if she'd solved a great mystery and, keeping both of Ronnee's hands tight in hers, pulled her close to her chest.

"So, Eve, I need to talk to you. How can we do that? Aren't they going to wonder where you went?"

The girl turned reluctantly back toward the bonfire. "I *guess*. Sssss." She exhaled disappointment.

"Ssssss," Ronnee repeated. "You sound like a piece of wet wood, hissing."

Evie laughed. "Maybe I can tell them I have to go call home. I'll go stand by the phone. See that building way over there?"

"Give me a hug before you go."

Evie clutched her around the waist, tight, looking up at her. She was a wonderful size, and she still had the automatic confiding warmth of a far younger child. Ronnee could feel a complicated little shiver of excitement ripple through her. "I'll think of some other excuses for later, okay?" Maybe this was what the girls who had babies knew, this sufficing warmth of trust and eagerness, hunger and acceptance. Maybe this was what her mother had had with her before she was stolen away. Even with all that staticky black-white business, it seemed much simpler to be loved by this child than by anyone else she'd met up with lately. She ached to think she had to walk away from it.

Ronnee kissed the top of her head. This little white girl, this perfect stranger who had been the one her mother got to raise. "Okay," she whispered, overcome with surprise at how instantly she had been trusted. "Let's see what kind of liar you are."

When they met at the phone, Evie said, "Why can't you just come in my bunk and everything? Why do we have to hide?"

Ronnee thought about it. She didn't want any phone calls to Houston to check her out. Just now, between lives, she supposed she wanted to be hidden. "It's just better that way. So, Evie . . ."

The child sat down at a picnic table where the light didn't reach. "So, Ronnee . . ."

"You having a good time? Is it a good camp?"

Evie shrugged. "I don't know if it's good. My friends are here and we—like, we do a lot of fun things. You know. I'm used to it. Did you ever go to camp?"

"Day camp. Went home every night, so it was sort of more like school. Except you play all day."

"Where do you really live?" She took Ronnee's hand and played with it casually, bending her fingers back very gently and letting them snap straight again.

"Smart girl." Ronnee told her a few facts. The empty place between them was the how and why of her presence in her life, Evie's and her mother's. She didn't know how to fill it now.

"Can I tell you something I already told you in a letter?" Evie covered her mouth with her hand, embarrassed.

Ronnee bent down to hear it, a buzz of a whisper.

"I don't like my brothers. I always prayed I would get a sister." This was clearly scandalous information.

"You think you'll like a sister better?"

"Will you stand up to my brothers with me?"

"Well, you're scaring me about them. Will I be able to handle them, do you think?"

Evie came and put her two hands on Ronnee's head and dug her fingers into her hair and wiggled them, giving her an imaginary shampoo, as if it were perfectly natural. Ronnee wondered if she'd have been like Evie if she'd grown up in this family. It seemed unlikely.

"They'll listen to you because you're bigger than they are and you look strong. And because—one other reason." She giggled again.

"What?"

Evie removed her hands and looked away, toward where the campfire had begun to subside. "Never mind."

"*What?* It's bad manners to start things you don't want to talk about."

"Well, it's bad manners to say."

"Say what, girl?"

Evie looked desperate. "Because you're a—you're—you know." She whispered it. "*Black.* They're scared of black people, they run away from them on their bikes. There are some, like—out farther. Not near our house."

"No, not near at all. So are you afraid?"

Evie put her hands on her hips, like a mime demonstrating defiance. "No I am *not.* Really not. But—I don't understand. I mean— And anyway, you aren't black at all, really. You're sort of—coppery."

The child needed a lesson in genetics. There were dozens of things Ronnee could teach her.

"We had this black cat once that had a litter of regular kittens, you know, they were black and white? And this perfect Siamese.

My dad said this seed was just, like, lying there inside her, waiting for another seed just like it to come along."

Ronnee liked the idea of a seed coming along, but she shook her head. "No, honey, it's a little different. You know your mother is my mother, right?" She realized she was crinkling up her face as she said the words, as if she were in pain. "But my father is somebody else, okay? And he's black."

"Brown, you mean."

Literalist. "Browner than me. Right."

Evie nodded without argument. "Is he nice?"

"Very nice." Keep it simple.

"Did they get married?"

Ronnee played with Evie's fingers to reciprocate. It was odd to touch someone you'd just met. "No, but they—" The old sentimental thing, still necessary even when it wasn't a fairy tale you were telling "—they loved each other a lot."

"So how come you didn't live with us?"

"I'll tell you what, Evie. Let's save some of that for another time." God, she sounded like her mother, stalling. "We're here now and I can't stay too long, so we better get to know each other a little. Otherwise the time'll be gone and we won't—"

The child looked outraged. "Where are you going? You just got here!" She actually stamped her foot. "Why won't you answer why you didn't ever live with us, anyway?"

"Honey, you're in camp. I can't stay, I don't belong here."

"I don't know where you belong! You never lived where we were, you never even met Seth and Eli. That's so stupid!" She was flailing as if to keep Ronnee from touching her. "You just show up like—magic—and now you're disappearing again." She was near tears.

"Evie." Could she say, Your mother didn't want me? Could she say, I didn't know your mother was alive?

"It isn't fair. I wish you never came!" She slapped Ronnee on the arm, hard enough to sting, and pulled her leg back as if she was going to kick her, but thought better of it. She vibrated with anger.

"It's complicated, honey."

"I hate when people say that. My mom is always telling me I'm too young to understand stuff. Well, I'm not."

All Ronnee could do was hug the sulky girl, overpower her against her chest, holding those spiny little arms inside her own. Evie's pointy elbows stuck in her ribs so hard she took Ronnee's breath away.

And then it was time to go. Evie, when Ronnee told her she'd better get back to her friends before they sent up an alarm, hit her in the arm and then hit her again and yet again, windmilling furiously with both hands. How helpless a child is, Ronnee thought. How little she can control anything at all. She felt irrevocably adult.

"Why did you even come if you were just going away so fast?"

"Because I wanted to see you so much. Anyway, isn't late better than never?"

"Maybe it isn't."

"Well, I think it is. But you really want me to sneak around in the woods like a criminal? Sleep under a tree and then steal you again in the morning?"

"Why can't you?" Evie was pacing around, furious. "I want to go with you! Where are you going now?"

She really didn't want to argue. This whole thing had begun to feel stupid and self-indulgent, something to do while every certainty went up in flames around her. Limbo, she knew, was somewhere on the way to hell. Camp Limbo. Though what would happen if she and Evie ran off together, found their way back to the city or lived in the woods? Maybe they could tell people they were orphans—she was almost one, in spirit. She could get any old kind of job—waitressing or something—and they could rent a room and really get to know each other.

Right. And dogs could fly. Meanwhile, she realized, she'd never find her way back to a real bed if she walked out onto the road at this hour: they were where camps always set themselves, in the dark and leafy middle of nowhere. It might even be dangerous.

"You know where you could sleep? This'll be perfect!"

What the hell. She let Evie take her hand and lead her self-importantly through a maze of wooden buildings, some lit, some dark, and then up the steps to a screen door. "It's the Infirmary. Tiptoe," she cautioned. "Let's see if there's anybody in here."

"How will we know in the dark?"

"Well, maybe it doesn't even matter. Just lie down and then you can just—like—get up really early and sneak out before anybody wakes up!" She was a very self-confident little girl, and she was having her way. They advanced on the room in perfect silence. The place felt deserted; the air didn't seem to hold any breathing, any movement muffled by bedclothes. God only knew what she'd find when the sun came up.

"Okay," Ronnee whispered. "I'll lie down here. And then how will I find you in the morning?"

"Go in the woods right where you were before and I'll bring you some breakfast. You like muffins? Or a bagel?"

"Doesn't matter. Are you sure you can do this, Evie? I don't want you getting in trouble."

Evie gave her a very quick shrug and made a face. "I don't care. What are they going to do if I get caught? Keep me from swimming for a day or something? That's one thing about this camp, they don't have very big, like, punishments. They *understand* everything."

Ronnee put her arms around the child and squeezed. "You better get back to your bunk before they count up and find out you're missing. Which reminds me. Maybe we can keep this a secret, okay? Let's not tell your mom that I was here."

"Why not?"

"Just—it'll be like our secret for now. Like a test to see if we can both keep secrets."

Evie shrugged. "I don't care." Absently, affectionately, she ran her index finger back and forth, up Ronnee's wrist and back down.

"Good girl. We can have a lot of secrets from now on. I'll bet your brothers have plenty of them." She was so calculating she disgusted herself.

"I wish you could live with us," Evie said petulantly. "It's not fair."

Ronnee laughed, hushed. "You already said that. There's lots of stuff that's not fair, Evie. This is only the tip of it." She gave her a little slap on the behind. "Now get out of here."

She took off her shoes and her blouse and jeans, wrenched the blanket from its tense clutch of the mattress and climbed in. The sheets must have been washed a thousand times, they were so soft. A woody smell lodged way up in her nose and something specific to nurse's offices, a slightly acrid cleanliness, a reminder that serious hygiene was not a natural state.

If Evie thought it was unfair that she didn't live with them, she considered what the child would think if she could ever explain— not that she would, ever, ever—that if she had, the way she understood her mother's past, Evie might not exist. Then again, she would have had a mother. She couldn't seem to get away from the what-if game. It stirred up her chest and this was worse: she felt guilty, somehow, for knowing such a secret thing about Evie. Could anything be scarier than to know you might not have been born? She remembered the part of her mother's story about walking along with Jewel and deciding—a snap of the fingers, that chancy meeting with the pregnant girl (blue dress, round white collar, stomach like a ripe melon, how dare her mother think she wasn't listening to every word, memorizing it?)—deciding, because she didn't think she should have a privilege that girl by the side of the highway couldn't afford, she said yes, I have to have this child. Not because Ronnee was going to be who she was but out of some weird sense of fairness. Because of who *she* was. So Ronnee had continued (her face was hot now, and her eyelids quivered over tears) to exist.

Now when she kept her eyes closed she saw her mother's disappointment—devastation, you'd have to call it, and she didn't even mind if Jewel heard it, like a witness—when Ronnee had allowed the truth to stand: Her mother at the side of the pool, dressed in those stiff cottons, looking like Donna Reed. But it was an old truth. (She was arguing for herself as if a judge were up there in the rafters, urging her on.) It was an old motive that needed modifying. Her daddy always said Trust your first instinct, it's always best, but that wasn't fair, it wasn't the whole story. Because it had come to her suddenly that her mother was the only one, in the end, who didn't see her color first, and she would miss that. Whatever she was, however she had burst forth from her body, bright or dark, her mother didn't care. Maybe she worried about it in public, maybe she hesitated in that store back in New Hampshire, with the woman in the gray hair like a Russian hat. But not for herself, she didn't hesitate. "Your little brown shoulders," she had said, so yearningly, remembering when she was lost to her. It was motherhood that did it—that mystery. Even her daddy said, "Black girl! Bearer of our racial destiny. Counter in the struggle." Then he loved her, loved her plenty. Fair enough, not untrue. But off, a little. Too specific and too general, all at the same time. Her mother seemed to embrace the simpler fact of her. Her shadow. Essence and existence, *she'd* have said they were indivisible. For example, her father had thought she could be kidnapped. But he hadn't managed to steal that essence. Her mother kept that, without her all these years, that was what had humbled her, quieted her, kept her sad. It was a kind of victory, wasn't it—upside-down or inside-out, but still a victory—that having to live without her had caused so much pain.

IT WAS STRANGE TO HEAR HERSELF WEEPING in a room where she might not be alone. When her eyes adjusted to the darkness she saw four beds in a small square, where sick kids must pass around their illnesses like a medicine ball. There was no one to rise and ask who she was or why she was so desolate, which, though it left her safe, left her more abandoned still. She used to cry like this, and soak the top strip of her sheet sometimes, when she knew her father was going out and leaving her. Since his business was music, a night-time profession, he didn't leave most evenings until after she was asleep, but often enough he set out early, stamping her forehead with a kiss, which led her to develop an alarming noise, a bleat of objection, hoping he would hear and take pity on her. Instead he perfected a technique that worked mysteriously, terrifyingly: he would hold up one finger as if he were about to count off her offenses and, at the end of an indeterminate number, punish her severely (though, in fact, he rarely punished her indelibly for anything). She got to the point where the finger was sufficient to make her stifle her sobs, but her baby-sitters inherited the anger she suppressed, or the neighbors who looked in on her, or the ex-girlfriends who, forever optimistic, continued to do him favors. With everyone except her father she had a terrible reputation for unruliness and anger, until she became sober and reliable, and parental toward him. Evie probably wouldn't have liked her when she was ten.

She was going to have to lie to Evie in the morning, Evie so delicious in the energy of her new love that it made her furious. She would have to stand there in that grove of trees and console her, reassure her that she'd see her soon in Houston when, in fact, she would never see Houston again. She would cringe for the rest of her life when she heard the name of that city. Selfish con, she called herself, inflicting the words like the slash of a razor, hoping they would hurt. You stupid selfish con. Her mother's face would not go away. She would have loved having a little sister. So many people to care about her. No more excuses. You lie, you pay for it.

IT WAS THE LIGHT THAT WOKE HER, soft dusty sunshine sifting through the pines, hazy, like a stage scrim. She loved it when they lifted the scrim and everything came into sharp focus, shocking when you hadn't even realized you'd been looking through cheesecloth. Along with gels when they made dawn, overlay of more colors than anyone would guess, it was her favorite effect.

While she lay studying the light she heard reveille, also dusty and distant-sounding, something vaguely familiar—some Jewish song like an anthem, shakily played on the bugle. She remembered where she was. Where she wasn't. Camp Limbo. She was the defeated daughter who was going home to Brooklyn to hear I-told-you-so, or she was homeless.

It occurred to her suddenly that some nurse might be showing up to get the sick bay started. She jumped up, tried to tuck the bedding back into its straitjacket, failed. Shoved her feet into her sandals, found the little wooden bathroom, contemplated her round, sleep-smoothed face in the mirror and decided she could not start this day with self-pity. Emerged washed and shining. Her hair was unmussable.

At least she'd lose some weight this way. She pictured Evie pocketing a muffin for her, feeling secret and specially blessed. Bagels did better in pockets. Okay. No matter what happened she would be bigger for it. Ma Thelmie liked to say, "Whatever don't kill you makes you fatter!"

It was going to be a lot harder to hide in broad daylight, though. She hung back in the trees, humming to herself, hoping no one could hear her. The mosquitos loved her; incited by every fading perfume on her, or maybe by her sweat, they veiled her head.

And if Evie didn't come?

But there she was. Angry or not, no way she was missing this. Ronnee, from behind a sign that said, DRIVE WITH CARE, WE LOVE YOUR CHILDREN!, watched her slip out the door of the mess hall, looking back over her shoulder like a true criminal. She had her hands in her jacket pockets, which must be crammed with breakfast. She called to her, little sister, who came toward her in the crazy heel-first gait of a speed walker. Did she think that was the way you tiptoe outdoors?

"Bagel *and* a danish, is that okay?" She removed them with a flourish and held them high up, the way you make a dog beg.

Ronnee walked them into the trees, munching on both halves of her breakfast at once. Evie had the brightest eyes she'd ever seen, like gray stones under clear water. "I couldn't sleep, I was so excited. I wasn't even this excited for my birthday!" She linked her arm in Ronnee's.

"I slept like a stone."

"A stone. A bone. A lone." Evie jiggled her arm. She seemed to need a response a minute.

"You do love to talk, don't you?"

The little girl looked like she'd been slapped. "I'll keep quiet. I won't say a word." She locked her lips with a quick turn of her fingers.

"I'll bet. No, I don't mean that, honey. I like it. I'm just—not used to it." The underwater silence of her mother's house. Sleeping Beauty's tranced castle.

They were coming into a little clearing, a boulder in the center and fire-blackened grass around it in a circle. "Boy, this place likes fire, doesn't it?"

"Fire's, like, the best thing! Some camps you can't have a fire on shabbat—they're really religious. We're less. I wouldn't like it if we had to, you know, just lie around all day on Saturday." She stopped to give her knee a vigorous scratching. She did everything emphatically. "When you're with a lot of kids and there's ghost stories or—we have all kinds of, like, ceremonies. Rituals, they're called?"

"You're really something, you know that?" Ronnee caught hold of the little girl, her energy, her boniness, her eagerness against her chest. Ronnee revved at such a different speed, she felt stolid and middle-aged beside her. The last person she'd held close was her new grandmother. New-old. The sad one. And Jordan. Jordan, like it or not.

They clambered up the steep sides of the boulder and settled themselves like conquerors at the top, which was conveniently smooth and flat. Looking down its hard gray sides, she felt like they were sitting atop an elephant.

"I was thinking . . ." Evie laid her thigh against Ronnee's, one leg so short, the other so long it was funny. "Maybe they've got some kind of a job you could do here, so you could stay. Maybe you don't have to—where are you going, anyway?"

She wouldn't say, Damned if I know. "I've got a lot of things to do before I start college, chicken. Does anybody call you chicken? That's what you remind me of. A little chick rushing around without its head." Things to do: Find a pile of money, for starters. Rob a bank, win the lottery.

Tomorrow she would worry all that. Today she was being a sister. They giggled a lot, Evie taught her the camp song, she told her exactly how her father had taught her to hit a ball, the way you turn the label on the bat just so, she itemized her brothers' considerable shortcomings.

"You, of course, are perfect, right?"

Finally Evie said, "Phoo, I've got to go back for lunch. I got my friend Suse to say I was going to the infirmary this morning, but now they're going to be looking for me. Are you hungry?"

"Don't worry about me. I'll walk you back."

"Could we at least go someplace this afternoon? Please? Like into town or something special?" Everything was urgent.

"Oh, I'm not special enough now? I thought I was worth losing sleep over." A flash, again, of the two of them cuddled in a room somewhere, a rogue family, comforting each other.

"You know something, Ron?" She gave Ronnee's arm a familiar squeeze. "I'm never going to feel lonely again."

She contemplated the child, who had stopped her incessant movement. "Do you get lonely?"

"My mom says everybody does. She says it's okay to be alone with yourself sometimes, you can be your own best friend."

Ronnee nodded. "That's a nice way to say it." She seemed to like her mother better through Evie's eyes than through her own.

"What's it like to not have a mother?"

"Oh, goodness, Evie, I don't know." There was no predicting what she would come out with, was there? "It isn't—you don't exactly go around thinking about what you don't have. Like not having a sister. You didn't go around thinking that every minute, did you? I mean, sometimes—" She told her how, in the fifth grade, the very grade Evie was in, they had to make Mother's Day corsages out of irises and florists' wire and green paper wrapped around the stems, fake orchids, the teacher called them, which was so painful she skipped a whole week of school so that she wouldn't have to finish hers and have no one to give it to. "But usually, you know, you have whatever you *have*. It's what you're used to."

True and not true. Like those people who say they didn't know they were poor. Some of them spent the rest of their lives making up for it. "It would have been lovely to have a whole family and be able to take it for granted, but, you know, an awful lot of people don't have that. More and more."

"Well, you could be my other best friend, besides me. And I can be with you on holidays and things. You'll come to Houston and see me if you're my sister and my best friend, right?" She looked up slyly.

They were swinging hands. Once Evie held their interlocked fingers up to be admired, but it wasn't the checkerboard of their color that seemed to please her—at least Ronnee didn't think so—it was the tight cinch they made. "We're like those pot holders you do on the little loom, did you ever do that? With the stretchy things?"

"Everybody who goes to camp has to. Didn't you know it's a law? You have to agree to make half a dozen of those things or they won't let you come."

"And then you give them to your mom and she never uses them." Her eyes widened as if something had bitten her between her shoulders. "Ooh, sorry! That just came out of my mouth!"

Ronnee laughed. "That's okay, Evie. Mother's not a dirty word, you know."

"And now you've got one anyway. Hooray, I forgot we've got the same one! Why couldn't you—" Evie began when a firm voice—Ronnee couldn't tell if it was male or female—said from behind, "Just a minute there, please, young ladies." A very round woman all in khaki, like a little bear, with a whistle around her neck on one of those camp-made lanyards, came up even with them in soundless sneakers. "And you are—?" She gave Ronnee the up-and-down-and-up-again look.

She sighed hard, resigned. "I'm her sister."

A small unreadable smile on the woman's face. "And have you registered at our office?" The woman walked her up the porch steps and in.

"And was—"

"Evie."

"Evie expecting you?"

"Not exactly."

"Do you have any record of your, uh—" She had begun to riffle though a large file. "Tannenbaum, isn't it?"

"Tannenbaum? No, that's Evelyn, she's in bunk seven. Vener." Evie was clutching Ronnee's hand till her bones hurt. If she had any defiance in her, it wasn't serving her just now.

The woman had pulled up a folder, and out of it she extracted a sheet that must have contained the campers' vital statistics, which would not include a sister. She held it up toward Ronnee as if it were self-evident that she did not exist. There was something insolent about her look of triumph.

"Why don't you ask Evie if I'm her sister." The little whore was back in the hands of the cops. Why had she ever left home?

"Well, now," the woman said. She had the patronizing air of someone who would insist, if you objected, that she was only doing her job. Didn't the sign outside say they loved everyone's children? "I don't think that would tell us much, would it."

"This is stupid. What would she be doing with me if she wasn't my sister?" Evie demanded. She looked like a child who was used to being listened to. "Anyway, we weren't doing anything."

Here comes the lesson on how you don't talk to grownups that way, Ronnee thought. But instead, the woman, holding up one finger as if to detain them or they might just head out the door, was dialing the phone. Don't be there! Don't be home! Which was perverse; what would they do with her if this officious little teddy bear couldn't connect with the truth? Back to jail? It was wearying. Ronnee sat down in a folding chair and beckoned to Evie to sit on her lap. Suspicious-looking, wasn't it. God only knew what she was planning to do with the child. "Don't worry," she whispered. Evie's neck smelled cindery, as if the ashes of last night's bonfire had gotten into her hair. Her part was straight and white as a chalked line on a blackboard. "Your mom will tell her it's okay."

"*Our* mom."

"Oh, right. Our mom will tell her to relax and then they'll be so sorry they'll invite me to have lunch with you." She saw her mother standing at the edge of the pool in her pristine cottons, being failed, being betrayed, being humiliated. *She thought she wanted me, but think again. Which of us didn't want the other one first?* Ronnee failing her, then, betraying her back. Her mother was going to say, "My daughter? What daughter?" This was her chance to get even. And Evie would stand there between them bewildered, like a squirrel in the road who doesn't know which way to run to safety.

The woman—Evie said she was Mrs. P., one of the big bosses of the camp—was mostly listening as somebody went on and on in Houston. She nodded a lot, stole illegible glances at her captives, and when she spoke she used her hands as if she could be seen at the other end of the phone. Ronnee was counting one, two, and just before three dropping Evie through her thighs. She varied the count: sometimes it was one, whoops!, sometimes two. Evie was more noisily amused than she might otherwise have been by the babyish trick. She was showing off her affection, in case it might help.

Finally Mrs. P.'s phone call seemed to be winding down. She nodded into the empty air one last time and then she came toward Ronnee and Evie, holding out the receiver. Sternly, she shook it at Ronnee like a maraca. "Come here, dear." All of a sudden, *Dear*. Oh, sympathy. She'd rather not know what for. "Put your sister down, she has to go to lunch. Here, take this now. Your mother wants to talk to you. You had her very worried."

Evie was bouncing up and down with excitement, the way you cheered for your ball team when something big was about to happen. Ronnee didn't raise a hand to take the phone. She looked at it levelly, picturing her mother in the shady kitchen, that island of cool. Her almost familiar face. If she accepted the receiver she wanted to be able to say, This is my choice. Nobody could stop her if she turned on her heel and walked out the door and kept on walking. It was important to know that. Some things are given, but nobody was going to have the last word. There was no last word, only a first one.

She took the receiver out of the round little woman's grip, ignoring the strained patience on her face; ignoring Evie, who was still bouncing, as if in pain.

She closed her eyes on all of them. "Mom?" she said.